FOREVER THE HORIZON

– PART I: FORTUNE'S CHARM –

Colorado Marshal

Prologue

The horse's hooves made almost no sound on the soft sand. Waves, shimmering gold and orange under the light of a sun barely over the horizon, splashed placidly on the shore, rippling over the hoof marks left in their path. The horse that cantered slowly along the water's edge was only lightly tacked, the soft, pliable hackamore draped around its sculpted head the only sign of control. Long reins passed along the neck, dangling lightly down its right side from the hand of a tall, quiet young woman who rode bareback. She and the horse were nothing more than silhouettes, outlines of movement; just another pair of shadows skimming in perfect harmony over the sand.

The girl pulled her horse to an easy stop, sliding down to land beside it. She was barefoot. The sea was an endless expanse before them, painted beautifully by the light as it danced and shimmered and feinted under the rising rays of the sun. She sighed, almost sadly, stepping closer to the warm body beside her and wrapping her arms around herself as a cool breeze swept in off the ocean. It was one of those days. Birthdays usually are. Days of remembrance, of reflection, days one sets aside to wonder if they've done the right thing. The loveliness of this place served only to remind her of the things she missed.

It had been a year since she bid farewell to what she once knew, a year since she finally found the courage to give it up and start anew. A new country, a new career, a new lease on life. No one – herself included – thought she'd be able to do it, find the strength to see herself through. She had. She had surprised them all, for time is far too precious a thing to waste. She was tired of having hers run by those who cared only what they could get out of it, tired of having it steered it mercilessly through rough waters while she drowned in the waves, unnoticed. She promised herself when she left that she would not run back. It was hard; life often is. As one of the first to leave the well-traveled main to seek new roads, she had encountered many challenges, and was sure she'd meet many more. Blazing the trail was never a simple task. It meant bucking the tide, challenging accepted wisdom and going against tradition, defying odds that only continued to grow with each failure that had come before. There was no certainty of success. Entering the wilderness was merely a beginning, and this was just the first step in a long, winding journey, the rest of which was still to be unveiled.

It was the hardest part of life to accept. Waiting, wondering, waiting to see what the future would hold and wondering where her own destiny would take her. The only time things truly became clear was when they emerged in the past, and by then it was too late to do anything but watch them disappear, learning from them as much as possible while they faded away like ghosts to leave new questions looming ahead.

The breeze died down, and she let her hands fall to her sides, watching the black shape of a gull swoop low over the water, casting a shadow over the sooth, undulating surface. It really was a beautiful morning; it was going to be a beautiful day. She couldn't have asked for better. In point of fact, she was not here to applaud the beginning of the day, nor was she here to admire the sunrise; rather, she was here at a request. His request.

She felt the butterflies that had plagued her earlier start fluttering again, beating their tiny, trembling wings against her insides. She knew she shouldn't get her hopes up. His note had said only that he wanted to see her. She didn't dare let herself imagine why, didn't dare let her thoughts dwell on it. Or him. She had done quite enough of that over the past year, and it had nearly driven her mad.

Bowing her head, she thought fleetingly of another relationship that had been on her mind lately, one that happened so many years ago and so far away, before she was even born. Back when her mother was young. It had been on her mind because it bothered her; it bothered her because she knew things could have –

no, should have – been different. But that's the way it was. Sometimes, no matter what you do, no matter how hard you try, even true love just doesn't succeed.

The waves continued their endless symphony, crashing rhythmically upon the hard surface of the sand, and their song brought a smile to the face of the girl who watched them. Today was going to be perfect; she'd make sure of it, no matter what. She had beaten the odds, proven herself worthy of the freedom she desired, and above all, it meant she was the answer to a fervent hope.

For it had been she who found the courage to choose differently.

Whatever you do, you need courage.
Whatever course you decide upon, there
is always someone to tell you that you
are wrong. There are always difficulties
arising that tempt you to believe your critics
are right. To map out a course of action and
follow it to an end requires some of the same
courage that a soldier needs. Peace has its
victories, but it takes brave men and women
to win them.

- *Ralph Waldo Emerson*

Chapter 1

Some say treasure and treachery go hand in hand. Like cookies and milk, bacon and eggs, rhythm and blues. But a bit more volatile.

For Gregg Nicholas, treasure and treachery and all that came with it was part of his life. Treasure, treachery, accessories, and the irrefutable evidence that, as a dedicated pursuer of these things, he would spend much of his time alone. In darkness, like tonight, pouring over material that would cause most people to glaze over.

Outside, the insistent patter of November rain was nearly unbroken; the constant, low gloom of city light pierced by the occasional passing car. It was a dreary night, to be sure. The kind of night that made sitting at one's desk almost bearable. Rain lashed at the windows, spurred on by a cold wind that seeped through the cracks and seals and whispered through the back recesses of the house. Gregg, however, was impervious to the cold. He neither noticed nor heeded its presence, so intent was he on what was before him. A small desk lamp illuminated the shiny, laminate surface of the table beneath his palms, on which lay a newspaper, soggy and feathered from the rain. It wasn't open. The headline was nothing more than black splashes.

IS IT REAL? Read the laser-perfect text. *Goldsteins uncover priceless necklace in Mexico, hint at ties to Robin Hood legend...*

The Goldsteins. One of the most powerful families in Europe. Lineage stretching back to AD double digits, maybe further, if the stories were to be believed. Lineage that included, among other notable people, none other than England's most notorious rascal: Robin Hood. One of the original superheros, the kind of legend Clark Kent of could only dream of becoming. A knight whose armor was a worn cloak and a deadly bow, whose allegiance lay with king and country... and whose undiscovered stash of treasure was said to be one of a kind.

Again, if the stories were true.

The historical community was sent into a frenzy today when Nicolo Goldstein, long believed to be the unofficial head of the Goldstein family, announced the discovery and collection of a piece most thought to be, at best, fictitious. The rare and priceless piece, known as Marian's Necklace, was uncovered in Sonora, Mexico, where it is believed to have resided for at least one hundred years. If the piece is proven genuine, it could uphold the long-debated claim of the Goldstein family to share lineage with Robin Hood, a claim that stretches back into the 1600's and has added a distinct air of mystery to those bearing the family name. It also might shed light on the legend of Robin Hood himself, pointing the way toward the vast treasure trove supposedly amassed during his campaign to free England's infamous King Richard the Lionheart from imprisonment in 1194.

Treasure. What legend was complete without it? The term itself was enough to make any capitalist lick their chops in anticipation. For centuries after Robin Hood's alleged existence, adventurers searched in vain for the cache said to be hidden by the outlaw's gang, a fortune worth billions in today's world. Men were driven mad by the possibilities, the clues, the endless riddles; much like those who searched for Bigfoot or the alien enthusiasts staking out Roswell, the modern-day community of Robin Hood aficionados was small, fragmented, and generally misunderstood by society at large. Unlike its "conspiracy theory" brethren, however, the men and women who frequented the Robin Hood camp tended to be average-Joe citizens; in normal clothing, with normal jobs, and from all walks of life. Hard to categorize.

Gregg, for example, was a university professor. A successful man in his field, well traveled, well educated, who just happened to believe the legend of Robin Hood and had personally been after the treasure for the better part of twenty years. He'd been introduced to it the same as anyone else: through movies, literature, backyard games. It was only when he really started looking into the events and time period behind the story that he began to see another side, pursue another avenue: gold.

He'd started his own hunt for Robin Hood's treasure right out of high school. In the pre-internet days of the Dewey Decimal System and rotary dial phones, tracking down leads was a mission, and finding people willing to share their own leads – acquired through methods that predated even Gregg's – was more so. It was quite by accident that Gregg met Walton Davis, an old man who had been searching for the treasure since before Gregg was even an idea. They struck up a conversation at a beachside bar; Gregg bought Davis a beer, and the two of them launched into discussion about Robin Hood.

Davis was from an old, New England family and had ancestors that crossed the Atlantic on the Mayflower. They brought with them tales from the old country, trinkets; one of these items, a small piece of rolled parchment, was inscribed with a symbol that tied in directly with the legend of Robin Hood – more importantly, the tale of lost treasure. It was one of those family things, passed down through the generations, with origins possibly rivaling the legend itself. Davis described the symbol to Gregg and sketched it out on a napkin he begged from the bartender. It was a simple drawing, pared down much like a tattoo with no detail, no embellishments; just a raw, sketched-out series of lines joined at the base around a triangle-shaped area of negative space and spreading outward like antlers on a buck. Beneath these lines, separated by no more than half an inch, a small triangle hovered alone. According to Davis, this drawing was the key. The key to everything. When it made sense, the rest of the puzzle would make sense, and the treasure would be within reach. He gave the napkin to Gregg, promised to someday pay him back for the beer, and wished him luck in his quest.

Gregg was twenty-two years old when he met Davis; eight years later, when his own hunt was well underway, he'd received a phone call from an estate attorney in Seattle who told him Walton Davis had recently passed away, and Gregg was listed in his will. Gregg was presented with a small envelope. It contained a note, thanking Gregg for an unforgettable conversation; five dollars for a beer; and the original symbol, scratched out on an ancient piece of parchment that nearly disintegrated in his hands.

For nearly a decade Gregg had harbored this secret scrap of evidence, in the hope that one day it would prove its worth. He'd had many breaks since then and just as many setbacks, but still he'd kept at it, in the hope that it would all amount to something someday. Like with anything, it required patience. History and her recollection of events was clear. But separating fact from fiction in a time period lined with not only secular but religious myths was complicated, and not for the faint of heart.

In the late 1100's, England was a place of turmoil. Nearly one hundred years of war both within and beyond her borders had decimated the country's resources, and continual, internal strife between the Norman and Saxon populations provided a breeding ground for opportunistic politicians and anyone else on the hunt for greater power. Though the Norman Conquest of 1066 was long over and the prize obtained, the more recent period of anarchy (characterized by several messy transfers of power with the Church playing both sides) left the general population split irrevocably. In simpler terms: easy pickings. A divided populace is, after all, much easier to conquer than one that stands together.

Such was the state of this once grand and prosperous place when Richard the Lionheart pointed his men toward the dry sands of Jerusalem, intending to free the Holy Land from what he and his forebears saw as the clutches of barbarism and once more setting it on the path to righteousness. The Third Crusade was meant to be his crowning achievement. It was meant to be the thing that would define him for all time. Seeking out, as men of his position do, the riches that would surely await them and the fame that was destined to accompany it, he pressed forward, marching toward the finale of this campaign to end all campaigns. On one hand, he succeeded. After an unceremonious parting of allegiances at Acre with the Duke of Austria, a former ally, Richard went on alone with his army and accomplished what he set out to do. While the ultimate goal of retaking Jerusalem was not realized and the city remained under Muslim control, history would mark the campaign as a success; in 1192 a truce was reached, known as the Treaty of Jaffa, that allowed Christian pilgrims access to Jerusalem and guaranteed three years of peace between the armies of Muslim leader Saladin and their

Christian opponents. Richard departed the Holy Land in October and headed for home a hero, the barbarians vanquished and the Holy Land secure. The fact that he, himself, committed acts of a most egregious nature in the process was merely jotted down to religious fervor if mentioned at all.

It was on his return journey when things began to go pear-shaped. Richard's ship went down in a storm off the coast of mainland Europe; while he and a small band of men managed to survive, they soon found themselves wandering like fugitives through the heart of territory belonging to Leopold of Austria, the very man Richard had offended so badly at Acre. And their bad luck didn't stop there. They were discovered, by none other than the duke himself. Having far from forgotten what happened at Acre, the duke was only too happy to take advantage of the situation; thus it was that King Richard the Lionheart was captured, and went on to spend a long stretch in prison, held for ransom in the dungeon of the man he had slighted. Some would call it a malicious trick of fate. Others, just karma.

It was during this time of Richard's imprisonment, when his younger brother Prince John got his mitts on the country's finances and started that all-too-familiar grab for other people's money, that a young knight by the name of Robert of Locksley decided he'd had enough of the royal treatment and fought back. He was soon joined by others. Hundreds of others. Together they formed a deadly alliance against Prince John and stooges like the Sheriff of Nottingham, protecting the public from tyranny while they worked tirelessly to scrape together the money needed to fund King Richard's return.

By the time it was all said and done, Robin Hood and his Merry Men managed to write themselves into the books as England's most lovable (and loaded) rascals. Tales of their exploits would crop up for centuries to come, inspiring history and myth and pop culture in a way few other legends could rival.

Many of the theories surrounding Robin Hood's questionable existence are bizarre. Amid the plethora of obligatory explanations concerning aliens, CIA conspiracies, and time-traveling monks, it can be difficult to spot the grains of truth hidden away in the chaos. And since none of these grains of truth, no matter how rational, has ever come out on top when put to the test, the story of Robin Hood remains just that: a story.

And the treasure? Well, that was just a story, as well. No tale would be complete without a hidden stash, and the rumors of gold had been around for as long as the legend itself; whether they were real or not... well, that was another matter altogether. Even Robin Hood remained an unproven enigma. Conspiracy theorists had their ideas, of course, their stories. To date, none of them had been proven.

For some, lack of proof meant lack of truth. For others, it presented an opportunity ripe for the picking. It was the link to Robin Hood and his elusive treasure that originally brought light to the name of Goldstein, and began laying the groundwork for what they were today. It could be said for both, legend and family, that the existence of one aided the other. It was a symbiotic relationship. And it all kicked off with the appearance of that necklace.

1454 found an England still obsessed with Robin Hood. By this point, of course, the deeds of the man were far outweighed by the lure of unending physical fortune, and every other day seemed to bring forth new evidence, new ideas, new places to look. It was into this society, where the quest for the treasure was well and truly cemented in the collective conscience of the working-class, that the next clue was injected. A man turned up in London by the name of Veit Goldstein and went straight to the grand ballrooms of the aristocracy. He claimed to be of noble heritage, descended from the great Robin Hood; while he seemed to blow in with the wind from the wilds of central Germany, the strange and enigmatic man went on to back up his assertion by producing a necklace, constructed of silver and sapphire. If the legend was to be believed, the pendant was approximately six inches wide, attached on either end to a pair of six-inch segments of silver chain. Its design was particularly unique, seeming to depict the lengths of two leafless tree branches whose bases were interlocked delicately around a large, blue sapphire before they spread and entwined, prettily, toward the outer edges. The detail was said to be amazing; the craftsmanship, even more so.

This necklace was far more than a work of fine art, however, according to Goldstein. It was an heirloom that was passed down through his family since it was first given to Maid Marian the day she married her outlaw lover, created from another piece Robin had stolen from a particularly hated foe during his campaign to free the king. He had gifted the original piece to Marian in the same way high school sweethearts would exchange promise rings: as a sign of his love, loyalty, and dedication. In times filled with such turmoil, it was unlikely they would ever have a life together, if Robin even survived his assignment; when he did survive and a life together was exactly what they were going to achieve, he had the necklace recrafted into its latter form to symbolize their bond, and the future that would emerge from it. This was more than just a necklace. It was a direct link to the time and the man; more importantly, Goldstein espoused, it proved the existence of Robin Hood's lost treasure trove.

Unfortunately for Goldstein, his journey was less than successful. Broken English made his story hard to follow, and even harder to believe. There were already so many theories making the rounds. So many quests. So many failures. So many things, some with much more credibility, that should have yielded results and didn't. The grand ballrooms of the nobility were becoming jaded. As a result, those Goldstein wished to impress were not moved, and only people of a decidedly different balance of income and scruples took his word for granted. Several attempts on his life were made before Veit Goldstein vanished in the same manner by which he first appeared. The necklace went with him. Ironically, once that happened, the mood shifted amongst the upper class, as it so often did, and the chase was on again. The piece dubbed "Marian's Necklace" became the talk of the courts, and the stories and legends tripled overnight. Every nobleman in the country suddenly found himself on the hunt for it. But these renewed efforts, while grand, were also in vain.

Veit Goldstein was never seen again. His purpose for entering London in the first place, for speaking up about his alleged family history, was never known. Perhaps he wanted notoriety for himself and his descendants; perhaps he wanted the real story to be heard, as he knew it. Perhaps, and this was the most likely scenario, he believed the necklace really did prove the existence of treasure, and was on a fishing expedition to secure funding to go search for it. Whatever his reasons and whatever consequence he hoped it would bring about, he failed.

The Goldstein family remained quiet for nearly one hundred years. Somewhere in that time, Marian's Necklace disappeared. But if anyone was under the impression that such a detail would cause any more inconvenience than a minor speed bump, they were mistaken. Proof or no, the Goldsteins were ready to make their mark, and while Marian's Necklace was making its epic journey across the world, the Goldstein family was embarking on its own: one of power. From the humble beginnings of Veit they advanced; slowly, steadily, building their empire on the mainland of Europe as merchants and shrewd businessmen, conquering minor titles, weaseling their way into the French inner circles before once more attempting to tackle the holy grail of the London courts as nobility. It had been generations since Veit had made his memorable appearance, and the stigma of his embarrassing rejection had never been forgotten. Not by these people.

Like most historians, Gregg would argue that what really propelled the Goldsteins into the big leagues in the end was their ability to cultivate the aura of mystery surrounding them. By 1600 their finances were stable. The wheel of fortune had been carefully, studiously crafted and preserved, through marriage arrangements and deals brokered behind closed doors; these calculated liaisons and alliances, passed on through the generations with the same care as the money they were meant to protect, ensured the family's continued survival in their chosen level of society. Money could buy many things, and the Goldsteins bought themselves a past. They took the story of Veit and his necklace – now a minor legend itself – and built on the foundations it provided, using that notoriety and the blank canvas of yesteryear to their advantage. By the time they were finished, the only thing people saw was the splendor of the present and a family tree lined with money. Old money. And power. With careful strokes, the Goldsteins had painted for themselves a history, one that was rich enough to be acceptable, yet vague enough to keep people guessing. Always guessing. Always wondering.

And always, always talking.

It had taken time. But eventually, it was the combination of intrigue and obvious physical wealth that lifted them to the top and held them there. One hundred years on and the Goldsteins were hot property. And so they remained: rich, powerful, almost inhuman in their collective perfection. Their lineage was impressive. It was said they were related to kings, emperors, pharaohs. It was said they were descended from the gods. Many things were said. How much of it was true remained a mystery, but plot holes were so much easier to swallow when they were delivered in gold.

Marian's Necklace didn't reappear until the late 1800's, when it was uncovered by a United States' Marshal who stumbled across the unusual piece while hunting down a fugitive in Mexico. From the Marshal it apparently passed on to his Spanish bride; from her, to their children.

Of course none of this latter story was known for nearly one hundred and fifty years. The necklace's journey from England to the Western Hemisphere remained an untold tale, and its sojourn in Mexico was only brought to light after the fact when, over a century and several generations later, a letter arrived on the opulent doorstep of one Nicolo Goldstein, informing him of the necklace's whereabouts.

The piece has been collected and taken to a jeweller in Texas for authentication. While it is nearly impossible to verify the story associated with it for obvious reasons, the jeweller has been able to establish that the necklace was, indeed, made of silver and sapphire, and created sometime in late-1100's Europe. That, in and of itself, is enough to make this piece worth a small fortune. But to its new owners, the psychological value is much greater. For a long time, the necklace was merely speculation and hearsay. And while it is impossible to verify one hundred percent that this piece is the piece from the legend, coincidence is also a very strong word to use. Amantha Goldstein, second-cousin to Nicolo and long considered the official spokesperson for the family, said in a press conference Tuesday that their modern quest for answers was only beginning, a quest that undoubtedly hinged upon this discovery.

To the Goldstein family, one of the most high-ranking and watched families in Europe; indeed, the world; the find was their crowning achievement. Their vindication. Skeptics would always abound, but their efforts did nothing more than to fan the flame of infatuation. In the modern era of pop culture, anti-heroes, and celebrities, the youngest generation of the Goldstein family reached an almost rock star status. Amantha in particular had attracted a ludicrous amount of attention over the past five to ten years. As the public face of the family she had become synonymous with perfection, catapulted into the stratosphere of fame right along with the royals, Madonna, and social media. It just went to show how fickle was the entity known as collective consciousness. After such controversy surrounding Amantha's life as a child, a past so carefully obscured and glossed over by the Goldsteins' ever-on-the-ball publicity department, now she could do no wrong. No one needed to know where she came from anymore. All that mattered was she was rich, beautiful, and knew the princes.

For Gregg, all that mattered was that she was a Goldstein and had possession of Marian's Necklace. For those after the legend, the Goldsteins had always been the missing link. It was a well-accepted fact among "hunters" that following the family would someday yield results. Gregg agreed with them. He opened the newspaper, reverently, as he had so many times this evening, to stare at the publicity photo of the Goldsteins' now-infamous discovery.

A pendant approximately six inches wide. Two six-inch segments of chain. Two leafless tree branches with bases interlocked around a large, blue sapphire while the arteries spread toward the outer edges. The Goldsteins had found their family heirloom, and Veit's infamous proof was plastered all over the headlines.

But it was more than that. Below the bottom edge of the newspaper lay another piece. A piece of parchment; old, worn, with edges disintegrating under the pressures of time; inscribed with a simple drawing pared down like a tattoo. A raw, sketched-out series of lines joined at the base and spreading outward like antlers on a buck. Walton Davis' symbol. The lines were, in fact, not antlers, nor were they joined only to each other. Rather, they depicted the leafless branches of trees, stripped bare as in winter, and the dark mass at their base was none other than a stone. The symbol Gregg had been given was nearly identical to the outline of the pendant photographed in the paper before him. Marian's Necklace was more than proof; like the symbol, it was the key to everything.

This was Gregg's moment. This was when he needed to make his move. And Gregg knew he needed to move fast if he was going to have a shot at the ultimate prize. He was close now, so close he could almost see the treasure. Now all he had to do was contact one of the most powerful families in the world, arrange to get a look at their discovery, and hope it somehow led him to gold. Piece of cake.

He'd just have to get in line with the time traveling monks and the aliens.

The Goldsteins had always complained of problems with the paparazzi, and if Gregg was correct things were only going to get worse. Once more, the story had come full circle. Whether it proved the theory or not, Marian's Necklace had been found, the box of secrets opened; Robin Hood fever and the search for treasure was ignited yet again. And if the Goldstein family thought they had it tough with the media before, they had only to wait. Because when it comes to the art of getting rich, treasure and treachery most certainly go hand in hand.

Or so some say.

****

The shot was sudden. Loud. It sounded like it was right next to her. Fear hit. Anne Gordon dived to the side, her running shoes sliding precariously over the gravel layer covering the edge of the sidewalk. She could still hear the splitting, clapping, shattering sound of the shot around her; she didn't know where it came from. Who fired it. Why they wanted her dead. Maybe there was no reason.

"Come out, come out, wherever you are!"

Anne felt herself shaking. Frantically, she dug her phone out of her pocket with scraped hands, nearly crying when it came up with no signal. Damn cell phones! The voice that called was creepy, menacing. It echoed across the alley, reverberating off the cold, metallic walls of nearby buildings, stretching around the dumpster she now crouched behind so pitifully, like a cornered animal, useless phone in hand. The faces of her family stared back at her from the lock screen. She knew she shouldn't have come this way; her husband begged her every day to take another route. She should have listened. Had she even said goodbye to him this morning?

"Come on, Marshal; stop wasting my time!"

There was no response. Anne held her breath. Marshal? Was she not the target?

A barrage of gunfire erupted behind her, and Anne clapped a hand over her mouth as a scream again threatened to tear itself from her throat. She heard bullets ricocheting. A spent shot hissed past her hiding place, finding its way onto the deserted street. Only one. And it was by hazard.

She wasn't the target.

Who was?

She didn't know. The only clear thing, and that painfully so, was she was in big trouble; her late-afternoon jog home had landed her right in the middle of a feud. If that first shot had not sounded when it did, before she took that initial step across the yawning mouth of the alleyway; had she not run for cover at exactly that moment, leaping backward into the small crevice beside the dumpster, she would have walked directly into it. So far her presence seemed unnoticed. But for how long? She didn't know where they were. She didn't know how many. And worse still: she had nowhere to go. If she moved at all, she would be seen.

"I'm getting impatient, Marshal! You wanted this fight, now come finish it!"

"Why not come finish it yourself!"

The answering shout was hoarse, strained; the owner of that voice was in pain. But it was decisive. Taunting. It held an accent, Anne could hear, but what she didn't know. She'd never been much use with accents.

She checked her phone, moved it around a little. Still nothing. Weird how signal through here seemed to come and go with the breeze most days.

Footsteps advanced. Another shot. Louder, closer. It was answered immediately by a different gun, larger caliber. Anne covered her ears, trying not to panic, not to imagine what would surely happen to her if she were seen.

She'd treated gunshot wounds before. Life in a Chicago hospital was never boring. She didn't want to end up bleeding out on a table or in this dingy alleyway with a hole in her body, didn't want her children to lose their mother, or her husband his life partner.

Hell, she just didn't want to die.

Carefully, silently, she stretched backward and leaned against the wall, peering around the dumpster. Her light windbreaker whispered against the brick. A signal bar flicked onto her cell phone, then off; she was so close! If only she could get that one, lonely bar to stay. She slithered into the small, nondescript space between the dumpster and the rough wall, her breath coming in short, quick gasps; her heart was pounding in her throat. She felt sick. She needed help. *Help me, please!* She thought, desperately. She hedged to the left, trying to corner the elusive band of communication flicking so spitefully across her screen.

That was when she saw him. The man hiding in the alley. He was resting back on an empty drum, surrounded by garbage. Against the dark, oil-smeared metal and black plastic, he stuck out. His hair was long and reddish, dirty, framing a face taut with pain. His left leg was bleeding. It was stretched out in front of him, harnessed by an old belt wrapped around his thigh.

With eyes accustomed to such things, Anne assessed the damage. Clean entry, clean exit, and while it was bleeding steadily the shot appeared to have missed the artery and the bone. Just a flesh wound. The kind that would hurt like hell but heal with little more than aesthetic damage.

The voice spoke again.

"I know you're back there; you can't hide forever!"

Anne looked for its owner, couldn't find him, as the stranger's face twisted into a wry sneer.

"If that's what you think I'm doing, you're a bigger –"

A shot cut him off and the bullet whacked into the drum, sending fragments of rust spewing out. The man swore under his breath.

"Is that the best you've got, mate!" He taunted, swiping irritably at bits of disintegrated barrel that had rained over his leather flight jacket.

Australian. The accent was Australian.

Another figure crossed Anne's line of sight, and she hid deeper instinctively as he looked in her direction. He was short, built like a bull, wearing a trench coat. He was walking straight for the fugitive's hiding place, the gun in his hand at the ready.

The man in the alley knew he was there. Anne knew he could hear the advancing footsteps, just as surely as she could. He checked his gun and swore again. His face was resigned, like he knew how little chance he really had. Peering out from behind the barrels, he took quick stock of the situation, ascertained his position, and fired. Once, twice, three times, leaping as he did out of hiding to take on his opponent head to head. Someone shouted. A gun went flying. A shot was squeezed off from the second as it too was flung away, the bullet pinging off a wall to ricochet over Anne's head. She ducked, convulsively, the movement causing a bar of service to pop up on the phone in her hand.

The bar caught. Held. Signal!

Type, type, type! She admonished herself.

9.

Her fingers shook so violently she almost missed the digit completely.

1.

Another shot. This could only end one way.

1.

Frantically, Anne reached for the call button, pushed it, held the phone to her ear.

"911 emergency service –"

"Help, please help me – "

A hand clapped over her mouth. The call ended. Anne screamed into the thick palm, in vain, and struggled to break free, her phone falling to the ground. Too late! Her kids' faces stared back at her from the pavement.

No, it was *not* too late! She would not give in!

"Calm down!" A man hissed in her ear. "Calm down, I won't hurt you."

Another accent. This one British. She knew because his voice sounded like one of the princes. Or was it Rex Harrison? Anne twisted. Amid the crashing chaos around them, the man whose immovable grip held her in place seemed unusually calm. His dark eyes betrayed nothing as they fixed on the struggle not twenty feet from them. Anne didn't know which antagonist he watched, whose side he was on in this fight to the death.

The two men were circling each other like panthers, each waiting for the other to make the first move. The one with the gunshot wound limped heavily as he stepped. The other one, the short one, seemed confident. They lunged. Punches were traded, heavily, without mercy, bloodying faces and hands. The body beside Anne tensed with every blow; she realized this man must have a large stake in the outcome, wondered what he would be doing if he wasn't here holding her to silence.

Suddenly, so suddenly, it all came to an end. The bull took a swipe at his opponent's injured leg, sweeping it from under him. The man went down, yelling out in pain. He hit the ground, rolled away from a crushing blow, reached his knees, lunged toward the discarded gun. His hands found the butt. The bull was almost on him, dragging at his injured leg.

With surprising agility, borne most certainly of desperation, the man on the ground flipped around. He lifted the weapon, aimed, and shot the bull at point blank range.

Anne shrieked again and squeezed her eyes shut, but not in time. It happened too quickly. She would never forget the images, the sounds, that assailed her. While she had dealt with the aftermath of this very thing many times, she had never seen someone shot firsthand. She was quaking, her limbs vibrating of their own accord as the adrenaline and fear coursed through her blood like the drugs so many of her patients overdosed on.

The man next to her slowly, cautiously, removed his hand from her mouth. Through her hazed senses, she felt his relief. Clearly, his side had won. What did that mean for her?

"Will you be quiet?" He asked.

Anne simply nodded, shaking uncontrollably. She felt sick. The hand moved further away.

"Stay here."

"And why – would I do that?" She snapped. Her own voice sounded alien.

"Because that man out there will shoot anything that moves."

Anne glanced at the stranger who lay motionless on his back across the alley, momentarily transfixed by his face as he stared at the sky above; somehow, she didn't doubt her companion's words.

"Stay. Here."

She watched him rise. His movements were those of someone who knew the art of restraint, and the grip he'd had on her earlier suggested a man of great control. His hair was cropped in a very short buzz-cut, accentuating a strong jaw and dark, steady eyes. He reached down and retrieved her phone, handing it to her. Without another glance at her he stepped away, walking toward the man in the alley who had slowly, painfully, sat up and dragged himself to the wall. As soon as Anne's companion rounded the side of the dumpster, into view, the gun swung up. Eyes sharpened. Survival instinct flared.

"Easy."

For a moment there was hesitation, then the hand with the gun was dropped with tired laugh.

"I should have known you'd be here," he said.

"You all right?"

"Yeah. Just out of ammo. Glad you weren't somebody else."

Anne's companion glanced at the body lying prone amid the garbage bags and debris.

"One left," he said simply. "Sounds like time for a celebration. Buy you a drink?"

A shrug.

"What the hell."

The man allowed himself to be pulled to his feet. Anne rose too, slowly, and walked into view. He turned to look at her, his body tightening again in reaction, but a quiet word from his friend stopped him.

"She's all right," she heard him say.

His eyes were intense. That was the first thing she noticed as they met hers. They were piercing, focused; they held intelligence. His features were strong. He would be an attractive man, Anne thought, had he not been so unkempt and haggard, but there was something about him, something indefinable, wild, that she didn't understand. Power; it was a sense of power. As he limped toward her, she could feel the hardness of his personality. The coldness. This man's stature held no give, no emotion, as if he were chiseled out of a marble block. He approached cautiously. Anne regarded him with equal wariness, taking a slow, involuntary step backward. She could see the gun still in his hand. The fact that it was empty, at least according to him, gave her little comfort.

He stopped a few feet away, and she moved her gaze to his face; noticed a surprising, underlying streak of emotion in his eyes that she hadn't expected to see. Compassion, sadness, a certain fatigue. It caught her off guard.

"What's your name?" He asked. His voice was calm, soothing, like velvet.

"Anne. Anne Gordon."

This time the kindness in his face was unmistakeable, as he smiled, ever so slightly. Anne was taken aback by the sincerity of that expression and how it transformed his face, the crows' feet edging outward from his eyes, the lines of humor around his mouth.

"Are you all right, Anne Gordon?" The question, spoken in that low, accented tone, was gentle.

"Yes."

He inclined his head toward the phone that lay, forgotten, in her palm.

"Wait until we are gone before you call the police." He began to move away, then turned back to her, almost as an afterthought. He reached a hand into his jacket pocket and pulled out a piece of paper. Staring at it briefly, with a somewhat quizzical look, he extended it to her. "Have someone call this man," he said. "He will understand everything, and he can identify the body. You can trust him… it will be good to have him on side. For your own safety, it would be better if no one else knows you were here for that. Not even the local coppers."

The piece of paper fluttered in her hand under a slight breeze as she accepted it. It contained a hand-written phone number, and a name: Peter Gates, Deputy United States Marshal.

"Thank you."

Nodding, he walked off, slowly, limping, his left leg still oozing blood. His back was hunched; the gun in his right hand dangled uselessly. Stiffly, he reached up to tuck it in the back of his waistband. He looked exhausted.

"You shouldn't leave that for long," Anne said. When he paused and looked at her, she gestured to his leg. "It needs to be taken care of. I have a friend… over in Englewood… as you might imagine, he deals with this kind of thing a lot. His name is Justin. Justin Kim. He lives in an apartment on Sixty-Eighth and May. Anyone in the area will know of him."

"Business must be booming."

"It's Englewood," Anne said, returning his smile. "Business is always booming. The complex is sketchy and all of his supplies tend to fall off the back of a truck, but he's good, and knows how to keep things quiet."

Another nod, one of thanks, and he was gone. Anne stood in silence as he walked away from her and approached the pair of men standing by the edge of the building. She hadn't seen before, but there were two of them now. Her companion had been joined, she noticed, by another; she couldn't see him clearly. The vague outline to which she was privy caused the unease, unease that had gradually begun to lift from her soul, to return. She felt the hairs on the back of her neck prickle. Where had he come from?

His posture was strange. Anne couldn't have said why. He was slight of build, light-skinned, medium height. His hair was nearly white, gelled into a small series of spikes over his head.

"I see my information proved useful to you," he said without preamble.

Even his voice, soft and shadowed like the rest of him, was menacing. From her vantage point, Anne could barely make out a pair of icy, light blue eyes.

"It did."

"Of course I expect to be paid."

"You will be. I have a few options lined up."

Anne stared after them as they walked off, wondering what they meant. The Australian looked back once, nodded. His friend did the same. As their forms receded into the dimness of late afternoon, Anne felt her skin begin to crawl. She was alone. Alone with a dead body. In an alleyway, and the sun was going down.

Bolting onto the street for signal, she dialled 9-1-1.

***

It was nearly midnight by the time Deputy US Marshal Peter Gates made it to the morgue. Ordinarily, it would be closed up tight by such an hour, but due to the nature of his visit the director had seen fit to leave one, unfortunate staff member lurking in the building until Gates' departure. Glenelg Mortuary was a rather outsider affair, dealing mostly with bodies lacking in official support networks; if they didn't have family when they kicked the bucket, they came here, in the hopes that one could eventually be found. If not, they were cremated and sent on their merry way. Chicago's never-ending supply of homeless transients ensured that Glenelg and places like it always had a steady stream of business.

When Gates walked in, he was greeted by flowers. Lots and lots of flowers. In vases, in bouquets, hanging from baskets. The smell was almost overpowering. Under lights that had been dimmed for the night, the carpet was old and stained, dark red in color with a faint, cream-lined square pattern etched with leaves. Looked like the front for a speak-easy. Sans music. Opening hours had long since passed, so there were no visitors to harangue with its monotony. Couches that appeared to be far too expensive for a place like this were tucked among the myriad of forest bushels; in one of them, furthest away from the door, a young woman sat quietly, eyes closed, listening to her ipod. Gates wondered if she was the one who had asked to see him.

He took it all in with the practiced eyes of one who missed nothing, sorting out the important from the inconsequential as he strode over to the reception desk in a couple, quick strides. No one was around. He dinged the small bell, and waited. At precisely the same moment he heard the distant, delayed chiming of a shop bell, triggered by his entrance through the door. He cringed inwardly. Well he remembered his first job in a local deli, where the combination of impatient customers, ringing counter bells, and chiming entrance sensors used to drive him nearly to the brink of insanity.

The call he'd received earlier from the local cop shop filled him in on everything that had happened, at least for the most part. A vicious fight in an alleyway. One man shot dead, blood trails suggested another wounded. No one seemed to know who it was or how badly. Gates had been called because the jogger who found the body had requested his presence. While that point offered up more questions than answers, Gates had no desire to start that conversation over the phone. He agreed to come, speak with the girl, and identify the body. According to the officer on the phone, it was a man he should be acquainted with; when he heard the name, the entire situation took on a newer, darker element, particularly in relation to the owner of the unidentified blood trail.

Gates wouldn't have admitted it to anyone, but he was worried. He knew he shouldn't be. It was, after all, none of his business anymore. But the heart and mind often disagree over protocol.

The insistent cacophony of bells had brought forth a young man from the back room, and he advanced in a spritely fashion to the massive, bar-like structure where Gates waited. He looked like a sheep dog. Very alert, dedicated, but hampered in a comical fashion by the hair hanging down around his eyes in a solid mass.

"Deputy Gates?" He asked expectantly, and at Gates' nod, held out a hand. A vibrant, blue eye was visible through the curtain of dark blonde. "Dusty. Boss-man's son. Right this way."

"Thank you. Sorry about the bell."

Dusty just laughed.

"You have worked behind a counter at some point," he observed.

He was a friendly chap, Gates soon found out. He chattered and talked with his hands all the way out of reception, in the office to get a key, and all the way down the long, sparely-lit corridor to where, Gates assumed, his objective awaited him.

"Apparently, his name is Bryan Culp," Dusty said, consulting a piece of paper, "but we were told to check with you. I guess there is no one else to confirm it."

Gates quirked an eyebrow in acknowledgement.

"If it is him, there are plenty of people, I assure you," he replied. "Trouble is, they're all in prison, in varying levels of security."

"Point taken."

The environment into which Dusty admitted him was even more offensive than the reception area, if that was possible. The flower smell wilted under the harsh ministrations of chemicals and sterile washes that mantled the gloomy room where Glenelg Mortuary kept its bodies. The lights were already on, their fluorescent, blue light flickering and jumping over the walls and stainless steel doors stacked one on top of the other like so many chess squares. Dusty advanced to the furthest row and pulled open the bottom door, sliding out the slab with an apologetic air.

"We did what we could for him, but it's a bit…" He trailed off with a vague gesture that Gates was able to interpret as "messy". "We don't get many like this," he finished. "There's enough of his face left to tell who he is – was – but below that…"

Gates just nodded.

The sheet covering the body rustled as it was pulled back, and Gates got a look at the body. The first thing that crossed his mind was that, yes, this was Bryan Culp; the second, Dusty was right. Aside from the head, there wasn't a lot left.

Well, he's done a good job with this one, Gates thought to himself, but said nothing aloud aside from the necessary statement to indicate that this was, indeed, the correct body.

So, there was number nine. Dead and gone. After ten years, there was only one left. Gates wondered how long it would be before that last man would be seen lying on a slab much like this one, and what would happen once this long, horrible campaign was finally over. What could happen?

"I wish I knew," he said quietly.

"Sorry?"

Gates shook his head. He knew all too well that final body lying on a slab might not be the one he anticipated.

"Nothing. Where's the girl?"

"Out in the waiting room." Dusty covered the body of Bryan Culp and shoved it unceremoniously back into the locker, closing the door. "She wouldn't leave," he said with a shrug. "Said you had been called, and she would stay until you got here."

"She say why?"

"Nope. I think she was jogging and found the body in an alleyway."

Same as Gates had heard over the phone. Whatever this girl wanted, she was playing her cards close to the vest. While he talked, Dusty led Gates back out of the sterile environment, back into the slightly-less-offensive space of the front reception area.

"You see this?" He asked, whipping a thick newspaper off the back side of the desk. On the front page was a half-page article about a blue sapphire necklace that had been unearthed in Mexico, whisked away to the UK by a rich family.

IS IT REAL? The headline read. *Goldsteins uncover priceless necklace in Mexico, hint at ties to Robin Hood legend...*

Gates smiled to himself. He hadn't seen, but there was someone he knew who would have been all over that.

"I usually start with the sports section," he said lightly.

"I did until I started betting on all the wrong horses." Dusty made a face and dropped the paper back onto the table. "She's over there," he said, obviously meaning the girl. "All right if I leave you to it? I need to lock the back up."

It was the girl Gates had seen on his way in. He wondered what she wanted.

"Be my guest. Thanks for your time." He shook the proffered hand and waited until Dusty took his leave before walking toward the couches on the far side. The girl didn't see him coming. She was cat-napping on the corner couch, hand resting underneath one delicate cheek while a collection of white wires crisscrossed and tangled over the front of her blue, cotton sweater. Dark hair fell across part of her face. She was a pretty young lady; probably in her early to mid-thirties, her delicate features held that classic, girl-next-door type appeal so often overlooked in a society fixated by exotic beauties. She reminded Gates of his wife. Gently, he touched her on the shoulder with a quiet word, and at the motion she sat up, smiling as she pulled her earphones out. She was surprisingly calm.

"Hi," she said, holding out a hand. "I'm Anne. You must be Mr. Gates."

"I am." Gates sat down next to her, settling in to the plush couch that was, indeed, as comfortable as he imagined. "Dusty over there told me you wouldn't leave," he said without preface. "You mind telling me why?"

Anne's pretty face held no reservation.

"I wanted to talk to you."

"So I heard. And your family…"

"They know I'm here," she said immediately. "My husband drove me from the police station. Funny, I'm in a hospital every day without a problem but that cop shop made me nervous."

"You're a doctor?"

"Nurse. Five years. You?"

"US Marshals Service based in Texas. Fifteen."

"Texas… long way to travel. Ever have a day off?"

"Occasionally," Gates said dryly. "My leave falls in June this year. I'm taking the missus to London. Will be the first time for both of us; at least, in a recreational capacity."

"Sounds exciting."

"I hope not," he laughed. "If things keep going the way they've been, I'll wind up spending my whole trip in the pub."

There was a brief moment of silence. Anne wound her headphones up and put them in her pocket.

"So what's all this about, Anne?" Gates asked, folding his hands in his lap. "You found the body this afternoon, and now you won't go home until you talk to me."

"I was there," was the unexpected response. "In the alley, when the fight happened. I saw the whole thing."

"I see…" Gates was always glad for the immaculate poker face he'd developed over the years for moments exactly like this. He sat back in the comfy couch and crossed his arms, staring across the room. "This does put a new spin on things," he mused thoughtfully. "Why didn't you say so before? The police report indicates you arrived after the incident was over."

"He asked me not to say anything. For my safety."

The statement hit him like a ton of bricks.

"Who?" Gates glanced at her quickly, not daring to think she might mean the person he hoped. The one he wanted to hear about but daren't ask after; the man possibly responsible for the blood trail no one was able to identify.

"He didn't tell me his name," Anne said gently.

"Can you describe him?"

"He was tall… strong features, Australian accent. Reddish hair. His eyes were hazel but very intent. He gave me this and said to call you; that I could trust you and you would understand everything. And that I shouldn't say anything to anyone else." She pulled out a piece of paper, on which Gates recognized his name and phone number, written in hand writing that was also very familiar. Even through regret that surfaced, Gates was unable to stop a small smile. It was him. The clever scoundrel had gotten away again; more lives than a damned cat, he had.

"Well I'll be damned," he said softly, and took the paper delicately. Never, in a million years, would he have thought he'd see that penmanship again.

Anne was studying his face closely.

"It's been difficult, hasn't it?"

Gates merely nodded.

"Is he your son?"

"No… no, he's not. What else did he tell you?"

"Not much. He…" Anne paused, collecting her thoughts. "He asked me if I was all right. He'd been shot, in the leg, but it wasn't critical. He was dirty and ragged and looked like he hadn't slept in a week, but still he seemed…" She considered. "It's strange, really. There was something about him… I don't know what it is…"

"No one knows what it is," Gates returned lightly. "He's just one of those people who is larger than life."

"Invincible."

"I hope so." Gates tucked the paper in his pocket. "I'll keep this, if you don't mind," he added. "It would be better if this conversation remained between the two of us."

"I understand," Anne said.

"And, Anne…" Gates considered a moment. "What you were told this afternoon is right. I can't go into detail, but for your safety and that of your family, I think it best that you were never in that alley," he said pointedly. "The man you met this afternoon has some powerful enemies, spread throughout a number of disreputable circles. You've spoken with him, seen him alive. I don't think I need to tell you how dangerous that is."

"I thought as much." Anne smiled slightly, a bit ruefully. "I can keep a secret if you can."

"You have my word."

"Now what?"

Gates reached in his pocket and pulled out a small business card, handing it to her.

"If you need anything, call me. If you see something weird, call me. If this day comes back to you in any way, call me. You've done the right thing and kept your involvement quiet, so the chances are low, but just in case."

Anne accepted the card delicately and her eyes flicked to the badge on his chest, partially covered by the fold of his sport coat.

"Who is he?"

"An old friend," Gates said. "An old friend that I hope, for both of our sakes, I never have to see again."

Chapter 2

It was hot for June. Anyone in San Luis Obispo would have readily stated that. For residents of coastal California accustomed to a gentle, seventy-five to eighty degree spectrum of early summer sunshine, the sudden blasting they were receiving of one hundred and ten degrees was unreal, and highly inconvenient for those still stuck in the final weeks of class. This included the lecturers.

Gregg Nicholas would have rather been anywhere but here: boiling like a pot roast in his miniscule Cal Poly office staring at the desk; no AC, no hope of escape. The view from the window taunting him with the promise of freedom. Term papers everywhere. Taunting him with the reality of lecturing.

News blips in the paper and on tv, regaling him with stories and theories about that cursed necklace. Taunting him with the passage of time. Taunting. Like everything else.

He had really thought that was the key, back in November. He had thought, finally, he was on a roll. When that necklace surfaced, everything made sense, and he had been ready to go treasure hunting. He had tried for weeks to get in touch with Amantha Goldstein to secure an interview; through her publicist, through the news, through every channel he had possibly thought could bring him some success. Nothing. The woman and her necklace were as untouchable as Jupiter.

Then, not three weeks later, the site works began. A block was purchased by the Goldstein family in the middle of London, and was immediately leveled, a collection of historical buildings taken back to bare ground in the blink of an eye. The official reason was to make way for a bigger, better building. A museum. The Goldsteins already had one such masterpiece, a monster of a structure that had opened its doors last July; they claimed they wanted another. An extension, to "expand the current enterprise". For all anyone knew, that brief press release might be telling the truth. But to Gregg, the sudden hive of activity meant only one thing: those people were onto something. Something big. Triggered by the finding of Marian's Necklace.

He'd begun to get discouraged shortly after when he received the fourth rejection letter. Form letter. Again. By then the necklace was safely ensconced in the Goldstein Museum, on display for the public to drool over, and completely inaccessible. Anger followed his discouragement, and he had delved vengefully into his research once more, bound and determined to find answers, if for no other reason than to prove a point. But it had been an uphill battle.

Ever since that computer crash in January, things had been rotten. Gregg was stopped in his tracks. He had been so close. After twenty years, to have it all nearly snatched away by such a heartless turn of events was gut-wrenching. It had taken him another month to find someone good enough to get the data off of his fried hard drive, and until last week the work was still ongoing. Funnily enough, it was the computer nerd himself who kept Gregg's spirits up and determination firing during the long process; without this kid, Gregg seriously doubted he would have been able to keep the dream alive after all that had happened.

Jared Casey. An indispensable ally with all his work and endless computer magic; an amusing image with his corny sense of humor and devotion to anything and everything edible, despite the fact that Jared was skinny as a rail and would probably never change. Behind his wire-rimmed glasses, baby-blue eyes looked twice their actual size. Innocent as a child's those eyes were, but observant and accurate as any lie detector. And Gregg was pretty sure there was more than a little bit of hacking experience in Jared's past.

Another ten minutes in his office and Gregg needed out. This was ridiculous. He packed up his things, waved good-bye to the HR girls, and bolted out of the stifling building. Outside wasn't much better. But at least it was expected.

The sun blasted across landscape still clinging stubbornly to veins of green that stretched through California's infamous golden hillsides. Tall prairie grasses undulated under the hot breeze blowing through the valley, shimmering like strips of precious metal. Majestic oaks waved, their deep green leaves casting shadows, a stark contrast to the grass they were surrounded by.

As he passed by the arena in the "aggie" section of campus, he paused for a moment to watch a couple of brave souls take on the heat to perfect their team-roping. Lathered horses fidgeted in place and cowboys wiped sweat from their brows, waiting for the signal. On cue they swept down the arena, lariats winging rhythmically over their heads, their horses with flattened ears and keen strides.

The sight was one Gregg knew well. In another time, and another place, one of those boys would have been him. He popped his door open to let his car air out a minute before getting in, staring mindlessly at the activity in the arena. This was a beautiful time of year, he had to admit, despite the heat. A beautiful time of year and a beautiful gem of a town; after visiting the area during college and embarking on an unexpected string of adventures, Gregg knew he would want to return here. When the opportunity presented itself, he had pulled up stakes without a second thought. He had been living and working in "SLO" for nearly six years now and had never regretted the decision. The scenery was gorgeous, the people were friendly, and the wine was excellent.

It was a good place to settle down.

Gregg had always been a little bit of a wanderer. Even as a kid, growing up in Lockhart, Texas, he'd felt there was something more, something bigger. Since the age of five he had known he wanted to see the world, experience all its wonder, and he had spent the majority of his younger years doing just that: exploring, conquering, learning. He and his best friend, taking on the world together. First as schoolboys, then as servicemen, and finally as deputies in the US Marshals Service. But things change. People change. Paths are taken. Sometimes those paths, outside the law, cannot be followed by someone else. And Gregg found himself continuing his journey of discovery alone.

He looked back at the team-ropers in the arena. Not a week went by that he didn't think about those times. About him. The friend Gregg let stumble, fall, and disappear from his life. He'd been dwelling on it a lot more recently; why, exactly, he couldn't say. It could have just been the guilt catching up with him. Failure was something that tended to gnaw away at one's soul.

Perhaps that guilt, that feeling of failure, was why the story of Robin Hood still meant this much to him after so many years. It was the one thing in Gregg's life that had survived, remained constant despite the drastic changes that had happened in the past. And yet, for all that, it remained a mystery. Incomplete. An open-ended question just waiting to be answered. Maybe by finishing it, Gregg could sort of hit a reset button. Maybe, he felt, putting a full stop at the end of this one project might help right some wrongs, change the trajectory of his own history. Of course he knew it wasn't possible to physically undo what had been done, but a little closure never hurt anybody. Gregg wanted to put the past to rest. And the greatest symbol of his past was this story. It had been there at the beginning in his youth, and it was the thing he had buried himself in when his whole world was falling apart. He felt, after this final quest, that he might finally be ready to hang up his adventurer's hat and call it a day, at peace with himself and his role in life. Build a white picket fence, find a girl who could put up with him, buy a dog. Move on.

It was time to move on.

"You look like you want to chase some cows," a voice said behind him.

Gregg jumped and spun around.

"Jenny, hey!" Cringing inwardly at his own vocals, Gregg covered it up with a smile he hoped was even remotely convincing in its nonchalance. "I was just letting the car air out a bit... you know... didn't want to turn into a human barbeque..." He cut himself off before the rabbit trails got too ridiculous. "The office was killing me," he finished lamely.

"Tell me about it." Jenny Eleanor laughed and adjusted the baseball cap situated on her head, the movement causing the ponytail she had stretching through the back to bob prettily. Her hair was an unusual shade of auburn; Gregg found it highly distracting. He scrambled around in his brain for something to say, found nothing. But then, Jenny always had that effect. It was what happened when a beautiful woman greeted a guy who was not overly experienced in the dating scene.

"I hear Jared and the boys are hosting another Halo battle tonight," Jenny continued. "It promises to be – and I quote – 'epic'."

"It always is," Gregg said dryly.

"You going?"

"I'll see how I go with these." Gregg made a face and resignedly held up the pile of papers he'd been hugging for moral support. "For the time being, I would say it is unlikely."

"You realize, of course, that Jared probably wrote half those."

"Yeah, I can find a pattern after a while," Gregg chuckled. "The kid's good, but his use of split infinitives gives him away every time. I mark accordingly."

Jenny laughed.

"Well, let me know how you do," she said. "Give me a buzz if you end up going – you know where to find me."

Gregg just smiled and nodded, cursing himself as she walked off. He wished he could come up with something clever to say. Unfortunately, it was becoming painfully obvious to him, and who knew how many others, that attempting speech with Jenny tied a trucker's knot around his tongue. Highly inconvenient.

He didn't know Jenny that well. She had come to Cal Poly about seven months ago, the new replacement for Professor Burns, who suffered a stroke and was forced into early retirement. Gregg heard quite a few stories about the young lady taking his place (nice legs, smart, nice legs, very sweet, nice legs) but it had been a good two or three weeks before he actually had occasion to see for himself.

That occasion had been one of the campus staff briefings. Gregg had walked in the room and spotted Jenny, just like that, leaning against the wall next to the far window. Her hair was pulled back in a loose ponytail, the auburn lengths flopped carelessly over one shoulder, framing her face with color. Although he didn't know who she was and didn't learn her name until a few minutes later, Gregg was completely astounded. This girl was so beautiful, so delicate, yet showed such poise and strength of character that he was afraid to even approach her. He'd been doubly unnerved when he turned to answer a greeting directed at him from that side of the room and found her watching him.

Not that she meant anything by it, of course; once he knew who she was, her intentions were all too obvious. She was new, the place unfamiliar, and she was studying her colleagues so she could recognize them in the future. Still, Gregg had found himself in no slight panic when he had chanced to meet those eyes, so soft and serene, yet full of a desire to learn about life. From afar he had studied her, the gentle curves of her figure, the way she walked and gestured, how she was continually tucking that stray tendril of hair behind her ear. In Jenny he had found many an interesting conversation, however short, on some of the rainy afternoons when they were all stuck indoors. She was a fun girl with a quick wit; positive, but in a very calming, down-to-earth sort of way. Pragmatic.

Gregg suddenly wondered what she would say if he asked her out. His stomach clenched at the thought. What if she said no? What if he suddenly became incapable of speech, which seemed quite a strong possibility? He truly had come to like her... *really* like her... but did she see anything in him?

With the idea and all its implicative scenarios knocking around in his head, Gregg drove home. While he owned this house outright, most of the others around him were rentals taken up by college students. Sometimes this was a good thing. Sometimes not. It depended on how much one actually wanted to accomplish on a given day and how much sleep was necessary. A few houses down was the house Jared rented; typically, it was full of geeks and engineers every weekend, when Jared and his housemates hosted legendary land parties. Gregg could sometimes hear the shouting and swearing all the way at his house, right along with the familiar soundtracks to Call of Duty, Grand Theft Auto, and Halo.

The house was cool and dark when he walked in. Throwing the remaining term papers on the counter, Gregg skulled a glass of water and wandered aimlessly into his living room. He thought about turning on the tv, picked up the remote, thought better of it and dropped the device back on the couch. He'd probably just get distracted anyway, and he still had a lot of work to do.

The realization that tv was potentially a greater priority than his Robin Hood research was, by now, a fact Gregg accepted resignedly. He knew, as he had for months, that he was nearing the end of his tether. He was getting discouraged; battling time, battling will power, battling the little voice in the back of his mind that told Gregg he should really be growing up by now. He glanced at the new computer Jared had spent so many hours setting up for him and once again discovered that his primary emotion was guilt. Not anticipation.

Maybe it was time. Even the best relationships can turn toxic, given the right set of circumstances. Everyone had things they regretted; perhaps this was just meant to be one of his. Gregg figured if this was the worst thing he'd regret in life, he was doing well. He had a good job, a good house, and lived in a nice town. He knew a few people that would literally kill to be in his shoes. Aside from the nagging feeling of unfinished business hanging over his head, life was pretty damn good. And Gregg was realizing it was up to him to decide whether or not he was going to allow that feeling to win. At a few months shy of forty, it was possibly high time he gave it all up.

He only had one life. He was approaching the big 4-0. Might as well get on with it.

****

It was hot for June. Anyone in London would have readily stated that. With the sudden spate of temperatures soaring over twenty-two degrees Celsius came the usual reports of chaos: crowded beaches, suffocating residents, and the typical segment on the evening news detailing *exactly* how hot the city had managed to get. ("Today, London was hotter than Athens, Los Angeles, Paris, *and* Sydney!") As the earth moving equipment continued making slow, plodding steps across the land, Marcus Remo ran the back of his hand over his forehead, grimacing at the sweat beading on his brow. He'd worked in Cairo during the height of summer – even that failed to compare with the miserable, heavy, sticky heat of London during one of her fickle hot spells.

It was going to be a long afternoon. Bare ground stretched around him on all sides like a desert, dotted by men and equipment and a few prefab buildings along the back side of the lot. It was surrounded by a rented chain link fence and guarded twenty-four-seven by private security, mainly to ensure that the continual stream of people bunched along the fence didn't get too cozy.

The site was originally a block of flats that butted up against the back wall of an old, rundown pub; both buildings had failed government codes of varying degrees and titles in the not-so-distant past, allowing the land to be bought and redeveloped. The buyer of the small selection of lots was a rich family by the name of Goldstein. Marcus had, of course, heard of them (unless one lived under a rock they were quite hard to miss), but he had no idea just how loaded the people really were until he saw the proposed budget for this project. And he had no idea how famous they were until he found himself hounded for autographs and bribed by journalists for inside information.

It had taken Marcus, and most of his workers, a good few weeks to get used to the stares, cat calls, and uninvited visitors that came along with working for a celebrity family. It had started as soon as Marcus set foot on the premises the first time, and continued with unrelenting consistency. Even now they were there, standing, waiting, photographing; Marcus recognized many faces as paparazzi that came by every day in the hopes of gathering some new, juicy tid-bit, but mainly they were tourists. Yanks with their sneakers and knee-high socks; Canadians decked out in maple-leaf outer wear in a desperate attempt to alienate themselves from their southern neighbors; Asians who stopped every three meters along the fence to take a photo; a few Australians sporting "green-n-gold" accessories and Bin Tang singlets, boardies, and thongs regardless of season and weather conditions. It was an odd assortment, and it proved just how far the Goldstein name reached. Marcus often wondered how hard it would be to recruit a few of these bystanders to do some unskilled labor for him… maybe even take over the whole project. He was tired of standing here accomplishing nothing.

Before him, the ground was as bare was it was yesterday, and the day before, and the week before that. Nothing had changed. Only the equipment shifted position, moving around the perimeter like monopoly pieces. Supposedly, in the near future, this location would be home to a museum – rather, the continuation of a museum – and was slated to be open to the public by Christmas. Considering that demolition work had begun in November, seven long and arduous months ago, Marcus somehow doubted it.

It had started out with such grand and marvelous flair. When Marian's necklace had been found, the Goldstein family had been on a high; not without coincidence, this project had been announced shortly afterward, and work had commenced almost immediately. It had dominated the headlines from the beginning. Now, as the months dragged on and nothing happened, the excitement was beginning to fade. Only those within the Goldstein clan, who had always been tight-lipped about the project, remained unchanged.

They had bought this block of land with the intention of expanding their museum. At least, that was what the public knew. The Goldsteins already had one museum across town, which, in and of itself, was massive; twice the size of the location Marcus was helping develop, it was a monstrous affair that stretched several stories both above and below the surface streets. It was attractive, undoubtedly, but Marcus still failed to see, as he had from the start, why these people even needed that much space. He also failed to see why that building took only a few months to fully complete, whereas he and his team had barely begun to properly break ground in a much longer amount of time.

And no one could even begin to explain why this addition was located where it was: halfway across the city and a good forty-five minutes to an hour's drive, when there were at least three sites in better locations, and much closer. Somehow, he didn't think it had to do with cost.

The whole thing was weird. In any ordinary circumstance, seven months would have been enough time to clear the ground and see a suitable completion to not only the foundations, but most of the structure; as it was, Marcus and his men were still stuck digging holes in a seemingly-random pattern over the two thousand square meter landscape, while Goldsteins hovered like vultures over their shoulders and tourists added their photos to "my holiday in London" albums. And then there was the press.

Marcus had heard of this kind of stuff on telly: reporters going through rubbish, staking out the yards of famous people… this was the first time he'd ever encountered something of that nature in person. He had been chosen to head the project on recommendation of someone who knew someone who knew a Goldstein; to this moment, he still had no clear reason why. He had a hunch it was because he showed little interest in the family and was therefore a safe bet for keeping his mind to task. Marcus had the laborious chore of sourcing and hiring an entire crew, outfitting them, and checking I.D. every morning before they clocked on; during original interviews and over the proceeding few months, he had already weeded out a number of reporters trying to sneak on site and get the scoop. Security had been doubled as of a few weeks ago when one of them tried to hop over a nearby fence and join the crew. Numerous break-ins had been thwarted, mainly by Robin Hood nuts who were after treasure. Amazing how the crazies surfaced in times like these.

Even before he had come on board, he'd heard stories of what was happening on this site. The inevitable protests as old buildings were pulled down, the praises for renovation, the speculation. Always speculation. Where there was a Goldstein, questions and theories were soon to follow. Why here? Why now? What do they hope to get out of it?

The press and the public were utterly relentless. Goldstein mania had hit a fever pitch right before the start of this project, when a one-of-a-kind, blue sapphire necklace had been discovered in Mexico, the finding once again catapulting the Goldsteins, their money, and their history, back into the front pages. Just in time for Marcus' crew to start work.

After that first week on the job, Marcus had several very definitive opinions about life in the fish bowl. Even his family and the families of some of his foremen had found themselves in the firing line a time or two, as the press sought gems of information and the public just wanted snapshots. Seven months was a long time to be working for someone as famous as a Goldstein. Especially when, as Marcus often considered with no small amount of resignation, there was no end in sight. If this was a museum, Marcus reckoned he was a bloody Chinese emperor. He had worked on construction sites around the world, had been involved in everything from the planning to the demolition to the construction of brand new, gleaming towers of glass the likes of which were so common in Dubai. The Goldsteins might think him a fool, a mere layman, but Marcus Remo understood far more than they gave him credit for. He was in charge of digging foundations for a building with no blueprint, in a location that made no sense. It hadn't taken him long to see things for what they really were: the Goldsteins weren't building another museum. What they were doing here was more like… searching.

Maybe the Robin Hood crazies weren't so crazy after all.

"Marcus!"

The authoritative voice even put the rumbling dump truck to shame. Marcus sighed.

"Yes, boss!" He called back, turning to face Nicolo Goldstein, self-appointed leader of the Goldstein mob. And probably the last person Marcus wanted to come in contact with today. The man was an absolute cad. Behind the double-breasted, tailor-made coat and perfectly-positioned tie existed a bizarre mixture of greed and perfectionism. In the old days, villains did the courtesy of dressing the part; now they wore suits and ties like everyone else.

Marcus made no move to leave his position, watching Nicolo with a subtle, wry smile as the latter made a finicky way across the site. Behind Nicolo, the fence line along the dig was still packed with people; cameras flashed and people pushed each other out of the way in the hopes of getting the shot of the day of the famous Nicolo Goldstein.

Nicolo was second generation of the modern Goldstein clan; his mother, Teresa, was originally part of the Greek upper class, and got shipped over to the UK when she married Michael Goldstein, Nicolo's father. Nicolo had inherited a striking combination of his father's prominent features and his mother's Mediterranean skin. Along with that he had picked up the family's insatiable love of anything profitable, and the brains to both hatch and see through schemes too shady for most to attempt. There was no one to get in his way. With a family like the Goldsteins backing his every move, he could not fail.

Like his mother and his two siblings, Nicolo entered into a semi-arranged marriage in his early twenties. That was how things were done in their circle; Marcus could easily imagine each young person of marrying age being handed a list and told to choose. To him, the idea was revolting, but then, he didn't have ten or twelve generations of wealth to safeguard. He guessed, being that high profile, it was only to be expected. Of course, things didn't always go to plan. While Nicolo did as he was told and married for money, two of his cousins, sisters, were not so pliable. The older of the two married a carpenter and removed herself from the family entirely. Her younger sibling tried something similar but was not so fortunate.

This sister attempted to do as her sibling had done, obtaining an unsuitable lover and severing all ties to her former life as a debutante. The situation was particularly offensive to the Goldsteins due to the fact that until the moment she disappeared, Stephanie Goldstein was the golden child: beautiful, ethereal, and perfect for the limelight. It was supposed to have been she who took up and carried the torch of honor for the family. As it was, that role fell to

Nicolo, when Stephanie bolted with her lover, leaving the Goldsteins little choice. The world outside her comfort zone, however, was too much for Stephanie's sheltered, cultivated soul. She finally dragged herself back into the fold, defeated, but her place had been lost and she was cut off as cleanly and mercilessly as a cancerous tumor. When she died in a car wreck five years later, only the tabloids were around to care… the tabloids, and her young daughter, Amantha.

"Marcus, we need to discuss progress," Nicolo was saying as he approached.

Of course they did. Like last week. And the week before. Marcus wished Nicolo would just drop the pretense and level with him, so he'd have a better idea of what results the man was after. For all he knew, Nicolo might think the treasure of the century was buried here; Marcus could be staring directly at it, but because he didn't know what to look for would probably miss it entirely.

"We've got the foundations for east wing nearly completed," he replied, gesturing broadly. "The west side is giving us a bit more trouble. A fair amount of rock, it has."

"Yes, yes, I can see that." The impatient response was delivered as Nicolo took stock of the situation with eyes shielded by sunglasses that cost more than the average car. He surveyed the workers, the landscape, the growing pile of earthen rubbish – composed namely of the rocks Marcus had mentioned – that was posted off to the side. "And when can we dispense with this?" He asked. "It's quite unsightly."

"I have men breaking it down as we speak."

"And what was beneath the rock when you took it out?"

"Nothing. More rock," Marcus answered. He crossed his arms. It was going to be a long day.

He kept his answers short while Nicolo plied him with questions; about the ground, the terrain, the type of earth being dug up and what it contained. Absolutely nothing about the schematics. Or the progress of the building. Or why there were six holes of varying depths and widths, as per request.

Nicolo finally ended the Q&A with a terse nod.

"Very well, then. Keep me updated."

"Certainly."

As always.

A car horn beeped along the front of the dig, causing both men to turn. Marcus couldn't stop a small smile when he identified the vehicle, a familiar one on site. The classic, old-school Mercedes whispered to a halt, and a hand emerged from the driver's side with a friendly wave. While Marcus returned this gesture in kind, Nicolo merely sighed in exasperation.

"What is she doing here?" He said under his breath. Unless he was mistaken, Marcus got the sudden impression Nicolo was rather like the kid with his hand caught in the cookie jar.

The car door opened and a tall, slender woman got out, leaning in to speak with the passenger before weeding a careful way through the throng of people that ceased loitering along the fence line to converge on her position. Marcus was immediately aware of the lessening of noise around him as several groups of workers lowered their tools to stare.

Amantha Goldstein, center of a scandalous paparazzi blitz as a child and now the object of many a male fantasy, cooked-up tabloid article, and much speculation, made her way easily over the rough ground in high heels, her slacks and fitted top hugging an enviable figure. Unlike Nicolo, she took to the trek with gusto.

"Morning, Marcus!" She called.

Marcus noted Nicolo's cross stare out of the corner of his eye. Nicolo hated informality of any kind, and Amantha was sort of the queen of it. Around him, the work was steadily slacking off; he zeroed in on a particularly smitten group of young men who had dropped all pretense of progress, and singled them out.

"Oi, you lot!" He shouted. "Get back to work!"

The four heads readily dipped back to task, but Marcus saw them casting furtive glances in Amantha's direction. He couldn't blame them. Aside from seeing her on a daily-to-weekly basis at the dig, she cropped up all the time in the magazines his wife was so fond of. If he did say so himself, the photoshopping and formality did her little justice.

A photo could give only outward appearance: the ash blonde hair pulled in to a loose ponytail, several flyaway wisps framing a face of fair complexion and delicate of feature, one that could easily be seen turning to a smile. Grey eyes. What was missing, and what Marcus found so irresistible about Amantha, was her personality. She was a good boss and an even better poker player; quick-witted, feisty, and funny. She had come into her own out of her teens, proving herself to be not only a bright girl but a beautiful one, endowed with natural sophistication, and the Goldsteins were too savvy to let that lie in darkness. They took her media-ready persona and ran with it. As the lure of her mother's trespass faded, Amantha had taken on an ever-increased role among her familial counterparts, until now it looked like she just might take over where her mother left off. More than likely, she would have already been handed that list of suitable applicants to fill the job of husband; however at twenty-eight, she was already well past the age at which most of her cousins had wed, and while she would more than likely take on that role eventually, it would be to someone who not only made the family's list but hers as well. The Goldsteins were proud. Amantha was even more so. She had seen a lot in her young life: lost her mother under such horrible circumstances, spent the majority of her existence in a fish bowl of publicity. And then there was that incident at Heathrow Airport a few years back where she'd been nearly arm's length from two hostages who got shot in cold blood in a bizarre set of circumstances that dominated world news for months.

She'd seen a lot. But she'd emerged stronger. And working with her as closely as he had been, Marcus was able to make a well-educated guess that she was the one calling the shots. Amantha was no fool, and she knew how valuable her person was to the entity that was the Goldstein family. Cave to their demands she might, but it would be on her terms.

The pot-stirring half of Marcus' brain almost hoped she never took that path. It would be so satisfying to see someone of such a restricted profile break free and fly away. Of course, he would never admit that to anyone; such a confession would simply label him a tabloid junkie.

"Good morning to you, Miss Goldstein," he said respectfully as Amantha reached them.

"Really, Marcus, you know how I hate that. It's Amantha."

Nicolo stopped just short of sighing aloud.

"I thought we discussed the issue of befriending the workers, Amantha."

"We did," she replied sweetly. "It was the same conversation in which we decided it would be best if I liaise with them, not you." Her smile was innocent. "Too many chefs in the kitchen, and all that."

She turned back to Marcus with a bright smile. "So. How is it going? It's all very exciting, isn't it?" She asked, her eyes dancing as they met his.

"It's different," he acknowledged. He didn't elaborate, as he'd had a few discussions with Amantha already concerning the process beleaguering his team at the moment.

"Well, since everything seems to be under control here, I must be off. I have an appointment to make." Nicolo was already checking his watch as he spoke. "Remember," he added, "we have a press conference in the museum at one, and lunch directly beforehand with Lady Austin and her husband, so do not tarry here long." This last was said distastefully. It was well known that Nicolo had a distinct dislike for "the husband", who was Welsh, and married into the Austin fortune. As he once again made his way through the mud toward his car, parked like a shining beacon of over-indulgence in front of Amantha's much more subtle choice of wheels, Amantha crossed her arms.

"Was he very rude to you?" She asked once he was out of earshot. "He can be positively unbearable. At times it's hard to believe we're related, the way he speaks to me." Even as her grey eyes rolled in exasperation, her face held that concern, that kindness, Marcus was used to. He just shook his head with a smile.

"It takes more than a sharp tongue to bring me to tears, Miss Amantha," he said. "And, no. On this occasion he was almost bearable." He winked at her.

"Almost," they said together.

"Well, from what I can see, everything seems to be on schedule," she said observantly, matching up their surroundings with the plans Marcus knew she would have been studying earlier.

Whatever that schedule was. Marcus said as much, causing Amantha to quirk an eyebrow in acknowledgement.

"Don't I know it," she replied. "It appears to be keeping the press busy anyway, even if the premise is completely false."

It was no surprise to Marcus that Amantha was aware of the obvious difference between what was being said and what was being done. She wasn't that clueless.

"What are they looking for?" He asked.

"I don't know…" Amantha's face was pensive. "Nicolo doesn't tell me much about these things. All I am to him is a face people can identify with; there isn't much need-to-know on that level. He has something going on, but it's so hard to figure out what he's thinking." She frowned prettily. "Whatever it is, we'll find out soon enough, I should think," she continued. "Anyway, I must be off. I was on my way to his beloved lunch meeting when I heard someone mention that Nicolo was coming here first; I thought I would drop in to be sure he wasn't too much of an –" She stopped herself and gave Marcus a sideways glance. "– unpleasant individual."

Marcus laughed aloud. As Amantha smiled at him and took her leave, he returned his attention to the small bobcat scraping at the base of the most recent hole. As of this moment it was still shallow, merely a smoothed depression in the ground. As requested, a bobcat would continue working its way over the earth until the hole was precisely one meter deep, before stepping back and allowing the backhoe to take over until the desired depth of four meters was achieved.

A loud banging noise followed by scraping and the useless revving of the bobcat's engine brought the machine to a grinding halt. The driver repeated his attempts a few more times, then backed the machine out of the hole and signaled to Marcus, who waved back in acknowledgement. Another layer of rock. One of many things that had been slowing the work up this morning.

"Thomas!" He called, then whistled shrilly to get the attention of the nearest plant operator, waving him over. "We've hit more rock!"

Thomas lifted a hand in response and fired up the large backhoe, rumbling across the ground. The bucket poised momentarily over the hole, then delved downward, breaking up a massive chunk and lifting it unceremoniously from the ground. The bucket swung to drop the load into a dump truck that had crept up beside it. The bucket fell again, clanging into a particularly stubborn piece. It rose, then dove again with greater intensity. This time, it not only broke the rock apart, the bucket itself disappeared nearly half a meter into the ground.

"Wait, wait! Whoa, hold up!"

It was hard to tell who was more surprised: Marcus or the plant operator. As Thomas carefully extracted the bucket from its unlikely nesting place and reversed, Marcus jogged forward to have a look at the situation.

He found himself staring into a black hole.

"Let me see those plans," he said directly, and studied the printout of underground services with care. Sewer, power, water... nothing on his map was in this location. Power and sewage for the previous buildings had all been accounted for, on the far side of the dig. Even the multiple subway plans he'd been privy to, some stretching back to the very first tunnels ever constructed, showed nothing.

What was this?

"Ben, let me see your torch," he said. Carefully poking his head into the hole, he shined the light around curiously. On three sides, he saw nothing but wall. Wall, wall, wall...

Stairs. Stretching downward into the darkness at a steep, almost dangerous angle, reaching eight to ten meters in depth before winding to the left, out of sight.

Marcus took a long, slow breath and sat up.

"What is it?" Ben asked, retrieving the torch Marcus robotically handed to him.

Marcus didn't respond, merely indicated for Ben to poke his head in and have a look. Even as Ben's surprise exclamation reached his ears, Marcus was already trying to restructure this area in his mind, as related to the previous buildings. If he was not mistaken, the apartment block and pub were almost perfectly situated to frame this location. Their foundations, covering an area of approximately one thousand meters squared, would have acted like a shield; no matter how advanced the city became, so long as those buildings remained in this location, there would have been no change. Marcus recalled some of the protests surrounding the demolition of the structures, mostly concerning their age and historical value. 1800's vintage, on foundations that were much, much older. Which meant that, someone not only knew this mysterious stairway was here, they'd gone to great lengths to cover it up – and keep it that way. In that moment, Marcus realized they'd just found whatever it was the Goldsteins were so desperate to uncover. Were the crazies right? Did it have to do with the necklace? Robin Hood's gold? He didn't know.

Workers had gathered at the sudden activity, scrunching in and rubbernecking for a better look at the hole. Marcus caught a couple tourists by the fence taking interest in the proceedings, one with a small, digital camera trained directly on them. While the device was limited in its capability, assuredly, Marcus had a feeling he and his team had just contributed to the top story on the evening news.

"Call Amantha back," he said immediately. "And get this covered up. Now, before one of those monkeys with a high-tech camera gets a glimpse of it. I think we found what we were looking for."

Even as a tarp flapped into place over the broken segments and workers began to disperse reluctantly, Marcus knew it was only a matter of time before word got out. Over by the fence, the paparazzi had begun to smell blood and were closing in, positioning themselves for attack. The chess pieces were set, and the board was in motion. Whatever this was, and whatever it meant, they wouldn't be able to keep it a secret for long.

Not in this city.

Chapter 3

"Jared, come on! We need to get these monitors set up!"

"Yeah, give me fifteen minutes!"

A head of tousled blonde hair poked through the doorway.

"You said that fifteen minutes ago… you're starting to sound like you work for an airline."

"And you're starting to sound like my mother." Jared Casey made a face at his housemate and went back to work. "I have to get this done today, Andy," he elaborated. "It's due tomorrow."

"And whose fault is it for procrastinating?"

"I wasn't procrastinating!" Jared retorted. "I can't help it if everything happens at once. The next time you need to finish two essays and a PhD thesis in five days, you let me know."

Andy rolled his eyes and retreated.

"Just tell me when you're done!" He called from the other room. "The best way to ruin the world's most epic land party is to run out of player space!"

"Or Pringles," Jared muttered. He continued slogging through the sixth page of references he'd tacked on to the end of his aforementioned thesis, a two hundred-page beast of a document covering the social and political implications of the internet, and the possible effects such a technology could have had on the direction of humanity if applied during crucial moments throughout history.

The room around him was that of a typical rental in San Luis. Possibly a little cleaner, as both Jared and Andy had at least a basic set of standards, but definitely nothing fancy. The carpet was old and worn, the windows barely latched, the paint on both the interior and exterior was badly in need of an update. On particularly rainy days, a bucket had to be placed under a leaky spot in the kitchen ceiling. The septic system was as ancient as the rest of the place, and just as faulty, as evidenced by the circular, brown patch in their two-by-four slice of lawn in the back.

Out front, the narrow street was lined with cars. College kids, like himself, clogging up the arteries of SLO's back streets with varying degrees of parking skill. Jared glanced out the window just in time to see Gregg tootle by in his '95 Ford rust bucket, dash board decorated with a stack of papers.

While his original guess of fifteen minutes turned out to be slightly ambitious, it wasn't outlandish. Half an hour later, Jared was printing off the final pages of his labor of love and carefully sliding it into a large, yellow envelope. With a sigh of ultimate relief, he sealed it and, rising, sauntered to the edge of the desk to drop it on a pile of identical envelopes. Whipping out a Sharpie, he labelled his latest creation in the same manner he had all the others: project title and author. In this case, the text read "Social and Political Implications of the Internet", and was written by Justin Gardner.

"You're crazy," Andy said from behind him. "One of these days you're going to get caught."

"I already have been." Jared finished off his label with a flourish. "And by this time tomorrow I'm also going to be well paid," he said in satisfaction. He flicked the Sharpie back into its holder and clapped Andy on the shoulder. "Now. Let's get this party rocking."

The boys went to work, unpacking and setting up the twenty monitors Jared had found for a bargain on Craigslist the week before. He and Andy got along well. They'd been friends since elementary, back in the days of cream-colored, Apple computers with black screens that were really only good for word processing and making cool little drawings. They'd met when they both caught each other trying to sneak into the computer lab (temporarily located in the corner of the school gym, next to the locker rooms) in the hopes of catching a glimpse of the girls' basketball team sans uniform. They failed, but had been best friends ever since.

While Andy lacked the same drive to accumulate wealth, he was every bit as tricky. If either of them had been asked who was better, it would have been a grudging, overall draw, with each party taking credit for various facets of trickery.

"We should have a good crowd tonight," Andy said, surveying their handiwork. The house was covered in cords, power strips, and zip ties, sporting that all-too-familiar smell of technology. "Gregg coming?"

"I haven't heard back from him yet."

"He's probably stuck grading all those term papers you wrote for his students," Andy cracked, and Jared laughed, knowing that was actually probably the case.

In point of fact, it was a situation precisely like that through which Jared first met the quirky, likeable professor. Gregg had somehow cottoned onto the fact that one of his students had handed in a project that had not actually been created by that student. He had then somehow gone on to figure out that Jared was the one who actually wrote it. Jared still didn't know how; at the time, he didn't even know he'd been had until he walked out to his car one day and found some guy leaning on the fender, dressed casually, dark hair neatly cropped into a crew cut. That person of course was Gregg, complete with fraudulent paper in hand and a quizzical smile on his face. Blue-green eyes surveyed Jared keenly, but not angrily.

"You must be Jared Casey," he'd said in an amicable tone, and held up the paper. "I have to say I admire your work."

Jared tried to bluff his way out of it and failed miserably. When he finally admitted his crime, he was surprised at the response.

"Well, at least you're honest," Gregg had said cheerfully. "Meet me in my office in an hour; I have a project of my own I want to discuss with you."

"And… your office is where…?"

Gregg just smirked at him.

"You're the computer wizard. You figure it out."

So, Gregg had been doing research of his own. As soon as Jared showed up, right on time, the professor had sat him down and told him a story. A story about treasure, knights in shining armor, damsels, and riddles. Truthfully, Jared had never heard anything so ridiculous. It was so ridiculous, in fact, that it had him hooked. When Gregg finally got around to the crux of the conversation – a crashed computer that needed data rescued – Jared knew he'd been very handily roped in to be the sucker to fix it. When he got it done, he noticed how disorderly Gregg's digital filing system was. So he fixed that too. He'd spent the next few months cataloguing, sorting, sifting, and generally familiarizing himself with nearly twenty years' worth of information. Somewhere in there, he earned himself a friend.

Gregg was not one to acquire friendships easily, he found out; Jared had a hunch there were a few burned bridges back there somewhere. He knew Gregg was from Texas, a fact not hard to ascertain given the slight accent that still mantled his easy voice, and that he had a few siblings roaming around. They weren't close. It wasn't a great secret or anything, as Gregg was not at all close-mouthed about himself, just quiet. A thinker. He had done quite a bit with his life, and every time they spoke it seemed Jared was learning something new. At last count, he knew Gregg had been involved in a trucking company he'd helped start from scratch during high school, attained an officer's rank in the Navy, and had spent a couple of years as a US Marshal. He'd traveled extensively, completed a teaching degree, and now taught at one of the best universities in the state of California. And he was a qualified pilot. Not bad for an old guy. Jared could only hope he'd be able to accomplish even half that much by the time he hit forty.

He stood mindlessly, arms crossed, as Andy turned on their massive, fifty-two inch tv and started flicking through the illegal cable network he and Jared had managed to hook in to, possibly hoping to find a good movie to backlight their afternoon. Jared looked on wordlessly, mesmerized by the changing colors with each station. Subtle, bright, dark, floral…

A program suddenly flashed across and he jolted to life.

"Wait, Andy… go back to that."

If Andy hadn't hit the channel exactly then, Jared doubted he would have even cared. His brain had already labeled the color scheme as "drab". What caught his eye wasn't the scene, or the audio, or the people in the shot; rather, it was the single phrase flashing across the screen at that precise moment: *"GOLDSTEIN GEM"*.

Jared grabbed another remote and turned the tv up as it came back on.

"For those of you who are just tuning in," the program broadcaster was saying. *"This is an aerial view of what was supposed to be the second portion of the Goldstein Museum, the completed half of which has been wowing visitors from all over the world since it*

opened in July. But, as you can see, construction crews have come across something a little more interesting than they thought. Mere hours ago, work was progressing on schedule when, apparently, crews nearly lost a piece of equipment down a hole. And when project manager Marcus Remo looked inside, he was shocked with what he found."

The scene swapped to the shaky, pixelated video of a digital camera that was honed in on a group of men crouched around the very same hole in the ground, looking stunned. In the background, Jared could hear a Japanese speaker, probably the owner of the camera, talking to those around her in curiosity. He couldn't pick all of it out; his Japanese was a little on the rusty side. In the video, the man clearly in charge could be seen gesturing to his workers, and a large tarp was dragged over the opening while all involved looked around furtively. Clearly, they had hoped they weren't seen.

"For more on this developing story, we're going to take you down inside the dig, with Carl Heyward, for an exclusive look at what has been found here in London. Carl..."

"Thank you, Julianne..." The scene switched to a middle-aged newscaster with a beard and a full dad-bod standing on the lip of a four-foot-wide hole. Beside him, the construction worker from the previous video stood patiently, his posture indicating he'd rather be anywhere but on international television.

"This could easily go down as the discovery of the decade," Carl was saying, *"and if it wasn't for a young tourist from Japan, who captured the amazing footage on her digital camera, we may never have had the opportunity to see what really lies beneath the surface of this site. I am joined by project manager Marcus Remo, who is undoubtedly the man of the hour..."*

Jared took brief note of the resigned look on Marcus' face before he slowly sat down on the bean bag in front of the tv. His mind was whirling. This dig had been all over the news for months. Since it began, Jared had been bombarded for information whether he asked for it or not; it seemed every time he turned on the television there was a new tidbit concerning the progress or the site or the myriad of break-ins that had been attempted by people who, Jared later found out, were much like Gregg. Men convinced that not only was the story of Robin Hood a real thing, it held the key to a vast treasure trove. Gregg had been nearly obsessed with this project. And now, for all intents and purposes, his obsession appeared well-founded. Everything Jared had seen and heard from Gregg since they met was hitting his brain as the newscast rolled, and it all came back to one point: Gregg was right. He'd been right all along. Since the beginning of Jared's involvement he'd harped on and on about the Goldsteins and their legend and how it was all connected to that necklace and how this construction project somehow tied it all together. Jared had started as a skeptic, then became a mild believer, thanks to combination of Gregg's enthusiasm and the massive amount of data Jared found himself sorting through.

Staring at the broadcast right in front of his face, he felt himself graduating to full-fledged groupie. For all intents and purposes, it appeared Gregg Nicholas had hit the nail on the head. He'd been right about the dig; if he was right about that, he was probably right about the rest of it. But what now?

"In just a few minutes," Carl said, *"we will have the honor of escorting you inside this newly discovered wonder of history to see it for yourself. But first, right after the break, I will be joined by Amantha Goldstein for some additional insight into the project."*

"Oh, my…" Jared finished the sentence under his breath and grabbed his cell phone. Dialed Gregg. There was no answer, so he tried again. Nothing. Swearing silently, Jared yanked his sneakers on over bare feet and ran for the door. "Andy, I have to go," he said over his shoulder. "Won't be long."

"Dude, really?"

"Yes, really."

Without another word, Jared snatched his laptop bag and dashed out the door, heading for Gregg's. This changed everything. Simply everything. And he didn't know what would happen now… but Gregg was going to want to see this.

****

"Gregg! Gregg! Turn on the tv!"

Gregg looked up at the yell and put his red pen down, which had been seeing quite a lot of use on the paper he was currently going over. He'd heard his phone ringing from across the room but, as he had with the television earlier, chose to ignore it for reasons of productivity. It didn't take a rocket scientist to figure out the call had been from Jared, and he wasn't too keen on being brushed off.

Enter, Jared Casey, stage left, he thought. "Afternoon to you too, Jared. Sorry to say, but I don't think I'm going to make it to your Halo party tonight."

Jared didn't even dignify him with a response. He simply walked in, snatched the remote off the couch, and flicked the tv on.

"Observe," he said simply. "And know that I am master."

"Of what?" Gregg retorted. He wandered over and leaned against the back of the couch. "You may be a genius, but your grammar in some of these papers is deplorable. I hope you gave your clients a discount." He caught the tail end of Jared's eye roll as he turned back to the screen, watching London's recognizable skyline hove into view onscreen. Within a few seconds, he not only saw what Jared was talking about, but wholeheartedly agreed the kid was master. Of everything.

"And, welcome back to our special, live broadcast. We are at the center of what could prove to be the most significant find of the century. One week ago, this area was nothing more than a construction site, preparing ground for the proposed second half of the Goldstein Museum. But at eleven o'clock this morning, everything changed..."

"Ha! I knew it!" Gregg celebrated. "I *knew* those people were up to something!"

"Wait, Gregg, it gets better," Jared said.

Gregg was stunned. Slowly, surely, everything he had been convinced of for the last seven months came to light on his television screen. The newscaster, listed as Carl Heyward on the bottom of the screen, took his time over the small hole in the ground, which was surrounded by caution tape; around him, activity continued as normal. Gregg stared at the screen, eyes taking in everything. He'd *known*! From the minute that newspaper article hit his desk. He should have realized that reaching out to the Goldsteins would yield no results. Even if they believed him, those people wouldn't want his information; they wanted the treasure just as much as he did, probably more. There was no way they would be willing to share credit with anyone. They wanted nothing more than a clear path as they bought, demolished, and lied their way to the prize. And if it hadn't been for one nosy tourist with a camera, taking video at just the right moment, that's exactly what would have happened; no one else would have known the truth about this site, and the Goldsteins would have simply continued on their merry way.

"Well, I guess the playing field is even now," he said, almost to himself. Every Robin Hood fanatic in the world would be tuned in to this.

"And now, as promised, I have the privilege of introducing a very special guest who is with us today, Amantha Goldstein. Before we begin, Miss Goldstein, I had a few questions for you, if you don't mind."

"Not at all. And may I say, Carl, it is a privilege to be here today. I'm sure you know how much the project means to me, personally."

The camera had pulled back to include a second figure in the frame and at the gentle, cultured voice emanating from the speakers on Gregg's aged television set, Jared's eyebrows shot up.

"Who's that? She cute."

"She's also half a shade away from being royalty," Gregg said.

"Goldstein, Goldstein…" Jared was reading the caption that had popped up. "Yeah, that's right. Amantha Goldstein. She's the chick they tried to get to do the *Playboy* centerfold but she turned it down."

"Is that literally the extent of your knowledge?" Gregg asked quizzically.

"Yep. But give me a minute." A couple seconds of silence as Jared pulled out his laptop and ran the name through a Google search. A couple minutes of typing, clicking, and surveying, before:

"Wow… this cameraman doesn't do her justice. She's beautiful."

Striking would have perhaps been a better word for it. Amantha Goldstein had the build of a model and the elegance of a queen, an inherent poise that all women wish for but only few ever manage to achieve. If memory served she was in her late twenties, but wore very little makeup, exhibiting a natural, subtle beauty acceptant of the passage of time. Smooth, blonde hair fell around her shoulders, shining a light golden color. Her eyes were grey. Amantha studied her interrogator keenly with those eyes, treating him to a confident, direct gaze that missed nothing. The conversation continued easily, hitting the subjects of charity, education, the World Equestrian Games, and the age-old push to land equestrian vaulting in the Olympics before finally settling on the topic at hand.

"The story of Robin Hood," Carl started. *"Is there any truth? Your family's reputation – indeed, their history – has been founded on it."*

"I certainly hope so!" Amantha laughed. *"Of course it is impossible at this point to say definitively… the twenty-first century requires more than just hearsay."*

"I'm from Nottingham…" Carl spread his hands expressively. *"As a kid, this legend was huge for me, for my siblings. We grew up with this incredible bit of history right on our doorstep, and we took it all for granted. As I'm sure many children around the world did. But it was different for us because we were so close to where it all happened. We had Sherwood Forest; The Major Oak, where Robin Hood and his army took shelter; right in our backyard. Up the road was Nottingham Castle, a magnificent mansion built in the 17th century on foundations of the original dwelling; I remember tromping through the grounds there as a child searching for characters from the legend… we'd be given a little piece of paper with their names, and had to roam around until we found them all. It was great fun! This story has touched so many people, for so many years… how utterly fabulous would it be for such a legend to be proven true?"*

"It would be fantastic," Amantha said, smiling genuinely. *"I remember as a little girl, my mother always promised to tell me the legend as she had been told it, handed down by my grandmother, and her mother before… of course my mother never got the chance to pass the story on to me, but I think I should like to see it verified."*

She was so matter-of-fact about things. It was like the fame she'd been handed from childhood didn't exist. She stood with a quiet dignity, listening attentively to Carl as he plied her with questions. Her answers were direct and to the point, spoken calmly, without a hint of the aristocratic conceit that dignitaries from all countries had a tendency to acquire.

"All right, here we go…" Jared had hit Wikipedia and settled in for a read. "Amantha Felicity Goldstein. Born June 25, 1979, height five-foot-eight… mother died when she was five and she was raised by relatives in Kent, wherever that is… ok, career. Socialite. What? Is that even a career?"

"You can edit that, you know," Gregg said, smirking.

"Education. She's got a Bachelor of Science, majoring in archaeology… post grad in cultural heritage management…"

That was to be expected. Gregg had it on good authority Amantha had been groomed for the museum project for at least four years before she officially became curator when its doors opened. He found himself watching her curiously, wondering. Who was she, really? While he had done his fair share of research and seen her features on his fair share of gossip mags and internet articles, he'd never invested the time to watch a proper interview. He quickly found her to be funny, witty, and genuine; very much a lady of class, but also very much an independent one. Her clothing was fine but subtle, and the Jimmy Choo heels she was gallivanting around in found not one misstep on the rough, uneven ground of the dig.

"Dude, before all that, she finished a degree in Mechanical Engineering," Jared piped up suddenly. "A Masters in Aerospace Engineering… she got a commercial pilot's license when she was seventeen and enough ratings to fly pretty much anything with wings… owns a Spitfire called *Penny Copper*. Qualified stunt driver… has been in a couple of movies as a double… won a bet by getting the best lap time of the season in *Top Gear*. She's incredible. Why'd she give all that up to work in a museum?"

"Does the term 'family interference' mean anything to you?"

"Someone this cool deserves a better family."

"Shall I start planning your wedding?" Gregg snickered. "I think Motel Six might have a vacancy for your honeymoon."

"No mere mortal will do for this girl." Jared's voice nearly dipped with reverence.

"I guess that's me out."

"You, me, and pretty much every other man on the planet. Besides," Jared said practically, "Jenny would be devastated if you turned up with a girlfriend."

"You think so?" Gregg asked, much too quickly. Maybe there was hope for him yet.

An overly-patient expression was pointed at him before Jared returned to his research project.

"Your obliviousness to all things female astounds even me sometimes, Gregg," he said absently. "Well, I was right: she's single."

"Who?"

"Amantha. Dated a couple guys here and there, but not for long and she's never been married. Not surprising, looking at these cats." He'd pulled up a short series of photos depicting red carpet arrivals Amantha had taken part of in the last several years; three of them were of her flying solo, and the other four had men attached. Gregg was trying to figure out how she'd even have time to date, after the list of educational obligations Jared had rattled off earlier.

"I take it none of these mortals are up to standard," he surmised in amusement.

"Gregg. Man." Jared gave him a look. "This woman is… she's like Princess Leia, dude. She needs someone who's –"

"Frozen?"

"Invincible." Jared's eyes were glued to the computer screen, lapping up information like a smitten puppy. Suddenly, his mouth fell open. "Gregg," he said conspiratorially, "now I know why they asked her to do *Playboy*. She was an honorary Victoria Secret model in their fashion show last year. *She walked the catwalk...*" Another few keystrokes. A video played; pumping, vibrant music with lots of bass. "And she's hot," he added. "Like, super hot. Are those feathers?"

Gregg could easily believe that; the woman certainly had some legs on her. He stole a glance at the video and stopped just short of a whistle. Whoa. He didn't know if it was the knee-high boots, lingerie, music, or maybe just the peacock feathers falling in a cape down her back, but that girl strutting down the catwalk was incredible. Clearly Amantha Goldstein was a woman of many sides. It was with difficulty that he dragged his eyes back to the tv screen.

"Now for this construction project," Carl was saying. *"Museum or not? I think the rest of the world is dying to know if you knew this was here."*

Amantha's expression took on an immediate façade of professionalism.

"As far as I am aware, this is, and always has been, a project begun with the intention of expanding our current enterprise."

So she'd known. But perhaps not everything.

"And how does Marian's Necklace fit in to all this? It seems work here started very soon after the piece was discovered in November."

"Yes, it would certainly appear connected, wouldn't it?" Amantha asked in return. *"As far as I am aware, the two events are unrelated. We did find the necklace... this project was announced soon after... but of course something of this scale would have had to be in the planning stages for months, if not years. I'm sure you can see how the two events cannot possibly be related."*

"Unless you are a mega-rich family that can make your own rules," Gregg said, more to himself than anything. He was still distracted by the vision on Jared's computer screen of Amantha doing a hip-bump at the end of the runway, flinging the feathers from her shoulders, and sashaying away from the camera while dragging the cape seductively behind her.

"And?" Carl was pressing. *"What is in store for this location now that such a momentous find has been discovered?"*

"We will have to simply wait and see," Amantha responded smoothly.

"Fair enough." Carl wasn't going to get any further with her, and he knew it. *"Shall we proceed, then?"*

"Certainly."

Together, Carl and Amantha walked over to the caution tape, passed it, approached the small, meter by meter hole beyond. Jared, overloaded to the point of insanity with information, finally closed his clunky laptop and tuned in to the broadcast.

"Beneath this incongruous hole in the ground is a maze of tunnels stretching at least a kilometer into the earth," Carl was saying. *"And that is just the portion we've explored so far. Already numerous tombs have been found inside, dating back anywhere from 1000 AD to the early 1300's. It is obvious that this place had, at the time of the last discovered burial, already been in use for at least several hundred years, if not half a millennium."*

For the next twenty minutes or so, Gregg and Jared sat engrossed in a report that was happening half a world away, but right before their eyes. Carl Heyward and Amantha Goldstein wound their way down through the earth, halting now and then to make clear a point about certain places, highlighting things of interest. The tunnels were dark and small, the endless expanse of wall broken at relatively even intervals by those black, open doorways.

"Oh, look at that," Gregg said, pointing in amazement. For the hundredth time.

The camera had panned left, its all-seeing lens probing into a dark opening that was clearly the doorway to one of many tombs.

"As you can see," Amantha said, shining a light inside. *"This room contains several coffins carved out of stone. An exact date has yet to be determined, but they are believed to be from the twelfth century. And..."* She angled the light upward. *"...like so many other tombs, it is marked with symbols that are being studied with great interest. If you'll note this one in the middle..."* The camera panned closer, revealing a trio of interlocked triangles. *"It is actually a Norse symbol, the Valknut, or 'slain warriors knot'; while there are many theories about what this symbol means, it is associated with a warrior's death in battle and has been used many times to symbolize the afterlife."*

"And here is the end of what has now been called 'The King's Highway,'" Carl said importantly. *"For the time being, at least, it has certainly lived up to its name."*

Jared snorted.

"How original. King's Highway. Every main road in the *world* is called the King's Highway."

The pair had stopped along an unbroken section of wall covered in writing and drawings. In the low light being cast on the two figures in front of it, the text looked alien; covered in deep shadow and barely legible.

"Of course this is only a fraction of what remains to be discovered here in this underground labyrinth in the heart of London," Carl continued. *"Tell me, Miss Goldstein, what else might we expect to see coming out of this find?"*

"You know quite as much as I do, Carl," Amantha returned, laughing. *"I'm sure one thing we can agree on is that it will be spectacular."*

"What sort of dates will we be looking at, do you think?"

"Very old," Amantha said, *"based on what we've seen so far. Whilst this tunnel ends here, at its head is another leading due west. That artery has not been fully explored yet, and who knows*

where it will end, but preliminary findings suggest we will be looking at dates older than much of what we have seen anywhere else."

Gregg shook his head, slowly. He knew there was something here. There had to be. Nicolo Goldstein was obsessed with finding the treasure; he had acquired this lot, leveled it, and found the tunnels. Whatever he was after would be here, somewhere, in these walls. Gregg just had to find out what it was, and how to use it to his advantage.

The screen darkened momentarily as Carl blocked the light source. He quickly stepped aside, still talking, and prepared to make his way back up the tunnel with Amantha on his heels. He took a small step to the left, and then Gregg saw it.

"Jared," he said, almost whispering. "Look..."

Carl's body was still partially in the way, obscuring the symbol as he moved. But it was there, plain as day. On the wall, part of a larger carving, was an exact replica of the line drawing Gregg had been given by the old man, Walton Davis. The one he'd been told was the key to everything. The one that matched Marian's necklace.

Jared his pause on the DVR and stared at the symbol, mouth open.

"You were right," he said.

"I was right..."

"The answers are in the dig..."

"No, Jared. The treasure is in the dig."

Gregg could feel the gears clicking into place. Gears that had been grinding for the last seven months, finally, meshed together. He'd been oh so close, but oh so far away. Like a musical arrangement in which one, tiny instrument is out of tune or a jigsaw puzzle with a missing piece, his research had lacked something; that one, intangible something as baffling as the legend itself. But the tune was finally complete. He'd been right all along.

The panic set in almost immediately. Half of him expected the two people onscreen to turn and see the drawing. How could they not? How many other people were watching this broadcast, right now, and seeing what he was? There had already been no fewer than a dozen people who had tried to get into the place, and that was without seeing the evidence as it stood now. Gregg couldn't be the only one with this information. He couldn't be the only one waiting with bated breath for Walton Davis' symbol to appear. Now that it had, this was most definitely going to be a race; the treasure was hidden away, somewhere in that construction site, and people would come from all over to have a crack at finding it. There would be no prize for second place; second place was just the first loser.

There was, literally, only one thing to do. And it had already been tried a dozen times.

"I've got to get in there," he said quietly. "Jared, I hope your passport is in order. We're going over to London and breaking into that dig."

"Ha! Get in line," Jared cracked, watching another catwalk video. When Gregg didn't join in on his joke, he looked up. "Wait. You're serious?" He questioned. "What? No. That's not why I – can't you just call them?"

"Tried that. Got no response."

"So you're just going to waltz in and have a go? How? Why? And what is this 'we' business? I might be mistaken, but I don't believe theft was part of my original job description."

"Things have changed."

"Not that much! Let's face it, Gregg; you don't know if the treasure even exists. There may not be anything to find in the dig! Is that chance worth a London prison? Is *gold* even worth a London prison? Guys have already tried this! Remember the dude three weeks ago who tried to parachute in and got caught on the razor wire? Take this from an expert; security at this place is going to be monstrous. You have absolutely no – Gregg... hello!"

Gregg walked off, occupied with his own thoughts, grabbing an old, leather bag off the table to leaf through the sections as he went. Where was his passport? He'd had this thing for twenty-five years and still couldn't find the right pocket. Jared leapt up and pursued him into the kitchen.

"Gregg! There could be guards. Dogs. Guards *with* dogs. *Bombs.* Machine gun wielding Samurai, you have no idea what kind of a death trap we could be walking into, here. The Queen's own army could be standing guard at the front gate. What do you propose to do about that?"

"I don't know yet..." Gregg said absently. Found his passport. He'd forgotten how young he looked.

"Not to mention that London itself is one of the most heavily monitored cities *in the entire world*. England is like, what? Spy-camera capital of the universe? Breaking into the dig is one thing, getting *to* it and getting *out* again is something else. You're not even a criminal! You wouldn't have the first clue about how to break into a pawnshop let alone this place! Come on, Gregg, be your normal boring self and *think* about this for a minute - it's not worth it!"

Gregg completed his lap of the kitchen and stopped, staring at the tv screen for a moment.

"Jared," he said, "I have been dreaming about this for most of my life. When I'm awake, when I'm asleep… call it an obsession if you will, but it has always been there. And this –" He gestured vainly. "– opportunity is probably the best one I'm going to get. Ever. If I don't take it…"

"I know, I know," Jared grumbled. "Someone else will. Fish that got away and all that." He sighed. "So you really think it's in there?"

"I know it's in there."

"I mean for real. Don't go all motivational-speaker on me and tell me the world is my oyster… if I'm going to end up in jail for this, I want to know why, so just tell me truthfully. Do you think it's there?"

"You remember what I told you Walton Davis said when he gave me that drawing?" Gregg asked. "He said it was the key to everything. That symbol has been my ace in the hole for years… I would be a fool to ignore this. The treasure's there, all right. Marian's Necklace has just shown us where to look."

Jared looked at him skeptically.

"You don't have to come," Gregg added. "I'd rather not see you end up in jail."

"What, you think I'm going to just let you walk in there like a loon with no backup? I may be a mere college student, but I'm the best chance you've got."

"I'm not entirely inept, Jared," Gregg laughed. "There was a time when I dealt with the seedier element all the time. I used to be a cop, remember?"

"What, and that makes you a good criminal."

No, no it didn't, and he knew Jared was right. The kid was only a college student and Gregg… well, his experience was more of a preventative nature. And that was a long time ago. Things change.

Minds get rusty, and that might just be enough to get them caught. He just wasn't on the edge anymore.

But he knew someone that was. He had stumbled and fallen from Gregg's life ten years ago.

Even as the thought hit, Gregg wished it hadn't. He tried to reject it, banish it, cast it aside; it scratched open too many hurtful memories... he couldn't go there. He simply couldn't. But still the idea persisted, ringing in his mind despite Gregg's attempts to tune it out. And he realized: just as this dig might be his answer, this person might be the only way he'd unlock it.

"I know someone who can get us in," he said simply.

Jared rolled his eyes, walked over to grab his laptop and bag off the couch.

"Why am I not surprised?" He muttered. "Ok... you deal with that, I'll get transport sorted out. When do you want to leave?"

"As soon as humanly possible."

"Right. I'll get on it."

"And Jared... thank you."

Jared grinned at him.

"Are you kidding? How many people can say they went on a treasure hunt? Even if I do wind up in jail, I wouldn't miss this for anything."

Jared clicked the door shut behind him and cantered down the steps out of sight, leaving Gregg alone. Alone with his thoughts and packing and the tv. The broadcast still played; now it was back to the news anchor and a few guests discussing the find. "Experts". Gregg kept it on mute. His mind was full enough already. He had to arrange cover for the last few days of class, get time off without somehow getting fired for it, make sure there was someone there to continue going through term papers... and then there was that other thing.

Him. Their way in, should Gregg choose to take it. With a heavy sigh, he straightened and turned his eyes to a small shelf next to the kitchen; almost of their own accord, his feet took him there. On the shelf was a collection of things: a couple photos framed in cheap plastic, a dried rose, a box. It was a small item, no more than four by seven inches, and maybe an inch deep. It was made of redwood, sealed and stained a deep, russet color. A gift from his mother many years ago. Gregg picked up the box, almost gingerly, and held it, blowing dust from the surface. He hadn't opened this in a long time. Hadn't touched it in a long time. It had gathered dust for nearly four years before finding a spot in one of the few parcels Gregg had brought with him when he moved to SLO County, and it still sat right where Gregg put it on the day he unpacked. Since then, as before, it had never been touched, not even with a cleaning rag.

There was a way into the dig. A person that could help. One that would almost assuredly get Gregg the results he was after. But did he dare open that door again? Did he dare risk what might be behind it? He raised his gaze from the box and took a final look at an aerial shot of the dig.

It wasn't about whether or not the idea would work. It was about how bad he really wanted this.

He lifted the lid and stared at the contents. Inside the box was another collection of photos, a pair of dog tags, and a few assorted pieces of paper. Gregg picked up the dog tags, let the chain run through his fingers as he looked at them, at the names on their shiny surfaces.

Lowell, Ian C.
Dancer, Robert W.

No one knew he had these, and no one would have known who those names were, why Gregg had their tags instead of his own. Had anyone asked, he wouldn't have bothered explaining. It was a story that stretched too far, covered too much, and cut too deep. It was of him and his best friend, taking on the world together; first as schoolboys, then as servicemen, finally as deputies. And then those paths had been taken and nothing was ever the same.

Ian Lowell.

Their friendship had always been strange. It began that way, continued that way, faded that way, and encompassed some of the best times Gregg thought he had ever known. And some of the worst. It had spawned many a bizarre mishap, humorous catastrophes that spanned the globe, fueled by Ian's immortal, fearless confidence and survived by Gregg's good sense. Ian Lowell had always been a wild one. Gregg knew that from the moment they met, first day of Kindergarten. They'd both wound up on the wrong side of the school bully, Gregg for his glasses and Ian for his accent, and from the first punch thrown that day they were best friends. They spent the rest of the afternoon in the principal's office. They spent the next twenty years bailing each other out of trouble.

Ian was the instigator of most of it. He had a dynamic energy about him that most people found impossible to resist, a mind like a steel trap, and the absolute determination to succeed. That determination was more than likely sparked by a home life that left a lot to be desired. His father was an alcoholic with a history of domestic abuse, and his mother was a good Catholic woman who felt divorce was unacceptable. It wasn't uncommon for Gregg to get a midnight call from Ian as his friend lay curled up in some obscure corner of the house, protecting his mother from her husband and his little sister Arielle from horrors she was far too young to understand. Often, after one of those calls, Ian would show up to school the next day with bruises he did his best to hide, knuckles skinned to the bone, and despair in his eyes.

Gregg had been there when a few of those bruises were delivered, had seen the brawls. He had been there to see the results. And there were times when he cried. He prayed, he begged, he pleaded with his parents to help, but it wasn't until Ian's mother was nearly beaten to death that she realized there was no hope for her husband, or the marriage she had suffered so much indignity to protect. She filed for divorce and prepared to move her children to Houston. Unwilling to see Ian uprooted and his mother overworked, Gregg's parents offered to take Ian in until the boys were done with school, an offer accepted gladly by all parties.

The following four years were limned in Gregg's memory as being the definition of awesome. As well as taking part in the buzzing Texas rodeo scene, he and Ian had already started a small freight business, which had been in operation from the moment both boys were legal to drive… maybe a bit sooner than that, off the record. Once both of their heads were under the same roof, the scheming and the fun kicked into high gear. Any self-respecting businessman needs a decent set of wheels; Gregg pursued and acquired a 1979 Dodge Powerwagon, styling the impressive beast after Rick Simon's truck in the *Simon & Simon* tv series (complete with a solid iron bumper and five thousand pound winch), and Ian had Sadey, the souped-up 1966 Mustang that basically made him famous in his final two years of high school.

There were the drag races and drive-ins, the girls and the rodeos, school dances and fights out in the parking lot at two am under a blanket of Texas stars. Endless summer evenings spent on the porch with Gregg's family, swatting flies and mosquitos and drinking sweet iced tea, relishing in the absolute simplicity of life while the sun sank in a glowing, orange ball in the west. And then there was the flying. Gregg would never forget the moment it happened, that day two inquisitive teenagers stumbled on their future in the middle of a hot, sticky summer afternoon, with the wind rustling the cottonwood trees and a storm on the horizon. The massive padlock on a barn door that clicked open under Gregg's amateur lock-picking skills; the warped, wooden doors rattling apart; sunlight streaming into a darkened barn and casting curious fingers through the room to reveal the faded, dusty wings of an old crop-duster tied down along the far side.

It was the beginning of an obsession. Gregg's idea of a coast-to-coast hauling company took flight. He still didn't know how the two of them made it work, how they managed to scrape the money together, but they did it. They became pilots. Leased a plane. Added to their already-booming freight line, and by the time college rolled around the bend, they were ready to play.

And play they did, although far differently from many of the people they graduated with. While the others were out partying all night and wasting their parents' money on booze, Gregg and Ian supported themselves, working their way through and managing to have quite the time while they were doing it. Between various odd-jobs, rodeo winnings they worked hard to get, and the transport business, the two of them amassed something of a small fortune and quite a novel of stories as they traveled the country, assignments in tow. They even had a rather extensive fan club at the bevy of local honkytonks, where they dropped in to play on the weekends they were in town. They finished their respective degrees two years ahead of schedule and prepared to jet off into the sunset as legitimate businessmen.

Everything, of course, became null and void when they joined the Navy. Looking back on it, Gregg knew they really should have thought about it more, for the decision turned both their worlds upside down. But then, that was probably why the recruiting stations were located where they were: right outside the theater during the mid-May release of Top Gun in 1986. The movie was a huge recruiting tool for the Navy, playing to the dreams, ambitions, and egos of an entire generation of American males. Gregg still remembered cussing himself out for a complete idiot afterward when, waltzing out of the theatre on an adrenaline high, he allowed Ian to talk him into signing up in the hopes of becoming fighter pilots. It was a long and arduous road they traveled, striving to reach that moment when they were deemed worthy to enter the naval aviation community. They were among the fortunate ones. Most of the other boys who signed up outside the theater in 1986 wound up as midshipmen cruising the Atlantic Seaboard. He remembered meeting Rob Dancer that first day in basic training, the quiet, witty Englishman who became their third musketeer; remembered the exhilaration of flying in a real fighter jet, watching the earth's surface drop out from underneath to leave nothing but liberty.

Then that dream ended, very suddenly. Another, darker one began. And then it ended as well. Events took place, mistakes were made, lives were changed. And in those hours friendship had faded away; unceremoniously, irreversibly, without warning. It was not a bitter parting. It was simply what had to happen. Strange. Like the day they met.

Gregg sighed. It felt like a lifetime since then. A better life. Someone else's. He'd accomplished so much since then, but for all that it still felt empty. Slowly, he wound the tags up and put them in the pocket of his jeans, reached back in the bottom of the box. He hadn't looked in here for a long time, but he knew what he was after, and exactly where it was.

He should. He'd nearly worn it out when it had first been handed to him.

He pulled out a small, three-by-five scrap of photo paper. Film. Faded, 80's color. Old school. His own, smiling visage stared back at him as he stood near the head of a tall, bay gelding. Ian's sorrel mare was a couple feet away, Ian sitting astride and leaning on the saddle horn with a big grin on his face. They were a study in contrasts; Gregg with his hat squared over dark hair and the innocent expression many people said he had, and Ian with that impish, devil-may-care smirk and a thick lock of hair escaping from his hat, which was tipped back in typical Ian fashion. They looked young and cocky and accomplished, just a couple of down home cowboys out to take on the world. Gregg remembered that day; it was just after they'd won their event at the state championship in 1986... merely a month before they'd joined the Navy. They were both twenty years old. He recognized the photo, knew it by heart, but still it seemed somehow foreign to his eyes.

Slowly, Gregg turned the photograph over and looked at the back. He remembered when this photo had been given to him. The yellowed surface glared back at him as it had then, decorated with two simple lines of text, written in black ballpoint. Hen-scratched, familiar writing. Several words had water spots from the tears Gregg had silently shed onto its matte surface.

I'm moving around a lot, but I'll keep this phone with me, the top line said.

Beneath it was a number. Gregg held the photo up carefully, staring at the image on the front, at the familiar handwriting on the back, the marks on every edge left by his nervous fingers all those years ago. Ten years... a decade... how time had flown.

He was thinking hard. He wondered if this idea of his was really so good. Honestly, he didn't know. He didn't even know if the man on the other end would help, didn't even know if the phone was still connected. Didn't know if Ian Lowell was still alive. It had been some time since he'd asked after him. He spent the better part of an hour staring at that piece of paper, the phone number, the handwriting. Let the memories flow, felt the regret. Pulled out his cell phone. Dialed several times but never hit call. Hung up. Stared at the paper some more. Dialed. Hung up. Sat down. Paced. Worried.

And then, finally, made the call. He didn't know what to expect.

The length of time it took to ring suggested the call was being rerouted through several channels before reaching its destination. But it went through. Connected. It felt weird listening to the ringing on what was possibly a fugitive's phone. Gregg found himself contemplating again if the number was even correct, or current.

He was about to hang up when the phone engaged on the third ring. A cheerful voice answered. A familiar voice.

"Gregg Nicholas," Ian said genially. "I was wondering if you'd ever call."

And Gregg, for better or for worse, knew his quest had just ramped up a couple of notches.

Don't be afraid to go after what you want to do, and what you want to be. But don't be afraid to pay the price.

- *Lane Frost*

Chapter 4

Cold was the only thing she was aware of for a minute. Cold and the awful feeling of waking up alone. Amantha Goldstein woke with a start and stared around the room, the silence almost overpowering. Only her clock could be heard, ticking dismally off in the corner. Faded moonlight shone softly through the window to her right, sifting gentle patterns over the light blue carpet at the base. The rest of the room was pitch black.

The dream had been a strange one: a combination of screaming voices and metal and gunshots, a car being torn apart as it sailed off the road through a crowded airport terminal. Her mother had been slumped over the wheel, lifeless; she was wearing a blue top. Everything else was grey. Even the blood. And there had been a lot of it.

Slowly, Amantha slipped out of bed and pulled a jumper over her loose night-shirt, the letters adorning a small charm bracelet on her wrist glinting dully as they caught the light. The bathroom door made not a sound as she pushed it open, the floor not a creak as slowly she crossed to the sink and splashed several handfuls of water on her face to clear her head. The water was cold and sharp on her skin, driving any remaining hint of sleep far from her mind.

She'd never slept well, for as long as she could remember. It had started shortly after her mother died, and continued to this day. The incident at the airport had only made it worse; death seemed to be an inescapably violent part of her life, and these things stayed with her, living in her mind, troubling her sleep. She thought about her mother a lot. That was a given. But that day at Heathrow... Amantha wouldn't admit it to anyone, but she was still scared. Still worried about it, six years later. The whole thing had happened right in front of her. The shooter was never caught, somehow managed to escape despite the best efforts of police and technology. His name, Parker Lewis, was burned into Amantha's memory. She felt vulnerable. Every now and then she felt watched. For on that day, she hadn't seen his face clearly, but she had seen it. And while she might not be able to recognize him, he would know her right away.

Such was the price of fame.

It was for these reasons her sleep remained unsettled. On nights like this her fears would combine, turning the illusion of peace into a horrific playground of personal demons. She thought for a short while that she might finally be making a corner, turning over a new leaf. She'd always been a late bloomer, and as she started to escape herself, to change, those nightmares began to fade. But lately even this fragile structure had been invaded, broken by restlessness and a sort of hopeless despair that crept in to haunt her. Her sleep had once more grown less fulfilling, her dreams darker and more violent. Events combining, churning, becoming one. It had been nearly a year since she'd had this dream, this sick combination of everything she dreaded coming back to haunt her; there was a time when it was nearly a constant companion. She guessed that went to show how far she'd regressed in these few, short months; these few, short months that were like a pathetic denouement to the last nine years of her existence.

It should have been easy. Just a simple favor. Nicolo wanted to build a museum, full of historical treasures he had fastidiously gathered from all over the world, showcasing the Goldstein family not as a crazy group of money-hungry treasure hunters in search of notoriety, but as serious contributors to the historical community. And Amantha was beginning to attract attention, the kind that would be highly advantageous to a publicity run given her stable personality and solid work ethic. She was becoming famous, for all the right reasons... and who better than a level-headed celebrity to espouse their message to the world?

She was halfway through her initial degree in Mechanical Engineering when Nicolo first broached his brilliant plan for familial redemption to her, nearly seven years ago. Clearly the idea had been

~ 72 ~

in his head for some time; Nicolo never did things on a whim. While reticent, Amantha had agreed to help so she could at least say she had done her part, and had an excuse to move on. Four additional years of university had seen her qualified to take on the role required of her, and Amantha had put her dreams on hold. Dreams of her own life, her own identity, without the weight of the Goldstein name. She'd never been one of them. The promise that she would, indeed, be free to do as she wished once her end of the bargain was completed and the Goldsteins had made it into a history book or two was her incentive. The museum was built, filled, opened. Amantha took on her role as curator and, funnily enough, found herself enjoying it.

She kept it up for a solid year, long enough to put procedures in place and ensure the place was running smoothly. Thanks to the business qualifications she'd undertaken in her first university stint, none of it was difficult. The museum was doing well; the books were balanced, the visitors were happy, the staff was productive, and the Goldsteins were beginning to see the first glimmers of their much-anticipated fame as historical connoisseurs. Amantha had done her part, had given them what they wanted. She sat down with Nicolo and, after a long conversation, was granted her freedom. Amantha had only to find her replacement and set them on the right course, and she would be free. She could return to anonymity, as much as possible, and live her life.

And then November had come.

With it had come the return of her sleepless nights, and the nightmares she thought she'd managed to dispel at long last.

Amantha stared at the face meeting her eyes in the mirror, the face that greeted her every morning from this gilded prison, the face that was so close to flying away. She had been so close. So very, very close to living her own dreams, finding her own reality away from the Goldsteins, away from all this. She should have known it was all too good to be true. Nicolo hated her almost as much as he had her mother. It was, after all, Amantha's mother who was handed the Goldstein title when Nicolo was deemed unsuitable. The fact that he'd inherited the role anyway after she died was of no consequence. To his mind, Stephanie Goldstein represented everything in life that had done him wrong; as her daughter, Amantha now symbolized the very same. Only this time, instead of casting his nemesis to the winds, Nicolo planned on holding his enemy close. Very close. Amantha was beginning to realize he'd never intended to let her go, that he was using her like a pawn to complete his chess board. And now, her dream was over and she was trapped by the discovery of one, simple thing: the piece known as Marian's Necklace. With that single event, her world – and her future – had been carved in blue sapphire. It was all the excuse Nicolo needed. He could sit back and enjoy the spoils of his conquest of vindication, watching his museum flourish, leaving Amantha, with a persona already accepted by media and public alike, to present this historical playground to the world… indefinitely.

He'd made this last very clear. In a meeting merely a week ago. Amantha had listened in silence as her suspicions were verified and their entire agreement, and her future, had been ripped apart, as Nicolo reclaimed her for the Goldstein family and labeled her an asset. She wasn't going anywhere. When Amantha had protested the decision, he had immediately, subtly, reminded her of her duties. Not only as a Goldstein, but a Goldstein with a very fragile reputation to uphold.

"Remember your past," he said. "It is only now that we are beginning to truly put it to rest. If anything were to jeopardize our efforts… we would be unable to protect you from the turmoil that would most certainly ensue."

The turmoil he referred to so circumspectly was in relation to a dirty little secret kept so deep in the family closet not even a skeleton would survive.

In 1976, Stephanie Goldstein was a superstar. She was revered by the public, both for her beauty and her compassion, and it was for this reason she was chosen as the heir through which the Goldstein name would continue. Amantha's father was far below her by Goldstein standards. Amantha had never met him. She knew he was a pilot, and that his name was Stephen Fox. She knew he had flown with the RAF for a time before moving on to work for the airlines, that he was a gentle man, a good man, a man with a big heart and wild dreams, one who had as good a hand with a skittish horse as with the controls of an airplane. He met Amantha's mother at a gala that he wasn't even supposed to be at. She had just finished university and was on the cusp of taking over the reins of the massive enterprise that was the Goldstein legacy – the first time the responsibility had ever been handed to a woman. They fell in love at that gala, courted in secret, created Amantha through their bond. But Stephen Fox never got to see his daughter. The young, star-crossed lovers were discovered; the ensuing media storm, fueled to even greater heights over the frenzy already surrounding Stephanie Goldstein, drove them apart more cleanly and permanently than a surgeon's knife. Stephen fled, Stephanie retreated, and by all accounts they never saw each other again.

But the public was not yet finished with Stephanie Goldstein. Alas, the perfect storm had only just begun. Discarded like a soiled cloth by the Goldsteins for tarnishing their spotless name, Stephanie found herself alone, pregnant, and hunted. By the time Amantha was born, her mother had been completely rejected by everyone except her elder sister, Marilla. And the paparazzi. They never left her.

Amantha was five when her mother died. She recalled very little. She did remember a very kind person, a good mother, very caring and considerate. Very sad. That impression stayed with her more than anything. Children are masters of intuition, and Amantha had felt that sadness every time her mother looked at her, every time she held her and spoke her name, every moment of every hour of every day. She felt it and knew even then that she would never be enough, no matter what she did. Because there was always something missing. Always. Something missing. Stephanie had lost the man she loved and had been rejected by her own kin, left alone in a world that wanted only one thing from her: a headline. And a headline was what they got, on a cold winter's night when Stephanie Goldstein's car careened off the Hardknott Pass to crumple like an accordion into one of the gullies along its route. The claim of brake failure was not disputed; the single-track, thirty-three percent grade connecting Wasdale and Eskdale was already responsible for its share of tragedy. It was only after nearly a decade that Amantha finally learned the real story: the car crash that had claimed her mother's life was no accident. It was, in fact, Stephanie's final decision.

That was the dirty little secret, Nicolo's ace in the hole. The press would have a field day if they found out that Stephanie Goldstein had committed suicide. And Nicolo was smart enough to understand that Amantha would do anything – *anything* – to keep that secret buried. For she, of all people, knew what it was like to be the daughter of a dead starlet: utter chaos.

Amantha's childhood became a nightmare, punctuated with anguish and loneliness and fear. It was little more than a fugitive's life. One quick getaway to the next; one car with darkened windows to the next with the time between lit with the relentless glare of flashbulbs and shouted questions. At five years old, Amantha had no idea what was happening. Only that she was in pain, crushed by grief, and was being hunted mercilessly, relentlessly, for reasons she didn't understand. Which was why now, when faced with the reality of her situation, Nicolo's veiled threat was enough to strike fear abject into her heart. Her mother had been poised in the limelight to take on the title. She had tried to escape it. She had failed. Amantha, for all intents and purposes, had been lured like a moth to a flame into an identical situation. If she tried to do the same, whether she succeeded or not, that dirty little secret and all it implied would surface so fast it would make her head spin.

Holding one's enemies close, and all that.

So this was to be her life. Nightmares and all.

As was usual in moments like this, when the world became too cold, too heartless, to deal with, Amantha found herself wishing she was in the air. Away. From life, from family, from the name that seemed destined to control and annihilate her future.

The decision didn't take much thought. Amantha tiptoed back to her room, making as little noise as possible to avoid waking her aunt, who slept down the hall. She dressed in silence, left the flat, started the car. Pulled away from the curb and, without looking back, headed southeast. Her plane was kept at Old Hay Airfield, a small, private strip just east of Paddock Wood in the borough of Tunbridge Wells. Amantha had attended the Old Hay Fly-In every year since she was a girl. The airfield was within a stone's throw of her aunt's property, where Amantha had spent most of her childhood. While Marilla kept the farm in good order, most of her time was spent in the city these days, keeping tabs on her niece.

A little under an hour later Amantha was pulling in behind the small unit that housed her Spitfire, a powerful beast of a plane with a history rich in lore. She swung the doors open, switched on the light, and smiled.

"Hello, you," she said softly.

Bare bulbs bounced a stream of white light off the cold, metal sheeting and exposed steel beams, illuminating the Supermarine Spitfire Mark IX situated regally in the center of the building. Amantha slowly walked around the stilled aircraft, running her hand along the cool metal as one would touch the shoulder of an unfamiliar horse. The top of the cockpit, over three meters above the ground, seemed to survey her in interest. The paint on the exterior was matte, closely resembling the original colors. The only variation to this scheme was a modern decal that had been added during the plane's extensive restoration process, which paid homage to the female ATA pilots of World War II; in particular, the notorious rabble-rouser of a woman after whom Amantha's plane had been named: Penelope Maureen Christopher, call sign "Copper".

Copper Christopher was of half Spanish descent, half Irish, born in France to parents who spoke mainly Italian. She escaped the clutches of the Third Reich and fled to the hills, looking back in time to see her town looted and burnt to the ground by invading forces. She spent the next three weeks on the run. During that time, she studied the German strategy, their positions, equipment; by the time she strode into an Allied base in September of 1941, she had an arsenal of information to hand over. In return, she wanted only one thing: to take her fight to the air. As women were still relegated to transport roles in every air force aside from the Soviet Union, Copper was tacked on to the ATA ("Air Transport Auxiliary" or "Ancient and Tattered Airmen", depending on who was talking). In this role she was trained to fly everything from Spitfires to bombers, and was one of over one hundred and fifty "ATA-girls" to grace the covers of magazines and newspapers worldwide for her achievements in transporting valuable fighting equipment, men, and airplanes to the Western Front.

But in October of 1943, Copper Christopher got her chance at revenge. And this plane, PB-559 of No. 10 Group, a fighter squadron based out of RAF Filton, was how she got it. It was while flying this very bird from a maintenance unit to a front-line squadron in France that Penelope Christopher ran into opposition in the form of one very determined German fighter. The Focke-Wulf, piloted by ace Heinz Bauer, was on her before she had a chance to evade. Help was out of the question. Copper was on her own. Not much was known about the ensuing dog fight that raged through the skies of France, only that, in the end, it was Penelope and her Spitfire that emerged victorious.

The plane and her pilot parted ways after the incident, one of only a handful of recorded encounters between female pilots and the enemy in the air; Penelope Christopher continued her service with the ATA until the end of the war, and PB-559 hers. 1944 saw the day the plane was sent back to Britain after a particularly nasty encounter, and she was stationed at Detling Airfield, where the remainder of No. 10 Group joined her later in the year. PB-559 was retired from service in the sixties. She then spent fifteen years in the back of a workshop until she was uncovered by an eagle-eyed enthusiast, who had the plane fully restored and given a name: *Penny Copper*. This benefactor spent nearly a year searching for the perfect person to do the nose art, and when the plane was rolled out at an airshow for the first time in 1984, she turned heads. The name *Penny Copper* was emblazoned on the side in a masculine script, next to the colorful image of a saucy, female pilot with green eyes standing solidly with one hand on her hip and a helmet under her other arm, flaming red hair and a white scarf blowing back along the Spitfire's body.

After the restoration process, the plane passed through two private owners before Amantha bought it at an auction in 2003. While it had been continually maintained during its service and done up to a beautifully high standard after its retirement, no one (Amantha included) felt any need to rid the fuselage of the ten bullet holes that *Penny* received in the dogfighting encounter that made her so famous. She was one of approximately sixty Spitfires still airworthy. Her last home base, Detling Airfield, was likewise now unused for aviation, with its main attraction being the annual Kent County Show that swung through for three days every July.

Under the strong light of the hangar, Amantha inspected the aircraft with a practiced eye, taking particular care in examining the condition of the elevators; distortion of any kind made the Spitfire difficult to control. It was a routine she knew by heart, this, and an essential element to safety. When one played with gravity, one needed to make sure their partner in crime was up to the task. Satisfied that all components of the Spitfire were airworthy, Amantha prepared to roll *Penny Copper* out of the hangar. She fired up the old, pushback tractor kept in a small service shed out the back and hooked up, carefully pulling the Spitfire's nearly three thousand kilogram frame out into the faded moonlight.

Camo on grey. That was the appearance of the plane's dim outline under the dim external lights as Amantha approached. Only the distinctive decal on the side was readily discernible. She gave a quick look behind, making sure the hangar was secure, then donned a light pair of gloves and entered the cockpit. *Penny Copper's* interior was much like the external body: spare, designed with intent, aesthetically trimmed down. It was made to fight. Comfort was secondary.

Amantha spent the next few minutes completing final checks in preparation for takeoff.

Master switch, on. Dials responding as normal.

Settings, correct. Among them, rudder trim wound right to counteract the Merlin's torque-induced swing.

Flight instruments, checked.

Engine instruments, checked.

Throttle lever, half-inch open.

As the engine was cold, Amantha unlocked the Kygas primer and primed the pump with six slow strokes of the handle, ending the procedure with the handle out.

Magneto switches on…

And now the fun began.

Due to the massive drain on the aircraft's batteries during start-up, early versions of the Spitfire such as the Mark VC required the use of a ground accumulator to generate enough power to start the engine. These accumulators were essentially a massive battery pack on wheels, and a common sight at any airfield during World War II. Later models, including the Mark VII and VIII variants, featured an electric starter. A variety in the middle, which was comprised of an early Mark VC body outfitted with a new and improved Merlin engine, relied on the Coffman Cartridge… also known as the "shotgun starter". *Penny Copper* was one of these. Made famous in films such as *Flight of the Phoenix* and *Six Days, Seven Nights*, the shotgun starter was what the name implied: a blank cartridge loaded into a purpose-built breech that could be set off either manually or electrically. When fired, energy produced in the form of pressurized gases would engage the starter, create movement, and start the motor.

It was a sudden, loud phenomena, liable to turn a few heads.

Amantha gave a final check to her instruments, made sure the brakes were securely on, and commenced the start-up.

The cartridge discharged with a loud bang, shattering the stillness, sending a puff of smoke billowing outward that was barely visible against the low light. The four-blade prop twitched, turned, responded to the ignition and booster buttons, came alive. Amantha pressed in the priming pump handle and the powerful, V-12 engine roared to life, prop splitting the air as another puff of exhaust rose into the night. This was what she lived for. The sound of over one thousand kilowatts of power, rumbling inside the Spitfire's conical nose, energy flowing through the machine like blood through the arteries of a living thing. Slowly she swung the plane out and taxied toward the far end of the grassed strip, firing off a general call while she was still clear of possible, last-minute traffic.

"Old Hay traffic, Spitfire Papa-Bravo-Five-Five-Niner intersecting runway zero-niner in preparation for take-off, Old Hay traffic."

There was no response, as was typical this time of night – or morning, rather. Amantha repeated the call again as she intersected the runway; with no further response forthcoming, she spun the Spitfire around and prepared to take off, running through her pre-flight run-up. It was dark; lit only by the moon wafting through inconsistent wisps of cloud, the runway stretched before her like a grassy stairway to freedom, little more than a pale strip of perfectly-mowed land reaching for the trees along the horizon. Amantha stared ahead intently, eased the power up, felt *Penny Copper* begin her run. The engine pitch changed. Louder, more intense. The speed increased. The tail lifted off the ground. Amantha pressed the throttle forward to full power, feeling that familiar rush of adrenaline as the Spitfire rushed the airfield like a racehorse, the distinctive sound of the Merlin cutting through the night air as it swept into the sky. Gravity pressed, then gave up in defeat. Land fell away, replaced by the inescapable feeling of freedom Amantha and others of her breed craved.

She climbed to two thousand feet, circling, and took a deep breath as she reworked the instruments and settled in for the flight. It was so peaceful up here, she thought, staring downward, spying the dotted lights that occasionally broke through. People's homes. Their lives. Were they happy, she wondered? Were they content? Up here, surrounded by the comforting smells of the plane, the darkness, and the familiar rumble of the engine, Amantha was the closest to contentment she felt she herself might ever know. Her life might be dictated on the ground, but not here; here, roaring through the clouds, she was queen of her own destiny. Untouchable. Heading north, she followed the River Medway as it wound its way through darkened countryside; occasionally spotting a glisten of water under faded moonlight, a pair of headlights on an old, deserted road, she tracked east, passed low over the North Kent Marshes, and swung out over the coast.

The lights of the Medway Towns reflected out over black waters, reaching out strange, yellow fingers inquisitively. The Thames Estuary was still, a dark expanse broken only by the looming outlines of fishing boats and the odd yacht heading to port. Beyond, the gloominess of the English Channel remained undisturbed. Already the fog was rolling in. Amantha crossed over the face and returned closer to land, following the jagged coastline. She flew for nearly three hours, winging over the landscape like a bird of prey and reveling in the feeling of power. She forgot the hour, the world below her. For this small amount of time it was just Amantha Goldstein and her plane, and nothing else. She followed the River Thames as far as she dared, then resignedly pointed *Penny Copper's* nose southward once more, and returned to the airstrip.

"Old Hay traffic, Spitfire Papa-Bravo-Five-Five-Niner... three kilometers west of runway two-seven on a straight approach, Old Hay traffic."

There was no answer. This time, Amantha didn't bother repeating the call. She touched down easily, rolling to a gentle stop over the six hundred and sixty meter expanse. Taxied. Shut down. Sat silently for a moment, listening to the quiet popping and shifting of the metal as it cooled under the consistent ministrations of the night air.

Reality slowly, steadily, returned.

Not many could truly claim to know Amantha Goldstein; she rarely talked about herself, and when she did, she kept it short and superficial. All her life, she had wanted to do only two things: fly planes and restore them. When she enrolled in uni as an engineering major it was under her father's name, Fox, and while the attention she received never really lessened, she found even that small degree of separation from the Goldsteins to be satisfying. She had worked so hard to be free, independent. Worth something. Something more than a name that wasn't her own, something her parents would have been proud of. She hadn't dated much. At twenty-eight, she could still count the number of beaus she'd had on one hand, two if she added in the two single-dinner dates she'd been drawn into by friends. Growing up as she had made trust a difficult thing, indeed. She had little time. And she was picky. She was always trying to move forward, focused on her goals, her dreams, staunchly committed to the future she had planned. A future that now was in serious jeopardy.

By the time *Penny Copper* was safely stored in the hangar once more and Amantha slid the squeaky, metal-framed doors shut, it was nearly four am. She'd be pushing it to get back to the city before dawn and catch an hour or so of sleep before she had to attend a bevy of meetings set up by Nicolo to further promote the museum. More people walking around staring at the same things, asking the same questions, ogling Marian's Necklace… The idea that maybe she could "forget" about these meetings was rejected as soon as it surfaced in her mind. So slowly, reluctantly, she locked the doors, got in her car, and left Old Hay Airfield for the city.

The street was cool and dark when she pulled in, dotted only with entry lights, reflections of the same dancing off the blackened windscreens of autos parked along the blacktop. To the left, the low, early-morning rumble of traffic in King's Road had begun humming along, its sound reaching even Amantha's flat in the quaint sanctuary of Margaretta Terrace. She locked the car and headed to the door, sliding the key into the lock furtively, like an outlaw. Opening the door with hardly a sound, she slipped into the kitchen and flicked on the light, stifling a yawn.

"It's about time."

Amantha jumped at the voice and spun around mid-yawn.

"Aunt Marilla!" She slumped back against the door as it clicked shut. "You gave me a fright. What are you doing sitting here in the dark?"

"Waiting for you to come home." Marilla Clancy surveyed Amantha keenly for evidence of injury or shenanigans with a pair of sharp, blue eyes that missed nothing. Ordinarily the look was hard to weather without cringing, but Marilla's rusty brown twists of hair, put up comically in curlers, rendered any seriousness ineffective. "Out flying again, were you?" She asked after a moment.

"Yes." Amantha set her small handbag aside and pulled out a chair.

"Thinking?"

"Just getting away," Amantha said quietly. She let her keys fall to the table. The yawn finally completed itself as she sat down, facing her aunt. She said nothing, and Aunt Marilla wisely allowed her to remain silent.

Marilla was probably the one person who could understand Amantha's difficulties more than anyone else. She was Amantha's biological aunt, her mother's eldest sister. Her only sister. It was she who had taken Amantha in after Stephanie's death, the closest – the only, really – relative that would have anything to do with the illegitimate child. She was also the only one to have escaped the Goldstein net. Half of it was luck. Half of it was will. As the first in a high-class family to defy tradition and marry outside their net, she had dissolved all ties with the Goldsteins by the time she reached twenty-four years of age. She was lucky in the sense that all the attention was on her younger sister; however at the end of the day, it was her strength of will that truly saw Marilla set free. At least for a while.

Her husband was a carpenter named Edmund O'Clancy. They met on a subway. He was on his way from work, and Marilla was sneaking out of the house to attend a party. They hit it off, and ended up in London's historic Farrington area until nearly three in the morning, deep in conversation over a thin-crust Margherita pizza. After that night they were inseparable. With the attention firmly squared on Amantha's mother, keeping their relationship a secret proved to be relatively easy; by the time the family found out, it was far too late for them to do anything about it. Edmund was neither rich nor famous, nor did he plan to be either by the time he died, but Marilla accepted his proposal of marriage without reservation. For she knew, without a doubt, there is far more to life than money. She and Edmund shared a lasting bond, a bond that stemmed from their love of life, love of independence, and the desire to make the most of every minute. Marilla's offense brought swift consequences from the Goldsteins. The family simply sewed up their empty space on the tree and moved on, continuing to cultivate those true to their name, seeming to forget that a young woman named Marilla ever even existed.

Marilla couldn't have cared less. Her life had been happy, full of joy and love, one she wouldn't have traded for anything. She still held the record for being the blackest of the black sheep. But alas, ten years after her escape, the death of Amantha's mother brought with it an unwelcome intrusion into her life... in the form of the publicity surrounding the little girl given over to her care. It was a role both Marilla and Edmund volunteered to take on without a second thought, in spite of everything it implied. Amantha remembered the day they'd come to collect her, saving her from the turmoil that was her existence, whisking her away to their farm in Kent where she might have a chance at a normal childhood. Amantha knew she would never be able to repay the debt of kindness she had been shown. They had come to her rescue when she needed it most, without being asked, and in Edmund's case without even being bound by blood.

He took to his responsibility as Amantha's protector with the same intensity he took to everything else in life. Looking back on it, Amantha felt he may have even enjoyed the challenge. His battles with reporters over Amantha's privacy became something of a running joke; Edmund was a clever, resourceful man, a deep thinker with a barbed wit, and was more than willing to stretch the boundaries of legality to make his point known. Between his dedication and Marilla's composure, Amantha's life took on a sense of regularity. Slowly the harassment stopped. Tragedies took place that overruled hers, and the story went from the front page of the paper, to the middle, to the back, and finally dropped away. Amantha's routine became steadier; her surroundings more secure. She remembered being shocked one day to wake up and find the rubbish bins untouched, as usually they were picked clean by the paparazzi that hovered around the house like vultures. That was the day she knew it was truly over, that she would finally be left alone.

She was eight.

Marilla and Edmund did their best to prepare her for a future they felt to be inevitable: the day when the Goldstein family would choose to forcibly drag Amantha back into the fold and thrust her into the limelight. That day finally did come, when Amantha was seventeen. With the story of her beginnings carefully blotted out and Stephanie's death still carefully concealed behind the tragedy of circumstance, Amantha was suddenly seen as a beacon of opportunity. She and her three cousins were pooled together, relentlessly touted as the younger, beautiful generation; the ones who would take the helm and valiantly lead their family into the future.

After her cousins cracked under the pressure, Amantha was left alone, deemed the only sane, somewhat predictable one able to shoulder the responsibility; be the public face of a large, distinguished family and carry on the torch of high class despite the crumbling times. The irony was not lost on her. From condemned to savior, illegitimate offspring to poster child stardom.

A stardom she could never have imagined would be hers, one she would give anything to trade. All she wanted was for her life to return to normal, as it was when she'd lived with her aunt and uncle on the farm. Fame wasn't so splendid a thing as people thought. For it wasn't just her life impacted that day when she was seventeen years old. It wasn't just Amantha who had been dragged back like a lamb to slaughter; Marilla, too, had been caught up in the mess. In the end it was her sense of responsibility to Amantha that eventually made her relent and turn back to her former kin, twenty years after she left them behind. With Edmund gone, having lost a hard-fought battle with cancer three years previous, Marilla had no one left *but* her niece… and she was given an ultimatum: return with Amantha or stay forever distanced. She chose the former, swallowing the bitter fine print that presented itself later in the form yet another Goldstein decree to drop the "O" from the offensive Irish surname of her late husband. Thus Marilla Clancy was plunged mercilessly back into the lions' den, the spoils of a long and bitter war between family tradition and independence. If she harbored any regrets, she kept them to herself; like the husband she had loved so much, life to her was too short to waste on reflections.

"You'd best get some sleep," Marilla said, rising. "If I recall, you have about four meetings tomorrow. Or, I guess I should say later today." This last was amended with a smile. "Don't fret, Ammy," she added gently. "You will find a way to make this work."

Amantha rested her forehead on her palm.

"How?" She asked softly.

"The same way I did. One day you will just have had enough."

"It's not that simple."

"Yes, it is."

"Aunt Marilla, they'll – they'll bring it all back again… all of it. If I leave, it will start all over again. And Mum…"

"Yes... they will. And your mother will take center stage if they do."

"I'm scared. I don't want to go through that again. I don't want her memory to be..." Amantha gestured futilely. "Not again. She doesn't deserve that."

"I know, Ammy," Marilla said. "But she's gone. You are here. And it is not selfish to seek your own path."

Amantha held back a tear as she looked at her aunt, such a tower of strength. If there was anyone who could say those words and mean them, it was Marilla.

"How did you do it?" She whispered.

"I was lucky," Marilla answered. "I had your uncle." She smiled kindly. "And you," she added softly. "I knew I had to be strong for you. Well, darling, I'd best be getting back to bed. You're not the only one with a big day." She patted Amantha's shoulder. "You'll be here a while, I take it?"

Amantha just nodded. Marilla leaned down and gave her a quick hug, then left the kitchen and slowly climbed the stairs. A door closed, then there was silence. Amantha lingered in it numbly, watching the very first grey of morning begin to shade the window to her left. Here it was again, she thought; the dawn of another day. A day to be filled with meetings and planning and deciding, another step in her prison term at the museum. Amantha wished she could escape. She wished she was brave enough.

Rising, she retrieved a mug from the cupboard, a teabag; filled her old, shabby teapot with water. While the water heated, slowly, she twirled the peppermint-tinted teabag in a lazy circle around her finger, liking the smell that lingered in the air. Peppermint was one of her favorite scents. It reminded her of Christmas. Snow, mittens, hot chocolate, carols, Christmas lights, and contentment. A real family.

She had never known what it was like to be truly happy. There were moments... rare, fleeting times she wanted to hang onto with every ounce of strength she possessed; however, as was the irony of life, the tighter she held, the faster those moments flew from her grasp. Becoming a pilot had been her dream since childhood, the goal that made her feel closer to a father she never knew, the thing that drove her. Completing that process had been the moment she thought would make her whole. Happy.

But still she wasn't satisfied. Still she felt… incomplete.

The teapot interrupted her thoughts, whistling in an insultingly merry fashion as it finished heating. Amantha dropped the teabag in place and dumped the piping hot water over the top, watching the liquid darken as little tendrils of color started seeping outward from the fine mesh. She took an experimental sip and sat down, resting her forehead on her palm. The window had brightened. The day was near at hand now.

It was funny; she'd grown up hearing about Robin Hood and his merry men, had oftentimes reenacted the legend out in the garden, chasing down the sheriff of Nottingham and vanquishing him to protect the good people of Nottingham. When she was little it had been exciting, a wonderful story. The Goldsteins had their own version of the legend, of course, passed down through the ages. Her mother had often promised to tell her the tale, when Amantha was old enough. Alas, the time had never come. Amantha had grown old enough, but her mother was no longer there to tell it. In place of fondness, bitterness had sprouted, and Amantha came to hate the story; to her, it no longer stood for adventure, but rather captivity.

This goal of Nicolo's, this quest for a place in the collective memory of society had overtaken them all, enslaving them a surely as poverty. To be a Goldstein was to be at the mercy of high society, and Amantha didn't want to be part of this latest project any more than she wanted to be part of the family itself. But her fate, like that of the rest of them, was tied to the very name she hated. The legend that held them all prisoner. The necklace that had finally been found and, in effect, sealed Amantha's fate.

She was a young woman haunted. Haunted by a family she didn't belong to, guilt from a past she couldn't change, desperation over a future she couldn't control, and resigned to a life she couldn't love. But, true to her culture and her class – more importantly, true to herself – Amantha said nothing of this to anyone. Her problems were her own, not public knowledge to be viewed at will, and her own they would remain.

So this was to be her life.

****

Some say that treasure and treachery go hand in hand. If anyone were to ask Gregg Nicholas about it right now, he would have agreed. He knew he was taking a chance that would probably end with prison time. That was if he didn't get killed first. He was flying to a foreign country with the sole purpose of performing illegal deeds in order to secure a treasure that might not exist, using as his guide a legend that had never been proven true, all because of a news broadcast he saw only yesterday. And he had as assistants one college student and a criminal he hadn't laid eyes on in a decade.

If that didn't have disaster written all over it, he didn't know what would.

The funny thing about long-haul flights is the amount of time they allow one to think about their sins. Gregg did a lot of that, sitting in the induced darkness of the 747, crammed in with a couple hundred other people on their way to the UK to accomplish perfectly normal things: family vacations, business trips, weddings.

The plane looked like an elegant, over-sized bird as it coasted in for a landing at Heathrow Airport about mid-afternoon. It had been touch and go for a while at LAX, with something in Jared's being continually setting off the alarms in the screening area. Just when the TSA guard was on the verge of hauling him off to prison on principle, Jared found the culprit: a miniscule paper clip that had somehow wedged itself into the lining of his pocket. Finally making it on board the British Airways flight as their names were being shouted over the loudspeaker in five languages, their adventure was underway; another twelve hours in the air and a five-hour layover in Boston's Logan International Airport, they made it to London.

"Gregg."

"What?"

Jared pointed toward the ceiling, where the seatbelt sign had just blinked off. The sudden, impatient rustling of motion all over the jet acted as further proof they had reached the gate. In truth, Gregg's mind wasn't really on the present activity; he barely even reacted as someone's travel bag bounced off his head on its way out of the overhead locker. He turned to the right and peered out the window, taking in the hustle and bustle of behind-the-scenes airport action in a quick glance. He thought he saw his suitcase wending its way guiltily toward the terminal on one of the little baggage trains.

"So, who's this guy we're looking for?" Jared asked suddenly.

"His name's Ian. Ian Lowell."

"Hey, isn't he the one from the story you told me? About buzzing Pirate's Cove –"

"– in a Cessna, yes," Gregg said, and chuckled. "Same guy. That was a long time ago."

But still funny. It was 1984, middle of summer, the first time Gregg had ever been to SLO County. He and Ian delivered a load of cotton just outside of Santa Barbara and decided on the spur of the moment to pop up the coast and see a friend, Graham, who was going to college at Cal Poly. They had no sooner touched down and taxied in before Graham launched his first brilliant idea. Looping an arm around each of their shoulders, he had drawn them aside and said he had to show them – to use his words – "an awe-inspiring sight" he had discovered along the coastline. It didn't take much convincing; with three guys, an idea, and a mode of transportation all in the same vicinity, things were bound to get interesting. And, ten minutes after taking off at San Luis Airport, they flew over a ridge and popped out directly on top of a nude beach. Pirate's Cove.

It was, indeed, an awe-inspiring sight. Gregg could still recall the facial expressions of some of those shocked patrons, running for cover as the plane buzzed low along the water with three hooting college guys waving from the windows.

And, as usual in any story involving Ian Lowell, there was this one woman.

Ian, his hands full of airplane controls, got so distracted watching some gorgeous, double-D babe frivolously do the Can-Can for them in knee-deep surf he almost ran right into a cliff. He did manage to miss it, barely, banking to the right and careening crazily out to sea, sinking them right in the midst of the nearby fog bank hovering in its ever-present fashion off the coast. Of course, after they got out of the soupy whiteness and got their wits back together, they did what any decent, self-respecting, American college boy would do…

Made another pass.

"We had a lot of stories like that," Gregg said, almost to himself. "Knew each other for a long time. We went to school together, competed in rodeo for several years… he was the one I started that freight business and joined the Navy with. And the US Marshals Service. We got put onto that by..." Another smile leapt to his face. "Actually the other guy from the nude beach buzzing. Graham Townsend. He was a friend of ours from high school. He'd been with the USMS for several years and brought us on board."

"Wait. Ian's a cop?" Jared asked. "How does that help us any?"

Gregg paused. He really didn't want to get into this. Not here. Not now.

Not ever, really.

"No, he… he isn't. Not anymore. It's a long story."

"What about Graham?"

"No."

Jared looked like he knew there was more to it than that, but didn't ask. Which was good, as Gregg didn't know what to tell him. What could he say? Answers to those questions represented the single biggest regret Gregg had in his past, and the most poignant concern he had over the future. He and Ian had known each other since they were five years old, but had not spoken in nearly a decade. Gregg would be the first to admit he missed those days of camaraderie. And now, standing in a hunched, twitchy position next to his seat, staring at the bald crown of some guy's head while the plane waited to disembark, he would also be the first to admit he was scared as hell to break that silence.

Who knew what he was tampering with by doing so.

"You all right?" Jared asked. His voice broke through Gregg's steadily-darkening thoughts.

"Yeah." Gregg smiled. "Just the jet lag."

Again, Jared let it drop. Gregg knew he wasn't fooled. His own worries had returned, worries that ticked at his mind like a tiny thorn in the sleeve of his shirt. He was nervous, as he had been since yesterday, since the moment he'd decided to stretch out an olive branch on a whim, risk opening Pandora's Box. Thinking back on the following moment, the moment he'd actually made the call and spoken to a man who used to be his friend, he found it almost inconsequential. He'd simply raised the phone. Dialed. Spoke, listened, exchanged pleasantries like nothing had ever happened. He could recall hearing the menacing, almost sinister lilt in his old friend's voice. The same, but different. It was the first time they'd spoken in so long. He wondered where Ian was while he was talking, why he was there, what he was doing. Gregg explained the reason for his call, the treasure, the archaeological dig in London and its host family that refused to respond to Gregg's advances. Ian knew him well enough to piece together anything Gregg didn't say. He remembered a lot more about the legend than Gregg would have thought.

And of course, at the end of the day, it came down to money. The simple fact that Gregg might have a vast fortune just sitting at his fingertips waiting to be plucked. Ian was a capitalist, and saw the opportunity. Even if the outcome wasn't written in stone, it was clearly a good enough chance for him to invest some time in. He had been abrupt but jovial; blunt, but eager to partake in this new adventure. By the time Gregg hung up, he'd been assured everything would be taken care of and not to worry about a thing.

But Gregg did worry. He worried that he might have made a big mistake.

Pandora's Box.

At long last, the line of people began to edge haltingly forward; watching the sight of movement beginning at the very front of the plane and its perking effects on people closer to, Gregg was always reminded of the opening line to Banjo Paterson' poem *The Man From Snowy River*.

"There was movement at the station, for the word had passed around, that the colt from Old Regret had got away…" he thought to himself as the ripple slowly worked its way back and he and Jared were allowed to exit the aircraft. They made their way through immigration, baggage claim, and customs, and finally got dumped out with the rest of the arriving troupe in the main terminal. By now, the never-ending noise of an airport was normal. So was the jet lag.

So was the unease. Wasn't this the airport where some guy had gotten shot a few years ago? Ernest somebody.

"Well, we're here," Jared said as they entered. "What now?"

"Find Ian. He's picking us up and will be our transportation from now on. I thought it might be a good idea not to be too dependent on public transport, considering the nature of our venture. Not ideal to get stuck over here, if you follow me."

"So, what does this character look like?" Jared asked, trotting to keep up with Gregg's long strides.

"About my height, mussed-up chestnut hair, a chronic chewer of peppermint candies, usually wears jeans and an old flight jacket." Gregg stopped mid-stride with an enlightening gesture. "Oh. And it usually helps to locate any exceedingly large groups of women first. He's most likely right in the middle."

"Mob of girls – real ladies-man, huh?"

"A mischievous rascal of an individual with Rick Simon's eye for women and Indiana Jones' penchant for trouble," Gregg affirmed glibly.

"Sounds like the tag-line for a movie."

"Would it help if I mentioned that he's a little bit like Han Solo?"

"I think I get the picture." Jared paused and took a cursory look around. "Let's see; no, no, no, *definitely* no, maybe but probably not... what about – wait, no, that's a woman. Hey, wouldn't be that guy standing over there in the corner, would it? Looks like a bit of a Han Solo/Rick Simon crossover. Tall guy, about two o'clock, right in the middle of that group of stewardesses?"

Typical. Gregg rolled his eyes as he took a cursory glance in the direction, found the object of Jared's question, and his heart literally sank.

So this was what ten years on the run looked like.

Even from that distance, Ian's person simply radiated danger. It could have been the way he was standing, leaning kind of careless and easy-like against the wall with his arms crossed. Or it could have been the closed, wary look that played about the face, even as he laughed heartily at a joke from one of his female companions. Gregg rubbed his forehead with a sigh, realizing the impression he'd gotten over the phone was right. His fears were right.

Pandora's Box had been opened.

Chapter 5

"Gregg! Gregg Nicholas!"

The Australian accent was the first thing Jared noticed as the shout and a sharp whistle cut through the terminal. The second was the energy. The presence. Ian Lowell, who Jared knew only as the cocky pilot who had buzzed Pirate's Cove in a Cessna, excused himself from the chattering group of stewardesses and vaulted lightly over a banister, bounding across the shiny floor as he ran a hand through his hair with a grin of welcome.

Jared could only stare at the guy. Whatever he'd been expecting from their new accomplice, it sure as hell wasn't this. He couldn't say *exactly* what he'd been looking for; a goofy forger, maybe, or a carefree car thief, perhaps a pickpocket who cracked safes on the side for kicks and carried women strapped over his shoulder as he wound his way through life basking in the limelight of disreputable fame.

Not this. Not this human whirlwind. It was like Sonny Crockett had stepped out of *Miami Vice* and waltzed a couple decades forward. Ian Lowell was fit, intelligent, and confident; a force field of personality; one of those dudes that had been there, done that, and made his own t-shirt. His features were strong, like his persona, and the chestnut hair he wore a bit on the long side was streaked with sun from long hours spent outdoors. He was a handsome devil, this one; Jared would have been jealous if he wasn't so impressed. Every female eye in the room was locked on, target acquired, drawn to the possibility – no, the promise – of danger that sizzled in Lowell's charismatic presence. Watching him stride over, Jared suddenly found himself comparing the man's movements to those of a jaguar or leopard. Or any type of big cat for that matter. Easy, relaxed, yet poised to spring. Controlled. Ian still looked thirty, although at Gregg's age he was surely a good ten years older, and Jared decided it must have been the constant, underlying glint of deviltry sparking in an intense pair of hazel eyes, humor that showed through even as those same eyes flicked warily from side to side before finally settling on Gregg and Jared.

"Hey, Genius, how are you?" Ian asked when he reached them, giving Gregg a jovial handshake.

"Great, Ian. And you? You look like you're doing all right."

"That I am, mate. That I am. It's good to see you again," he said gladly. "What's it been, now...ten years?"

Jared stopped a few steps behind Gregg and set his bag on the floor, watching the typical old-friends-encounter soap play out before him, characterized as always by the laughing and joking and carrying on that so often bursts forth upon the reunion of good pals long separated. He didn't know what Gregg was thinking. He wished he did. Big, red flags were waving around this Ian character like nobody's business right now, and Jared was afraid he was the only one to notice. Whoever, or whatever, the man was, he was *not* a friend.

Keep calm and run as far away as possible.

"Speaking of lining things up, Ian," Gregg was saying, "I want you to meet my other partner in crime. Jared Casey, say hello to Ian Lowell."

Jared stuck his hand out and almost winced at the power of the grip that met it.

"Glad to know you," he said.

"Jared Casey, huh?" Ian asked, sizing him up. "You must be the youngster Gregg told me about. The computer whiz."

"I know my way around," Jared said with a reserved smile.

"Good, good," Ian said. "Well, come on." He slung an arm around each of their shoulders and steered them toward the exit, a pair of dog tags around his neck clinking merrily as they slipped from the front of his collared shirt. "From what I've heard so far, this sounds like quite an adventure. We've got a lot to talk about."

"That we have," Gregg said.

They passed the group of stewardesses, who looked truly disappointed at Ian's departure, and Ian was quick to smooth things over before he deserted them. Jared watched him work a very skillful dose of bad boy magic, and suddenly realized just how good the guy was at being charming. Brilliant, actually. The kind of brilliance that comes with lots and lots of practice at being someone else.

Jared stole a look at Gregg's face, trying to ascertain what was going on behind his stilled features. He couldn't tell. Which in itself boded ill, as under ordinary circumstances Gregg's poker face left a lot to be desired; for him to actually achieve a credible result must mean he was trying very hard. Too hard. Jared still didn't know what caused these two to part ways, or why they hadn't spoken in so long... all he knew was that Ian was somebody Gregg had known for a long time, who used to be a cop (but for some reason was no longer a cop), and for some reason hadn't spoken with Gregg until yesterday.

This wasn't weird at all.

Outside, the airport was bustling with activity. Cabs lined up along the curb to let out their fares; people bade goodbye on the sidewalks; kids, unaware of anything but the present moment, cavorted gaily around stilled luggage while their parents sorted out belongings. It was all very much like LAX, except the voices coming over the loud speaker had an accent and said funny words for things.

What, for example, was a zebra crossing?

"So, what kind of plane do you have now, Ian?" Gregg asked as they headed out onto the bustling sidewalk. "I heard through the grapevine somewhere you had a Gulfstream."

Ian nodded, popping a peppermint candy in his mouth. Jared was suddenly reminded of a villain in a James Bond novel.

"Still got her, and she runs like an angel."

He and Gregg then went on to discuss the plane, its parts, engine, wheels, metal, innards, IQ, how the thing needed two pilots instead of just one and the instruments on the control panel differed from pilot to co-pilot.

Jared wondered briefly how Ian was going to manage up there all by himself, and had to stifle a laugh as several mental possibilities came to mind. Ian lounging across both front seats, operating one set of controls with his fingers, the other with his toes, sipping a martini as he read the latest edition of *Playboy*; standing on the nose John Wayne style, guiding the thing with a pair of reins hooked to the wings, reading *Playboy*; plugging in a little mannequin-shaped copilot, complete with flipped hair and requisite string bikini, still reading *Playboy*.

If Gregg noticed Jared's stupid, half-smothered grin, mainly brought about by nerves, he said nothing.

"We'll take a cab from here to Farnborough," Ian was saying, "then fly to a little private strip in east Surrey. Mate of mine pointed it out. Should only take us thirty minutes or so to get there once we leave the ground, give or take. It's a ways out of the city, but I don't want my girl too close to the action in case we have to get out in a hurry." He pointed at Gregg with a grin. "I've got one more surprise for you," he added.

Jared, walking behind as they entered the parking lot and headed for the far side where he assumed their ride waited, had sudden mental flashes of machine guns, explosives, a tank...

"Rob!" Gregg exclaimed, and Jared jumped involuntarily.

A tall man with close-shaved, dark hair had come around the back of a small car and ambled toward them, an easy smile lighting his features as he held out a hand in welcome.

Oh, great, Jared thought. *Henchman number one has entered the picture.*

"Rob Dancer," Gregg said gladly, shaking hands with the newcomer. "I can't believe it."

"It's good to see you, Genius," Rob answered, his low voice mantled with a markedly English accent.

"Rob was in the Navy with us," Gregg explained, adding Jared into the proceedings.

Rob was friendly enough on the surface. Like Ian, his handshake was hard, backed by muscle that extended far above his hand, and the black jacket he wore wasn't quite able to hide the power of his shoulders or upper arms. His eyes were dark, lined with an almost ominous intensity. Loyalty, determination, and confidence were all expressed there, even if in a somewhat overshadowed fashion, dominated by the same glint of cocky humor seen so easily in Ian's expression. The same glint of humor, and the same sense of inherent menace. It was easy to like Rob Dancer; it was also quite easy to remember that he was, in point of fact, no less dangerous.

His overall appearance reflected the impression. Aside from the bulky jacket and black jeans that had Jared looking around for a Harley, a seemingly-permanent shadow along the jaw line did nothing more than reaffirm Jared's previous assessment of "henchman", and pointed as further proof that this mission was already going south if Rob lived up to expectations. Jared had no doubt that more of that caliber would sally forth before this deal was done. He sighed heavily. Even if Gregg was right about the dig, even if it yielded the fortune to end all fortunes, the current situation wasn't exactly how Jared would have gone about it. Thanks to Gregg's picture-perfect rendition of Othello, their entire project – not to mention existence – was in the uncertain hands of two men that Jared wouldn't trust with the key to his mother's Volvo, let alone the kind of info Gregg was sure to have dished out. He couldn't help feeling that Iago and company were just about to run off with Desdemona.

It was with dour thoughts that he climbed into Ian's infamous Gulfstream nearly an hour later, and as the jet surged forward along the runway and arced into the sky, Jared hardly noticed. He did notice the turbulence. Their trip was rocked, starting when they were merely minutes into their climb, indicating that while Ian and Rob were both very capable pilots, they didn't seem to have an "in" with the Man Upstairs regarding the weather. The brief scenic tour Ian took them on didn't help matters any; by the time they lined out for their destination again, the jolting had only increased, and Jared spent the latter half of the trip wondering if there was some rule against priests issuing the last rites via cell phone. He had forgotten there was such a thing as solid ground by the time they touched down, and was quite thankful for the sensation.

Gregg hadn't seem to pay the slightest attention to the roughness of their jaunt, busy as he was catching up on ten-year-old news and recalling a bundle of stories. Jared could say one thing for these three: they weren't boring.

"Remember that Halloween party at Margie's?" Ian asked as they taxied from a large plot of mowed grass to a smaller one.

"You mean the one senior year?" Was Gregg's response to the arbitrary question. "Where we both dressed up as pirates and you got your wig caught on a tree while you were chasing Sally –"

"– Tretton around the back yard. Yeah, that one."

"Thought I forgot about that last part, didn't you?"

"Did you get the wig back?" Rob asked wryly.

"No," Gregg said, cutting off the white lie Ian was about to deliver to preserve his macho image. "He almost had it when Margie's dogs got a hold of one side and started a game of tug-o-war." He let the comment ride, and a moment passed with only the whining of the engines to break the silence. "I think that was the year we made the pirate flag and put it on Sadey's antenna," he added on suddenly. "That was interesting."

"Sadey?" Rob and Jared asked almost at once, and Rob couldn't suppress a snicker. "The girl with an antenna?"

Gregg laughed amusedly.

"It was a car. You know, like Eleanor? *Gone in 60 Seconds*?"

There were only four other planes in the whole place, Jared noticed as they disembarked; a small twin-engine, two single-engine jobs, an old biplane tucked off in an obscure corner... the Gulfstream was by far the most impressive. The airport itself was rudimentary and sported only basic amenities. Grassed runway, and little if any hangarage. Clearly a private enterprise, if the cows loitering behind sketchy fences along the edge attested to anything. There were probably hundreds of these tiny runways in the country. There was no control tower, so pilots were on their own when it came to flight patterns, controlling air traffic by talking to each other and working things out themselves. Most of the time, the place would run on a first-come, first-serve basis, with the only clearance being what one would get from anybody else cruising the area. But it was never a good idea to assume. Tying for first at the runway was not the best way to meet your neighbor. Likewise, coming over the trees and winding up face to face with another plane trying to either land or take off in the opposite direction was not recommended.

"So what kind of a deal do we have here?" Gregg asked.

"A sweet one." Ian snapped a bag shut. "I've booked us a hotel about ten minutes away from the dig, with freeway access and a comparatively straight shot to this airport if things get dodgy. Fortunately, they take Visa."

Gregg shot him a panicked look.

"You paid with a credit card?"

"An alias is such a comforting thing, Gregg," Ian said easily. "If anyone checks, they'll come up with an entire family history of one James Hyland, including how he flunked high school in 1969 and was drafted the next year. No family that anyone knows of, although there is a birth certificate registered in Arkansas and records are freely available at a number of orphanages. He's an animal rights' activist, world peace advocate, and his last known residence was in a remote village in Zimbabwe where he lives with his wife and three kids as a valiant crusader against disease. He uses his credit card only for travel to summit meetings, peace talks, and environmental conferences."

"Fascinating. So what's happening in London over the next few days?"

"Well, we've got an international refugee conference, several scientific breakthroughs being discussed, a protest against deforestation…"

"Right, right, right, I get the picture."

Thus the discussion continued, and Jared was left trying to put together the ever-increasing pieces of the puzzle beginning to weave itself around Gregg Nicholas and these two mysterious acquaintances of his. Gregg and Ian clearly went way back, so how did one friend end up a history professor and the other a professional thief? And then there was the subject of Rob Dancer. How, exactly, did he fit into the scheme of things, aside from just a random Navy pal who apparently had Ian's penchant for leather jackets and dubious life choices?

Of the three, Gregg was the slightest-built, walked with the least amount of a swagger, and had the most honest face. Shy around people he didn't know well – or, in Jenny's case, a girl he found attractive – he nevertheless was able to convey a sense of innocence and hope for humankind, an air that folks found comforting and easy to be around. He was just one of those people that could be trusted with the combination to the bank vault and no one would ever make any bones about it. A born card player, a poker face was, unfortunately, impossible for Gregg to achieve to any believable extent, although he gave it his best and lamented at his lack of success. It just wasn't in his nature to be devious; at least, not without good reason.

Jared couldn't say the same for the other two. But he could see why, in another time and another place, the three of them had gotten along so well. They thought alike, gestured alike, and aside from obvious differences such as hair color, there were quite a few physical parallels. All were tall and athletically built, expressing a sense of confidence more than likely instilled in them during their days in the military, and a certain something that reached even further back into their pasts. It was in the way they dressed, in the practical nature of their mannerisms. It was blue collar, small town, agricultural family history. Despite being from all ends of the earth and now existing on decidedly opposite sides of the law, the three were very much the same kind of people, imbued with the same basic set of similarities that bind lives together to create lasting relationships. It was more than simply sharing a list of favorite things. It was a meeting of the minds, formed from knowledge and talents and strengths and weaknesses, trials and victories and experiences, all balancing each other out to form a camaraderie that outlasted time itself.

Jared wondered briefly if that closeness could bridge the gap between good and evil.

Their ride arrived in the form of two black, London cabs that pulled up. Gregg, Jared, and Ian got in one; Rob disappeared into the other. Apparently he was on his way to pick up a rental, which would service their needs until they blew town as millionaires. They wound their way back into the heart of the city, their feet hitting the ground once more outside a small hotel on some little side block far from the bustling city center. It was, legitimately, nothing fancy, but under the layers of dust and cockroaches it was perfect for what they had to do. Sweetly pocketed on the corner of two streets behind a large tree, it was easily missed if you weren't looking for it, but easily spotted if you were. The small sign out front was old and needed painting; the building itself looked more like an old, oversized mansion than a hotel.

"Like I said, perfect for what we need," Ian said as he unlocked the door around a leather duffel bag and booted it open with his toe.

Jared looked around as he stepped inside. The room was neat and clean, about three shakes of a dog's tail away from the stairs, and another short distance away from the elevator. The one window it possessed was conveniently positioned right next to the limbs of the tree that grew outside.

"Just in case," Ian remarked at Gregg's quirked eyebrow.

Jared saw the "remember that time when..." look pass between them. He set his bag down. Any minute now, and they would launch into yet another story.

"Thinking of the Walter's case when we were in Milwaukee, were you?" Gregg asked.

Who called it.

"What else?" Ian flopped onto the nearest bedspread with an exaggerated sigh. "What a night that was. Pouring rain..."

"Wind, sleet..."

"Snow."

"Hail..."

"And the guy tries to go out the window and down a tree trunk. Stark naked. Brave man."

Gregg laughed.

"And if it hadn't been for the dog sitting under the tree, we'd never have seen him. You were too busy looking at that girl in the window. Also stark naked."

"You know me, Gregg. I never could resist a pretty face. Even mortal danger takes a back seat."

Why wasn't that surprising?

"Say, speaking of that dog, how's Gates doing? He still on the job?"

"Oh, yeah. You couldn't drag him away from his work if you tied a herd of wild horses to his feet." Gregg looked at the grey, London sky outside for a moment. "You know, he was mighty upset when you quit, Ian."

"Yeah... figured I had my own rainbows to chase," was the evasive response as Ian unwrapped another peppermint. His tone seemed to indicate dangerous ground. That was the closest they had come to discussing "it", the elephant in the room neither wanted to talk about. The reason two former best friends barely knew each other anymore and it took this situation to cause Gregg to call him after ten years. The reason Graham Townsend hadn't been mentioned. The reason Ian was no longer a cop, and more than that, their best option for getting into the dig illegally. "Well..." Ian broke the silence, rolled the candy around in his mouth as he checked his watch. "If you want to take a cursory look at the dig before the deed tonight, now's your chance. I've been watching it since yesterday, right after you called, but didn't want to take a chance on missing anything. I hired

~ 101 ~

a guy to keep an eye on it while Rob and I came and got you two. Need to head over and pay him for a service hopefully well done."

"Hired?" Gregg shot him a look. "Does he know anything?"

Ian produced a large roll of bills from his pocket and waved them around.

"He knows it pays well," he said. "You want to come along?"

"No... I think I'll stay here."

"Right. I need to head out; Rob should be pulling up front about now with the rental. We'll be back in an hour. You'd better get some sleep, if you can, both of you. I know you're not used to this, and whether everything goes as planned or not, it's going to be a long night."

As Ian disappeared out the door, Gregg sighed and sat down heavily on the edge of the nearest bed, rubbing his forehead.

"And jet leg's a pain," he muttered, almost to himself. Jared could almost feel the headache he knew Gregg would be suffering about now, same as he always did when he changed more than two time zones. Only his headache was likely to be a whole lot worse. For only he knew the truth. About the fate of his hunt, and about the two men he had drawn into it.

Ian Lowell, handsome, dashing, and debonair though he might be, was far more dangerous than the attractive scoundrel everyone saw. And Rob Dancer was far more than a willing fourth party, just along for the plane ride. They were here for one reason, and one reason alone: the possibility of a treasure trove lingering in the light at the end of the tunnel.

Jared Casey... mom's not going to be too proud of the company you'll be keeping.

Funny thing, Jared wasn't either. Suddenly, this "grand adventure" wasn't so grand, and Gregg's only opportunity for discovering the truth about his legend might just get them killed.

"Don't say it, Jared," Gregg said wearily, addressing the silence. "Bad idea to bring Ian into this, I know. Had I known he was going to drag along his own personal squad, I never would have called him. Rob was as much of a surprise to me as he was to you, so just don't even say it."

"I wasn't going to say anything," Jared replied quietly.

"No, but you were thinking it."

Well, that was true. At his silent, affirming look, Gregg spread his hands defensively. "Look, we need them," he said. "Both of them. You were right; we couldn't do something like this on our own."

"I know."

They sat wordlessly for a moment, each busy with their own thoughts.

"Wonder who the guy is that Ian hired to watch the dig," Jared mused.

"Somebody either very desperate for cash or very easygoing," Gregg answered, and yanked out the nearest pillow as he dropped noisily onto the bed, ignoring the few dismal puffs of lint that rose indifferently by his face. He looked tired. Clearly there was more to this theft/break-in business than he'd anticipated. Jared made a mental note never to do this again.

Mom was right, he thought. *Crime doesn't pay.*

"If we can just get in, we'll be all right," Gregg's voice said from beyond the wall of pillows he'd constructed near his head, almost more like he wanted to make himself feel better than anything. "The treasure is there; I know it. We'll find it, split it, and that will be that. Ian will go back to his life on the run, Rob will disappear in a cloud of dust and carbon monoxide, and we can go back home. Simple. Finished. The legend will be solved."

His words died in the stillness of the room. Dust filtered. Clouds moved outside. Traffic rumbled. And Jared knew there was one, small problem.

"What if we don't find anything?"

"We will. Better stretch out and get some sleep while you can, Jared," Gregg said resignedly, his voice muffled. "Ian's right about one thing: it's going to be a long night."

"Yeah," Jared replied. "And we have work to do."

Gregg didn't respond, and Jared was left to dwell on his own thoughts, make his own peace with reality as it stood. He had committed himself to this, and while he may have been able to back out of it before, there was no hope of that now. Jared was under no illusions. Whether they were successful tonight or not, found Gregg's treasure trove or – heaven forbid – not, their heads would be waiting to roll. The Goldsteins would be out to get them, and Jared had a hunch the cavalry those people could call in was far more extensive than even his imagination could conjure. Gregg was correct: they needed both Ian and Rob if this thing was to work, and just had to hope Gregg's treasure theory proved correct. If not, Jared had a hunch a mob of angry Goldsteins would be the least of their worries.

Success was the only option tonight. There was no door number two. With someone like Ian Lowell on the loose, anything could happen.

"What happened to Graham?" Jared asked.

He was greeted only with silence. Gregg was asleep. And Jared was left wondering: what did Graham Townsend, a friend from Gregg's high school years, have to do with Ian becoming a crook? What had he done? Probably most importantly: where was he now?

***

It was cold.

The air was still and silent, chilled, almost like someone had locked him in a freezer and shut the door. Gregg crouched silently behind the big desk, shivering, his hand shaking as it clenched the butt of the forty-five caliber pistol he had half-cocked just moments before.

He had to get out of here. He had to get out of this place, away from the horrors it held, away from the terror it was so close to presenting. The surroundings were familiar. Gates' office walls rose on all sides of him, the paintings and pictures blending seamlessly with the cavernous interior of an old packing warehouse that seemed to stretch on for eternity, fading into the shadows far beyond Gregg's line of vision. But this was no longer a place of friendship. Far from it. Now it was a place of death.

Despite the stifling heat of summer pounding just outside the door, the inside of the warehouse was ice-like. And silent. It was filled with the deafening sound of utterly alone, the despair of having absolutely nowhere to turn.

He was alone. Yet he was not alone. Gregg knew they were there, waiting, just as he was; waiting for him to make a wrong move as Graham had done. Gregg slipped to his right, around the side of Gates' massive desk and moved stealthily behind a small stack of barrels, leaning back against the cold, metal sheeting that covered the outside of the building. In the silence his movements seemed to echo like gunshots. He knew he had to get out of here. But where? Where was the door? Where was the way out?

A bullet smacked into the barrel above his head. The report of a high-powered rifle cracked and echoed around as a small cascade of oil spouted out, pouring into Gregg's eyes. Gregg dove to the left, firing blindly. He couldn't see anything. He could hear nothing but dull noises. He felt no pain from the dark liquid on his face, only desperation over vision he couldn't control. His eyes seemed covered by a blanket, allowing only filmy images to reach his mind.

A shot boomed directly behind him. Another off to his right. They were all around him, closing the distance, ready to do him in. They just kept coming. And there was nothing he could do but run. He seemed to be illuminated by some unknown light source, one that followed him relentlessly and left him exposed even as everything else stood in shadow. Frantically he ran, shoes catching on themselves and leaving dark, rubbery scuffs on the floor below, but there was nowhere to go. An image loomed up on his right; an old, metal barrel surrounded by oil that oozed ominously out through a series of holes near its center, oil that was mysteriously interlaced with something else. Gregg knew what it was. He knew what was behind that barrel... who was there. He didn't want to go back, but he also knew he had no choice. It was the only place to go if he wanted to live.

Graham Townsend's body lay just as he remembered, sprawled on its side, lifeless eyes seeming to stare right through Gregg in an accusing manner. He lay in a pool of dark liquid, a mixture of oil and blood that swirled around him in intricate patterns, seeping over the floor. It began to ooze over the toes of Gregg's shoes.

A shot sounded. Gregg saw the flash of one gun, then a second. Frantically he fired, again and again, but though he could now see his targets clearly, he didn't seem to be hitting anything.

And then Ian appeared. He was walking calmly through the middle of the warehouse, gun in hand, unaware of the chaos around him. His strides were those of a man with a purpose, eyes set and hard as the slugs from Gregg's forty-five. He was bleeding. But he didn't seem to notice.

Gregg tried to call out. He tried to warn him, tried to tell Ian to get down and stay under cover so he wouldn't get hit again. But his voice refused to work. He shouted louder, as loud as he could, watching men stand up from all sides and take aim... Ian didn't care. Slowly he walked, deliberately, across the room toward the door. Gregg knew where he was going. He was going to clean up the rest of them, just like he said he would. He was going to right the wrong and make sure the animals who killed Graham got what they had coming.

Ian opened the door and looked back once, a mere shadow against the blackness of night outside.

"Take care, mate," he said quietly. Then, with a sodden clang, he was gone, swallowed up by the night. And Gregg knew he wouldn't come back. One by one, he felt the enemies surrounding him succumb to Ian's vengeance, dropping from his mind's eye to sink away into oblivion. But still Gregg was afraid.

"There's no telling what he'll do now..."

The words came back to Gregg unbidden, a distant memory he had hoped to forget. It was too painful a recollection to hang onto. Something was beginning to niggle at the back of his mind. Some unknown sense of dread that he was not prepared for, something he did not expect. Suddenly, quite clearly, he knew what it was.

He was being hunted.

The hair on the back of his neck prickled in the darkness. Something was tailing him, coming closer and closer in the darkness, sneaking up behind him...

Gregg panicked. He bolted from his hiding place, leaving Graham behind, but no matter how fast he ran, he couldn't go anywhere. He slipped uncontrollably in the mixture at his feet, stumbling into barrel after barrel as he ran for the door. He lost his gun as it flew from his hand. He fell to his knees as the cement gripped his shoes. Desperately he lunged forward, falling and tripping over the smooth floor of the warehouse, his feet refusing to move correctly.

No shots were fired. No sound came. He knew his enemies were all gone, every one of them, and all that was left was the terror that pursued him. The room was as still as space. There was only the sound of fear, the heavy, thudding beat of his heart as he stumbled for the door amid the deafening silence and icy chill. He reached the door, turned the handle; the door wouldn't open.

Movement shifted behind him. It was almost on him now, ready to spring...

Gregg slammed his shoulder into the door and tumbled outside as it gave, banging it shut behind him. Soft sunlight hit his face. Gregg leaned heavily on the door, letting the warmth soak into his body and melt away the dread, letting the horror drain away with the memories. It was over. His nemesis was gone, trapped in the building where it belonged, in the past with the dreadful things that happened there, and Gregg was out. He was safe in the present. It couldn't reach him here.

Slowly, his eyes heavy with relief, Gregg walked over and sat down on his couch as the trees and bushes around him melted effortlessly into his office walls. He glanced behind him at the large clock in his living room. The hands moved silently, around and around, almost hypnotizing in their effect. Gregg leaned back and closed his eyes.

And it was then, in the cool of the room, that he felt it. It was back. Gregg jumped up, ready to face whatever it was that had been dogging him through the warehouse, through time, through the past. Behind him, a figure moved stealthily out of the shadows on the far end of the room.

Gregg spun around, prepared for anything... except for what he saw.

It was Ian.

***

Gregg sat bolt upright, his muscles stiff and cramped, a cold sweat beading on his forehead. Even now he was expecting to see it, see *him*, see the things he'd just imagined coming to life around him. But there was nothing out of the ordinary. Jared was stretched out on the other bed, using his bag as a pillow, sound asleep. The digital clock blinked silently on one of the small tables, flashing six o'clock as afternoon sunlight filtered in through the large window. Angrily, Gregg wiped the sweat from his face with his jacket, slamming the garment back onto the bed with a sound that seemed to echo through the room. He stood up slowly, a bit light-headed, and rubbed his forehead with stiff fingers. It was all so real, so fresh... it was like it happened yesterday.

Graham Townsend had been killed in the line of duty as a US Marshal on September 4th, 1995. He had bled to death in Ian's arms. Gregg found them both sprawled behind an old oil drum, Ian draped over Graham's lifeless body in a feeble attempt to save him, unconscious and slowly dying himself. The men they were after, a formidable ring of drug runners and human traffickers, disappeared without a trace, leaving behind only a trail of loss.

By Christmas it was all over. Ian had spent at least a month in and out of hospitals, had come back to the job a changed man. He was closed off, distant; Gregg saw him spend hours conversing with Gates, their senior officer, saw them talking through the closed pane of glass that was Gates' office door. He was never invited in. Ian had shut him out completely. He had shut everyone out. It had started several years ago, this estrangement; right after they left the Navy. But the tipping point had been reached at last.

Then came the day that Gregg always expected, but never quite imagined would happen. Ian turned in his badge, turned in his service-issued firearm, and went after Graham's killers alone. He didn't want to be constrained by the law. Didn't want to be bound by rules of conduct. He didn't want anything but a loaded gun standing between himself and them when they finally met face to face. There were ten men. And he intended to hunt each and every one of them down.

Gregg remembered the day Ian left, setting out on his self-appointed mission, dropping his badge on the table with a quiet: "Take care, mate." He had walked away without a backward glance, out the door and into the darkness outside, the purposeful stride of a soldier on duty. He never came back. There had been something ominous in his words, in his tone, as if Ian somehow knew it was good-bye. As if he knew where his journey of vengeance would take him and that he would not emerge unchanged. It was as if he knew, deep down, what was in store for him.

Three days after he left, Gates gave Gregg the photograph with the phone number on it. Gregg had stood there in silence and cried. He was still reeling over Graham's death, and from the moment he touched that piece of paper, allowed the reality to truly reach him, there was an incredible void in his heart he knew would never be filled. The best friend he'd ever had in this life was gone; there was nothing to replace that. His tears hit the ink, smearing it, as his fingers worried the edges. Gates had stood by silently, his hand on Gregg's shoulder, while Gregg felt his own heart break into a thousand pieces.

Recalling that moment still brought pain. It shouldn't have ended like that.

Gregg slowly pulled the dog tags out of his jeans, where they had been tucked since yesterday. He had vengefully thrown them in the trash, hurt, and went on a drinking binge that lasted for four days. It didn't end well, as normally he didn't touch the stuff. When he sobered up he didn't feel any better; didn't feel anything at all, really. Calmly, coldly, he had removed the tags from the bin and put them in that box, along with the photo Ian had left for him. He never looked at them since. He never used the phone number.

He'd managed to keep track of Ian for a while, through Gates and the others, kept track and watched in sorrow as Ian's situation grew worse and worse with each killing, each notch on the butt of his gun. One man down, then two, then three. There came a time when Gates, his face somber, handed Gregg an arrest warrant and told Gregg that Ian was beginning to commit crime in order to get close to his victims, infusing himself completely into their world. Not only was he himself becoming a crime boss, there was a target forming on his back that was impossible to hide. Some of the men he took out had their own syndicates, their own gangs, networks in play long before San Diego. Their deaths caused a lot of financial harm for a lot of unpleasant characters; Ian wasn't making himself any friends out there. His response was to go harder, be tougher, hit first. It was typical Ian. But it was a tactic he used with too much efficiency. For there came the time when even Gates admitted he was beyond help.

"I don't know, Gregg," he had said. "I've gotten scattered reports here and there, heard stories... things have been happening. I hate to say this, but I think Ian has gone off the deep end. There's no telling what he'll do now."

It was the final blow in a fight Gregg knew he had lost long before, and he knew the day Graham died was far from over for him. Just as time marched on with relentless precision, just as the unnamed fear in his dream had passed easily through years to pursue him into the present, so did the chain of events that had been set in motion the day Graham Townsend was killed, events still in play to this day. It was ironic, really; of the ten who had escaped, only one was directly responsible for Graham's death. And, true to the fickle whims of luck and fate, if Gregg's sources were accurate he was the only one Ian had yet to catch. To this day, no one knew the man's identity. The others had all been accounted for, one by one, but that tenth man still ran free.

Gregg had been a fool to call Ian. He knew, at the heart of the matter, it was not the Gregg Nicholas, Treasure Hunter that dialed that long-lost phone number on the back of a worn photo, it was the Gregg Nicholas who simply wanted his friend back. The Gregg Nicholas who thought, perhaps, after ten years, Ian might be tired of this life he was living and want to be saved. Gregg should have known better. Ian was no closer to being done with his hunt than Gregg was with his own. Ian would not stop until he had finished what he started out to do, and he would not finish until he had righted the wrong. Even if it landed him in prison, even if it got him killed.

Or worse, took his soul to the depths of hell itself.

There was no escaping the raw emotion Gregg was feeling at this moment. Fear. Fear of having his worst nightmare realized; the idea that, somewhere over the course of the last decade, Ian had set aside their friendship and now considered Gregg no different than anyone else. A stranger. A loose alliance. Someone who, if necessary, would prove expendable. It was the feeling of haunting, empty despair that came with turning around in a dream to find his best friend standing there ready to watch him die.

"I think Ian has gone off the deep end," Gates said again. *"There's no telling what he'll do now."*

He was right. Every human being has their breaking point; maybe Ian had finally reached his. Maybe Gregg wasn't dealing with an avenging warrior anymore but a hardened criminal, one that would sell any life, even those he knew, for a piece of gold. The thought was frightening. But Gregg was well aware that it was very, very possible; history was rife with examples. Ian had conditioned himself to kill, to hunt, to become every bit as vile and wicked and impossible to forgive as those he pursued. He had trained himself to set aside his humanity. And in the process – in that slow, agonizing, heart-wrenching process – he just might have gone too far.

Suddenly, Gregg was scared.

Chapter 6

"Ian, are you sure this is such a good idea... doing this tonight?"

Jared's question broke a long stretch of silence. They were on the way to the dig. Just another Enterprise rent-a-car roaming the streets, full of tourists. Except these tourists were tense, alert, and on their way to commit a crime.

Preparation for this job, although somewhat hurried, had been complete. Whoever Ian hired to watch the dig had done his job well, and acquired everything from detailed videos of the surrounding area to exact, down-to-the-second timetables for the guards, both front and back. From the time Ian and Rob sauntered into the hotel room with everything their contact had picked up, the four future grave-robbers had studied. And studied. And studied some more until they had every detail of the place down pat, every number locked away inside their heads. They'd eaten on the fly, sending off for an order of Chinese food that arrived five minutes early in the hands of an absolutely gorgeous blonde who had more makeup on than a stage performer and sported a manner that suggested delivering takeout wasn't the only in-home service she provided. A few uncomfortable moments elapsed as she stood in the doorway waiting to be paid, batting her eyes flirtatiously at anything and everything male within her line of sight. When she finally handed over the food and left, it was with no small amount of amusement that Ian discovered a discreet piece of paper with her phone number on it tossed in with his rice.

"I always was a sucker for blondes," he said in mock distress. Potential success with this lady fair, however, was rendered moot when Rob "accidentally" spilled his coffee on the paper.

Dinner had been brief. Then it was back to work. By the time their "grave-robbers' 101" course was over and they were ready to go, the only non-black anything visible anywhere was skin-colored faces and the drab, nondescript jackets they all wore for public appearance. Now they were here, and it was getting real.

Gregg wanted that treasure in his hands. He could see it already; now he just had to get to it. He and Ian sat in the back, Rob at the wheel, Jared in the passenger seat. Jared peered out the window nervously as the streets of London rolled by; his eyes were about the same size as a pair of dinner platters. He shot Rob a look as the latter glanced over at him, chuckling.

"What?" He demanded. "What's so funny?"

"You. You look like a squirrel."

Jared rolled his eyes.

"I'm sorry, I was going for more chipmunk action. But, really, guys, is it such a bad idea to wait a day... or two or three... maybe forever? I mean, it wouldn't hurt so much to study some more and break in later, would it?"

"We'll be fine," Ian said brusquely. He handed Gregg one of two silencers and screwed a second one on the barrel of the pistol he held in his hand. Jared had refused to even touch the gun he was offered, let alone use it, so Ian found him a large piece of pipe before they piled into the rented car. "Here. Just in case you get attacked by those Samurai lurking about," he'd said. Jared now clutched his weapon with white knuckles, clearly wishing he'd never seen a computer and wishing he'd never heard the name Gregg Nicholas.

"Rob," Ian said quietly, tapping their driver on the shoulder, "pull over and park near that bar."

The wheels of the car made a low humming sound on the pavement as Rob angled it toward a parking space not far from a busy, lighted tavern called the Pale Horse Pub. The place was packed, with people streaming out onto the sidewalk; over the door, a two-dimensional sign depicting what appeared to be the fourth horseman of the apocalypse holding a pint over his head welcomed clients to the venue.

"Great," Ian said enthusiastically. "This is better than I thought. Rob, I'll keep in touch with you on the walkie. If things go bad, pull out and meet us around the block. Gregg, Jared." Two sets of eyes turned to peer at him. "I know you both know what to do, but it gets a little different when it's the real thing. Right beyond this string of buildings is the dig, and the easiest way to get there without being spotted is to go through this tavern right here. Remember what Gates used to tell us before we went in, Gregg."

"Stay buttoned up and shut up," Gregg recited.

Jared nodded, even though he would have no idea what either of them was talking about.

"Gregg, give me a rundown of your job."

"I distract the guard and get him away from the shelter a ways so you can get rid of him. Then we make him disappear and slip in."

"Jared?"

"Take up the post out front and keep an eagle eye out for movement. If someone comes by, show life signs. If anything bad happens, radio you... what if we get caught?"

"Shouldn't we have some sort of a back-up plan?" Gregg asked.

Ian grinned at him.

"Yeah. Run like hell. Now, remember, your target is the bottom of the street. Follow it around until you reach the front of the dig, so they can see you coming. It will take us seven minutes to get to our station, and it will take you three to reach the front. That gives you four minutes to work your magic. Jared, you stay with me, and we'll just kind of ease on through the pub. Don't stop, don't talk, don't do anything that will set you apart. There'll be enough people in there to make us just a couple more faces in an ever-changing crowd, and nobody will even remember we were there. There are four cameras in this place: one above the door, one near the back entrance, two over the bar. Try to avoid them if you can but the most important thing is to look normal. Once we get out back, we'll be directly east and about three hundred feet away from the front of the dig, behind a pile of rubble. Now there's fence there, like the video showed, but it's nothing more than chain link with razor wire along the top. We get behind that pile of rubble, cut a hole, slip inside, and wait. Ready?"

Gregg nodded. Jared shook his head.

"All right, let's go get some treasure." Ian opened the back door and the three of them hopped out of the car. He grinned at Gregg. "The next time we speak, we will be breaking in on a fortune," he said, and Gregg could almost hear the cash register chiming in his head.

"Good luck," Rob said.

Gregg half-heartedly waved. He was on his own now. It was like going to his very first job interview alone… but ten times worse. This interview could turn deadly in the blink of an eye if he muffed it. He had to ingratiate himself with the guard at the front of the dig, hang around for the changeover, wait for the rear guard to disappear, and distract his new "friend" until Ian could take care of the issue and gain them entrance into the tunnel system itself.

He felt like a fugitive as he walked off down the street. He saw Ian and Jared grab their backpacks from the car and head toward the pub, through the smattering of people near the front door. Then they were gone, and Gregg was alone. He kept walking. Around him hummed the sights and smells of the party-town London he had read about: pubs and nightclubs filled with people who didn't care if they had work in the morning. Night air abuzz with the noise of traffic and drunken laughter and the clinking of glassware. The sidewalk beneath his feet lit with streetlamps.

He really hoped there was gold in this place.

He went around the block and approached the dig from the front. Checked his watch. Thirty seconds, then he would move in and start talking. He dug around in his bag for the small, digital camera he had stuffed in the front pocket, took a deep breath, counted to ten, and started forward. The long, chain link rent-a-fence stretched for a good one hundred yards to his left, and another twenty or so to the right. Along that right hand side was the back boundaries of all the pubs and nightclubs Gregg had just passed, and the one Ian and Jared were more than likely leaving right now.

The dig was well lit. He could see the tarp in the middle, covering the hole that delved so unexpectedly into the ground. There were a couple of guys hanging out near the caution tape, and Gregg knew they had seen him as soon as he first appeared. In their business, it didn't pay to be slack. The whole space surrounding them was a lot bigger than he imagined. Standing here, with all five senses engaged instead of the mere two stimulated by the broadcast made all the difference. It made everything much more…

Weird. Was there really treasure here?

He was nervous. No, he was terrified. The reality of the situation was slowly, surely pressing down on his shoulders; cruelly, the camera-eye perspective he'd been able to maintain since yesterday morning was fading, leaving him with the knowledge that the feet taking him so steadily forward were his own, the eyes that looked around so carefully were his own, and the heart that pounded so quickly was also his own. The consequences of this night would be his own. No one else's.

The fence loomed. Gregg knew his time had come. He looked to his right, at the rubble pile inside the fence line, wondering if Ian and Jared had managed to get through that fence to their posting behind the massive mound of concrete and brick. He supposed he would find out soon enough.

Casually, he raised his camera and took a photo. Another. Another. The guards near the shelter kept an eye on him, but otherwise didn't react. Gregg wasn't worried; both the front guard and the group posted behind the building still had to swap with their reliefs. He would get an in as the first one came out the gate. Strike up a conversation, and it should be relatively easy from there. He was the only one here at this time of night aside from the occasional party-goer who wandered by. He nonchalantly edged closer to the gate, happy-snapping away at anything and everything he thought might be of interest. As an added touch, he popped a piece of gum in his mouth and started blowing bubbles.

Two minutes. The guards near the shelter dispersed and went their separate ways, one heading around back and the other sauntering toward the front gate. He punched in a code to unlock it, stepped outside. He was mere feet from Gregg.

Gregg snapped. Blew a bubble for emphasis. Snapped again. Then, feigning inability to see, he put his foot in the bottom diamond of the fence and hefted himself up a few inches, snapping a bit higher. The bid for attention worked. The guard looked at him quickly.

"Excuse me, sir, might I be of assistance?" He inquired, rather stiffly. Gregg hated to think how many times he saw this every day.

"Oh. Hi, man," Gregg said, looking around innocuously as he munched away on his gum. He stepped back to ground level. "Is this the site for that museum expansion?"

"It is." The response was spare. Gregg's new mission was to transform himself from annoying member of the general public to BFF.

"Sorry, I'm being rude," he said expansively, and wandered forward to hold out a hand. "Nicholas Handler, reporter for *The Times*."

"Of New York?" Was the immediate question as his hand was shaken, rather cautiously.

"Yes. Well..." Gregg grinned. "If you mean New York, Nevada," he said, lying glibly. He was met with a dumfounded, but curious, expression.

"Nevada."

"Nevada," Gregg affirmed. "Won town of the year in 1910... population three hundred and twelve. I got sent over here by the local paper to do an exclusive on this museum of yours."

"I wasn't under the impression America was interested in our news. Particularly a town of such... concentrated nature." Clearly Dodge Rams, rednecks, Hell's Angels, and the occasional KKK meetup were running through his mind.

"Oh believe me," Gregg said emphatically. "We may be small, but we are an insatiable lot. I can think of at least...four people who would give an arm and a leg to have more access."

This time, his response elicited a laugh. Mission accomplished.

"Well, tell those four people that we appreciate their support and interest," the guard said. "By the way, my name is Jerry. Jerry Ellis. Pleasure to meet you, Mr. Handler."

"You, as well. I apologize for climbing on your fence; I promised my readers as complete a story as possible."

"It's quite all right. What is it they want to know about most?"

Can we come break into your dig to get treasure?

"Well," Gregg said, whipping out his notepad for appearances. "I think the readers I've encountered are most interested in how Marian's Necklace relates to the treasure legend."

"Well, that's not really a question for me. Miss Goldstein is the one to ask. I'll tell you what I know, however, and –"

"Jerry!"

The sound of a car door popping open caused Gregg to turn, and he found himself staring at none other than Amantha Goldstein as she hopped out of her car and jogged toward them through the moonlight, maneuvering expertly in a pair of stilettos. Tall stilettos; no kidding, the heels on those things had to be six inches. What was she doing here? Gregg got the distinct impression this was not part of the plan. It was, if nothing else, a major distraction. Amantha was dressed in beige slacks and a filmy, white shirt with three-quarter sleeves and a v-neck, her hair done up in a simple, yet elegant do. She wore little makeup; just a bit here and there to darken her expressive eyes and enhance features that, honestly, didn't need enhancing. She was shorter than Gregg would have imagined. Even with the heels, she stood eye to eye with him only. He figured that was what came with seeing her on TV. Not that she was actually short – five-foot-eight was nothing to scoff at – but onscreen she seemed like she must be at least twenty feet tall.

It must have been the legs.

Gregg looked.

It was definitely the legs.

"I do apologize for the intrusion," Amantha said sincerely as she reached them. "I was on my way to the banquet and completely forgot to give you the procedures you requested." She held out a small parcel to Jerry, then looked directly at Gregg and smiled. "I don't believe I've had the pleasure."

"Miss Goldstein, Nicholas Handler."

The hand Amantha presented him was soft and small, the hand of a lady, but one that possessed a surprising firmness of grip. Not hard, of course, just enough to get the point across that this woman was no shrinking violet.

"Mr. Handler."

"It's – nice to meet you," Gregg managed in shock, and gave a startled chew on his gum, realizing who he was actually shaking hands with. Funny, but as he looked at her, the only thing he could think of was how much easier her eyes were to meet than Jenny's, and wondered why that was so. No fireworks had mysteriously erupted at their introduction, no thundering crescendo of music had sounded, no stars had streamed through the sky as their hands met. Regardless of what romantic literature would want to see happen, there was not a spark of attraction between Amantha Goldstein and Gregory Parnell Nicholas.

Too bad. That would have been convenient. Well, there was always Jared.

Amantha had turned to Jerry Ellis and was plying him with questions, much like a sister would request information from her older brother. Her voice, too, was different than it had been on TV. It was livelier. Her manner was unassuming, ordinary, indicating a person who judged everyone by the same set of rules – ones not necessarily dictated by class. Gregg admired that. It would be easy for her to act differently.

"...have a few moments you could spare?"

"Yes, I do," Amantha said brightly at Ellis' query. "What can I do for you?"

"Mr. Handler is a reporter. He's come all the way from New York, Nevada, population three hundred and twelve. He was interested in hearing about the necklace you acquired in November," Ellis explained, and Amantha turned to Gregg with a winning smile.

"What did you wish to know?"

For a split second, Gregg was caught unprepared. What? Know? What did he want to *know*? He was just here to find gold. He hadn't actually planned on doing an interview. Least of all with Amantha Goldstein.

"I – well, I just was curious about it." He shifted the bag on his shoulders as a pick started to dig into muscle. "You're sure I'm not putting you out?"

"No, not at all."

Amantha Goldstein was easy to talk to; kind, direct, a keen listener and very informative. She talked with her hands. And she knew literally everything about any Robin Hood angle Gregg could ever hope to cover. Truthfully, if a joint vision of Jared rolling his eyes and Ian sailing in on horseback to sweep Aamntha off her feet hadn't suddenly cut in, Gregg would have lost all track of time – and the reason for his visit – so interested was he in this topic.

"Just one last question, Miss Goldstein," he said finally, scribbling madly on the small notepad he'd brought along. "Where, exactly, did this piece come from? You say it was acquired."

"It has been in my family since the late 1100's," Amantha said, "but as you know, when Veit Goldstein disappeared from London, it went with him. We bought it off a family in Sonora, when they wrote to us and informed us of its whereabouts. How it really got there, I suppose we'll never know; of course the family has their own tale, but, like ours, it is hard to prove. I imagine the piece would have quite the story to tell."

"How fascinating!" Gregg exclaimed. And it was. He would have loved to just stay right here all night.

Amantha suddenly checked her watch.

"Oh! I really must go, Mr. Handler," she said, and held out a hand. "Fashionably late is one thing, but I will be pushing the limit of that if I tarry. I'm sorry I couldn't speak with you longer."

"Not at all, Miss Goldstein." Gregg shook her hand lightly again and smiled into the clear grey of her eyes. "Thank you for your time."

"It was my pleasure." As Amantha walked briskly down the rough, gravelly path toward her car, Gregg stared after her in momentary amazement. Had he really just met her? She was, like, a celebrity. Wasn't she supposed to have bodyguards or something? It was just this morning that he saw her mug all over the front page of some chick mag in the airport. He was still struggling to forget that thing with the feathers.

Out of the corner of his eye, he saw Jerry wave, then check his watch.

Right. Duty calls. Gregg took the opportunity to check his own watch, ascertaining he had most definitely killed enough time for Ian and Jared to have reached their position. Now it was just down to the guard change.

Then let the good times roll.

"Always late," Jerry muttered, almost under his breath.

"Your replacement?"

A nod.

"A right clown, he is. I normally don't mind so much, but I need to spend time studying." He held up the packet enclosed in his left hand.

"Important?"

"Policies and procedures. I commence duty as head of museum security tomorrow."

"Sounds challenging," Gregg said empathetically. "Which reminds me, do you mind if I grab a quick photo of you? I would like to show my readers the face of the man who gave me all the good information."

Jerry laughed.

"Well, if you must," he conceded. "Although I warn you, I might break your camera."

Gregg laughed with him and took a couple of shots. And as he did, a car pulled up along the curb, followed by a van.

The first replacement was here.

Gregg's stomach tied another knot.

****

Gregg had long since disappeared down the street. Jared followed Ian like a puppy, aware that doing so was his only chance of getting out of this unscathed. Although he may not trust or even like the man personally, Jared knew Ian was someone who understood risk. Understood danger. Understood how to work with both. For better or for worse, Jared was committed to this now, and Ian was the thing that would keep him in one piece.

It was in strained silence that they left the car to make their way into the tavern, carrying backpacks that looked to be, to any casual observer, full of photographic equipment. True to Ian's prediction, they weren't noticed any more than had they been local hangers-out, and it was a simple chore to make their way through the bustling building and out the back door. Jared knew his face was being plastered all over the cameras; he'd seen two of them as he walked through. Oh well. In a few hours he'd be rich and could buy the footage. Ian paused right before they headed outside.

"King, can you hear me?" He asked quietly into a small radio.

"Loud and clear, Aussie; we're set."

"Good. Keep your eyes open, and don't call me unless it's an emergency."

"What, like some hot chick showing up with friends?"

"Exactly," Ian said emphatically. "Signal with a single beep if anything happens, and I'll pick up. We want to keep this as quiet as possible."

"You got it. And remind the chipmunk to keep me informed."

"Excuse me, but the chipmunk is right here," Jared cut in.

Ian turned the volume down a little on the walkie-talkie and opened the door. A few steps later, they creaked open an old, wooden gate and headed away from the tavern, past the bins smelling of stale liquor and rotting food. Neither said anything. Jared was anxious and quiet, the magnitude of what they were doing once again settling on his shoulders. Ian looked tense, but his attitude stemmed more from excitement than fear. Jared had a hunch he never tired of this, creeping around unnoticed, getting in without detection, the sheer magic of a job well done. He was probably always like that, even when he was a law-abiding citizen.

The fence was before them. Ian reached a gloved hand into his backpack to reveal a pair of wire-cutters, which he quickly plied to the thick wire, cutting it with no more than a few quiet clicks. The place he'd chosen was right behind an old pallet cast aside from the tavern's back enclosure, and shielded from the dig by a combination of several large pieces of earth-moving equipment and copious amounts of debris. He peeled back the wire and sent Jared first before slithering through himself and letting it down again. Then, like rats in a maze, the two of them crept around the pile of rubble on the near side of their goal and parked themselves behind a large slab of cement.

"Put these on," Ian said, handing Jared a pair of gloves. "Don't leave anything lying around that might possibly be used by anyone, anytime, in any form, and don't touch *anything* without gloves. The last thing we want is fingerprints."

He pulled a dark cap on over his hair and peered around the barrier. Below them lay the dig, radiant in the glow of stationary, white flood-lights. Moths darted back and forth in the harsh lighting, making runs at the bulbs. The still, almost lunar quality of the ground was eerie. Right in the middle of all that emptiness was a band of yellow tape strung in a rough square, and a tarp in the middle. Jared assumed it was covering the hole they wanted.

It took Jared a minute to spot Gregg, standing casually near the front fence, laughing and talking with – was that Amantha Goldstein? Jared felt his eyebrows shoot up. How had he accomplished that small miracle? Even as he wondered, Amantha took her leave with a winning smile, retreating from view to hop in a car parked along the front. A few moments and it drove off.

"Wow," Jared said, impressed.

"What?" Ian glanced at him quizzically.

"Nothing." Ian wouldn't get it, anyway. To him, Amantha Goldstein would just be another body in between him and the gold he was after. Jared cast a quick glance at the receding form of the vehicle, and went back to the dig. He could see the chain link fence along the front, where Amantha had been parked, disappearing into gloom on the far side; the fence along the back was obscured by several prefab buildings and silent construction equipment. Behind those buildings, he knew, was where five men were stationed of a night time, just to provide a little backup to the poor fellow put in charge of keeping this place secure after dark.

Funny: for a scene containing the possibility of a multi-million dollar payout, it wasn't guarded very heavily. One rent-a-cop with some friends didn't seem enough. Maybe… there wasn't anything here. Maybe there was nothing to guard. Jared thought back to the conversation he and Gregg had had earlier, at the hotel. They both knew how much of a gamble this was.

He peered at Ian out of the corner of his eye, silhouetted against the bright lights of a building behind him. What about him? What would he do if there was nothing there? Or Rob, waiting so silently and sinisterly in the car. Jared didn't even want to think about it. Ian was quiet and grave, having long ago slipped into "mission mode" and blocking out all thoughts but those important to the task at hand. He was on the job now, and it was going to be done correctly and without mistakes. Jared could feel the intensity radiating off his body, that infectious excitement that was dangerous as it was contagious, seeming almost to try and egg him into doing something regrettably heroic.

Oh, why did you have to get yourself into this? He thought to himself, idly wondering what would happen if he just hit Ian over the head with the pipe and took off.

Ian pushed up a dark sleeve and checked his watch.

"They should be changing the guard any minute now," he said, leaning his back against the slab. "After that happens, we'll have only a few minutes until the back-up team changes. We want the bloke out front neutralized as soon as the group and their replacements disappear."

Gregg swapped companions when the guard he'd been talking to traded places with another; after a brief introduction and jovial farewell, Gregg was left alone to continue his discussion with the newcomer.

"Any minute now," Ian said. "Remember. Always expect the unexpected and be prepared for anything. Just because something is supposed to work a certain way doesn't mean it will, so keep your eyes and ears open."

Now you tell me, Jared thought.

Right on the dot, the back-up team showed up and entered through the gate. Five men, armed to the teeth it seemed to Jared, stalked into view and changed places with their tired peers, waving to both Gregg and the guard on their way by. The off-duty team piled gratefully into the van that had brought their replacements, and within a couple of minutes, there wasn't a soul in sight except that one, lonely guard out front by the gate. And Gregg.

Game on.

"All right, Jared, now's our chance," Ian said. They crawled quietly down the rubbish pile, hit flat ground, advanced cautiously. The guard was unaware of their movements.

"I think you'd have to be a historian to really understand the real value of this place," Gregg was saying. "Have there been many artifacts uncovered?"

"Mate, heaps," was the emphatic response.

"Where does it all go?"

"The museum. Their storage room and cleaning department have taken on the extra load, and some of the pieces will be ready by the end of the week. They're dedicating an entire room to it, so I hear. I'll tell you, those people have been hopping lately."

"I'll bet..."

Jared peered cautiously around the wide, empty space, searching the darkness for signs of life. Nothing moved. To his left, Ian was halfway across the clearing, creeping up behind Gregg's acquaintance with the stealth of a panther. He held the pistol in his hand, raising it higher the closer he got.

One good whap should do it, Jared thought uncomfortably. He could almost see Gregg cringing.

"By the way, Jerry didn't introduce us properly," Gregg said casually, extending a hand. "I'm Nicholas Handler."

"That he didn't. Pleased to meet you, Nicholas, I'm –"

Whack!

Gregg's new friend dropped like a brick.

"Sorry," he said by way of apology and leaned down to grab the feet as Ian took off with the upper body.

"Who was your friend?" Ian asked with a grin. The lifeless hands of the guard were smacking into his knees as he backed up.

"What?"

"The blonde you were talking to. She was hot."

So he had noticed. Jared realized he shouldn't have been surprised. This was, after all, basically an Australian version of Han Solo.

"Oh." Gregg's sense of propriety was clearly offended. "Just a girl who works at the museum," he said. "Nothing to –" He paused as he almost tripped over the body. "– worry about," he finished.

The hole was before them. Surrounded by caution tape. Still covered by a tarp. Gregg and Ian stood aside with their bundle as Jared pulled it back as quietly as possible, then flicked on his flashlight and shined it around in the small, claustrophobic space below them.

"Creepy," he said.

And it was. The space couldn't have been more than six feet squared with a low, uneven ceiling; the walls were rough and textured, adding to the closeness. One by one, all three dropped down inside, dragging the body with them. Gregg was panting by the time they'd stashed the guard in a corner and stripped him of his outer uniform, gagged him lightly, and covered him with another tarp they found discarded in the tiny room.

Ian attached the end of a long string to the wall, the rest of which was wound around a thick roll in his hands.

"What's that for?" Jared asked, curiosity getting the best of him despite his nerves.

"Location," Gregg answered, and hefted a bag to his shoulder. "There's more than one tunnel down there and we don't want to get lost."

Jared grimaced at the thought.

"Jared," Ian said, tying the string off. "I need you to take this guy's shirt and pants and put yourself in his post out front. As long as everything looks normal at a glance, we should be all right. You need to be our eyes and ears, but you need to look the part."

Jared nodded and picked up the bundle of clothes lying on the floor next to the tarp. They smelled of sweat, dirt, and cigarettes.

"Are you sure this is the last guard change?" He asked, pulling the pair of overly-loose pants over his jeans. He was going to need a belt. Or some string.

"It better be, or this is going to be a real short trip." Ian pulled a second radio out of his bag and handed it to Jared. "If anything happens, let us know."

"Worst case scenario, come get us," Gregg said. "Just follow the string and we'll be at the end. Let's go, Ian. We don't have all year."

Ian grinned.

"Let's go get some treasure, mate," he said.

The beam of the flashlight bounced eagerly off the walls as Gregg started toward the steep staircase on the far side. It was cool and dry in here, perfectly preserved, despite its location under one of the busiest cities in the world. Ian flicked on a second flashlight and started down the stairway; behind him, Gregg paused. Looked around, sighed quietly. And for a split second, Jared could see the satisfaction on his face; of realizing where he was... in whose footsteps he was walking. He looked down at the hard, earthen floor beneath his own feet. Who had come down this passage in the past? Who was buried down here?

"What is it?" Ian asked from the middle of the stairs. His eyes were fixed on Gregg.

"Nothing," Gregg said, "I was just taking a moment. There is so much history down here... being in the midst of it is..." He shook his head. "...beyond description."

"Even for a professor?" Ian's voice held a sympathetic smile.

"Even for a professor," Gregg said softly, and passed by him to lead the way down the stairs, running his flashlight over every inch of wall. "We'll be back, Jared," he said quietly over his shoulder.

"Careful, dudes," Jared said in response. Ian briefly nodded at him and disappeared into the darkness, the string waving out behind him. Jared could hear their footsteps and smatterings of brief, muffled conversation. When it finally died away, Jared shrugged into the guard's shirt, carefully climbed the ladder, and crept outside again, into the faded moonlight to take up his post.

They had an unconscious guy wrapped in a tarp underground, and he was impersonating a guard. This just got real.

****

It was black. Blacker than Gregg could have imagined. Silent but for their footsteps. The air inside the tunnel was close, stale, surprisingly dry, and smelled of age and rock and time. Over his head, the rock was less than a foot away. At his feet, the fine layer of dust covering the floor was broken only by a few other sets of tracks; two of these, he knew, would be the prints of Amantha Goldstein and Carl Heyward. He was glad Ian brought the string. There were several tunnels, and Gregg was running only on the memory he had of the broadcast and the mysterious, guiding patterns of footprints in the dirt before him. Twice he followed a set sure to be Amantha's only to have the prints lead him in a direction he didn't expect, or back toward the surface. Once they hit a dead end and had to backtrack a good five hundred feet before choosing another path at a point where three intersected. It was slow, tedious, tense. Gregg was so excited he could barely breathe, and so nervous he was getting dizzy. Some tunnels were lower, smaller than others, requiring Gregg and Ian to stoop in order to walk through them. The claustrophobic atmosphere boggled his mind and sent his heartrate up. Gregg remembered a similar feeling hitting his chest the very first time he strapped himself into the seat of a fighter jet and felt the canopy close over his head.

It was with equal parts excitement and relief that he found the wall. *The wall.* The one he and Jared had seen on the broadcast, the one that brought him all the way over here.

"Ian, hold this light." He handed the flashlight over his shoulder and looked around. To his left was another wall, to his right the tunnel they had followed to get here. The one Carl Heyward referred to as "The King's Highway". In front of him was another surface, covered in drawings. This was it; this was what he had seen in the background of the newscast. And there was the drawing, Marian's necklace, right before him. This was the place he wanted to search.

~ 126 ~

On the way down he had explained to Ian the significance of the symbol, where he had obtained it and how it fit into the hunt for Robin Hood's treasure. Standing before it now, ready to steal whatever secrets it could give him, was surreal.

Carefully Gregg ran his hands the wall in front of him. He was seeking information, clues, old grooves or carvings that may have been covered over time, but nothing presented itself. The stone was cold and still as he ran his fingers over it, even through the gloves, smooth as a river rock to the touch. And then he felt it. An unnaturally straight ridge, perpendicular to the ground, reached from the bottom of the tunnel all the way up. Along the very top of the wall, where it joined the ceiling at a right angle, was another, a vein of loose stone, stretching about four feet along the wall where it was met on either end by another ridge heading down toward the floor. Gregg reached a hand toward the nearest one, brushed dust off, scratched at it. Several chunks fell out. Gregg grinned. He'd been right. Underneath the layers of grit, these crests were almost invisible. Ian leveled the light along the wall as Gregg whipped out his pocket knife and stood on tip-toe.

"Got it!" He said. "See, look... this was made to look like a solid wall, but..." Gregg ran his fingers along the top ridge, then clawed away at a portion of it with the knife. Relief – and excitement – flooded his system as an old, clay-like substance fell in large pieces to the ground, exposing what turned out to be a rather wide, deep crack in supposedly solid stone. "It's a door," he said excitedly, hacking away. "I'd say that, when this thing was built, it was undetectable. But after about eight or nine hundred years of earthquakes and natural earth movement..." He pulled the knife out, staring at the engraving in the middle of the door. "There's more of this stuff along the sides and bottom," he said, running his shirttail along the blade of the knife before folding it. "Get out the picks."

Dropping the roll of string, Ian slit open one of the backpacks and produced a couple of small picks. A few minutes of chopping, and the door stood exposed for what it was: a gateway to the unknown. Ian gave a couple last whacks for good measure, then leaned against the rock and pushed lightly.

"It'll give," he said. "On three?"

As Gregg pressed his shoulder against the door, he felt the old, familiar tingle of elation running through his veins, that feeling he got when he knew he was on the verge of an adventure. It had been a few years since he'd felt it, as the humdrum of normal everyday life was very good at beating it into submission. He was long overdue for an adventure. And he was definitely long overdue for the fortune undoubtedly waiting somewhere beyond this thick pane of rock.

I'm going to be rich, he thought to himself. Pressing his hand to the etching, he gained a foothold in the loose dirt and nodded. Ian smirked at him.

"Doesn't this remind you of Old Man Kraler's place in Lockhart?"

"I was just about to ask you the same thing. Ready? One... two... three!"

The boys leaned their shoulders into the task and shoved on the rock section. It gave, grinding reluctantly against the solid wall on either side, silt and debris raining down. With a moan of protest it gave, falling inward, and crashed loudly onto the stone floor beyond to shatter. While the dust settled in coats around them, Gregg shined his light around as Ian knocked a final chunk down to peer in. Both just stared in amazement. Another tunnel; small, discreet, lay revealed before them, its floor littered with several yards of rock from the wall they'd just taken down. The remainder of the large slab lay in motionless pieces at their feet.

The tunnel led away from them, stretching on into the unknown before it turned, sharply, and took off to the left, out of the beam of the flashlights. Picking their way through rubble, Gregg and Ian started down the hand-chiseled space. It was low, so low they had to bend to fit. Following it for about ten feet around the corner, Gregg suddenly found himself staring at a dead end in front, and an opening on his left.

"Look," he said, and angled the light inside.

The room was still, pitch black except for the bright beams of artificial light that darted curiously over the rough, stone walls. It was no bigger than any of the others they'd encountered; actually, when looked at closely, it appeared to be smaller. It was meant to be hidden, overlooked, and its size reflected the intention. Gregg's symbol was etched very clearly in a low brow of rock that bulged from the ceiling.

This was it.

I'm going to be rich...

Old tapestries draped like curtains along the perimeter, their soft colors vibrant and new-looking; armor from the Crusades for both horses and men were stored beside them, appearing as shiny as the day they were tucked away. Swords hung on the walls. The racks that held them were finely made, manufactured to be put on display. An old wardrobe took up a corner, filled with lovely, antique dresses barely visible through a crack in the door. A jewelry case sat next to it on a small table. Both were covered in a light layer of powder.

But where was the gold? Gregg's heart sank a little.

"Rob, we're in," Ian said quietly.

"How rich are we?"

"We're about to find out. Place looks a little small to hide a life-changing fortune."

"Traveler's checks?"

"There must be another room," Gregg said directly. He looked around. But where? There were about a million places to look. *It's not here,* he thought to himself in despair. His flashlight beamed around the room frantically, lighting up small portions. In the pitch blackness surrounding that limited shaft of light, nothing had changed. There must be a door. A room. Anything. This couldn't be it.

Could it? Had he come all this way just to be foiled by false information? A false hunch? Maybe even a false legend? Maybe there was no treasure. Maybe there was no Robin Hood.

Now what?

His light landed on the pair of objects in the center of the room. His heart stilled. Two stone coffins lay side by side under a shield bearing a coat of arms that hung from a wooden frame. Gregg walked slowly forward, his flashlight trained on the shield. It was old and well used, the colors softened from age, cut across with several slashes as from a sword or lance. It was familiar. Gregg shook his head in disbelief. Could it be? Could this really be what he thought? No way. He dropped his gaze to the two coffins. Dust had settled over the tops along with several pieces of ceiling that had come loose, hiding the inscriptions, dust from seven hundred years ago. Gregg leaned against the end of the nearest one and blew the dirt away, directing his flashlight toward the words at the head of the casket. He was unaware of the light that began to fill the room, unaware of the quiet crackling of flames as Ian struck a match and lit torches along the wall. He saw only the words before his eyes.

"Ian," he said excitedly. "Ian, look at this."

Ian strode over from the other side of the room and peered over his shoulder.

"'Sir Robert Fitzooth of Locksley'," he read, and turned to stare at Gregg as he jerked his thumb at the coffin. "Is this who I think it is?"

Gregg could only nod. Emotion such as he had never known was flooding his being, rendering words both impossible and ineffective. Quickly, he wiped a dirty hand over his eyes. How long had he dreamed of this moment!

Ian reached over to click off Gregg's useless flashlight, patting him on the shoulder.

"You okay, mate?"

"I just can't believe it," Gregg said. "We found him. Robin Hood!"

Chapter 7

Jared felt strange out here, seated on a bony wooden chair next to a small hole in the ground surrounded by caution tape. He was so isolated, so alone, yet right in the middle of one of the most industrious cities in the world. He could still see cars, the occasional pedestrian; his ears picked up noises that, at any other time, would have been normal. But here they just seemed... out of place. As if, for a deed of this importance, there should be complete and utter silence.

An hour passed. Jared sighed and leaned – slouched – against the back of his seat. The chair had clearly been designed by someone of Vulcan ideology, for comfort was not its primary purpose. Jared fidgeted as first his spine, then a rib, was attacked by one of the more zealous parts of the wooden frame. He felt vulnerable out here; aside from the relatively high probability of getting caught, any semblance of human interaction had vanished a long time ago, and the only link between Jared and the goings on below was the string he could barely see down the hole. It was mostly still now, only moving on occasion, fading between white and grey as it caught the light. Jared started to get jumpy again. What if something bad happened? What if they found something dangerous down there? Worse yet, what if they found something good and Ian got greedy? He could just kill Gregg off on the spot. There would be no indication, no warning, and then he could come back and... get Jared. And nobody would ever know.

Suddenly, from deep in the bowels of the tunnel, there was a muffled clunk.

Oh, no! He did it! He's killed him!

Jared spun around to peer into the blackness, trying not to panic. What was he going to do? How would he escape? Where would he go? Ian had to have people all over the world in case of a situation like this. All he'd have to do was hit the "escaped prisoner" button and Jared would be caught within minutes, brought back begging for his life and dispatched execution style...

"Wonder what they found," he said instead, speaking to nothing in particular.

Another hour passed, even more slowly than the first. A brief exchange between Ian and Rob on the radio that Jared didn't catch for static. He hoped the news was good; it had better be, or they'd all be in trouble for nothing. Just as he was about to manually pronounce the evening a victory on principle and break out the martinis and finger sandwiches, a car pulled up out front by the gate. Headlights flooded his position, and he shrank fearfully back into the chair, sure that he was going to be identified at any moment. There was no other way it could happen. The lights were right on him, revealing everything, exposing him and the others for what they were.

"Ian, someone just showed up," he whispered tensely into the radio. Nothing. "Ian."

The headlights flicked off.

"Ian!" Jared hissed. "Rob!"

No response. The radio remained as silent; belatedly, Jared noticed the light on the side had switched off. More than likely the battery was dead. He started to rise. What should he do? What if the driver came over to talk? What if they saw Jared? Suddenly he remembered what Ian had said when he handed him the pipe.

"Here. Just in case you get attacked by any of those Samurai lurking about."

Well, if this guy didn't qualify as lurking Samurai, Jared didn't know who would. He grabbed the pipe off the ground, clutching it with white knuckles. He'd wait until whoever it was got close, then put them out of their misery. But what about the guard in the rear? Surely they heard the car. Even if Jared was able to knock this guy out, what about the rest of them? What could one piece of pipe do against ten heads? He suddenly wished he'd accepted that pistol. Not that he'd know what to do with it, but he wished he had it, nonetheless. He scrunched closer to the chair at the sound of a car door opening.

"William!"

The driver got out of his car and strode toward the gate, a taller gentleman in what looked to be a uniform. The unnamed visitor punched in the code and opened the gate, walked forward a few paces. Called out again. Jared waited, shaking, willing himself to remain silent until the last possible moment; so far, the rear guard had not come to investigate. He had to get this right; Ian made it look so easy, hitting someone over the head. But now with Jared staring that very real possibility in the face, he wasn't sure if he could do it.

Then he recalled the alternative and knew he could.

His thoughts were spinning. His vision was hazy as panic caused him to hyperventilate. He hoped he didn't pass out. In front of him, the man walked closer, mumbling to himself about William's unreliability. Jared waited. Breathed. He was so close.

"Bill," the man said sharply as he walked within striking distance. "Mate, really? I told you once already, I'm *not* covering for you again." He stepped close and leaned down to roughly grab Jared's shoulder. "Wake up, you lazy –"

Jared struck out like a snake, all his pent up anxiety bringing out a strength he had no idea he possessed. The newcomer yelped plaintively as the pipe connected solidly with his head, and Jared felt the hand on his shoulder go limp. The man fell to the ground. Moaned. He was still conscious. Jared knew he should hit him again, raised the pipe. Lowered it. He couldn't do it. He wasn't Ian. Dropping the weapon, he made for the tunnel. He took only a split second to glance back at the man, mentally apologized, briefly allowed a "why does this have to happen to me" cross his mind, and darted down the ladder. It would only be a matter of seconds before his victim was up and about and all hell broke loose around here. There was nothing Jared could do but warn the others and hope Ian and Gregg had enough fox in them to figure a way out of this. If he could find them down there.

Even as the blackness of the tunnel closed in over his head and he ran, tripping, swearing, and stumbling, into the unknown with only a string and his cell phone screen as a guide, he heard a shout above the surface.

He'd just hit a guy over the head with a piece of pipe, and was now going to be involved in a hazardous escape plan.

This just got very real.

****

This moment was beyond incredible. Now, for the first time, the record could finally be set straight about Robin Hood's existence. His deeds, habits, comings, and goings might forever be shrouded in mystery, but at least there was something to base them on. A real life, a real human being, a real person.

"Well, they'll definitely have to rewrite a couple of history books now," Ian said.

"Yeah…" Gregg looked at him and grinned. "They certainly will," he said.

"Right. Let's get to it."

Ian knelt down next to the coffin and pulled out a pocket knife, chiseling away at the mortar caked along the underside of the heavy, ornate lid.

"Wait, what?" Gregg stared. "You want to open it?"

"Treasure's not here, Gregg. As much as I'd like to celebrate this victory for the historical community and call it quits, I need to get paid."

"But why the coffin? Maybe there's another room, a door somewhere. We need to check."

Ian sat back, pointed to the lid. At the very top was Gregg's symbol, carved with perfection into the stone like it had been cut with a laser. In his excitement, Gregg had missed the carving entirely.

"If there is another room, this is where we'll find how to get to it," Ian said. "Unless you want to spend half the night knocking on walls until we find something."

Gregg knew he was right. Reluctantly, he nodded, trying to mask his disappointment at having to desecrate this monument. By the glance Ian shot him across the lid, he knew he'd failed somewhat. They worked in silence, the sound of chipping clay and falling debris the only sounds between them. It took time, but at last the lid sat anchorless on top of its great, stone box.

Gregg took hold of one side. Ian took hold of the other. He looked down at the inscription, feeling a pang of regret – again – and wondered if all treasure hunters felt as chronically guilty as he did. Maybe it would be better not to continue, leave well enough alone. Should they really unearth the contents of this coffin? A glance at Ian reminded Gregg that it would be far better to unearth than not. He was waiting patiently, giving Gregg his moment, but Gregg knew Ian Lowell was far from satisfied with this single discovery. No matter how helpful and friendly he'd been in the last couple hours, he was here for one reason and one reason alone: treasure. If they failed to find any, who knew what would happen. Gregg's heart sank a little lower.

"You ready?" He asked sharply, and, at Ian's nod, they lifted the lid of Robin's casket. Moving slowly, they set it down on top of the second. The lid clunked softly as Gregg lowered his end.

"I guess we should have found out who was in there first," Ian said dryly, and gave the coffin a conciliatory pat. "Hope you don't mind, mate."

"I believe 'ma'am' should be your word, Ian," Gregg answered. "I think that's Marian."

"Oh." Ian lifted his cap. "Pardon me, ma'am."

Gregg rubbed his hands together. Upon lifting the lid, he had found exactly as he had expected; a skeleton lying on its back with the hands folded over a sword on his chest, but on closer examination, the sword looked to have something inscribed on it. Gregg directed the light at it and tried to decipher the tiny, scripted text.

Ian stood by the door while he worked, listening carefully to the silent passageway outside. He remained motionless for a moment, then disappeared out into the blackness of the tunnel, taking stock. He was not the type that liked to fly blind; even with Jared out front, that was essentially what they were doing.

"Anything interesting?" He asked, coming back in.

"A poem." Gregg bent a little closer, holding his flashlight at a different angle to get a better look. "It seems to be written either for, or in honor of, Maid Marian. Listen."

"'My beloved bride, the light of my life
These tokens have I for thee, who hast been my wife

May they guide thee on thy long road, through the sands of time
For now I give them all to thee, these things that once were mine

This, a stone of Hope, a mirror to thine eyes
Blue as the endless seas, and deep as the midnight skies
May it speak of distance, as it was meant to do
The sentiments therein proving Truth to you

This, an ivory piece, Wisdom that shall grace your wrist
Such a work of divine craftsmanship
May it prove right for you, this from the lady of the sands
And narrow the distance for you to those foreign lands

This, the sword of Truth, which hath known its day
It will be used with Wisdom, but only once, I pray
To serve as a dais for Hope, your guiding light
Washing away despair, fear of loneliness and night

And this, the Book, fit for one of sovereignty
The words of Wisdom have been good to me
Leading me towards the light of Hope and Truth
Guiding my steps, showing me what to do

May these treasures, these things that once were mine,
Help thee on thy long road, through the sands of time
May they light your way and help your quest
Toward richness in spirit, faith and happiness'"

 Silence greeted itself as Gregg's voice echoed in the room and died away. Slowly, he stepped back, staring at the motionless figure below him while light from the torches flickered and bounced around it in ever-changing patterns. Quiet crackling of flames could be heard, but nothing else. A thin veil of smoke danced along the ceiling.

 "So, what does that mean?" Ian inquired. "That can't be all he's telling her, right? Here's some stuff I used to own, take good care of it until you buy the farm and then pass it on to the kids?"

"You're right," Gregg said quietly. "There's more to it than that. Look at how he calls the blue stone 'a stone of hope', a 'guiding light'."

"You think it's some sort of map."

"Exactly. But how can a stone be a guiding light…?" Even as he said it, Gregg knew the answer.

Marian's Necklace. The damned piece of jewelry that was locked up in the Goldstein Museum. The necklace wasn't just proof, and it wasn't just a key to the treasure. It was a map.

Ian put his hands on his hips and looked around.

"Looks like we keep going, then," he said. "Damn I was hoping that gold would be here." He raised the radio. "I think we need to go back to the drawing board. Treasure's not here, mate… or if it is, it's well hidden."

Gregg felt a bit sick. The thought of doing this again, tomorrow night, and the next, was disheartening. Scary. He was done. He should never have called Ian in the first place; that good-bye from ten years ago should have been the last time they came in contact. It would have hurt, but it was better than seeing his old friend as he was now. Gregg had made a grave mistake.

"We'll have to bring that thing along," Ian added, pointing at the sword. "If that's our only link, it needs to stay with us."

Gregg nodded.

"Let me write this poem down first," he said. "And I want to replace the sword with another one."

Ian nodded and moved to a rack near the wall as Gregg stared for a moment at the body. It finally hit him, just how strange and wonderful this moment was, the magnitude of the discovery he had made. In his quest for treasure, he had unwittingly proven one of the world's most famous legends, taken it from the Roswell status only a handful of sketchy historians believed to legitimate, authentic history. Robin Hood was a real person.

The understanding was still tracking through his mind as he slowly, carefully, reached down and pried the sword from the skeletal hands. When someone inevitably came across this room after their departure, Gregg didn't want them to know what they'd been up to. Or what they'd found. Gently, he removed the engraved sword, pulling dried fingers away from the hilt. He realized he should be squeamish about this, maybe even a bit nervous. This was, after all, the body of Robin Hood himself he was tampering with. He felt none of that as the remains ground and crunched quietly, relinquishing their grasp. Instead, all that crossed his mind was that scene from *Titanic* when Rose so casually pried Jack's hands off her floating palace and let him sink into the depths of the North Atlantic. To this day, Gregg wondered if they could both fit on that bloody board.

"Here," Ian said quietly, and handed Gregg a replacement, which he tucked in as carefully as possible. It took a bit of doing, but when he was finished, there was virtually no difference.

"Just lean that on the wall," he said. "I'll copy it down in a moment."

The coffin lid made a hollow whump as they dropped it carefully back into place, concealing the body of Robin Hood from view. Oh, how Gregg would have loved to stay here all night! Studying, taking notes, taking pictures, just reveling in the knowledge that he had finally succeeded. But, they had a schedule to keep. So without a word, Gregg let go of his end of the lid, feeling troubled as he glanced at the sword standing so quietly next to the wall. He knew Ian wouldn't be content with simply the one coffin being open; as long as there was a stone unturned, he would want to turn it. It was with no surprise that he saw Ian immediately step to Marian's coffin and start chiseling away at the mortar along the seal. Stifling a sigh, mostly born of regret, Gregg left him to it and started copying down the poem from the sword. The process was irritating, slow; but Gregg pushed impatience aside and kept at it, copying the riddle down, word by word, letter by tedious letter. He was suddenly edgy. Things were going well… too well. Jared was still silent on the radio, but Gregg had seen enough movies to know this was about the point where it started to unravel. Quickly.

"You have any idea of what to do if we get walked in on?"

Ian shrugged, swiping away at some dust.

"Bust out the snags and chicken wings for a barbie?"

Gregg rolled his eyes at the blithe tone. Trust Ian to try and make a joke even now, right in the middle of a heist. It was a tendency that used to drive Gregg absolutely nuts. Hearing it now, he realized it still did. He had no doubt there was an alternate plan in the works, one Ian was just not willing to let him in on quite yet.

"Ian," he said, pausing in his task and taking a look at the pistol in Ian's waistband. "We shoot to scare if we're caught, right? I didn't sign up for murder."

"Right, Nick. We shoot to scare."

Gregg didn't like the tone. It was another one of those tendencies. Over the years, when Ian called him Nick instead of his real name – or Genius – it usually meant Ian was putting him on. Gregg's distrust meter shot up another few notches.

"Give me a hand with this," Ian said, rising. He folded his pocketknife and tucked it back in his jeans.

"Yep. Just a second." Gregg took a cursory look at the final verse of the riddle and copied it down from memory as he put his notepad away and trotted over to help Ian with the lid of Marian's coffin.

It seemed heavier than the first for some reason. Maybe Gregg was just getting tired. Maybe the guilt was getting to him.

Marian's coffin offered up nothing very interesting. It was just a corpse, in a dress, in a box. A famous corpse, to be sure, but it gave them no further clues as to what they might be looking for. The skeletal remains were simply adorned; the dress was fine but not fancy, and the only piece of jewelry Gregg could see was a small bracelet on the right wrist that looked to be made of bone. It was a unique piece, to be sure. Gregg was leaning in for a better look when the loud slapping of footsteps broke the stillness.

"Get behind the coffins." Ian took a quick, soundless step back. He seemed to melt into the shadows by the door as Gregg dove out of sight, peering between the stone boxes while the footsteps grew louder. Where was Jared? Had he been caught? Knocked out? Shot? Stabbed? Beheaded? He shrank down as a figure appeared in the entrance, hidden by the darkness of the tunnel. Another step and it was inside.

Ian sprang from his hiding place by the wall, and Jared yelped in surprise as he suddenly found himself wrapped up in a choke hold, dangling several inches off the ground. Vainly, he started swiping around with his hand in an ineffective fist, trying to land a blow. Gregg leapt to his feet.

"Ian! Wait, it's Jared!" He called in a panic, fearful that Ian might just go ahead and dispose of one of them right then and there. "Jared, what are you doing here?"

"I'll tell you if you'll tell him to eighty-six the choke hold," Jared said in a strangled voice. He dropped limply to the ground when Ian released him. "Save it for a throat that needs it," he spat. "We've got company."

Ian made a dash for the doorway.

"How long do we have?"

"Like, maybe three seconds."

"How many?"

"A bloody army, man! How do I know? I didn't sit there doing a head count!"

"Gregg, give Jared the sword and get over here," Ian said directly. "I need your help. Jared, why didn't you use the radio?"

"I *did*. It was dead."

Gregg paused for a split second as they argued. Looked at the sword leaning against the wall, at Jared. Did he dare make a switch? Did he dare try to bring the wrong weapon out of the room? When Ian found out they had the wrong one, he would be incensed. If he found out Gregg did it on purpose, he'd probably kill him. But Gregg was willing to take that chance. He and he alone knew where they needed to go after this, the priceless necklace they needed to obtain; he and he alone had the riddle written down. This was his hunt. He would call the shots.

He made the switch deftly, hanging the real sword backwards on the nearest rack to hide its inscription.

"Hang onto this and don't let it out of your sight," he said, handing the fake to Jared. He cast one, final glance at the genuine weapon where it hung so innocently, and ran over to help Ian. He had a funny feeling he was going to regret this later.

"What are you doing?"

Ian cut the string and tied the piece they'd been following around a heavy statue, tossing it out into the tunnel. He had switched into full survival mode, and was focused only on getting out of here in one piece. In the distance, Gregg could hear the echo of footsteps and voices shouting. There were quite a few.

"Remember in grade school?" Ian asked, rolling the remaining string up. "What we used to do to Joey Prickett and his gang when they started hassling us?"

Gregg grinned and ran forward as the idea dawned on him. He grabbed a couple chairs and piled them on top of a small table along the front wall.

The idea was simple: string a rope at calf-height across a doorway or narrow opening, tie one end off to a solid structure, and tie the other end to a mess of relatively lightweight objects. It was a bit like the various booby traps implemented by the VC during Vietnam utilizing trip wires and explosives. While Gregg and Ian's version had been far less deadly, it was no less effective. The trap would be triggered when someone ran into the rope, and whoever was behind them suddenly found a mound of junk catapulting into them with a fair amount of force. If the boys were lucky, they would sometimes have the added benefit of the front man face-planting into the pavement when they tripped.

Outside, a muffled yell sounded. The statue in the tunnel scraped roughly on the floor, and Gregg jumped. Their pursuers had found the trail. Another triumphant shout verified this point. Jared panicked.

"We're going to get caught!" He said nervously, twisting the sword around in his hands.

"No we're not," Ian answered. "And stop doing that before you cut yourself. Blood can tell a story just like everything else. Gregg, take this end and tie it off."

Ian tossed the end of the string to Gregg, who caught it mid-air and bolted to his mound of furniture.

"Where do you want me to tie this?" He asked with a quick gesture.

Ian glanced over as the statue grated again and footsteps sounded close by in the tunnel.

"The table legs," he said. "And make it tight."

Gregg made a couple quick knots and stepped back, balancing his furniture. This had better work. Across the room, Ian looped the string under a low-hanging rack, and gave a cursory yank to one of the higher racks on the wall. He tied his end off there, stretching the string tight.

"All right, everybody back!" He yelled, and dove in front of Jared just as a small army barreled into the room.

The one in front gave a startled yell as he tripped over the string and fell face-first, his weight yanking Gregg's furniture into the foray. It shot across the floor to slam into the next three, knocking them to the ground. Meanwhile the table overturned, spilling several chairs and a lamp on top of the downed guards and making several more trip over the mess as they tried to enter. Gregg tried not to think of all the history they'd just destroyed.

And then Ian waded into the chaos, blazing a trail through bodies and debris and flying limbs with Gregg and Jared right on his heels. Gregg made a dent in someone's head when they tried to stop him. Somebody else made a grab for Jared and, swiping quickly, Jared beat on him with the sword, leaping out the doorway. Gregg's flashlight lit the way and Ian grabbed the string he had tied off, looping it over his arm to follow it up the tunnel as he jerked out the pistol and his walkie-talkie.

"Rob, plan B!" He shouted, unscrewing the silencer and cocking his pistol with a sharp click. "Get moving, we'll be there in a minute!" Spinning around as they reached the main artery, he took aim into the blackness behind them.

"No!" Gregg side-swiped him and shoved him away from tunnel branch as the gun went off, forcing the shot to go wild. "We said no bullets, Remember?" He yelled. "I don't want a dead man on my conscience!"

"Come on, Gregg, what difference will it make?" Ian shouted back.

Gregg slapped his gun arm down, angrily, and pointed to the exit.

"Go!"

Footsteps and shouting could be heard behind them. Gregg hoped no one had been hit. They ran up the tunnel, scrambled up to the surface on the ladder. Another guard materialized in front of them, club at the ready, only to drop mutely over the chair as, in turn, Ian's fist slammed into the man's jaw. Gregg raced out and, with a snatch, Ian reached back and grabbed Jared by the collar, slinging him off to the side. He leaned backward and sent a couple cracking shots down the hole, and a surprised yelp and several scrabbling sounds could be heard down the tunnel as their pursuers tried to dodge the winging bullets.

"Are you *nuts*?" Gregg dug talon-like fingers into Ian's shirtsleeve and hauled him away, cursing himself for a fool. He didn't want to be responsible for the death of an innocent man.

The three of them scurried away from the shelter like rats, running low across the open space to disappear in the rubble. For a minute, at least, no one followed.

Ian kicked the fence open and herded them through, dropping the flap of chain link noisily into place. Behind them, the sounds of a belated pursuit lessened as distance increased, but they didn't slow down. Along the back part of the block they ran, behind the tavern with the dig off to their left, until they rounded a turn and spotted the car, parked on a side street, engine running, lights on. Gregg pounced inside the open door and retreated as Ian leapt in, jerking Jared in behind him.

"Punch it!" He yelled, and slammed the door as Rob burned rubber and sped off.

It was cramped in the back seat. Gregg and Jared were both breathing heavily, and Gregg found himself fighting off a persistent feeling of panic-induced nausea. He was stuffed like a sardine in the corner, cursing himself and all his brilliant ideas of fame and fortune. Things had gone from bad to worse. Ian had just tried to shoot someone. Three times. He might have succeeded; someone might be lying in the tunnel right now, bleeding to death, because Gregg had called the wrong guy for help. Even Gregg's worst nightmares hadn't truly prepared him for the cold light of reality. The lid to Pandora's Box had shut with him inside, and there was no way out. He had left the sword behind, yes, and Marian's Necklace remained the secret ingredient that only he knew about.

But Ian knew he had the riddle. With or without the sword, they still had a way forward. And he would not be keen to give up this hunt. The dig hadn't given Gregg the fortune he hoped it would. Instead, it had given him just enough information to dig somebody else's grave. Or his own. If they went onward together, someone was going to get killed. By Ian. If they didn't, Gregg was probably going to get killed. By Ian.

By the time Rob pulled off the road, into a quaint stand of trees bordering the River Thames, Gregg was on the verge of an anxiety attack. He was suffocated by the weight of panic and his own conscience, desperately trying to figure a way out of this but knowing, so well, how stuck he truly was. As soon as the car rolled to a stop he was out the door, putting distance between himself and that horrid space.

"What the hell happened back there, man?" He demanded, giving a hard shove to Ian's shoulder as he also stepped out. "I called you to get me into the dig, not break in and leave a trail of bodies!" He paced back and forth, delving his hands into his hair, feeling sick. Who was this man? What sort of creature had he conjured?

"Relax, Nick," Ian replied. "Nobody got hurt. Your conscience is clear."

"That you know of!"

Ian ignored him. Shafts of light from streetlamps and taillights eerily illuminated his features as he reloaded the clip in his pistol and clicked it back in place. He seemed unfazed.

As Jared came to stand by Gregg, Rob also left the car and wandered to their side, where he conversed quietly with Ian for a moment about things Gregg wasn't even listening to. He seemed immune to Gregg's outburst regarding Ian's behavior at the construction site, and his compliance only served to freak Gregg out even more.

They weren't human. Either of them.

"Well, Genius, let's see what you found down there," Rob said.

"Mate." Ian grinned at him. "We found the guy."

"*The* guy?"

"*The* guy."

"And the gold?"

"We uncovered a poem that Gregg thinks will lead us right to it."

They both looked to Gregg; here it was. The moment he'd been dreading. What could he do? He had the poem; knew where to go, what to look for. The necklace was being held in the Goldtstein Museum, and to continue this quest that was where he had to go. But he didn't want to go there with *them*. These two men who he had erroneously tried to rely on.

To his left, Ian regarded him silently. Rob's question remained unanswered. Gregg could see Jared watching him. What could he say? Tell Ian he'd go on alone and pay him at the end, assuming they didn't get caught? Tell him there was nowhere else to go? Tell him he was wrong about everything? That the legend was false and the treasure a myth? Admit this whole thing was a bad idea and dig into his life savings to square the debt?

How did one put a price on what had been touted as an immeasurable fortune?

"Nothing," he said. "We found nothing."

"Come on, Gregg," Rob laughed, the cynicism in his tone unable to be missed. "Don't hold out on us."

Gregg scrambled frantically for something. Anything. His brain refused to work. He didn't know how to steer the conversation away; he'd forgotten how to stall for time.

"Like I told you, nothing," he said again, and shrugged. "I was wrong. It was just a poem."

The look on Rob's face changed a little; became more closed, more distant. Gregg started to panic again. He sensed the distrust.

"What did you find, Ian?" Rob asked after a moment. His cool gaze shifted, away from Gregg, to Ian standing so quietly to the side.

"Show him, Gregg." The command – and that's indeed what it was – was spoken softly, almost experimentally in nature.

"No."

"Why not?" Ian asked, spreading his hands at Gregg's blunt statement.

"Because I don't want to be party to murder," Gregg snapped in frustration. "If I tell you where to go next, someone is going to get shot."

"I thought you just said there was nowhere else to go," Rob reminded him quietly.

"Is that all you care about?" Gregg demanded. "Really? You just don't get it, do you?" He looked at Ian almost pleadingly. "I told you," he said. "I *told* you no bullets. No killing."

"What are you on about? Are you still hung up on the fact that I took a pot shot at some bloke?"

"Not one pot shot. Three. You tried to kill someone three times… someone you don't even know. Someone who had done nothing wrong. If that doesn't qualify as murder I don't know what does. The Ian I grew up with wouldn't have done that." He knew he should shut up while he was still ahead. He knew he should let it lie. He knew he should back off and remain calm, but it was impossible. There was too much anger, too much fear that had been building inside of him. He had to get it out. "What has *happened* to the both of you?" He demanded. "Can't you hear yourselves? You're talking about shooting someone down as if there are no consequences! You think that force and guns and sneaking around in the dead of night are the only ways to do something, but you're wrong. You're wrong!"

"So, what you just hired us to sit around the campfire and sing Kumbaya?" Ian asked.

"I called because I knew you could get me in. Which, come to think of it, is pathetic. I finally pick up the phone to call a man who used to be my best friend, because he's the only one I can think of who would know how to break into a heavily-secured construction site." Gregg spun around and started on Rob, including him in a gaze that was both accusing and desperate for understanding. "And you," he said. "You've been here before. What about those months you spent running drugs for that low-life in New York? The prison time. Did they teach you nothing? Did you learn not one thing from all that? And what about the day we came home from the Gulf? You *promised* that day you weren't going to end up like this again, and look at you now. What happened?"

"Life happened, mate," Rob said. "Simple."

"That's one hell of a sorry excuse."

"Gregg, I'd advise you to stop right now," Ian said. "You know why –"

"Save it pal," Gregg shot back callously. "Just save the sob stories for some other audience. I know why you're here now, and it has nothing to do with honor." Ignoring the stunned look that crossed Ian's face, Gregg took a heavy, defeated breath. "Truthfully, you're – both starting to sound more like the guys that killed Graham than anything," he finished, addressing Ian directly. "And I don't even know you anymore. Either of you."

He was met with silence. Gregg looked up, immediately aware that he had overplayed his hand, that he had reacted too strongly and reached much too far. Two faces stared back at him, utterly still, like a pond frozen over during the winter months, devoid of life and emotion and compassion, showing nothing but ice. Slowly, Rob turned his back on the whole scene in an ominous gesture of dismissal, and Ian nodded.

"All right, Nick, if that's the way you want it."

"No, it's not the way I want it."

"You called me. You hired me to do this."

"And now I'm firing you," Gregg said flatly. "You can keep the sword. Good luck figuring out the riddle… I don't want anything more to do with this. Or you. I'm going on alone."

"I'm afraid that's not going to be a possibility."

"Oh, yes it is," Gregg said. "There's nothing you can do to stop me."

Ian's smile was cold.

"Let me be the judge of that," he said. "You see, Rob and I... we didn't live this long in this game by leaving a bunch of loose ends waving in the breeze. Ends that are either cut off or untie themselves have to be taken care of. Or they might come back to bite us."

Gregg didn't like his tone. It was almost like…

"Jared, let's go," he said, trying to keep the panic out of his voice. "We're walking."

He turned away and stopped dead. Where there had at one point been nothing but shrubbery, three men now stood illuminated by the light inside the car. Jared leaned away from them, his small bag clenched in a death grip in front of him, and Gregg felt his heart go cold as the two of them traded a look. He looked back at the men before him; of the three, his gaze was fixed on the one furthest to his right, the one with blonde, spikey hair and deathly blue eyes. He was truly a creature from another realm.

"May I present Troy, George, and Stan... also known conjointly as 'leverage'," Ian said from behind them. "Rob, of course, you know already. I brought them along in case I needed to ensure your cooperation. Now, I will ask you again. Is this the way you want it?"

"This is a cute addition," Gregg said, trying to bluff his way out. "Real cute. Get them out of here."

"I'm not sure you understand," Ian said. "You are no longer in charge of this expedition, Nick. As of this moment, I am. Cooperate with me and I might pay your expenses at the end… if I feel like it."

"A couple billion dollars in gold and you want to pay for my flights?" Gregg replied. "I'd do better selling Amway products."

"That's probably more your speed, anyway. My game, my rules. Now, you want to turn this into some kind of competition, mate, fine by me, but I can guarantee you won't get far. Just call the ball."

Gregg stared at him. Ian stared back.

"Well?"

"I guess we'll just see who gets there first," Gregg said simply...

...and jumped Troy. At least, the one he assumed was Troy. Aside from Spikes, he really couldn't tell which was which.

The move was completely unexpected, and it worked. For once. Gregg's victim catapulted backward, and then Jared was swiping at the other two with his bag of destruction. One almost managed to get a hold of it, but then drew back with a yell as Jared aimed a deadly swipe at his left shoulder. Gregg shoved Jared through the shrubbery, racing after him as, behind them, he heard the pounding of footsteps and Ian yelling directions of some kind. Jared's left leg gave way as he stepped in a hole. Gregg saw his ankle twist. Jared stumbled. He regained his balance and staggered forward, limping heavily but still mobile.

"Make for the river, Jared!"

Jared's head turned. He shouted something unintelligible that sounded suspiciously like a curse, and, apparently deciding his love for life was stronger than his pain, ran harder, his strides evening out to carry him faster toward the dark, still river flowed that flowed so sedately on its course. A few more steps, a lunge, and he was in the water, swimming fiercely to the right to follow the current. Gregg was right behind him.

With Ian on his heels.

And everyone else behind. Ian was quickly outdistancing the others, the years he spent on the track and field team serving him well. Gregg knew he couldn't outrun Ian. He never had. With a final leap, one borne of faith, he dove for the river. He went in head-first and swam down, to the left, hoping that small change in direction would save his life. Even this close to the bank the river was deep, possibly about twelve feet, but in due course he felt the thick, slimy smudge of the bottom against his palms. He stayed down and crept along as quickly as he dared, following the current. His lungs were bursting; he could see nothing. He could only hope he was swimming in the right direction and not straight back into Ian's sphere. He hoped Jared was still alive.

When he could no longer hold his breath, Gregg slowly, carefully, allowed himself to float upward. He held a hand over his head; as soon as it broke the surface he stalled his ascent as much as possible, finally poking his forehead out of the murky depths like an alligator. He refrained from gasping for air, instead opting for controlled, quiet breathing that took every ounce of willpower to achieve. He swilled back into the shadows along the shore and took stock of the situation.

The first thing he saw was Jared, shivering, hiding like a fugitive beneath the heavy protection of some riverside vegetation just upstream from him. They were about fifty yards downstream from the car. Ian's boys were still combing the riverbank.

"Jared," Gregg hissed, softly. "Psst! Jared!"

Jared jumped and spun around. Gregg put a finger over his mouth. Jared, seeming as relieved as Gregg, nodded.

Voices. Footfalls in the grasses. Jared shrank back under the thick plants as much as he possibly could, and Gregg, watching from his vantage point, did the same. They blended. Hid. Waited.

Ian walked into view, stepping from the trees along the shore. He walked to the edge of the river, mere feet from Jared's hiding place, scanning the still waters with a practiced eye. Gregg tried not to stare directly at him; his grandfather had told him many times that living things, human or otherwise, can feel the eyes of others on them. So he didn't stare. Didn't breathe. Didn't move. Jared's gaze was fixed on his across the water. He was almost directly below Ian, gripping the long fronds of river plants with white knuckles while he waited for, what he surely felt, was the inevitable. Ian didn't look directly down. Even if he had, Gregg was fairly certain Jared would remain hidden, but if he moved even the slightest muscle, it would be all over.

Ian stood for a moment, watching. Listening. Assessing. Then, deliberately, his face expressionless, he turned and walked away. Gregg could hear his footsteps receding into the distance. He saw Ian and Rob hop into their small rental and drive off, followed closely by another car that slithered out of the trees. A few more moments, punctuated by tires on gravel and small economy engines revving up to speed, and the area went quiet.

****

Her mobile rang at half two. Amantha jumped at the sudden noise, which came from the small phone jutting off the table by the door, and scurried over to answer. As per usual lately she was awake, reading a book; in her rush to still the incessant ringing of the phone, the novel flew from her grasp and disappeared over the far edge of the bed to land with a solid thump. Who could be ringing at this time of night?

"Hello," she said as quietly as possible.

"Miss Goldstein?"

It was Jerry. He sounded panicked, which was nothing new.

"Yes." Stifling a yawn, Amantha tried to pay attention, running her hand through her hair. She was tired. Sleep these past few nights had been more elusive than usual, and she found herself paying for it dearly.

"...by the time we got in there they were gone. We've called Commander Northam, and he's –"

Amantha suddenly paused mid-stretch.

"Wait, wait, what?" She cut in, much louder than she intended. "You said someone just what?" Too late she lowered her voice, and heard Marilla's feet thud to the ground down the hall.

Damn.

Jerry rattled off a rapid monologue of what happened – only half of which Amantha caught – and she promised to come right down. She had no sooner done so and hung up than her bedroom door burst open and Aunt Marilla charged in, ready for battle.

"What is it, Ammy? What's the matter?" She demanded.

"Someone just broke into the dig," Amantha said in disbelief.

"What?"

"Someone broke into the dig."

"I heard you the first time." Marilla stared at her. "That's *it*?"

"Isn't that enough?"

"Hardly. I thought the block was burning down!"

"Of course not, why should it be?"

"Oh, poppycock! All I can say about that dig is good riddance. It's unbecoming for a lady like you to go traipsing around in that overgrown burrow like one of those prairie dogs over in Africa." She folded her arms over her chest. "I suppose you'll be going over there now..."

"I'll be back in about an hour, maybe a little longer." Amanthe hopped to her feet and pulled on some clothing.

"Well, just give us a bell before you come home," Marilla said. "I'll be up."

"No need to wait up; I'll be fine."

"Ammy," Marilla eyed her warningly, and Amantha made a face in response.

"Yes, Aunt Marilla," she said, and cantered down the stairs, snatching a light jacket on her way out the front door.

The dig was fully lit and crawling with people by the time Amantha pulled to a stop out front. Right away she spotted Commander Edward Northam, her friend from Scotland Yard, talking to Jerry near the entrance to the tunnels. She was glad he was here. Of all people, he would know what to do.

Northam was a man people either avoided or were drawn to; his outer appearance was sufficiently aloof to scare off those not interested in looking any further, but behind the cop mask he was a gentle, caring soul. In any case, whether liked or feared, he held people's respect. He was mid-sixties; dark-haired and fit; with a steady, calming personality. He'd been on the beat for nearly thirty-five years, starting out as a country constable in Sussex before being poached by the Met, where he spent the next ten years rising through the crowd to obtain the rank of Commander. Contrary to cinema's (in particular Hollywood cinema's) portrayal of a Scotland Yard Commander, which limited their capacity to wandering haplessly in and out of brothels and sealing shady deals before meeting a rather untimely – and often messy – demise somewhere in the middle of the plot, Northam was a true gentleman. He was of the Commander Gideon variety; intelligent, noble, soft-spoken; a good one to have on side.

In Amantha's eyes, Northam was probably the closest thing to a father figure she had now; with her uncle long since gone, it had been a blessing in disguise to make Northam's acquaintance, even if the circumstances left something to be desired. Amantha had known him for nearly six years now. He was the officer in charge of the investigation at Heathrow Airport the day of the shooting, the one in charge of the ensuing manhunt until someone else, some American chap, was given control. Amantha never had understood why Northam was taken off the case. Perhaps it he hadn't been, the infamous Heathrow shooter Parker Lewis would have been caught, and Amantha wouldn't still be fretting about it.

Amantha put the thoughts aside. She didn't want to dwell on it right now.

As she approached Northam and Jerry, standing side by side next to the waving band of caution tape, Amantha felt a shiver of excitement. Only some of what Jerry said before had reached her – indeed, only some of it made sense – but after a dozen attempted break-ins that she hadn't heard about until the following day, all Amantha knew for certain was that whatever just happened, it was big. Very big. Otherwise she wouldn't be here. In all honesty, she couldn't wait to see what it was... and where it would lead.

Chapter 8

Jared hauled himself up the riverbank and flopped out of the water like a catfish, Gregg behind him. They lay side by side in silence, staring at the thick overhang of trees above. They had truly been lucky this night, and both knew it.

Jared sat up and slammed his balled fist into the ground.

"Great... Just great!" He snapped, divesting himself of the rumpled uniform he still had on over his clothing. He tossed it vengefully in the river.

"What?"

"What? *What!* Come on, Gregg! What you *think*? My laptop is dead, our passports are soaked, and our way to the treasure just tried to kill us. Not only will we have to figure it all out ourselves and deal with ensuing illegalities ourselves, we now have to outmaneuver the expert... who *will* be looking for us and *will* shoot us on sight. You realize that's what will happen if you and Ian cross paths again. Ever. In this lifetime, ever."

For a moment, regret flickered through Gregg's bedraggled mind.

"That's just a chance I'll have to take," he said quietly. "He wants to play rough, we can play rough."

"I think his rough is scarier than our rough. He's an expert."

Of course Jared was correct. Ian was an expert. An expert at doing things through force, without regard for consequences. Gregg had thought he needed someone like that; he realized now that he'd been wrong. He and Jared could do this thing themselves. They were both smart, adaptable, creative. They might not have the technical experience, but Gregg knew they had the ability. And he had a point to prove now. He wanted to show Ian Lowell that there was definitely more than one way to skin a cat.

"I take it you know where to go?"

"The Goldstein Museum. We need the necklace."

"Of course. So we're going for this thing, then?" Jared's question was spoken almost rhetorically. Gregg answered anyway.

"Yep."

"And then what?"

Gregg held up his waterlogged, soggy piece of paper with the poem on it.

"This will tell us where to go."

"What is it?"

"A riddle. We found it engraved on a sword."

"The one Ian has."

"Nope. The one that is still leaning safely up against the wall in the very room we found it in. I handed you a fake."

"Such a trusting bunch. You leave pieces of the puzzle behind to throw off the competition, and Ian brings his own death squad. Great."

"Well, to each their own." Gregg wrung out the tail of his shirt. "By the way, I don't know if you caught that bit of the conversation, but we found Robin Hood," he finished off casually. "No treasure… so I was a bit wrong about that… but proved the legend."

"Cool. My dreams of being the leader of a spandex-wearing entourage are vindicated." Jared yawned. "So where will this poem lead us?"

"I don't know yet. I know we need the necklace but that's as far as I've gotten so far. I just need to have some time to sit down and decode it all," Gregg said tiredly, and dropped back onto the grass. "I'll give you the whole story once we've found someplace to roost for the night. We'll figure something out, Jared. Soaked or not, we still have our passports and all the money we could possibly want. What more do we need?"

"Yeah, I guess you're right." Jared joined him in staring up at the darkened sky, fingers laced behind his head. "At least I can get all the data I need off the computer. Andy's designed a program I can run to get through security at the museum… and I know a guy here. Never met him in person, but we used to play Call of Duty online together. Between him and Andy – and my own awesomeness, I might add – we can do this."

"Can your mate be trusted?"

"More than your mate," Jared shot back. "The closest he's gotten to a gun is dual-wielding Needlers in Halo." He closed his eyes. "He's all right. Knows how to get his hands on any information you could possibly want, so in regards to the museum he's our best way in. He's got a good network. We need to find a way past security sooner rather than later… otherwise Ian will either find us or figure out the clue."

"Any chance you could contact your friend tonight?"

"He's a hacker. Night time is his playground."

****

The small torch in her hands did little to alleviate the utter blackness around them. Amantha felt crushed beneath the weight of some invisible force as she, Jerry and Commander Northam ducked out of the main tunnel and into a second, tighter one, picking their way carefully through the rock and loose gravel that used to constitute a solid wall. Their greeting outside had been brief; there was no need for introductions, and no desire to waste time. With Jerry again trying to explain exactly what had happened, the three of them climbed down the ladder and descended into the vacuous series of tombs. Sound from above had almost immediately been cut off through the dense ground. The air was stale. There was no second outlet. The fluoro lighting disappeared soon after the sound, cut off as they rounded a sharp bend, and once it was gone only the small, pinpoint beams of the torches and the sound of footsteps on packed earth remained.

Amantha stepped over a final mound of rock and paused, looking around. The tunnel was short, much shorter than she was herself; she estimated it to be no more than one hundred sixty cm in height. A similar width. Hand-hewn, with deep gouges and uneven gashes still visible in the walls. It was not as "professionally" carved as the rest of the network, and hidden as it was behind that band of rock, Amantha was shocked to see it revealed at all.

"How did they find this place?" She mused curiously. Her question broke a minute or two of silence.

Jerry shook his head.

"I don't know, Miss Goldstein. We won't know anything until we locate Bill."

Bill, the guard, had disappeared sometime between Jerry's departure at ten pm and his return at half twelve. He had come back to the dig to retrieve a bag he'd accidentally left behind, and found who he thought was Bill asleep outside. Upon leaning in to wake him, however, the person had come to life, clocked Jerry over the head, and took off down the tunnel. Jerry hadn't seen his face; he could see enough to know it wasn't Bill. And no one seemed to know where the real Bill was.

Amantha had a sudden flash of that reporter she'd spoken to by the front gate. Nicholas... Handler? He'd seemed pretty chummy with the guards. Maybe he knew what happened. She hoped he wasn't part of it; that would be just too much.

"Did you approach this area during that interview the other day?" Northam asked suddenly. He was crouched on the floor, holding a large piece of stone in his hands.

"Yes. We stood directly on the other side of this – well, what used to be the wall."

"Do you have a recording?"

"Yes, I do. Why?"

The stone was elevated. Jerry tilted his light towards it, illuminating a series of symbols.

"I think if you check it, you may find what they did," Northam said. "There must be something on the original wall that tipped them off."

"Which also begs the question... what do they know about this site that we don't." Amantha said softly, more as a statement.

Slowly, the trio made their way down the short hallway, around the bend and toward the soft lighting on the other side. The light source turned out to be a small room, lit only by torches that, surprisingly, still worked. Their bright flames danced hungrily off the cold, stone walls, the space in between lined with tapestries and racks of swords. Amantha simply stared in disbelief, Jerry at her elbow, while Northam walked the room in silence, taking it all in. His face was unreadable, but Amantha knew him well enough to see he was deeply intrigued by their surroundings. She was shocked; truthfully, she didn't know what to say.

"Watch your step, Miss Goldstein," Jerry said, pointing out another mound of debris just inside the door. A table, several chairs, and a number of smaller items lay sprawled in a general heap. Beyond the strewn mess, Amantha's gaze was drawn to two large, stone coffins sitting side by side in the still room. She gingerly stepped over the clutter. Who had done this? How had they known to look here? How many more rooms were there like this down here, hidden from the rest of the world? And, most importantly... what had been found in this one?

"Jerry," she whispered. "Jerry, it's..." Amantha felt her eyes widen as she got a good look at the coffins before her and read the inscriptions. "I can't believe it..."

This was far more than the mere artifacts Amantha had assumed were uncovered, more than trinkets of only limited importance. The men who managed to locate and break through a doorway no one knew existed had also managed to uncover a find no one was going to believe. The burial place of Robin Hood. Robin Hood and Maid Marian, together, in what had to be the most significant discovery of the decade. At least.

Her mind returned to Northam's question about the interview, his assumption that it was a symbol visible behind Carl and Amantha that had brought this situation about and led the bandits here. The possibility was intriguing. If indeed these mystery men had found something important in inscriptions carved on what seemed to be a solid wall, they were most definitely privy to information no one else knew. Nicolo – and all his cronies – would have wasted no time in tearing that rock limb from limb if they'd known what lay behind it.

What was the information these men had, and where would it lead them?

Northam and Jerry stood off to the side, Northam asking questions and writing things down, Jerry reenacting what had happened down here in this unusual room.

"When we came running in – and the table made its entrance, of course – this tall bloke made a dive for us and blazed a trail for his mates as they went out the door."

"Get a good look at him?"

"Not really. Like I said he was tall, over one hundred and eighty centimeters... wearing a dark cap, black jacket... looked like he had reddish hair or something under the hat but I couldn't tell."

"What about the other two?"

"Didn't see them. The first guy took a swing at me and I ducked... one was short, one was tall. That's all I could tell. Bryan might have gotten a better look than I did. He nearly had one of them."

Amantha listened while she studied the interior of Marian's open coffin, trailing her hand along the open edge as she wandered between the large containers of stone. It was more than she'd ever imagined was possible, seeing what she was seeing right now, touching what she was touching, smelling the ancientness of this place and hearing the beautiful, untainted silence of history. She gently touched the soft fabric of the sleeve before her, stroking the lace cuff. She was fingering it curiously, studying the pattern, when she saw what looked to be a bracelet underneath. She directed the torch at it.

It was indeed a bracelet, exquisitely made, with intricate designs on the band, made of solid ivory. Although large enough to fit with ease over someone's hand, it was quite delicate. Along the top, a wide heart distinguished itself from the streamlined band.

Amantha reached down to touch it, then carefully slipped it off the wrist, holding it up to the light. She ran her fingers along the gently curving edges, feeling the small heart with an almost reverent air. It may have just been her imagination, but that heart looked like it was a separate piece, perhaps hung on tiny hinges that stuck into the band. She pressed the top edge. A split second passed with no response, and Amantha pushed a bit harder. The heart swiveled. But that wasn't all. Seeing it now, at a different angle, Amantha could see that there was much more than met the eye. Not only could one see through the heart from front to back, but also down inside. Like a pocket. The top was open, framed by solid, flat sides that extended down to the point at the bottom. The front face displayed an odd pattern, as did the back. Amantha found that, by subjecting the object to light pressure, it would continue to revolve in a stationary circle until it reached an angle perpendicular to the band, with the pocket-side up. At that point, it would go no further.

The piece fell out.

Amantha started as it dropped into her palm, thinking she broke something (mentally cursing herself if she had), and quickly examined it. It turned out she had been right. Two small hinges protruded from either side of the heart, nothing more than a pair of oval tips that inserted themselves into a matching pair of sockets. Amantha put the piece back together and held the whole thing up to the light. As she did, she noticed a string of small, engraved numbers carved into the inside of the band, where it had rested on the wrist.

47, 4, 7; space; 19, 72, 15; space; 48, 1, 17… as the series continued, they became more and more faded, more and more indecipherable. Amantha knew she'd have to clean it off thoroughly to get a proper look.

"We'd best get back to the surface," Northam said. Behind him, one of the torches was flickering ominously. Another was already out. The smoke in the room was getting thicker, drifting down from the ceiling; Amantha hadn't noticed the change in air. She pocketed the bracelet quickly and stepped toward the door. A few more moments spent in the small room and she took hold of the string, leading the trio to the surface. They paused in the room at the very top of the tunnel system, the space Marcus and his crew had accidentally dropped in to. Amantha played with the string attached to one of the middle rungs of the ladder, making it bounce merrily; the movement continued until the point where the string disappeared down the staircase, and into utter darkness. Whoever had engineered this certainly knew what they were doing, she could give them that. Not only that, he could think quickly on the run. If not, all three would have been caught. A grudging admiration took root in her mind.

Admiration, and a burning curiosity.

Northam was near the head of the stairs, holding his smartphone up to a point on the wall.

"We have one contact here," he said. "How many shots did you say were fired?"

"At least three," Jerry answered.

"They *shot* at you?" Amantha asked. She'd missed that bit.

"Someone did," Jerry answered. "Missed us, fortunately. Mike nearly caught one in the arm but it lodged in a wooden board he had grabbed on his way out of the room."

Northam wandered over, producing a small, plastic baggie with a deformed piece of lead rolling around inside.

"Forty-five caliber," he said. He put the bag back in his pocket. "'God made all men, but Sam Colt made them equal'," he quoted.

"Sir?" Jerry quirked an eyebrow.

"Just an expression." Northam glanced across the small room. "What is that?" His gaze was directed at a mound of material in the corner.

"Just an old tarp," Jerry answered. "We had it over the entrance, but it had a few holes so we replaced it yesterday morning."

He had no sooner spoken than the tarp moaned and twitched.

"What the –" Jerry dashed forward and whipped it back. "Bill!" He exclaimed.

Amantha and Northam were already beside the delirious guard, who had clearly suffered some sort of trauma to the head, if his confused air and the dirty great knot over his left ear were to be believed. His hands were tied behind his back, his had a gag in his mouth, and he was stripped down to his underwear.

"No, no don't try to move; just lay still," Amantha said as the gag came out and Bill tried to sit up. Northam was already on the phone dialing for an ambulance. "Take a breath."

"How many fingers am I holding up?" Jerry asked.

"Five." Bill sat up slowly, painfully, and rubbed his forehead. "Where am I?"

"In the tunnel," Amantha said.

"How long have I been here?"

"A couple of hours."

"Did you get him?"

"Who?"

"The reporter. Said his name was Nicholas or something…"

"Nicholas Handler?" At Bill's nod, Jerry and Amantha traded a look. "I should have known," he said.

"As should I," Amantha answered. She sighed.

Northam hung up.

"Ambulance is on its way," he said. "Amantha, Jerry. Would you both be willing to talk with a sketch artist?" Clearly he was adept enough at multitasking to catch everything that had just been said.

Amantha and Jerry nodded together.

"Will we come with you, then?" Amantha asked.

"Yes."

"Very well. Let me quickly ring Aunt Marilla to let her know where I am." Amantha jogged out front to her car, through the bright lighting and past the ambulance that pulled up almost immediately. Fortunate timing; they must have already been in the area. She snipped her phone off the front passenger seat and held it up. "Uh oh," she said to herself, noting the twelve missed calls illuminated on the screen. Aunt Marilla was not going to be happy about being kept in the dark. Quickly, Amantha dialed her aunt. The ringing phone was picked up almost immediately.

"Amantha Felicity Goldstein, I have been trying to ring you for the past hour!" Marilla said without preamble.

"Sorry, Aunt Marilla; I was down the tunnel with no reception." A hilarious image of Marilla pacing around in her curlers popped to mind as her aunt muttered something that sounded an awful lot like a curse on all electronic devices.

"Well, as long as you are in one piece, that's what is important," she amended at last.

"I am in one piece, mobile, unscathed... and I have the most exciting news," Amantha said. "Aunt Marilla, you are not going to believe what they found!"

****

Commander Edward Northam of the Met stared with seemingly casual indifference at the stack of papers before him, his blue eyes thoughtful. Very focused, those eyes were, quick and bright as the mind behind them, not a single indication of having dulled in the least after thirty years on the job. The only proof of those years could be seen in streaks of grey nestled amongst Northam's dark hair, and the lines creasing his face from many days of quizzical squinting... and just as many days of laughter. His was a persona that many respected, even when his profession was unknown, for it was one that demanded such. He had spent the majority of his life serving his country, a life which had cost him any semblance of normalcy – as well as a marriage that had crumbled under the strain of occupational hazards – but if asked about regrets, his answer would be along the lines of: "What regrets? I have none."

Those he might have harbored had nothing to do with his job.

It was nearly quarter to four. The night's escapade continued. The guard, Bill, was in hospital under observation, and Amantha Goldstein and Jerry Kinsella had long since come and gone; after duly sitting down with a sketch artist and producing a very lucid image of the reporter calling himself Nicholas Handler, they were released at about half two. The sketch had been run, and now they were simply waiting for a match.

Amantha was nearly buzzing with excitement as she left, and Northam had no doubt she was, even now, sitting down to obsess over that interview she'd conducted with Carl Heyward, in an attempt to find out what, exactly, led this Handler chap into the dig. Northam half smiled to himself thinking about it; the lass should have been a cop, he reckoned. She had more potential than half the youngsters Northam worked with on a regular basis, one of whom was on this case.

That youngster was Benjamin Tunney, the newest lad to achieve the rank of Inspector. He was green, over-eager, and pumped full of testosterone, but he had potential. If he lived long enough to temper everything else, that is. Pulling him aside for a chat was something of a ritual now, and Tunney had managed to get himself kicked off several investigations thanks to this overzealous streak. Still, he was learning… slowly… and eventually Northam felt he would mature into a decent officer. He was from a wealthy family and had been a bit of a trouble-maker in his teens and early twenties, so his parents gave him a choice: Royal Navy or law enforcement. Tunney didn't like boats, so here he was.

Taking Tunney under his wing this time around was Shaun Howard, an experienced and loyal Inspector who had been on the job almost as long as Northam had himself. A few too many years spent behind a desk had seen his waistline increase exponentially, but behind the mild countenance and thinning hair was a sharp mind Northam had learned never to doubt.

The third individual Northam had on this escapade was Sergeant Leonard Howell. Ex SAS, Howell was imposing, tall, and built; after racking up nearly fifteen years in the service that saw him travel extensively in places most people didn't want to contemplate, he decided to change course and was almost immediately picked up by the Met. Funnily enough, Northam and Howell did not like each other when they were first thrown together. Howell was diehard military, especially in those days: by the book, regimented, and cautious. Completely opposite to Northam's free-thinking, rules-are-for-others outlook on life that had seen him both praised and reprimanded over the years. From the first, they were like oil and water. Opinionated, stubborn, and at least in Northam's case admittedly at odds with any sort of authority, they clashed constantly in personal worldview and working style, differences that saw them in a fresh row every other day without letup. Northam was fairly certain they would have killed each other if it hadn't been for Howard.

Gradually, however, time wrought a change in heart. Like so often happens between people of vastly different, but equally passionate opinions, Northam and Howell at last found common ground in a grudging respect for each other's refusal to back down. A few on-the-job crises and close calls later, and anger gradually turned to genuine respect, and respect to friendship. They'd learned to work with each other, trust each other's judgment, and had finally figured out that their different ways of operating were complementary.

Northam wandered over to the coffee machine and poured himself a cup.

"Sir, we have a match," Howell said, waltzing into the office, and Northam paused mid-sip to examine the results of the facial recognition software. "Nicholas Handler is actually a chap by the name of Gregg Nicholas. Born in Texas, 1965, now resides in California."

"What, does he herd cattle on his surfboard?"

"I wouldn't doubt it. You never know with Californians. Lecturer at California Polytechnic State University of San Luis Obispo…"

"Quite the mouthful."

"The locals call it Cal Poly, sir," Howard piped up from behind the large computer monitor he was studying.

"Cal Poly… I say that is much easier." Howell scribbled a note.

"What was that town called again?"

"San Luis Obispo?" Howell attempted, sounding it out as best he could.

"Luis," Howard corrected. "Said like Lewis, not Louie. Also known as SLO."

"Again, much easier, thank you," Howell acknowledged.

Northam arched his eyebrows in Howard's direction.

"I hired a motorcycle and drove down the coast from Canada to Mexico," Howard said by way of explanation. "I was originally only going for three weeks, but I found a room to let in San Luis and ended up staying there for a month before continuing on. Nice little place."

"So we have Mr. Gregg Nicholas from Texas, who lives in California and teaches *what*, exactly?"

"American History, World History… a few other bits and pieces. He has been employed at Cal Poly for six years." Howell produced a printed copy of an online newspaper article, featuring the staff of the history department at Cal Poly. "There he is on the far left, sir," he pointed.

THE FOSSILS OF CAL POLY HISTORY DEPARTMENT, the article title read.

Northam took in the photo with a practiced eye, studying faces and postures. They appeared to be a likeable lot, smiling and clearly hamming it up for the camera; a few of them were, indeed, fossil-like. Only Nicholas and one other appeared to be under the age of fifty.

"Girlfriend?" He asked, placing his finger near the image of the pretty girl with auburn hair standing near Nicholas. She was staring up at him, laughing merrily as he pulled a face; he, in turn, was giving her bunny ears behind her back.

"Maybe."

"Wonder if she knows what he's up to." Northam took another swig of coffee. "So our history professor comes across the Atlantic to break into the dig, for what reason…? Any priors?"

"Not as such, sir. But before teaching, Gregg Nicholas was a deputy United States Marshal. Three years. 1993 to 1996."

"A US Marshal. You're joking."

"Not a bit. He worked out of Austin… looks like he earned several commendations whilst in the job… I have a Peter Gates, Senior Deputy, who looks like he was around for a lot of this."

"Howard."

"I'm on it."

If they could contact this Peter Gates, that might shed some light on the motives of Gregg Nicholas, but what about the other two? Northam had found several decent CCTV angles from nearby cameras, where a rent-a-car could be seen pulling up along the pavement outside the Pale Horse Pub. Three men exited the vehicle, which then drove off around the corner to wait. Its rego plates were easily deciphered. Gregg Nicholas walked down the street, while his mates entered the pub; unfortunately the camera failed to give a good image of the two men. Northam intended to approach the premises later in the morning to see if the pub itself had cameras. The car, of course, was nowhere to be seen as of yet, and he had no doubt it had been left far behind by now.

"Commander?" Howard poked his head out again from behind the monitor. "Peter Gates is still a deputy with the USMS. I have spoken with a very lovely young lady from Austin, who told me Gates is currently in London, himself. Staying at the Savoy."

"What's he doing over here?"

"Holidaying, sir."

"Ah. Yes, well... Leo, when we reach more decent hours, let's see if we can't make Mr. Gates' holiday a little more colorful."

At precisely nine am, Northam and Howell strode into the quiet bustle that was the Savoy's front reception. The Savoy was London's claim to fame as far as historic hotels were concerned. When it was first constructed by the Carte family in 1889, it featured many innovations not yet seen in the world of overnight accommodation; electricity, running hot and cold water, and electric lifts were some of the opulent amenities guests could expect to encounter in the lavish building. It raised the bar for luxury and guest service, a standard it kept up to this day. Northam gave a quick study to the room, making his way to the opulent check-in counter. He waited while the room was paged, thanked the young lady at the counter when she informed him that Gates was on his way down. A few minutes later, the man himself walked into the room.

"There he is," Howell said, as the lift door slid open.

US Marshal Peter Gates was tall and slim, with a shock of thick, black hair brushed neatly off to the side and dark eyes that were both cold as ice and warm as the sun on a cloudless day. Northam felt, in a way, when he looked into the eyes of Marshal Gates he was seeing a reflection of himself. Gates looked to be in his mid-fifties, and had the appearance of one who would do what was needed to get the job done and do it right, one who would follow orders, but also one who would rebel if it proved necessary. By his side was a small woman, sandy-haired and brown-eyed, clearly his wife if body language were to be believed.

"Marshal Gates?"

"Yes."

Introductions between Gates and his wife, Sally, were brief.

"What can I do for you-all?" Gates asked in a decidedly Texas accent.

"Just a bit of information if you can," Northam said. "We have a small situation here... involving an American citizen, and we were wondering if you could lend us your assistance."

"How can I help? I'm out of my jurisdiction by a few thousand miles," Gates replied dryly.

Northam smiled and handed him a small, printed photo of Gregg Nicholas.

"Do you know this man?"

Gates surveyed it momentarily, then showed it to his wife, who sighed and shook her head in resignation.

"Oh, lordy," she said. "What's the boy done?"

"Broken into private property, vandalized the property, possibly stolen goods from it, but we can't be sure of that yet."

Gates nodded and handed the photo back.

"You mean the site where that new museum will be built."

It was a statement rather than a question. Northam glanced at Howell.

"Yes."

"Let's sit down, Commander," Gates said. "I think I know what this is about."

Over tea and scones in the hotel dining room, Gates told him a story. About Gregg Nicholas, his life, and a very strange legend that had been his constant companion for as long as Gates could remember. As he spoke, Northam found himself realizing the man was absolutely right: whether or not the legend was real, and whether or not it amounted to anything, Gregg Nicholas believed that it was and would.

Hence why Northam became acquainted with him through a break-in.

"Gregg was obsessed with the thing even when he was working for us. I suppose it would be hard not to be after chasing it down for as long as he has. According to him, he's been researching since high school."

Well, it certainly made sense. Not in the way that anything would ever come of it for Nicholas except failure and a stint in prison, but as motive it cleared things up.

"He had most definitely tried several avenues of approach before resorting to this," Northam said. "The Goldstein family has been getting written requests from him since November, after that necklace was found. They said no… to their detriment."

"Anyone else involved?" Gates inquired.

"Two people. We don't know who they are yet."

Howell produced a still from one of the CCTV cameras around the pub. While both of the remaining offenders appeared, the light was too low and the distance too far for little more than silhouettes to be perceived. Gates and his wife looked closely at the photo, traded a very slight, almost imperceptible look.

"Have you tried the bar for cameras yet?" Gates asked.

"On our way there shortly," Northam said. He accepted the image back and glanced at it, curious about that look Gates and his wife had shared. The shadowed hint of worry that lingered on Gates' countenance after the fact was even more puzzling. At least one of the men who broke into the dig with Gregg Nicholas was known to them, and known to Gates in a manner that caused him concern. Of that much Northam was certain. He had a sudden hunch he should give a closer check to the "US Marshal" segment of Gregg's life. It might yield some answers.

"I do apologize, Commander," Gates said at last, "but we have a tour scheduled at eleven and were told it would be wise to get there as early as possible."

"Of course, certainly," Northam agreed amicably. "Thank you for your time. I hope you enjoy your stay in our lovely city. If either of you think of anything that might help us, please don't hesitate to ring." He handed Gates his card, shook his hand, saw them out.

Outside the hotel, summertime tourist traffic was well underway. Of course the city never really slowed down, nor did it lose any of its local color; it simply gained more during the summer months. Northam and Howell bade Gates farewell at the entrance to the Savoy, waved to his wife, and watched them walk away together amid the continuous bustle of traffic, bodies, and the ever-present sounds of city life.

"He knows something," Northam said quietly. He and Howell stood at the door as people milled around them.

"Yes, sir, he does."

Gates and his wife entered a cab that slowed up along the pavement. The cab pulled away, merging effortlessly into the traffic.

"Let's pay a visit to that pub near the construction site… I'll have Howard start digging into Nicholas' service record with the US Marshals."

"You think Nicholas' partner was someone he worked with."

"Or arrested. Or got information from. At least one of them fits the description, and it was most likely a colleague. She knew the person, as well; you saw the way they looked at each other back there."

"Yes, sir, I did."

Northam rang Howard on the way to the pub, queuing him up for the search that would be headed his way.

"As soon as we have a photo, I'll send it through to you," he said. "See if you can match it up with anyone from Nicholas' past. Start with colleagues first, then work your way through any high-profile arrests or cases."

The pub was predictably dead at ten thirty am; why the place opened at nine, Northam had no idea. Only an odd assortment of barflies stuck to the bar, nursing their habits and heartaches, watched over by a young and bright-eyed waitress and a lad cleaning glasses, both of whom smiled in greeting as Northam and Howell entered the front door.

"Good morning," Northam said pleasantly, and introduced himself to the chap, whose name was Ben, briefly explaining the situation. "We are in search of video footage if you have any."

"Yes, we do as a matter of fact," the young man said. "Follow me." Leaving his female counterpart in charge of the barflies, he led Northam and Howell into the office. "We have five cameras on the premises," he said, booting up the surveillance program. "We record up to three weeks of footage and transfer it to a hard drive. Can never be too careful." A live feed from the front room came on, quickly replaced with footage from the night before as Ben delved into the archives.

"Twenty-one fifteen will be a close enough time," Northam said when Ben glanced at him, giving a quick check to the CCTV printout in his hand. The footage rolled. A couple of minutes passed with Howell and Northam observing the typical humdrum of a busy pub, and then Northam's two nameless thieves walked into view.

"Rookie," Howell said, indicating the shorter one, who was clearly aware of the cameras but unsure of how to deal with them, looking around nervously and unwittingly pasting his face all over the investigation as the feed froze and several handy images of his young visage were sent back to Howard.

"Yes, but he's not," Northam said. He pointed to the second figure in the frame, the one who was very carefully keeping himself out of direct contact with the lens. From one camera to the next he stayed away, wending his way through the crowd in such a way as to keep his face out of sight. "He's the one we want," he concluded. "You said you have five cameras?"

"We have another one in the hall outside the loo," Ben said. "In fact, if you're going to get anything, mate, it'll be from this one. It's well hidden."

"Can we see it?"

Ben swapped frames, rewinding the feed by a few minutes to make sure they didn't miss anything. Women lined up outside the loo. Men milled. A drunk couple started getting a bit overzealous in their affections and got herded out by the bartender.

"There he is," Northam said.

The calm, confident thief entered the frame, followed by the squirrely one. The one in front noticed the camera almost immediately and expertly hid his face, but not before they got a short look at him.

"Back it up a bit… freeze. Right there, freeze it."

The video stopped. Ben magnified the image as much as he could without undue distortion, and Northam leaned in for a better look. Tall, like Jerry had said, probably one hundred and eighty cm or so; reddish, sandy hair. This was the bloke. And this time they had a shot of his face.

"Leo?"

"I have it, sir." Howell had already saved a digital copy and was sending it to Howard. "This should do nicely."

It was a fuzzy image. But it was good enough.

"Got you," Northam said in satisfaction.

****

The sun was coming up. Amantha sat by herself in the lounge, watching the recording of herself and Carl Heyward over and over and over, trying to decipher what it was, exactly, that had led Handler, or whatever his name really was, to the discovery he'd just made. The man had gone to all this trouble to travel from America – judging from his accent, somewhere in the South? – and while breaking in to a heavily-guarded building project halfway across the world had uncovered what was sure to be the most important finding in a few hundred years. How had he done so? Why? What was he after? Had he found it?

Those questions and many more whirred around in her mind like fan blades. And so, here she sat, fiddling with the small, ivory bracelet she'd found in Marian's coffin and staring at the screen so intently her eyes were turning square. Watch. Pause. Rewind. Repeat. Watch. Pause. Rewind. Repeat. She nearly had the entire interview memorized. Every gesture, every sentence, every pinpoint of light on every rock, every crater and etching in every wall. Still, she found nothing. It was maddening!

She'd finally managed to decipher the remaining numbers on the underside of the bracelet, carefully scrubbing off centuries of oil and grime from the band until the numbers showed up clearly. She still didn't know what they meant. She wrote them down, tried different configurations, ran the whole thing through a series of internet searches. Nothing. Again, simply maddening.

"Ammy, I don't know what to do with you, really," Marilla admonished, bustling into the room with two piping hot cups of peppermint tea.

As if she was any better. After Amantha had talked with her aunt on the phone and brought her up to speed, she'd spent quite a long time speaking with the sketch artist Northam had called in; however, by the time she'd returned home at nearly three, Marilla was pacing the kitchen like a caged lion, third cup of tea in hand. That was judging solely by the number of used teabags laying on the counter; who knew how many more she'd already used and thrown away.

"Thank you," Amantha said distractedly, accepting the cup.

Marilla sighed and sat down.

"Anything?" She asked.

"No… I just don't understand. I was right there. What did this man see on the telly that I could not see in person?"

"Something small," Marilla answered. "Something simple. Sometimes all it takes is a fresh perspective." She leaned back, sipping her tea thoughtfully. Watching. Amantha was sure her eyes were square as well by now. Thirty minutes passed in silence: watch, pause, rewind, repeat. Watch, pause, rewind, repeat. "Isn't that Marian's Necklace?" Marilla asked. She pointed to the screen.

"What?" Pause. Amantha sat bolt upright, leaning forward to study the area her aunt had angled an index finger at. Just as Marilla had suggested, there was the necklace, engraved on the wall over Carl Heyward's right hip. "That's it," Amantha said quietly. "That's the answer… it has to be…"

The answer to what? And how did the thief know about this? Marian's Necklace had only been discovered eight months ago. How had he known enough about it to realize that piece held the key to whatever it was he was after?

"I wonder how he knew," she mused thoughtfully. "I wonder what he wants."

"We'll know soon enough," Marilla said matter-of-factly, then paused to look Amantha up and down carefully. "Oh, no you don't, young lady."

"Oh, no you don't what?"

"I know what that look on your face means, Mantha, and I absolutely forbid it."

Marilla sat back and crossed her arms as Amantha attempted to defend herself.

"Aunt Marilla, what do you take me for?" Amantha asked. "Do you actually think I'd go *looking* for the men who broke in so I could join them?"

"The fact that you know what I'm talking about says it all, and I wouldn't put it past you to at least put yourself in their way.

He's probably a bloody treasure hunter who will be rewarded for his efforts with a jail cell."

"Do you think it's even real?" Amantha asked. "The treasure, I mean." She returned her gaze momentarily to the stilled image on the telly screen, wondering what it all might mean: the bracelet, the dig, what it was those thieves found, if they could possibly be leads. Everything had changed now... and Amantha had a funny feeling something was about to happen. Whoever these men were, they'd already proven the legend's truth. What about the rest of it? Where were they going next and was there was any way to catch them?

Suddenly, staring at the symbol on the wall, she had her answer.

Handler was going for the necklace. He was going to try to break into the museum. The necklace was the only thing that tied everything together; that had to be it.

Amantha's intrigue rose by another level. If Nicholas Handler could pull this off, he would strike a blow to Nicolo's ego that he might never recover from; that, if nothing else, was well worth it. Amantha knew where he was going next. She just had to keep her mouth shut long enough for him to get in, get the necklace, and get back out again. If she wanted to see Nicolo burned, this would be the best way to do it, and the best person to do it through.

She was not tired anymore; far from it. She was more excited than she'd been in a long time. This situation had just taken a turn she would never, in a million years, have suspected, and Amantha wanted to see where it would end up. And who knew what else might happen? Any time the status quo changed in life, opportunities arose. The status quo was about to be knocked on its head by some guy from the fictitious town of New York, Nevada, population three hundred and twelve, and depending on the outcome it might remain unseated. If Amantha was really lucky, she might find a way to escape the clutches of this family for good. The thought was energizing.

"I wish Mum was here," she said softly, slipping the bracelet over her wrist. "I wish she would have had the chance to tell me the story."

Marilla was watching her restless movement carefully.

"Would it mean any less coming from someone else?" She asked.

~ 172 ~

"You know it, as well?"

"Who do you think told your mother?" Marilla smiled. "I know she always intended to pass it on to you, when you were old enough. I never mentioned anything more about it for fear of digging up old memories. But if you would like to hear it, I will tell you. It really is quite the tale… although I must warn you it is far too long to get through in one sitting."

"Then we'll have to do it in several," Amantha said. "I'd love to hear it."

"I shall tell you, then." Marilla smiled suddenly. "It has been years since I've had the opportunity to do this," she said. "I used to love telling it to your mother; she would pester me and pester me until I gave in… I must have retold this story a hundred times to her." Clearing her throat to quell a tide of emotion that was, frankly, unusual to Aunt Marilla, she set her tea aside, sat back, and began her tale. "It was nearly two years after the Crusades," she said, "when the queen received word of her son Richard's dire circumstances; that he and a small group of soldiers were imprisoned, doomed to death if the required ransom wasn't delivered. What had happened to the men between the shipwreck that cast them adrift and the present moment was unknown to her, but the state of both the messenger and the young man who knelt silently by his side was evidence enough. The messenger was young and slim, with a maturity about him that came from long days filled with battle and bloodshed, sleepless nights of watchfulness, and a long stretch of imprisonment. His face was lined with fatigue, his eyes with bitterness, but he was there, ready to serve his country yet again. His companion was smaller, hooded and cloaked, kneeling with his hands in front of him.

"The messenger and his companion had, however, had no sooner conveyed the dire tidings and left the queen's presence than they had to flee for their very lives as a royal posse took to their trail. The instigator of the disturbance, the queen's younger, power-driven son, John, had no idea that by acting as he did, he was about to create the worst enemy he had ever encountered. It wasn't long before that became evident, to him, as well as the rest of the world…"

Courage is the greatest of all the virtues.
Because if you haven't courage, you
may not have an opportunity to use any
of the others.

- *Samuel Johnson*

Chapter 9

The Prisoner

"Bring out the prisoner!"

The heavy chains around his ankles clanked loudly as the prisoner, Robert of Locksley was brought into the room. His hair was long and unkempt, as was the beard falling from his lifted chin. The clothes he wore bore vestiges of former beauty, yet were ragged from long hours of labor and lack of maintenance. However, though tiredness tugged at his face, the clear, grey eyes of this young man were hot and defiant. Not a hint of fear showed as he cast a glance around the well-lit, cavernous room into which he was being led.

Chandeliers and tapestries adorned walls and ceilings, giving the impression of unconcealed, audacious wealth. The long table in the center was decorated similarly. It was piled high with food, enough to feed an entire city, but only one of the thirty or forty chairs lining its sides was occupied. The Duke of Austria, captor of King Richard the Lionhearted, set aside the goblet he held and sat back, watching mildly as, at a wave of his pale hand, the guards alternately shoved and yanked the prisoner down the long stretch of cold, stone floor and threw him to his knees.

"Here he is, my lord."

The words echoed in the nearly empty room. Through the shifting light, the young prisoner could make out the thin features of the duke, he who had so unscrupulously seized King Richard and the few who traveled with him. He was a handsome man, in a boorish, malicious way, but as far as conquering victors go, he was anything but fair. A year's worth of imprisonment for his captives wasn't enough for him, a man of power who had been wronged; rather, he would have it that they remained in prison for life. But a year was all he got. For the king's friend, a humble minstrel by the name of Blondel, had found Richard at last and alerted those back home, forcing a few drastic measures on Leopold's part. At least, that was the rumor floating around. Lifting his head rebelliously, the young prisoner never let his own eyes stray from those of the duke. What could this man, a mere mortal, do to him that God had not already? He watched as the duke bit off a thick, inviting chunk of bread and set the loaf aside, tipping a large sword back and forth in his hands. The first gesture was one of temptation; what the second boded, who could tell.

"You are a soldier in the army of Richard of England," Leopold said. "What is your name?" He received no response. The young man never said a word. "Ah. I see we have a foolish one. Foolish... yet brave. It is lucky I am in a mood to admire that quality this morning. Have you nothing to say, boy? No name by which I should call you?"

"Robert of Locksley," one of the guards supplied.

"Sir Robert," the prisoner corrected, speaking for the first time.

"So! We have a knight among us! How very awe-inspiring. Sir... Robert, is it... of Locksley? I like it. Very... *English*." The duke paused a moment and contemplated the decorative pattern on the hilt of his sword. "Have you any family members who came with you on this... most unfortunate venture?"

"My father."

The chains rattled again as Robin of Locksley straightened, shifting his weight.

"I see. He was killed, was he not?"

"Yes. But it took fifteen men to do it."

"Pity... pity the Holy Land should be tainted in such a manner..." The sword must have been telling the man what to say, for he stared at it quite intently.

Robin of Locksley remained motionless and silent. He knew the Austrian duke was trying to anger him into either a rash action of violence or escape; he was not about to do either.

"Robert of Locksley," the duke said finally. "I have brought you here this morning because you happened to be nearest the door when my guards came to collect someone."

"My lord, if you please, I was already halfway *out* the door by the time your men arrived," Robert said with a wry smirk.

"Of course. An escape artist. Well, well. I trust this assignment will not be too unpleasant for you then. Tell me, do you love your king?"

"With all my heart, sir."

"And your country?"

"Equally."

"And your fellow invaders?"

"Sir, my fellow *soldiers* are some of my closest friends," Robert said, and there was distinct pride in his voice. "And I would appreciate it if you would not let your personal feud with our king undermine the integrity of my men." He raised his eyebrows pointedly. "We were on the same side when this began, after all."

"Yes, yes... well then," Leopold said, letting the subject slide away, "you are just the man we need." He sat up and clapped his hands twice in a commanding beat, and instantly two more servants, each as pale as their master, appeared with a small, jeweled case. "Come here, Robert of Locksley."

Clanging with every movement, Robert rose and approached as the duke reached into the chest and removed a piece of parchment, rolled and sealed with his crest.

"This," the duke said. "Is a letter to your queen corroborating the rumor that I now hold your king's life in my hands. Only for the sum of one hundred and fifty thousand marks will this life be returned. The remaining soldiers, of which there are very few, will also be returned at the time the money is received, for an additional fifty thousand marks." He pulled out the seal of King Richard. "It is obvious to you, what this is, yes? The seal of your king, so his fate will be known. And this..." Leopold reached up and removed his own seal. "Is a guarantee that you speak the truth. Take these things, Robert of Locksley, and make yourself a hero in your country." His voice was patronizing as he dropped his own seal into the chest with a clack and slammed the lid. "Now we must discuss the terms of this endeavor," he said practically, speaking in the same irritating tone as Robert accepted the small box. "First, I have already heard from your own lips your love for king, country, and fellow invader. I will now put your words to the test. You are to take these things to your queen and demand your king's release. You may be tempted to run. Let this be made clear: I will give you one month to either return yourself or send someone in your stead. After that, each day at sunrise one of your men will be executed. When the last man has died, your king shall be taken apart piece by piece, limb by limb, until you either come to collect him or we feed to the dogs what is left. Am I making this understood?"

"Yes."

"Good," the duke said in the tone of one just discussing a minor business detail. "May I remind you that the party we captured, yourself included, was small –"

"Twenty men, sir."

"Yes. Twenty men. And I believe there are only eight left, yourself included. That gives you thirty-seven days before I begin taking your precious Richard apart. I will send a man along to accompany you. Any tricks, you will be killed and the news brought to me. You can guess the rest. If other circumstances prevent you, however, from reaching your queen – or returning here – such tidings will also be relayed, and I will give someone else the chance to finish what you have started. Does this strike you as fair?"

"Strangely so, considering who is making the offer."

"Don't press your luck, boy," the duke snapped. "I could kill you all right now and not lose any sleep over the matter."

Robert ignored the threat.

"I have two requests," he said instead.

Quick as it had appeared, the flash of temper was gone, and two jeweled hands were spread expansively. The duke liked to be asked favors. It made him feel powerful, in control.

"Name it, young Robert of Locksley."

"It may take time, sir, to collect the amount of money you require, longer than the time you outlined. I must ask that, as long a message of agreement from the queen reaches you by the end of one month, the lives of King Richard and my fellow soldiers be spared."

The duke nodded slowly and reached behind him.

"Done," he said, and handed Robert a bagful of coins. "This is for your passage across the sea. What is your other request?"

"That I have the chance to see my king and my men before I leave."

For a moment, the duke hesitated, and Robert feared he might refuse. Then, as before, the duke spread his pale hands, put aside the sword, and stood up with a magnanimous smile.

"Very well," he said smoothly. "You shall see your men. And your king. Leave the case here for now, and you can collect it on your way out. It would be unfortunate to lose one's only salvation in the dungeons."

The key made a harsh scraping sound in a lock that seemed to need some cleaning. One that gave the appearance of little use and long stretches of idleness. As he stepped into the stairs and the blackness of the dungeon closed in around him, Robert of Locksley – known as Robin to those close to him – began to wonder if maybe this was such a good idea. What if the duke changed his mind and locked Robin down here out of spite?

The door banged shut behind him and it was too late to do anything but proceed.

The duke had refused to enter the dungeon himself, claiming the smell made him ill, but Robin was unaffected by it. It was something he had grown used to, a stench that, for the first few weeks threatened to make him sick as well, but later became a part of his existence. He forgot what it was like to smell flowers and fresh air and green grass... the odious, dank odors of the sweat and blood and rotting food of his prison cell was all he had known for the last year. Most men would have had occasion to be angry and resentful towards their leader for getting them into something like this, and, indeed, that may have been the duke's idea. Robin, however, felt nothing but empathy and support for his king, who was in much direr straights than he.

It had all begun at Acre. After King Richard insulted Leopold of Austria, the duke had gone home with wounded pride and a rather large chip on his shoulder. That chip had grown to the size of a Yule log during the remainder of the Crusade, and, by the time Richard and his army were on their way home, the duke was in a fine state of temper. He'd had all that time to stew and fester and rot and plan until finally, through the tempestuous hands of destiny, he got his chance at revenge.

Of the men who survived fate's strange intervention in their future, several were of the opinion that the trouble was caused by a witch putting a curse on the fleet. What her motive was or even where she came from was unclear, but there she stood, the day they left to sail home, cursing the fleet and all its occupants, telling them off for traitorous dogs and shrieking that she hoped the sea would swallow them up. It was a tense voyage, one that eventually ended in tragedy as, true to her wishes, the sea overtook them, allowing few ships to go free. Richard's was not among them.

He and a small band of survivors reached land and, after days traveling, found themselves staring at the castle of Leopold of Austria. And there, riding towards them was the duke himself. A mild attempt at deception was tried, but it failed miserably. Leopold would have known Richard with his eyes closed. He unceremoniously locked the few soldiers up together in one large cell and put King Richard in the dungeon, where he remained to this day, one year later. If it hadn't been for Blondel, a rambling minstrel and friend of Richard, who knew how much longer he would have been down there. Considering the duke's vengeful nature and wounded pride, the rest of Richard's life would have seemed far too short. But Blondel had come, searching for his friend, and after finding him, had gone back home to tell the queen, thus inspiring the duke's actions. If one couldn't keep the man himself, one could at least make a country pay a heavy, heavy price for his return.

Robin was grateful for his chance at freedom, grateful for the duke's frustrated decision, and mostly grateful to Blondel, whose loyalty had gotten them all out of a terrible bind. For Robin and his fellow soldiers were witnesses, party to the secret, and could not be set free for the duration of their king's imprisonment. And that could have ended up being a very, very long time. Winding his way down the stairway behind a man who was, essentially, a mobile boulder, Robin determined to make sure his men lived long enough to come home. It was what they deserved, and it was all they wanted.

All around him were sounds of agony. Behind these heavy, wooden doors were human beings, human beings confined to a life of misery for something they may not have deserved. Men and a few women begged for their lives, bony hands clinging painfully to the bars in the high-centered, tiny windows. At the base of the large doors separating these people from the rest of the world, smaller, secured flaps where food trays were passed in and out were chained to rungs on the floor. As he passed by one of these small openings, Robin caught sight of a slim, feminine hand and wrist, mantled with a delicate bracelet that looked to be made of ivory. How the piece survived in here or how it managed to get into this place to begin with was unclear. Robin averted his eyes and continued on as the hand retreated into its dark prison.

After a seemingly endless venture downward into the depths of the castle, he was halted and pushed to the side as his bulky escort stepped to a door on their right and inserted his key into the lock. It looked even more rusted and unused than the last one, and Robin felt his heart sink. The door swung open, and he was ushered inside.

"No tricks," a gravelly, monotonous voice said behind him. Two torches were lit; their hard, dry tips catching instantly, filling the tiny enclosure with eerie, yellow light.

Richard Plantagenet sat with his back to the wall, arms draped over his knees. Crouched there, in the semi-dark of the room, he appeared anything but a king. The third of five sons, he had made a name for himself as a fighter throughout his life; by the age of sixteen, he had already taken command of his own army, helping to suppress rebellions against his father, King Henry II. He was a big man, rough and uncouth at times, but a brilliant warrior and loyal friend. To see him as he appeared now was shocking. Long hair, matted and dirty, hung around his hunched back, cascading over thin, lifeless shoulders. A long beard stretched down his chest, and hair fell into his eyes, half-concealing them from view. But the look Robin saw in those eyes was enough to convince him there was hope. Fire still flashed, and though it was faint, it was there, nonetheless, plain as the stars in the sky.

"Your Highness," Robin said quietly, kneeling. "I cannot tell you how glad my heart is to see you alive."

Richard coughed forcefully when he chuckled, the noise disheartening.

"I have life, yes," he answered hoarsely. "But I'm not alive. Not in here."

"That is soon to change, sir," Robin said. "I have been appointed to return to England to secure your freedom."

King Richard was silent. The news for which he had lived and breathed the last year was at long last in the air. Finally, after a minute or two of silence, he nodded, his face breaking into a slight smile.

"It is good to hear." He surveyed Robin for another moment. "There were twenty of you, were there not? Those who were washed ashore with me. Tell me, how many are left?"

Robin bowed his head.

"Sir, there are but eight of us left," he said softly. "The duke has promised us our freedom as well."

"So... Leopold has grown soft in his age," Richard replied dryly. "Blondel moved his spirit."

"No, sir, scared is more the word you are looking for. Blondel went back and told the queen of your imprisonment. The duke knows his time for vengeance is almost up. He wants 150,000 marks for your return, 50,000 more for the rest of us."

"Is that all..." The shaggy head shook back and forth in wry disdain as King Richard sighed heavily. "He certainly knows how to hit where it hurts, doesn't he?"

"He does, sir. He does."

"What is your name, my lad?"

"Robert of Locksley."

The king nodded slowly.

"I remember you, Sir Robert," he said, recalling the title with no prompting. "Your courage in battle was commendable." He studied Robin a moment. "I knew your father, too," he said quietly. "A good man, a kind man... much kinder than I." Slowly, painfully, he stood and put a hand inside his dingy outfit, retrieving a small Bible and holding it out to Robin with trembling fingers. "This has been the only thing to get me through at times," he said. "I cannot read it in the dark, but just feeling of it has given me hope. May God light your path, and may His words of wisdom be good to you as they have to me."

Robin, still kneeling, gently accepted the gift.

"Thank you, sir," he said softly as he rose.

"Go, Sir Robin. Your country will thank you. As will I."

The last thing Robin saw of his king was Richard standing proudly and stoically at the back of his cell, head held high, the light in his eyes flashing back into existence as he realized that freedom was on the horizon. Then the door swung shut, and Robin followed his escort back up the stairs, the Bible clutched under his arm.

Robin's talk with his fellow prisoners was short and to the point, but filled with feeling. Standing in a small group at the far end of the cell, they were a varied assemblage: several foot soldiers, Robin, and two other knights made up the lot. They had come into this place on different social levels, with different standards, but the time spent in this tiny, changeless place had broken those class chains, building them from the ground up as equals. As Robin spoke with them now, he no longer saw men of better or lesser backgrounds; just soldiers. Soldiers who wanted to go home.

"Can he be trusted?" This from Gideon de Rosel, a knight from Normandy with distant ties to England on his mother's side. He had stood aside silently while Robin told of the duke's offer, his tall frame leaning on the wall with arms crossed, brown eyes reserved. Thick, black hair obscured part of his face, making him seem far more intimidating than he really was. He was a pragmatic, logical man, excellent at the planning and execution of ideas. At his straight question, Robin shook his head.

"Not at all," he said. "But I also think he has no choice right now."

"He could try to have you killed."

"I have thought on that… but what would he gain? If England knows we're alive, that the king is alive, shooting the messenger isn't going to do much good, is it?"

Gideon nodded in acquiescence.

"When do you leave?"

"Now."

"Well, then…" One of the other men, also called Robert, stepped forward and held out his hand. "Take care, Robin," he said quietly. "God go with you."

There was hope in his eyes, in the eyes of everyone present. Even Gideon, as realistic and down-to-earth as he was, had a small, enigmatic smile on his face as he too shook Robin's hand.

"They couldn't have chosen a worse person," he joked, and clapped Robin on the back. "Try to save the wenching for after, hey? We'd all like to go home."

"I can't make any promises," Robin returned.

There was another round of banter, another round of goodbyes. And then he left that place; watched those seven faces disappear as the door closed, walked with the guard back out into the fresh, aromatic air of freedom. He did not take lightly the task that lay before him, as it would be the hardest thing he'd ever done in his life. But he wanted to get this show on the road.

"So, you are ready to depart, young Robin," Leopold said as Robin was brought before him once more and shoved to the floor. "Take care you heed what I said – no tricks."

"No tricks, sir," Robin answered calmly.

"Good... I trust you were sufficiently shocked by the appearance of your king to give his salvation your best effort?" He took in Robin's wordless expression of contempt with a cold smile.

"Ah, the splendors of youth. If I didn't know better, I should think you would like to kill me here and now."

"If so much was not at stake, sir, you would already be dead," Robin stated flatly.

Leopold rose slowly, elegantly from his plush chair, still fingering that sword and studying it carefully.

"Well, not to tempt you unnecessarily, but I do believe you will need protection on your journey," he said smoothly, and held the sword out toward Robin's kneeling form. His eyes fell on the Bible. "What is that?"

"King Richard's Bible," Robin said quietly.

The duke nodded, still extending the weapon as another condescending smile breached his face.

"How could I dare come between the mighty King Richard and one of his faithful subjects?"

His tone invited Robin to do something stupid. Indeed, it seemed to beg for such an act, one that would mean the immediate extinction of both Robin and his king, as well as the seven men still locked up. And thus would end the problem. But his hopes went unanswered as Robin reached out and took the sword, sliding it with an icy, silvery sound through the duke's hands.

"This sword will not kill you, my lord," he said. "It will defeat you through different means. By means of truth and justice and righteousness, love of country and honor... these will be the things that this sword will bring upon you."

Leopold retained the smile on his face, even as his eyes chilled noticeably.

"As I told you before, *boy*, don't press your luck," he said.

"And I told you, *sir*, if it were just my life at stake right now, yours would already be nonexistent. Now, if you please, before the temptation becomes too great for me to bear, I will take my leave."

"Your attendant awaits you outside." As Robin began to turn away, Leopold added: "A word to the wise... as soon as you leave the premises, your king shall be moved to another location. Do not try anything you will regret later while mourning at his burial."

Robin just kept walking, the king's Bible in one hand, the duke's sword in the other. Two opposing forces; one of healing, one of destruction; one of forgiveness, one of vengeance; but before this was over, both would meet under the banners of wisdom and truth, both doing their part to right a terrible wrong. Slung from his shoulder was the small case, bearing the duke's terms. And, if Robin felt funny about carrying the lives of eight people around with him on his shoulder, he said nothing.

The opposite of love is not hate, it's indifference. The opposite of art is not ugliness, it's indifference. The opposite of faith is not heresy, it's indifference. And the opposite of life is not death, it's indifference.

- Elie Wiesel

Chapter 10

Across the Ocean

As specified, there was a man waiting outside when the tall door swung shut. A long, brown cloak trailed rather aimlessly toward the cold stone of the courtyard, revealing nothing more than a dark hole where a face would normally rest, and pair of pale, soft hands that remained clasped in front of the man's waist. Somehow, Robin was not surprised at the quality of those hands. Like servant, like master, after all.

The man was small in stature, very slim under the bulk of his cloak, the build of one who had been alive long enough to warrant this kind of job but who hadn't done much with his time on earth aside from sit. He gave no sound as Robin approached, and Robin waited for none. He strode on past, hearing the soft scuffle of footsteps as the figure turned to follow him toward the stables. They wasted no time. Robin only had thirty days before Leopold would go after his men, and only seven days after that before Richard himself would be caught in the line of fire. Time was of the essence.

"Thank you," he said as a pair of long reins was flopped into his hand.

His escort accepted the horse handed him without so much as a nod.

Robin's horse shifted irritably as it waited for developments, eager to be on the move. It pranced into the courtyard and aimed a delicate nose for the gate at the far side. The gates swung open, revealing a beautiful expanse of open road, a beautiful expanse of freedom.

Robin paused for a moment. He realized where he was, what he was doing. He realized that all of the things he missed, all the things he craved, were right there in front of him. He could smell the grass and trees and damp earth; the horses; the sheer purity of the air around him. It was all he'd wanted, all he had dreamed of. And quite suddenly, it was staring him in the face.

"Move along, now, if you please."

The sentry by the gate was starting to get impatient. Robin slowly filed past him onto the open road. For one, brief moment uncertainty touched at his heart, causing him to question if everything would go according to plan, what would happen over the next month... if he could really do this.

"I guess we'll see." Robin's comment was directed more to himself than anything, and it was a good thing. His escort still hadn't said a word. Robin was beginning to wonder whether the man had somehow lost his tongue along the way. He took a quick look behind him, gave a brief thought as to whether or not words would ever emerge from that quarter, then turned his back on the place that had caused him so much pain and faced forward once more. "Let's go, Bob," he said, picking a name at random. "We have a long ride ahead of us."

****

It took Robin and Bob two days of hard riding to make the mainland coast. Once there, Robin made himself slow down to take the time to clean up, ridding himself of years' worth of grime and beard. It felt good to have breeze on his face again. Then they boarded the first available boat headed in their direction... and waited. Finally, late at night and far behind schedule, they departed, and set sail for England.

And home.

****

The boat rocked in a slow, consistent motion beneath him as Robin sat with his back to the large mainmast, staring out over the water. It was almost dawn, the end of a long and bitter night finally beginning to recede as light seeped in from the east, trying to bite through the thick fog that covered the channel. The horses were down in the hold, waiting with annoyance to be rescued from this treacherous, rocking piece of wood, their occasional neighs of impatience drifting up on deck. Robin could hardly blame them. He listened to the quiet slapping of water against the hull, the whisper of the salty, sea air. Bob sat beside him. Neither spoke for the time being, Bob keeping to his seemingly-permanent vow of silence and Robin just deep in thought. He had long since given up on trying to get a word out of his companion, deciding Bob had either been forced to come on this venture and was determined to punish Robin psychologically for the inconvenience, or he literally *had* had his tongue removed at some point and couldn't say anything even if he wanted to. Whatever the reason, he remained silent, and Robin remained within his own mind.

He still couldn't believe he was out. Out! The year he had spent inside that cell had felt like an eternity, an eternity whose existence was marked only by the rise and fall of the sun and designated by scratches on the wall. They couldn't even see the sun, really; just vestiges of its passing on the topmost corner of the wall.

It had been fairly easy to cope at first. Surely they would not be forgotten. Surely they would be rescued. Surely *someone somewhere* would realize there were still men out there waiting to come home. But as days turned into weeks and weeks into months, as the months crept by without development and the marks accrued on the wall without change, slowly hope began to fade. Slowly, surely, it drifted away to be replaced by melancholy, and ultimately despair. It was a desolation that nothing could break. Memories that had, at one time, been uplifting, became little more than cruel reminders that memories might be all they had left. One by one they'd failed, leaving Robin and the others empty, their hearts devoid of everything but resignation that this would, indeed be their life from now on. This constant cycle. Unending. Unchanging. Unbroken. Unbearable. This would be their life until the day they died.

Thoughts of his father, his family, his home, his country, all fled in the wake of harsh reality, chased away like mere fugitives to be replaced by only bitterness and dark recollections. Even the memory of being knighted, kneeling down in humble acceptance as the king himself declared Robin a noble man, became little more than a shadow, unimportant and indistinguishable. Funny, it didn't seem to matter so much after all. It was just a title. And there were those far more commendable, far more worthy, who had not lived to see their efforts rewarded. One of these had been Robin's best friend.

Robin would never forget the look on Peter Fitzwalter's face when his friend realized he was talking to a real, live knight. He would never forget how Peter decidedly declared that he, himself would become a knight one day. And it might have been so, but that final battle in Jerusalem, where Peter had proven beyond a shadow of a doubt that he was worthy of such an honor, had been the battle that put an end to his plans. Peter had proven his merit. He had proven it by dying. It had haunted Robin for months, shadowing him in wakefulness and sleep, playing and replaying and playing again that final, terrible scene when Robin rounded a corner after the fight and saw his friend, lying facedown, a mere number among a thousand other bodies littering the ground. Robin had rushed to his side, begging Peter to come back, pleading with him, but his efforts were in vain. And he, too, became just another number. One man among a thousand grieving for those they'd lost.

It was in that moment and in the months following that Robin questioned. Time only increased his uncertainty. The shipwreck changed his mind on life; prison changed his heart. Everything; good times, positive thoughts, even God; all became disgusting pieces of guilt-ridden baggage spoiling his mind, reminding him again and again that everything in life is subjective, debatable, indefinite. Nothing is for certain. Not even God. For what kind of God would command that so many be sent on a quest from which most would not return, a quest whose reason was questionable at best and, at worst, nothing more than a political ploy. If God really cared so much, why did he let it happen? If it had to happen, why did so many have to die? And if so many had to die... why did it have to be Peter Fitzwalter?

Robin prayed for answers. He tried to find truth. He failed miserably. And he finally came to the grim realization that God was no longer with him, and indeed, may never have been. Those last weeks of prison caused even his faith to desert him, slipping away like a shadow, and Robin was left alone. Utterly and completely alone. Only one memory remained in his heart, one memory untainted by the squalor and guilt and vileness, one that he clung to with all the strength he possessed. And now that it had served its purpose, he tucked it away, burying it deep in his heart for fear of contaminating it as well. He wanted at least one good thing to remember in the years to come.

He played idly with the sword he still held in his hands, running his fingers over the queer pattern on the hilt. His thoughts were scattered and disorganized, flitting across the board as they often do in the mind of someone who has too much to think about.

"It's hard to believe, Bob," he said, tracing a small square with his fingernail. "I'm out. Going home, at last..." He didn't expect a response. He didn't expect a reaction. He just needed to speak; to know that, whether or not there would be any return, someone would hear the words he spoke. At least then he'd know they were real.

What would home be like now? Not like he remembered. Strange, probably. Foreign. Unfamiliar. Things would have changed. Robin knew he would return to nothing, his residence merely a relic of former beauty and home only by ownership. He knew most of his friends would be gone, having joined the Crusade and never returned. As for his family... he had no family anymore, for his father, too, had been one of those who never left Jerusalem. Robin had, in fact, nothing left but his country. The rest he had lost a long time ago.

It had been over fifteen years since his mother, aunt, and three-year-old cousin William were killed in an indiscriminate raid by person or persons unknown who managed to remain anonymous to this day. Robin and his father had been out hunting and returned to find their house on fire, anything of value gone, the entire place ransacked, Robin's mother and her sister Elaine lying outside. William, they'd never found. It was likely he never even made it out of the house.

Theirs had not been the only residence to be raided that day, and the random streak of violence literally decimated the tightly-knit community of Nottingham. Desperately people searched for answers as more and more of their friends and family turned up dead; slowly the small, family cemeteries around the county began to be filled with the sight of freshly-turned earth. No one knew the reason. The culprits were never found. But the act was no haphazard affair. Its precision, its speed, the timing; all of it pointed to a job done by someone who knew exactly what they were doing, and exactly how to do it. The only question was why. It was a question that still remained unanswered.

After helping pick up the pieces to start over, Robin had put it out of his mind, deciding to forget about it and move on. Many years passed before he could think about what he'd seen, what he'd felt; many more passed before he was able to talk about it. He couldn't understand what drove people to such extremes, what animalistic nature must be at work inside their minds to produce evil of that caliber. There were times he'd wondered the same about himself and his compatriots during their time in Jerusalem. Some of the things he'd seen had been of sheer brutality; acts motivated, he was sure, by the same sense that had impelled the men who'd run rampant through Nottinghamshire to do what they had all those years ago.

Human nature. That's all it was. The darkest side of mankind could be found with ease, interspersed with incredible heroism, at times when the human spirit was tested to its limits. People would either go one way or the other, up or down, turning into heroes or cads in a heartbeat, showing their true colors in the rawness of trial. Robin had seen this at work many times, seen men he'd admired morph into beings of incredible cruelty while others he'd never noticed transformed themselves into men of genuine character. Men like his father and Peter.

Robin sighed, leaning back to close his eyes. His father. The leader, the peacemaker, the one people always turned to when they were in trouble, the one who lived up to expectation amid hardship no matter what he was going through himself. It would be very strange not having him around. Not sad, for Robin was far beyond feeling that kind of emotion anymore. Just strange. He doubted people would accept him as they had his father, doubted they'd accept any leadership he could offer. Just because he'd been in a few fights and hung out in a jail cell for a while wouldn't make him worthy of trust; he'd have to carn it. He reached carefully into his pocket and pulled out an intricate, gold ring, one he'd managed to keep hidden for an entire year, the last thing his father had given him.

"Robert... I feel uncertain of what might happen today. If I don't come back, will you see to it that Bishop Lorien is given this ring?"

Robin hadn't wanted to. In some perverse, uncanny way he was afraid to accept the request, afraid it might somehow jinx the situation; afraid that, by taking that ring, he was signing his father's death warrant. And, for all intents and purposes, he seemed to have done just that. His father hadn't returned. Now it was Robin's task to complete his last request, taking the ring to its intended recipient.

Bishop Paul Lorien. A good friend, a good man, a man who could be trusted simply for his sheer humanity. He had been a close friend of Robin's father for many years, had been the man before whom Robin's parents said their vows, the man who baptized Robin as a baby, the man who dropped everything to come perform the service the day Robin's mother was killed. He always kept in close contact and had come to their house countless times; usually unannounced and just in time for supper. Jovial, tall, and quite round, Lorien didn't quite fit the mental profile one usually brought up when thinking of bishops or men of the cloth; he was far too kind and unassuming. He was far too human. Though Robin hadn't seen him in over five years, still he could picture Lorien's face, and as clearly as if he'd seen it yesterday.

He knew the bishop was one of only a couple people he could count on being the same. The other one was Marian. The sister of Robin's best friend. How was he going to tell her about Peter? How would he break this, the most terrible of news, to a woman who had already lost so much in her life? He opened his eyes to stare at a variety of fading stars visible beyond the flared sheeting over his head, but if he sought inspiration, he found none. All he found in the lightening expanse was a memory, one that made planning his impending task all the harder.

Marian Fitzwalter had always been a wild girl. Robin had met both her and her brother when they were kids, the day they all got caught climbing several of the old, distinguished trees adorning the lawns of the king's palace in London. After that, the three of them had been inseparable. They had been best friends and co-conspirators in many a prank and many a merry horseback chase; where one was found, the other two were sure to follow. It was a friendship from which much youthful trouble was caused. Marian had her own little place in the trio, as she quickly proved beyond a shadow of a doubt that she could out-shoot and out-ride either of the boys. The horseback riding didn't matter so much, really... but the archery...

It was quite embarrassing to be out-shot by a woman, especially when it was your best friend's sister. *Especially* when she wasn't supposed to be doing it in the first place and had to sneak out at night to learn.

"I wonder how Marian is," Robin mused thoughtfully. "She must be married by now... a couple of kids... surely she wouldn't stay alone forever." He paused, running a hand through his hair. "How am I going to tell her? About her brother? It would be one thing if I was someone she liked..."

Bob's silence asked a question Robin knew was coming.

"Does she like me? Well... no, not exactly. See, it's because of me that she was forced to have her hair cut short when she was ten. *I* didn't do anything, really... I just accidentally held a candle under her hair and set it on fire. It was an accident, I swear!"

Bob stared into the distance, and Robin nodded in grudging acknowledgement.

"All right. Maybe it wasn't *quite* accidental. I just wanted to see what her hair would look like with black tips. How did I know it would light up like a haystack?" He chuckled, gesturing mildly with a hand. "She did look rather funny, running around like that, her hair flaming behind her... little bits of fire falling to the floor. Finally Peter came running up and doused her with a bucket of water. Look here." Robin unbuttoned his shirt and pulled back the collar, revealing a small scar at the base of his neck. "That was from the butcher knife she was holding." He sighed exaggeratedly and gazed out over the sea. "She never was quite the same toward me, after that," he said in a dramatic fashion. "Every time we met, she made sure I saw the various knives and weapons she had hidden on her person. One time, I think she had a sword."

That had been about nine years ago, when Marian was a tall, gangly twelve-year-old girl with remnants of pigtails. Although she had become fairly pretty over the years, she had never lost that skinny look, not even when Robin and Peter left just after her seventeenth birthday. Robin couldn't help but wonder what she looked like now. Probably either chunky and red-cheeked like most of the family, or skinny as the proverbial knife blade. She never had been what could be considered gorgeous; the blue-green eyes had always seemed a tad big for her face, which was narrow and cheeky. Way too cheeky, as a matter of fact. She did have pretty hair – what was left of it – deep brown and wavy from the braids she always kept it in.

They used to have a lot of fun together, he and Marian. There were times when she was almost a better friend than Peter. And then there were the times when Robin was sure his worst enemy was standing right in front of him, the one every true hero must face sometime in his life; only it was made of the wrong gender and appeared a few years too early for him to do anything about it. They would really go at it sometimes, fighting like cat and dog over something as simple as a wind-ridden archery competition or a stick-throwing contest, brother Peter standing aside just watching the fireworks. It was all quite harmless. But there did come a day when their words were laced with far more bitterness, and were far more permanent.

Robin did have to admit to a slight jealousy when Sir Richard Norrington started paying attention to Marian, but he told himself it was because he had known Marian for such a long time and hated to lose her to a complete stranger. Four years older and a handsome, dashing rogue who had been newly knighted, Richard was the talk of the countryside from the moment he arrived. He could have had any girl, of any age or class, but for some reason it was sixteen-year-old Marian Fitzwalter who caught his eye. Not even Ellen de Gant, Marian's beautiful and charming friend, was able to sway him.

And it was then, quite suddenly, when all the young, single men who had known Marian their whole lives realized they must have missed something important. Up to that point, Ellen had always been the one to attract the interest, her thick, blonde hair and blue eyes and lovely figure unintentionally stealing attention away from her modest, unassuming friend. Where Marian was usually dressed in clothes suited to the rough-and-tumble lifestyle she loved, Ellen was always proper, always regal, always dressed to kill. The difference in their appearance and resulting attentiveness never seemed to harm the relationship between the two girls any; it was almost like Marian enjoyed being one of the boys and had no intention of caring about any of them as anything more than a friend or potential archery target. And then, out of the blue, she up and bags the most eligible bachelor in town.

Robin had stood back and watched the progression of the relationship like everyone else, wondering just how far it would go, how it began in the first place, and most of all questioning himself as to how he could have missed whatever it was that so captivated Richard Norrington. There had to be something...

But then, maybe not. Robin had never gotten along too well with Norrington, anyway, and they certainly differed in the opinion department. It wasn't that they were unfriendly or hostile towards each other, just aloof. Robin always felt belittled and unimportant when Norrington was around, and his ensuing discomfort had a tendency to result in a distant attitude and occasionally sharp tongue. Richard never bit back. And, although the fact did add to Robin's annoyance, he consoled himself with the thought that the man had always been a bit too perfect and was only living up to his goodie-two-shoes outlook on life. But that, of course, could have been simple jealousy talking.

Peter had teased him about that very thing once, saying jokingly that Robin's amorous feelings for Marian were obvious to all and he might as well stop pretending. It hadn't helped the situation any. In point of fact, it only made it worse. These supposedly "amorous feelings" being a complete newsflash to Robin, Peter's comment managed to not only make him incredibly tense when around Marian, but sent him into a mental state roughly associated with the town drunk. Since his nerves were already fried for some reason even Robin couldn't explain, he suddenly came to the realization that the situation had grown far too deep for him and he had to get out of it. In short, he panicked. Fearing that anything he did would be misconstrued as a come-on, Robin had started trying to alienate his friend's sister in hopes that the whole thing would just go away. It hadn't. Marian sought him out. Not understanding his motives and unwilling to let an old friendship die without a fight, she tried vainly to patch up what Robin was tearing down, the efforts of both sending their relationship into an entirely new and rough sea. They fought more than ever; not in the playful, careless manner of a couple of kids but in the biting style of ex-lovers. There had come a day when they didn't speak at all, finding no words other than in anger; there had come a day when Marian refused to even look his way. And then had come the day no one would have expected: Richard Norrington and Marian became engaged to be married. Three months after they met. Four days after Marian's birthday, she would become the wife of Sir Richard Norrington.

Robin didn't know whether he was happy about it or not. It was a relief, knowing soon that all pressure would be off and things would be back to normal, but at the same time the news struck a funny chord in his heart, one that he wasn't used to having tugged on. He ignored the feeling and kept all thoughts on that matter in the shadows, immersing himself in the wedding plans like everyone else. The weeks rolled by, the day approached... and, once more a turning point was reached, a single moment in time that took the rickety bridge between two childhood friends and smashed it into complete oblivion.

It was supposed to be a simple joust. A competition staged the day before the wedding as added excitement, bringing the victorious groom-to-be against a man considered by many to be his equal, in a match that everyone was sure would stand alone in the tides of history.

The protagonist was Richard Norrington. His opponent was Sir Eustace DeMarke. DeMarke had the reputation of being a shrewd, deliberate man with a lot of money, a lot of power, and the desire for a lot more of both. The castle of his family, near the town of Nottingham, was one of the largest in the region, an example of ostentatious wealth jutting out from the green hillsides like an oversized prison. Not liked by many but feared enough by all to merit respect, Eustace DeMarke had slowly but surely acquired influence, using his inherent people savvy and slippery charm to his advantage. A good deal of fighting power never hurt anyone either, and DeMarke had plenty of that, organized with precision under the direction of his right-hand-man – who was also, coincidentally, his cousin – Guy of Gisbourne. Hence the fear and subsequent respect in people residing within a twenty mile radius. Anyone who got in the way of Eustace DeMarke had a funny way of disappearing.

That DeMarke had long coveted Marian Fitzwalter – or rather, the close proximity to the throne that could be had through her – was another one of those things that everybody had an opinion about but never mentioned. Marian's parents were close to the royal family, Marian was close to the royal family, Eustace DeMarke wanted to be much closer than he was. After the death of Marian's parents, it seemed there would be no obstacles. Until Norrington threw himself into the mix. DeMarke was as surprised as anyone else about this new development, but no one else could begin to match his irritation. He thought he had a clear field, a clean shot, then in comes this young brat with fancy clothes and a glistening title, stealing Marian right out from under his nose. And for DeMarke's golden goose to be suddenly snatched away by someone who didn't need Marian politically was not only in sharp defiance of his plans, but an absolute waste of a good connection.

Considering the events, it was with no small amount of curiosity that Robin anticipated the joust between these two men in Marian's life. Through one string-pulling technique or another, he wound up as the squire of Norrington, a position which allowed him close proximity to the field and the action. It wasn't a job he particularly relished – when his relationship with Marian went downhill, civility between himself and Norrington vanished altogether – but at least the view was well worth any hassle. Ten knights participated in the event, from all over, pitted against each other in five, spirited matches that led up to the main event. The tournament was exhilarating, highlighted by challenges and cat-calls, victories and defeats, the pounding of hooves and clank of metal on armor, just what the people were looking for.

Finally the finale arrived. Robin was jogging to his post, hurrying to get there while he listened to the clashing metal and thundering bodies of the latest encounter, when he happened to notice DeMarke's squire, a young man named Silas, carrying a lance whose blunt nose was covered by a sheet of cloth. In a rush to reach his own post in time, Silas let slip the cloth and it slid back, revealing not the relatively harmless, rounded point of a jousting lance, but the hard, arrow-shaped head of a spear. Silas didn't see Robin and just covered the thing up to go on his way, casting several surreptitious looks around.

Of course the idea of actual treachery was nonsense. Robin put it aside, reassuring himself with the fact that DeMarke wasn't that stupid; he wouldn't attempt murder in broad daylight. And he really couldn't be that desperate.

Could he?

The next few seconds had proven Robin dangerously wrong. He watched as the two horses charged from their positions for the final joust, thundering down the brightly-colored lanes, enormous hooves pounding the earth. People shouted in expectation, the lances of the knights were lowered menacingly... and suddenly it was all over. A sharp clank, a yell, a fall, and Richard Norrington was lying prone in the center of the arena, the shaft of a spear protruding grotesquely from the crease of his armor. A truly brilliant shot, aimed by a master. The crowd went silent as the blow landed. Somebody screamed. Somebody called out. All chaos broke loose. People poured from the stands onto the field, fighting their way to the fallen knight, but there was nothing anyone could do for Richard Norrington. He was dead before he hit the ground.

Despite the fact that the word "murder" had never officially been attached to the incident, there were few who deemed it otherwise. Including Marian Fitzwalter, although her chosen place to lay the blame was far different from everyone else's. Unfortunately, Robin's comment earlier regarding the rather strong lack of feeling between them was far closer to the truth than he wanted to admit. He would never forget that day in the arena, the day Marian looked up into his face with her eyes swinging eerily between grief and absolute loathing, and told Robin she hated him.

"I will never forgive you for this," she had whispered brokenly. "You were here to keep him safe... I will hate you for as long as I live."

Robin had no answer for her. He had run to her side as a friend; he hadn't realized he would arrive an enemy. Until then, it had never occurred to him he might be at fault. Looking in her eyes, however, he knew she meant what she said. And always would. He had turned and walked away, not looking back once, leaving the scene as far behind as he possibly could. In the space of about two minutes, his heart turned to stone.

Richard Norrington had been buried, Marian had gone into a long and bitter mourning, and it had been right around that time, with things at their worst, when King Richard announced his intention to retake the holy city of Jerusalem. Robin signed up before he even heard the reason. He wanted to serve his country. He wanted to help whatever cause his king was vying for. But more than anything he just wanted out.

Marian said nothing when she learned of Robin's intention, said nothing when Peter decided to go with him. She just stood there, watching them both with accusing eyes, begging Peter through her silence to stay, cursing Robin through the same. She wasn't going to like this sudden turn in fortune, the ironic twist of fate that sent her brother to his doom and brought Robin back to her doorstep, the one person she hoped would return replaced instead by the one she hoped never to see again. She would hate Robin more than ever now, as the truth became a certainty.

Robin bowed his head. He didn't want to come home like this, to the world of anger and bitterness he was undoubtedly going to enter. But it appeared he had no choice in the matter. With his father gone, the only family he'd have at home would be those buried in the small cemetery out back. The only friends he'd have would be those he made along the way. It would be a world of alienation and peculiarity, where he was the outsider in a place he used to call home, unknown to many, recognized by few, and those with no small disdain. For most of those few would be people whose own sons did not possess such luck as Robin. And then there was Marian...

"Land, ho!"

Robin leapt to his feet and dashed to the railing.

"Look... look! There it is!" He called excitedly, pointing into the distance as Bob trailed slowly behind. "I'm home!" He whooped in exhilaration, punching at the sky with a hard fist. "You know the first thing I'm going to do when we dock," he added happily. "I'm going to run. I'm going to come off this ship and fly away and never look back. I can't believe it! I'm home!"

Bob said nothing in response to Robin's exuberance. He just observed, studying the shoreline, the long hood still shielding his face from view, and Robin could tell nothing of the expression that lingered behind it. He didn't care. For that one moment, while the sun's rays began slipping over the eastern horizon, he was able to forget his troubles and find happiness, standing gladly at the railing as his homeland came into view. At long last, after all those years.

He was home.

Chapter 11

Bob

The boat docked without incident, and not a moment too soon. The gangplank had barely touched down before Robin and Bob charged shoreward on a pair of frisky horses, galloping through the crowded dock area. People yelled and waved at them to slow down, but the calls went unheeded, alarmed citizens diving to the side as the two horses plowed through the center of town.

Robin held his horse in a bit, watching the edge of the village come closer and closer, staring at the great, open road stretching beyond. He could hear the distant sound of hoof beats behind him as Bob's horse closed the gap and came up on his heels, but Robin didn't look back. His own horse was almost out of control. Its hooves beat erratically on the ground as the animal tried to take the bit in its teeth, lunging angrily over the damp ground and throwing its head and shoulders into the air. It had been cooped up in the hold of a boat for far too long. It wanted to run.

They made it to the road. The last person went flying by on the right, the last building on the left, and Robin dropped the reins. His horse took off like an arrow. The hind feet dug into the soil, sending great chunks of it slinging out behind as the scenery whipped by in a flurry of flying colors, so fast it almost blended together. Robin threw his hands in the air.

"I'm home!"

He laughed ecstatically and pulled back a little to allow his escort to catch up, letting Bob swoop beside him on the left. The little man was sitting his mount with surprising ease, holding down the flap of his long hood with one hand while he guided the horse with the other. The horse was running flat out and soaring, mane and tail streaming behind it, the sculpted head held high. Bob let it run. For a moment Robin thought he heard a laugh; a high, sing-song intonation of joy coming from the mouth of his companion, but he couldn't be sure of that.

They let the horses run until the tall stallions tired of the pace and slowed of their own accord. Heading north from the small seaport, they traveled steadily through the day and well into the night, stopping only when they could no longer see the road ahead of them. By the next morning, they were that much closer. The sun was pale around them, peering every now and then through the traditional layer of clouds, hitting the grass in beautiful rays. Robin was in seventh heaven. Gazing all around him at countryside that, at one time had bored him, he now felt it was the answer to a prayer. Beside him, Bob's body language indicated that he seemed somewhat annoyed by the constant greyness about the place.

As stride after stride of grassy, English country rolled by on either side, the road ahead of them appeared unending. It was lined with trees, branches stretching low over its earthen surface and bathing it in a dark, mysterious shade. Already things were beginning to look familiar. Robin watched it all seem to change right before his eyes, turning from unknown places to ones he recognized, becoming more and more like what he remembered. Morning passed swiftly, melting into noon and noon into the latter part of the day, all of it disappearing in a succession so rapid it didn't appear possible. The light changed, intensifying ever so slightly, but the day remained cool.

The third morning found them nearly within sight of their destination. Robin knew right where he was, and he knew right where he was going. He was now about half a day's ride south of the place he used to live; closer to the village of Nottingham, which lay farther to the west and almost in sight of the large castle inhabited by Sir Eustace DeMarke; and closer still to the home of Lady Marian. Both residences were near the edge of Sherwood Forest to the east, which Robin could already see stretching out to meet them.

"You see those stands of trees, Bob?" He asked covertly. "That is the beginning of Sherwood Forest. It's said to be haunted. People have heard strange noises coming on nights when the wind blows and the moon is full; they say it's the witches roaming the forest in search of prey." Robin studied the dark tree-line slowly coming into view. "I never thought much of those stories," he said. "But then, I've never believed much in ghosts, either."

"Is that a fact, old boy?" The voice came from behind. "No! Don't turn around," it added commandingly as Robin tried to spot the owner. "Stop your horses and put your hands over your head."

Robin pulled his horse to a halt, as did Bob, and raised his hands as two bushes up ahead suddenly grew legs and sprang to life. So this is how it was to end. Everything that could possibly save the lives of his king and his men swept away by a crew of bandits.

Not likely, he thought.

"I said *both* of you put your hands up," the voice from behind said again when Bob didn't move.

"Bob... do as he says," Robin whispered. "If we can get them to come in close, we might have a chance."

Behind the branches ahead of them, the faces staring back were unkempt, dirty; beards matted; all of it adorned with disreputable material. The only visible portion of the men was the pair of arrow-loaded bows pointed right at chest level.

"Whoever is out there," Robin tried lamely, "don't shoot. My friend doesn't speak English." He wasn't sure of that, but it was worth a try.

A low chuckle came from his right side as the owner of the voice stepped up next to them. He was like his companions: scraggly and rough-looking, small-eyed, with a beady expression probably drilled into him by the nature of existence he led. At Robin's excuse for the lack of compliance, he cocked his head to the side.

"He doesn't, eh? Well, let's see if we can teach him."

He nodded to his companions, and Robin and Bob were yanked roughly from their horses and pushed to the side. The horses were led off a few feet.

"Now," the leader said. "Let's try that again. Hands up."

The results were the same. Quickly, fearing that his escort would be mowed down without so much as a second thought, Robin reached over and took Bob's small hand, putting it up over the shoulder.

"Please, Bob," he said. "You've made your point."

Apparently not good enough. The hand was jerked back. The three highwaymen laughed at the situation, shaking greasy heads in unison.

"Looks like your way isn't good enough, old boy. I think I'll have to take over." And with that, he stepped up and reached up a hand for Bob's long cape. "You are a –"

Bob suddenly came to life. There was a jerking motion, the flash of silvery metal, and the grease-ridden highwayman jumped back with a yelp, his arm sporting a long gash. Robin jumped into the game. Bolting out of the way, he sent one of the men beside him to his knees with a well-aimed kick, slammed a fist into the other one and dashed for his horse, grabbing the sword given to him by Leopold of Austria. He spun around and prepared to direct a deadly swipe at the leader, who was trying to wrestle Bob to the ground. But he didn't get halfway there. Suddenly the man's body stiffened, and, with a choked cry, fell backwards to flop lifelessly onto the road. A dagger protruded from his chest. Robin kicked away the two unmanned bows and stepped toward the other two.

"Leave now if you wish to live," he said.

The men took his advice. They disappeared without another word.

Robin turned back to Bob with a friendly comment on his lips.

"Bob, for being silent, you're –"

He stopped mid-sentence.

– not even a man.

Black hair had slipped out of place from under the long hood covering Bob's head to fall softly about slim shoulders, framing the beautiful, oval face and dark eyes of a woman. Her skin was brown in color, its pigment much darker than Robin's, but pale, as if she had not seen the light of day for many months. The girl swept the remainder of the hood of her head and eyed him suspiciously.

"You are surprised?"

Her accent was familiar, yet foreign, one Robin had heard many times during his stay in Jerusalem but never with kindness. For a moment, he had no words.

~ 204 ~

"Slightly, yes," he said at last.

A small, detached smile tipped at her mouth as the girl reached down and retrieved her dagger without so much as a shiver. As she did so, Robin caught sight of her wrist as it extended out from the long-sleeved garment she wore, and he saw it just when a delicate, ivory bracelet slipped down to her hand.

"Is something wrong?" The girl asked, still aloof, as she straightened.

"No, I... I just didn't expect a woman," Robin said quietly, and his remark caused the suspicion to return full-force.

"Are you going to try and do something about it?"

"After what happened to him? Uh-uh."

"Good. I'd hate to have to kill you too."

She wiped the dagger across the man's pant leg and slipped it back into a sheath inside her cloak.

"I assume your name isn't Bob, is it?" Robin suggested.

"Thankfully, no," was the response. "It is Jasmine."

"You are not Austrian, Jasmine," Robin said curiously, hoping to elicit a few hints about the presence of an Arab woman in a European country.

"I am Saracen. Daughter of al-'Adil."

"You mean..." Robin stared. "...al-'Adil, brother of Saladin... you're his *daughter*?"

"Yes. Niece to Saladin. I was one of those locked in the dungeon at the duke's castle, but I managed to escape the day you were set free. I killed your man Bob and took his place."

The dungeon. When Robin was allowed to see the king. It had been *Jasmine's* hand he saw sliding through the bars of the window.

"I heard your voice pass by my cell," Jasmine added, as if reading his thoughts. "I did not know at the time we would come to make this journey together. It was not my intention to come with you at all."

"Are you trying to get home?

"I have no home," she said flatly. "I wish only to be left alone."

"Why haven't you a home?"

Jasmine swept a bit of dust from her cloak in annoyance.

"Did anyone tell ever tell you that you ask too many questions?" When Robin didn't answer her rather irritable query, she crossed her arms and looked off as one of the horses came over to snuffle her shoulder. "I had been promised to a wealthy sheikh. He sought an alliance with my father's house, and had we wed, I would have been his sixth wife."

Robin quirked a skeptical eyebrow.

"Sixth?"

"I suppose my people's performance of such practices is one of the reasons you consider us barbarians," Jasmine stated. "Had I married, my family name would have meant nothing, except as a – how do you say... a feather in my husband's cap. But I was destined for another road... you know most of it already, I think. About the women among my people who were taken prisoner by your soldiers in an attempt to make the cost of war too high for us to bear."

"I do. I was never part of it."

"It was the work of cowards," Jasmine spat. She lifted her head spiritedly. "But they do not know my father," she said in sudden pride. "He would never give in. Nor would Saladin."

"Is that how you were taken to Austria?"

"Yes. I was caught by a raiding party and sold as a slave. Eventually I came into the hands of the duke. He – made me do things that are not just sinful, but a sin that requires death." Her voice caught briefly. "I waited for a chance to escape, but impatience finally got the better of me. I foolishly tried to strike him, and the next thing I remembered was waking up in blackness. I have been in blackness from that day forward. I think it was his intention to break me, then return me to his service." Her voice trailed off after her eyes, which were fixed intently on the horizon. "Now you see why I cannot go home," she continued softly. "I am no longer pure and chaste." Jasmine looked down at her body, her hands, those of an impure woman. "And so I am no longer wanted, Robin of Locksley. I am not wanted anywhere, nor am I welcome."

Robin glanced at the ground. He knew well how it felt to have no home, no family, no one to care... even if his isolation was to be only temporary. Silently, he walked up to her and put a hand on her shoulder, against the rough material of the cloak.

"You are welcome here," he said. "And if you wish, you can ride with me."

"What of your people? What will they think?"

"Does it matter?" Robin asked gently.

She nodded gratefully.

"I would like to ride with you. At least until I can understand this country." Slowly, she reached over and gathered the reins of her horse, which stood patiently by her elbow, and smiled quietly as she stroked the velvety nose. "I have not ridden since my capture," she said. "I had almost forgotten how wonderful it was."

Robin swung into the saddle.

"You'll enjoy yourself here, Jasmine," he said. "I suspect we just met three of the nastiest characters in the entire region. The rest of them will be better."

He later remembered saying that and almost laughed at his own shortsightedness.

The trip after that was uneventful for a time; they saw few other travelers, and these were so busy going about their own business, they hardly noticed the features of Robin – or Jasmine, who rode beside him. It was just after noon when the lone figure appeared far up ahead, walking slowly along the road, a strange contraption strapped to its back. A closer glance revealed the figure to be male, and a minstrel, one of hundreds roaming the English countryside. But there was something else. Robin knew this one.

"Of all the people to meet," he said with a grin.

"Who is he?"

Robin cupped his hands around his mouth.

"Allan!" He called out. "Allan-a-Dale!"

The figure stopped. Robin urged his horse into an easy canter, the swinging stride carrying them swiftly over the dirt road. He shouted again, waving, and this time Allan-a-Dale, rambling minstrel of the dales, recognized him.

"Robert?" He asked with a broad smile.

"I told you before, it was just Robin!" Robin leapt off his horse and embraced Allan warmly. "I am glad to see you are well, friend."

"As am I," Allan answered. "I feared you were dead."

Robin patted him on the shoulder as he stepped back.

"I was, Allan. I was." He turned to Jasmine. "I would like you to meet my traveling companion. This is Jasmine. Jasmine,

Allan-a-Dale. Next to a choir of angels, you will find no greater music anywhere in this life or any other."

"On the contrary, Robin, mine are but simple tunes of the dales," Allan said, his voice edged with embarrassment, and nodded to Jasmine. "It is a pleasure to meet you."

"And you," Jasmine said, smiling warmly.

Robin could tell Allan knew at a glance who Jasmine was – or rather, of what people and religion – but he could also tell it didn't really matter. Allan-a-Dale had never been one to judge by merits considered important by the general populace. Even the vicious, ongoing feud between the Norman and Saxon cultures that so pervaded the country seemed to have little effect on him, and Allan continued to judge character only by what was important to him; integrity, honor, humor, respect for the earth and its natural inhabitants, kindness to one's fellow human beings, the willingness to fight for something worth fighting for. That he had seen more than his fair share of battle, whether personal or on a grand scale, had always been obvious to Robin, for no man could emerge from it unchanged. Allan carried in his eyes the tales of such events, remnants of times long over that were not so fair. Slightly taller than Robin and a handsome man in his own, subtle right, the most outstanding feature on the face of Allan-a-Dale was a pair of arresting, blue-green eyes, eyes that managed to express all the kindness in the world along with a striking tenacity. They were made all the more remarkable by the shock of thick, jet black hair that surprisingly managed to keep itself to a manageable length. Allan was slim of build, toughened on the outside by the elements and the effects of a life he'd led for many years, yet softened on the inside by the very music he played, and its influence on others. His way with words and the kindness in his smile had avoided many a senseless fight, and had helped to make him many a friend along the hard road he'd chosen for his life. Allan's face was still lighted with this unusual smile as he turned back to Robin.

"What end of the earth did you come from?" He asked. "I must admit it is no small surprise to see you alive."

"We have come from the castle of Leopold of Austria," Robin said. His tone was one of a storekeeper imparting a minor point. "The duke held this good lady captive for over two years and still holds the lives of seven men in his hands... as well as that of our king," he added with far more importance.

"His Highness is alive?"

"Indeed. I have seen him with my own eyes. He is the reason I am here."

"I am afraid you won't find many to believe you, Robin," Allan said. "We all heard the stories, but few had faith enough to trust in them."

Robin couldn't stop a smile.

"Fortunately for all of us, the duke has no knowledge of that. He knows only that King Richard was discovered and the secret is out. I was chosen to negotiate the release with the queen, and I must return to the duke with her approval within thirty days."

"Or?"

"Or Leopold has threatened to kill everyone he still holds captive," Robin answered. "The sum he asks is non-negotiable."

"And what sum is that?"

"Two hundred thousand marks."

Allan whistled softly.

"It will take every man, woman, and child in the country to raise that much."

"I'm afraid so," Robin said. "But the cause is worth it." He took up the reins. "Are you traveling to Nottingham?"

"I am."

"I'll trade you a ride for a tune," Robin said ingratiatingly, and Allan laughed.

"You have a deal," he answered. "I was tired of walking."

He seemed glad for the company. As the distance rolled by peacefully, Allan sat behind Robin, strumming a tune on his lute and humming along in a clear, easy voice. He wanted to know everything about what had happened to Robin and the others in the last year, and Robin filled him in. The shipwreck, the capture of King Richard, Robin's own imprisonment, the chaotic day of freedom and equally-chaotic venture to this moment. They had just caught up to the present when Jasmine pulled up and pointed.

"Is that not a royal procession?" She asked.

From the top of a small knoll up ahead, a fine, richly-designed carriage began to distinguish itself from the low trees, making its way slowly over the rutted dirt. The long curtains covering either side rustled faintly. Slowing just before it reached a small side road that swung in from the west, the carriage and its two black-clad outriders turned left and continued on their course, heading away from the main road.

"They must have come through Nottingham," Robin said. "I can't quite make out the colors from here..."

"It's Lady Ellen," Allan answered, just above a whisper.

"Then let us make haste!" Robin called. "Long has it been since I last saw Lady Ellen de Gant!"

Over-riding Allan's indignant protests from the back, he spurred his horse and charged gleefully up the road toward the slow-moving vehicle. But he had forgotten one thing: Robert of Locksley was supposed to be dead. It wasn't long before his joyful advance met its demise.

"Halt! Identify yourself!"

The imperial command came from one of the two individuals flanking the carriage. In a sweep of metal and black material, the two riders swung about to face him, drawing their swords in a single motion, and Robin pulled his horse to an abrupt stop, Jasmine right behind him.

"Easy, friend! We mean you no harm."

There was a momentary standoff; Robin, Allan, and Jasmine with their hands in plain view; the guards with their hands planted firmly on the hilts of the long swords raised in front of them. One was a tall man, stocky and solid; the other was smaller, more of a boy than a man. The lower half of his face was obscured from view by a mask, which Robin assumed was an attempt to hide his tender age.

"What business have you here?" The first demanded. "State it and then kindly move on."

"Lady Ellen is an acquaintance of mine. I wish only to speak with her."

He and the others were surveyed by two pairs of careful eyes.

"I was not aware that Lady Ellen associated with... persons... of your circumstance," was the condescending response, again from the first rider.

The second one remained silent, observing the situation as would a spectator at a jousting tournament.

"I doubt it, as well," Robin said, "that Lady Ellen knows many like me. How many of her acquaintances have survived war and prison?" He cocked his head. "Certainly not the likes of you. I doubt you've ever seen the inside of a prison. Or the danger of a battlefield, for that matter." His comment brought no reaction.

"Is there a message you wish to convey?"

"Yes. Tell her ladyship, if it pleases her, Sir Robert of Locksley would like a word."

"Robert? Of Locksley?"

Robin thought he detected a slight stress of recollection on the latter two words.

"Yes," was all he said.

There was more staring. Robin's guess must have been accurate, for a glance was traded between the two men before the first backed his horse up with a nod, studying Robin cautiously.

"I shall ask if Lady Ellen will see you."

The second guard remained in place. He still said nothing, keeping a watchful eye on these three newcomers, his hand perched restfully on the sword that now lay across his saddle. He seemed particularly interested in Jasmine. For several minutes the contest continued; Robin, Allan, and Jasmine silently defending themselves against the virtual barrage of unspoken questions leveled at them from the face of this opponent, all the while listening intently to the muffled conversation going on at the carriage.

Robin wondered if Lady Ellen would even remember his name, let alone what he looked like. Let alone *recognize* him as he was now.

"Robin? He's *here*?" He heard in Ellen's distinctly clear voice, and the words were filled with anticipation. "Yes, yes, please show him over."

Robin didn't wait for sanction from the guard who stood solidly in front of him. He reined his horse to the side to move past the little man, meeting the defiant, blue-green eyes with a knowing smirk. The rider swiveled to face him. A small, jeweled cross dangling around his neck glinted sharply in the light as he did, matching the near insolence sparking in his eyes, and for a moment Robin thought passage would be denied. Then, reluctantly, the smaller man drew back and moved aside.

"Thank you," Robin said, and stepped carefully to the ground beside Allan, handing the reins of his horse to Jasmine before walking toward the carriage.

"Robin!"

The joyful cry reached him at the same time he caught sight of Lady Ellen, and he smiled widely as he strode over. Ellen de Gant was a bright, enchanting woman whose love for life showed in every highlight of her fair face. She was kind, loving, and considerate to all, no matter their station, and even those of a more sinister nature seemed to respect her enough to leave her be. It was regarded as bad luck to do harm to Lady Ellen. For she had been a friend to many who had none at all. Robin knew of the things she had done, had seen some of them himself, and would always be grateful for the kindness she had shown him.

"Lady Ellen," he said. "It does me good to see you. You are as lovely as ever."

"And I see your silver tongue has not yet deserted you, Robin," she replied teasingly. Concern entered the blue of her eyes as she let them travel over his face with care, observing the lines and marks that, Robin knew, had not been there when they had last met. "We were told you had perished," she said quietly. "Your ship lost at sea. It is good to see you safely home at last."

"It's good to be home, m'lady. I only wish more could have been so fortunate."

"Is it true, then, about Peter Fitzwalter?"

"It is."

Elllen bowed her head.

"I'm sorry."

"So am I." Robin glanced around. "Does Marian know?"

"Not formally, but I think there is little doubt. Just as there was little doubt about you. You have been gone for a long time, Robin, much longer than the others... what else were we to think?"

"Nothing," Robin admitted. "There were times I wondered myself." He took a look at the impatient guard at his heels and stepped back. "I do not want to keep you, my lady," he said. "I didn't mean to cause delay, but the thought of your face welcoming me home was too good a reception to ignore."

"I'm glad you stopped," Ellen said freely. "It is a pleasure to welcome you back." She turned to Allan where he stood silently off to the side. For a moment, surprise flitted plainly across her face, but it was quickly disguised, and she only smiled. "Good-bye," she said softly.

Allan nodded to her respectfully.

"Lady de Gant."

A faint flush rose in her cheeks, however Lady Ellen said nothing more, waving quietly and settling back in her seat once more as the carriage began to roll forward. A few moments and the curtains fell back in place.

As Robin turned to walk for his horse, he smirked knowingly to himself, a hint of curiosity beginning to tug at his mind. The look he had seen on Ellen's face as she bade Allan good-bye was unmistakable and definite, spelled out more clearly than if she had written a letter and explained everything. There was a deep thread of feeling running between the two of them, very deep, stretching straight from one heart to the other in a single, unbroken band. Clearly Lady Ellen meant more to Allan than just a beautiful face. Clearly he meant more to her than a passing acquaintance.

And, very clearly, Robin knew there was much more than he knew to the tale of Allan-a-Dale and Lady Ellen de Gant.

The last enemy that shall be destroyed is death.

- *JK Rowling*

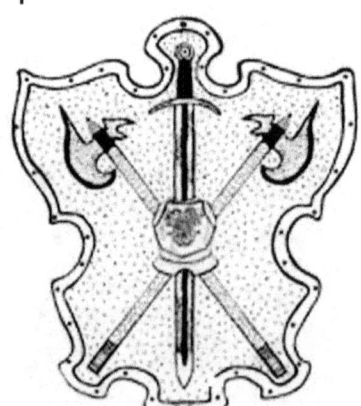

Chapter 12

Allan-a-Dale and the Lady Ellen de Gant

Allan-a-Dale would never forget the first time he saw Lady Ellen de Gant, the one moment he knew he'd found everything in life he could ever hope for. It was a dark night, lit only by lightning that split the sky in random bursts, silence punctuated by the pounding of thunder and pelting of rain on a hard, dirt road. Allan had curled up to wait it out, hiding under the dry, somewhat warm seclusion of a small grove to avoid getting too drenched and therefore any more sick than he already was. The illness that plagued him was mild, having begun creeping in a day or so ago, but it wouldn't take much time out in this weather to make it spiral into something regrettable. It was already showing signs of doing this already.

The rumble of the storm was rather soothing once one became accustomed to it, and it soon lulled Allan into a fitful sleep of sorts, the boughs above him whipping together under a strong wind. He had been asleep maybe an hour before he heard it. A sound. A human sound. Allan sat up and looked around. Only a fool or a ghost would be traveling in a storm such as this, and, although Allan didn't believe in such things as ghosts or goblins, he didn't know too many people who would be wandering around right now, either. It was with no small apprehension that he pulled back a low-hanging branch to peer out over the road.

It was pitch black. He could see nothing. Then, in a sudden flash of lightning, a figure took shape among the emptiness, the shape of a little girl. Even as he watched, the child raised her head and cried a name, her quaking voice little more than a frail strand of sound. The sight was chilling. Water ran in streams down skin that flashed almost pure white under the lightning, her hair was matted around her throat, the small body shaking visibly. Her voice was drifting when she called, floating through the air in the aimless, rambling manner of someone who doesn't know they're even speaking. She was delirious, raging with fever, stumbling around in circles in the middle of the dark, deserted road with a little doll clutched tightly under her right arm. Allan waited until another flash of lightning lit the area, then rushed out to get her, lifting the thin, frail form with ease into his arms before retreating once more out of the storm. But his haven would do the girl little good, and he knew it. She needed a warm bed, a dry room, care by someone who could afford the time.

A glance outside proved it was madness to try and make it through; a glance at the small figure curled up beside him proved he had no choice but to try. The girl was shivering uncontrollably and whimpering, a tangle of dark hair illuminated by flashes of light, green eyes glazed and blinking sightlessly as they wove sporadically around the small space.

Allan knew he had to do something now, get the girl to a place where she would be safe, or she would have no tomorrow. He never thought twice about it. He gathered his few belongings and strapped them to his back, whipping his cloak off to wrap it around the child before picking her gently up in his arms and stepping out into the open. The insanity of what he was doing hit him at once. As did the water. Rain lashed at his face in cold drives, soaking him to the skin before he'd even gone twenty paces. Slowly he struggled through the storm, his precious burden held close to his chest, ignoring the chill and thundering rain as he remembered again and again the sight of that little child wandering in this chaos. The picture alone was enough to drive all thoughts of personal discomfort from his mind. Nottingham was thirty miles away. He could not stop. Time seemed an interminable continuum, an endless circle, something that went on even when it appeared to stop completely.

Allan never knew what caused him to glance up when he did. He never knew what force pulled his head up at just that second in time. The wind was turned toward him, pelting his face with frigid, hard drops of water, but something tugged at his mind. He looked up, to the left, and in that one moment, he saw a light. Then it vanished. Allan stopped. Surely he'd been mistaken. Surely he couldn't be that fortunate. He took a quick step backward, staring into the distance, hoping he was right but certain he'd just fallen victim to a cruel illusion.

There it was again! A tiny, yellow dot of light beyond the trees. Allan wasted not another moment. Fixing his gaze on that small, flickering beacon of hope, he plunged off the road through the woods. He immediately sank up to his ankles in wet earth. He ignored the sensation and strode onward, felt the biting sting of branches slapping his face, the constant shivering of the tiny body in his arms. The light illness that had been plaguing him began to intensify, cold water and air wreaking havoc on his body. His own temperature was beginning to rise. A light dizziness was setting in. His feet were beginning to stumble of their own accord. The light itself seemed to move away, slipping farther into the distance even as Allan moved toward it, but finally he felt the hard, rocky trace of stones under his feet and stumbled through the darkness of a dimly-lit courtyard to reach the front door. His hand was so cold it refused to loosen itself from the tight fist he'd kept it in, and his first attempt at knocking was little more than a muffled tap.

The little girl coughed, her form convulsing with the motion, and Allan raised his hand and pounded on the door. The effort took all the energy he had left. He slouched against the deep frame surrounding the tall, wooden door, resting against the stone. He felt his skin burning up even as the inside of his body turned to ice, felt the heated chills of fever shivering through his entire body. It was about that moment he realized both he and the girl would be lucky to last the night.

The door opened. A girl stepped into sight. Allan was aware only of the clear, crystalline blue of her eyes, widened in shock, looking kindly into his as he held out the trembling shape of the child.

"Please," he said, and his voice was little more than a whisper. "Help the girl..."

The sensation of light brought him around. Allan awoke feeling better, but still very tired, and realized that wherever he was, it was warm and dry. He remembered little about the night before; nothing specific. Slowly, almost loathe to do so, he opened his eyes and looked around, taking in his surroundings. Where was he? This was no servants' quarters. The room around him held all the marks of being inhabited by someone of distinction, yet at the same time was strikingly home-like. As if the "someone" who lived here wanted, above all else, to have a happy household and not just one of plush comfort or empty elegance.

Allan couldn't have said what gave him that exact idea. Perhaps just the way the light filtered so kindly into the room or the graceful, subtle beauty that manifested itself more in atmosphere than actual belongings. The portraits on the walls were simply done, yet not dark or moody; the furnishings modest but obviously made of fine materials; the room itself very charming in an almost rustic kind of way. It was an effect probably added to by the hand-woven carpet in the middle of the floor. Allan was studying that carpet with interest, wondering how it came to be in a place such as this, when the door across the room squeaked a little and opened.

"Good morning," he said.

The young woman he spoke to averted her gaze for a moment, almost embarrassedly, before returning it to his face.

"Good morning," she answered, smiling as she stepped inside. A single dimple pressed inward on her left cheek. She held a bundle of clothes in her arms, which she hugged close in a self-conscious manner, once again looking away.

Allan realized suddenly that this was no servant he was speaking to, but rather a lady of the house. Her entire appearance proved it. Her hair was pulled back in a simple bun, a few blonde curls loose and falling around her face, shining in the sunlight that streamed unashamedly through the window. She was dressed in the attire of the upper class, but like the room in which Allan had found himself, it was not ostentatious. Rather, it was a simple extension of her natural beauty, adding to it subtly as a tier of clouds would complement a gorgeous sunset. For hers was far more than mere physical loveliness, but rather a charm that stemmed from deep within her heart, a kindness and compassion evident in her eyes and voice and movement, that gave her an almost radiant splendor. Allan knew it was the beauty of love he saw before him. The beauty of a woman who loved without vice.

"Where am I?" He asked as she approached.

"This is my home," was the response. "I am Lady Ellen de Gant."

Lady Ellen de Gant...

Allan wasn't sure if the surprise he felt was actually visible on his face. He had heard the stories pertaining to Lady de Gant, though he'd never seen her before this; tales of her beauty and kindness and loyalty; the unbiased attitude she presented to all she met, regardless of class. She was known as a friend of the people. Clearly it was so.

"How long have I been here?"

"Three days," Lady Ellen said, and set the bundle of clothing by the bed. She looked at him without hesitation now. "Might I know your name?"

"Allan-a-Dale."

She repeated it silently, to herself, seeming to try it on for size, as she reached over to lay a gentle hand on his forehead.

"Thankfully your fever has broken. You gave me quite a fright, Allan-a-Dale," she said seriously. "I thought we might lose you." Her voice was soft as her hand, cool and quiet, like a brook rippling peacefully over the rocks.

"How is the little girl?"

"Well. She is still weak, but getting better by the day." Lady Ellen studied him thoughtfully. "It was a very noble thing you did," she said. "Most would have been too afraid for their own lives to worry about hers. Where did you find her?"

"Wandering in the road," Allan said. "Did she say where she came from?"

"No. She only tells me that her name is Alexis, and she has no family here."

"Surely she has someone."

Ellen placed her hand by his shoulder and leaned over him with a caring smile, brushing her fingers through his hair.

"Do not worry about her, Allan-a-Dale," she said softly. "She is safe. Rest now. I will be here if you need me."

Allan found no answer. He wished for all the world the two of them could stay right where they were, for he could spend the rest of his life staring into the eyes of Lady Ellen de Gant and still be the happiest man in existence.

"Lady de Gant," he said quickly as she reached the door. "How is it you came to care for me instead of another? I am but a humble minstrel."

She turned slowly to face him, her eyes pensive.

"Humble minstrel or gallant knight," she said, "I do not find the two so very different."

"You didn't know me."

"No... but I knew what you had done. That was enough."

As she stepped outside and quietly closed the door behind her, Allan lay there staring at the ceiling above his head. He knew nothing about Lady Ellen de Gant, really; only what he'd heard from others over the course of a conversation or two. He never went out of his way to dig up facts concerning those of a higher class. Studying aristocracy wasn't something he took particular delight in. There were some, however, who reveled in it, and they were the ones from whom he'd learned the basics. Allan didn't know about all of it. Some of the things he heard were fairly far-fetched. He did know Lady Ellen was incredibly beautiful, kind, and must be an exceptionally special woman to care for all as she did. She had not the smallest clue of who he was, yet without hesitation she had taken him in, helped him heal, treated him as one of equal class.

That was something worth telling. Allan was still thinking about it as he drifted off.

When he awoke the second time, he was completely rested. His body felt alive again, renewed, not used and flat like an old, miller's flour sack as it had before. For a moment he didn't want to open his eyes, afraid he might find he was only dreaming last time and would find himself lying on the floor of a drafty barn or underneath the rustling branches of a small grove. He was almost afraid Lady Ellen might be a dream. But everything was just as he remembered when he looked around, and Allan allowed himself a smile.

The faint sound of music met his ears. Allan listened for a moment to the harmony of a quiet, cultured voice and a mild instrument, immediately recognizing the sound of his lute as its melody drifted in. He would know it anywhere. Rising silently, he slipped into his clothes, which had been cleaned, and walked out into a long hallway, turning to the left to follow it closer to the strumming music.

The hall opened into a large room. As soon as Allan took a step inside, he suddenly knew without a doubt that he was in the house of a noblewoman. The contrast was so apparent it was remarkable. Filled with the elegance of the day, this place was made to impress, and made to impress important people. A large fireplace took up half the wall of one side, the fire within sending orange light shimmering around the room, dancing off the walls and tapestries and furnishings that were the marvel of modern life.

Lady Ellen sat with her right side to him, the lute across her lap, strumming it with skillful fingers as she sang along. Her hair was down, falling over her shoulder and reaching almost to her waist, its smooth waves light and shining. She handled the lute like she knew what she was doing. Her fingers found with ease familiar angles and chords known only to those who have spent much time with an instrument, and her voice was clear, sweet, blending perfectly with the melody of an old ballad Allan hadn't heard since he was a kid. It had been one of his favorites back then.

He leaned against the door and listened without a word, not wanting to interrupt, reluctantly taking his eyes off of Lady Ellen to place them on the little girl she sang to. He knew her at once. This was the girl he'd found on the road, the one Ellen said called herself Alexis. She was much different than when he last saw her; the green eyes were sparkling like a pair of emerald stars, her hair was combed and smooth and done up nicely, and she had a good color about her face that came from being taken care of well.

Alexis was completely mesmerized by the music. She sat as if transfixed, staring wide-eyed at the way Ellen's fingers worked the lute, bringing each sound to life as her voice gave life to the words. It was a few minutes before Alexis noticed Allan standing in the doorway. When she did see him, her face lit up in a bright smile.

"Are you the one who saved me?"

The question brought an abrupt end to the music. Lady Ellen jumped visibly and spun around, setting the lute aside in the same instant as she apologetically sought Allan's face.

"I'm sorry," she said. "I didn't mean to –"

"Don't be," Allan said quietly, and turned to the girl. "Are you Alexis?"

She nodded.

"Then I'm the one who brought you here," Allan said with a smile. "Although I think you would have to credit Lady de Gant more than I." He looked back at Ellen. "You play beautifully," he added. "I haven't heard that ballad in years."

"Thank you," was the shy response. Lady Ellen hurriedly twisted her hair into a bun and stood up. "I had an excellent teacher," she said as she finished. "My grandfather loved the lute. He always said if the world weren't so complicated, he would like nothing better than to give it all up and become a minstrel, wandering the earth from end to end just so he could see to it all men knew the joy of music. I believe he meant it."

"It's not a bad life," Allan said. "Things take on an entirely new perspective." He glanced around curiously.

"I don't like it much either," Lady Ellen said, reading his thoughts. "But people expect things... They want to see the residence of nobility, and my father delights in such things." She held a hand out to the little girl beside her, and Alexis took it happily in both of hers, like it had been a long time since a hand was extended her.

"Lady Ellen said you found me in the storm," she said.

Allan knelt down in front of her.

"I did," he said. "It was fortunate we happened to be in the same area that night. Tell me, Alexis, where is your family?"

"I have no family here," she said quietly, still holding Ellen's hand.

"Have you no siblings, no mother or father?"

Alexis shook her head.

"I've been alone for a year. My brother went with the soldiers, and mother and father both died of fever."

How she had survived for a year on her own, Allan had no idea. He didn't ask.

"Lady Ellen said I could stay with her until my brother comes home," Alexis continued. "Will you stay, too?"

Allan would like nothing better. But he knew the impossibility of such an action, and knew he had better be moving along as soon as he could. He was about to explain when Lady Ellen cut him off.

"You most certainly are," she said primly. "At least for a while. I don't want you to get sick again after all the pains I took to see you through." She smiled and played gently with Alexis' long curls. "We were about to go have some breakfast," she added. "Would you care to join us?"

On second thought, Lady Ellen decided she'd only let him come along if Allan promised to stay. Allan finally agreed. Truthfully, he didn't take much convincing; with Ellen's father gone for a month to London and not due back for another two weeks, the opportunity was just too easy to take, no matter what his mind and good, old-fashioned logic were telling him. In the end, Alexis and Lady Ellen had their way. He stayed.

The following days were probably the fastest he'd ever experienced. And the happiest. Alexis continued to get better, day by day growing stronger and more precocious, becoming the child she should have been instead of the tiny adult she was. She loved the lute. Allan would sit with her by the hour, singing and teaching her old songs, teaching Alexis how to use the instrument itself. The girl was a natural musician, and her skill never ceased to impress Allan. It all came so easily for her, so simply, it was almost like she had been taught the whole lot already and was just taking a refresher course from him. The lute was as comfortable in her hands as air in her lungs, a song as natural on her lips as the beat of her heart. She was good at everything she did and was willing to try anything; one of those rare, once-in-a-lifetime people to whom living is a grand adventure and every failure is simply a much bigger triumph waiting to happen. It was this attitude that had kept her alive.

Alexis loved horses, Allan soon found out, and when the music was absent, one was more likely to find her in the stables than anywhere else, conferring with the beautiful animals belonging to Lady Ellen's father. She had her own, pet names for all of them, and took special interest in the care of a sleek, grey mare called Isabel. She wasn't all talk, however. Put her on any one of those spirited creatures and she would stay there. No matter how high it pranced or how fast it ran, Alexis was at home on the back of a horse. And, to Allan's surprise, so was their hostess.

Ellen de Gant was a living contradiction. In public she was a lady, aristocrat incarnate, exactly what anyone would expect from a woman of noble bearing. In private she was completely different. Still very much a lady, yes, but different. She became an Ellen unhindered by society, untouched by flattery or façade, an Ellen unafraid to take chances. The faster the horse or the more dangerous the situation, the better she liked it. She admitted concealing such secrets from the people she knew, and many of them considered her to be somewhat sheltered, soft, a woman with little sense of adventure.

"If only they knew," she would say with a smile.

Allan did know. He rather liked it. As the days flew by and Alexis kept improving, the time they spent indoors lessened. Riding became an almost daily pastime, one that had a tendency to last all day, as well. Ellen would take the lead, guiding them to some unknown, obscure corner she frequented as a girl, and there they would stop; she and Allan and Alexis, three tiny figures among the majesty of untouched territory.

Allan had traveled a lot over the years. He had seen some beautiful country, been to many exotic places. But somehow, none of them could compare with what he saw and heard on those rides; the muffled beating of hooves on damp earth, the music of laughter, the whisper of the wind. If there was a heaven on earth, he figured he had found it.

But, of all the memories he had of those times, it was his relationship with Lady Ellen that Allan held most dear. He recalled every moment he spent at her side, listening to her laughter and watching the poised grace of her movements; talking about things of great importance, talking about nothing at all. The easy companionship that stretched between them made it seem like they'd known each other for years, and Allan thought equally of her as a friend as he did a woman. With each day that passed he came to appreciate her more; admire her independence and respect her kindness, value her as a person. It had been immediate infatuation the first time he saw her. Their time together turned it into a true and genuine love.

Allan remembered long talks sitting by the fire at night, telling her about his life and listening to Ellen describe hers; remembered how much he enjoyed getting to know her better, how much he just enjoyed her company. He remembered little moments, sweet gestures; her hand brushing his as they walked through the stables or the way her eyes sparkled so happily when they were together. He remembered the first time he kissed her, under an apple tree by the river, how he had turned away from the rippling waters to find her watching him with an expression of such tenderness, he couldn't have resisted even if he wanted to. He had reached up to touch her hair, brush it from her face, and then he kissed her, very gently, his fingers trailing lightly across her cheek. She didn't pull away.

And for that one moment, that small space in time, Allan allowed himself to think this could be it. Ellen was the reason he kept going all those years, over the next knoll and through the next field, waited out the next rainstorm; she was the reason he had continued to wander through the countryside with nothing more than the clothes on his back and the worn lute in his hands, waiting, always waiting, for something he didn't understand. He had, at last, found his way home.

Reality set in right on time, exactly two days before Ellen's father was set to return. A rider arrived in the early evening, announcing the impending arrival of Lord de Gant sometime the following day. The way he had surveyed Allan as he spoke and hinted, very tactfully, that Ellen should have the estate prepared for her father's arrival, brought the world into sharp focus for Allan in a way he couldn't have imagined. This was the day he had been subconsciously dreading, one that kept coming back to nag him even as he pushed it from his mind over the past weeks. He was in love with a woman he knew as Ellen. The rest of the world knew her as *Lady* Ellen; a member of the upper class, sophisticated, a lady of quality.

Allan was a minstrel. A wanderer. A peasant. If it hadn't been for the extraordinary events surrounding Alexis, they would never have met. And no one would accept those events as a plausible explanation; not Ellen's friends, her family, and most certainly not her father. Discouraging as it was, this was reality; the reality of their situation, their positions, of the world in which they lived. It was the day Allan knew he had to leave.

The morning was cold and damp, echoing the chill in Allan's heart as he rose and began packing his few things. He tied them in a small bundle and tucked them under his arm, plucking his lute from where it rested by the bed. His fingers slid over the strings, causing the little instrument to sing softly, and Allan clenched it tightly, almost angrily, his hand silencing the music as he stepped through the door.

He met Ellen in the hallway. She smiled when she saw him, started to speak, then took in the rest of the scene. She looked at the bundle under his arm, the lute in his hand, the resignation on his face; and in those moments, all traces of joy vanished. Her eyes lost their luster as she gazed at him, her hands fell to her sides, and she quietly turned away to walk away without a word, her footsteps hollow and cold as they resounded in the empty space.

Allan heard her break into a run just out of sight. He didn't try to stop her; nothing he could say would comfort her, for there was nothing to say. He didn't wake Alexis to say good-bye. She wouldn't understand well enough to know why he had to leave, and it would only make it harder on her. And him. He bid her farewell as she slept, stroking her soft cheek, tracing a tendril of hair from her eyes. He would miss her. Very much. Alexis was the closest thing to a daughter he'd ever known, or probably ever would know, and to leave her was leaving a piece of himself.

Ellen was waiting for him when he came back. Her face was still, calm, but traces of tears remained in her eyes. She said not a word as she walked with him to the door, holding his hand tightly in both of hers, her every motion begging him not to leave her despite the assertions of logic that it was only proper. Allan stopped on the doorstep. He turned to face her slowly, trying to sum up an apology for what he was about to do, but it eluded him, fluttering out of reach like a leaf blowing in the autumn wind. He didn't know what to say.

"Must you go?" Ellen asked at last, very softly.

Allan just nodded. He had no words to tell her why. They both knew them all already. Those words would make sense to some, but they had no bearing here, nor were they even welcome. Mere words fell far short when it came to matters of the heart.

"I'll – I'll see to it Alexis has a good home until someone comes for her," Ellen ventured. She was stalling for time.

"I know you will." Allan wanted to say something. He wanted so desperately to say something, something meaningful and unforgettable, something that would touch Ellen's heart and let her know how felt. But even his poetic streak failed him, rendering him only a man in love, a man who was about to lose the one love of his life. "Good-bye, Ellen," he said simply. He turned away reluctantly, loathe to leave but driven to it nonetheless, and started slowly across the courtyard. It was going to be a long walk. He could feel her eyes on him, calling him back, could hear her voice, see her face lingering before him as does a lovely reflection on the surface of the water.

The edge of courtyard was as far as he got. He heard Ellen whisper his name, heard a muffled sob come from her throat, and it was more than he could take. He couldn't leave like this. What a fool he was to think he could! Allan turned and dashed back, running across the hard stones, and dropped to his knees at Ellen's feet.

"Lady Ellen de Gant," he whispered as he took her hands, bowing his head to rest his forehead against the cool of her fingers. "There is nothing I can say that makes this right. But I want you to know... that no matter where this life takes me, my heart will always be yours. I swear it."

Tears slipped silently into her eyes as she reached out to touch his face.

"And mine will be yours, Allan of the Dales," she answered softly. "Until the end of the world."

It had been two years since that day, two years since Allan had turned and walked away from the woman he loved. He still regretted it. He had never forgotten. He had traveled many miles since then, seen many dark, stormy nights like the one that first brought them together, thought many times of what it might have been like had he stayed by her side. He supposed he'd never know. He had seen Lady Ellen in passing, heard her mentioned in idle conversation... today was the first time he'd spoken to her. Her voice was just as he remembered, just as clear and sweet, still as full of love as it had been the day they parted. He could see she still cared. He hoped she could sense the same about him. Allan would never forget the days he spent in her company, the few, short days that were the happiest he'd ever known.

Until the end of the world.

It was a long time. And, seeing her today, Allan knew she meant it.

****

Robin could tell there was a great deal more on the mind of Allan-a-Dale than the tune he was idly creating. He had a fairly good idea of what it was. He kept his mouth shut, however, concentrating instead to the lazy clopping of hooves on dirt, the strumming of the lute behind him, the wind in the trees. Allan could keep his secret safely tucked away without fear.

That wasn't good enough for Jasmine.

"This Lady Ellen holds a special place in your heart, Allan-a-Dale," she said in satisfaction, more as a statement of fact. "And you in hers."

A string suddenly plucked off-key over Robin's left shoulder.

"She has been kind to me," Allan said. "She took me in when I was no more than a stranger."

Robin smiled. He would give up his inheritance to hear that story.

"Lady Ellen seemed to me unhappy," Jasmine said. "I know she smiled and – how do you say... put on a cheerful face, but her eyes were sad."

Robin had noticed the same thing. He'd thought it was just his imagination until Jasmine confirmed his theory.

"She is unhappy," Allan said. "She is being forced into a marriage of convenience with Sir Guy of Gisbourne."

"*Sir*... Guy of Gisbourne?" Robin questioned indignantly. "The dolt is a *knight* now? I didn't know he could even ride a horse."

"He can't."

Robin didn't need any convincing on that matter. Nor did he need convincing that it would take a spectacular horse, indeed, that was capable of carrying Gisbourne and his three extra chins, plus a full suit of armor.

"Care to explain this rather odd turn of events?" Robin queried curiously.

"It was all just part of the plan." Allan slung the lute moodily over his shoulder. "He was knighted a year ago," he added. "The way he acts, you would think there is no other knight in the country." His attitude proved Ellen was not the only one suffering from the intended union.

"What of Ellen's father?"

"He wants it to happen."

"Splendid."

"I never met him," Allan said, "but I guess I had this idea that he had to be a noble man. To be Lady Ellen's father, at least. Now I know better. He is willing to sacrifice his daughter's happiness for his own gain and for the gain of that trifling whelp in London."

"Prince John?"

"He was the one to confer knighthood on *Sir* Gisbourne," Allan said, and Robin glanced at him skeptically.

"Our good Prince John seems to be taking a few liberties with his influence."

"I think they all had their eyes on a marriage between Gisbourne and Ellen for quite some time," Allan added. "It is only one of several. Solidify the base a little more, create a union stronger than mere common interest. Making Gisbourne a knight was just to make it look more probable."

"Who is 'they'?"

Allan didn't answer directly.

"Many things have changed, Robin," he stated sagely. "You will see it before long."

Robin was already beginning to notice a few distinct changes. And very disquieting ones, at that. King Richard's younger brother John – often called John Lackland because of his tendency to get the decidedly shorter end of the lollipop when it came to favors from the queen mother – was actively conferring knighthood upon his own loyal populace, and conferring it upon people like Eustace DeMarke's power-driven cousin. Such an act implied a certain assurance, a certain... confidence... that indicated comfort with one's position. Too much comfort, as a matter of fact. With such an outlook, it raised the question of whether or not one would be willing to relinquish said position to the rightful owner. Somehow, Robin doubted it. Truly this turn of events boded ill; there was nothing good that could come from a man hungry for power finally achieving it, only to have it snatched away again. It promised to be, if nothing else, very interesting.

Robin reined his horse around a fallen branch. He would have to admit he expected a bit of resistance from certain fronts concerning the return of King Richard; fathers and mothers who had lost children in the crusade, bitter aristocrats like Eustace DeMarke, people Richard had offended over the years who were bound to be plentiful... but not from this front. Not from the king's own brother.

Yes, things had changed around here. It was beginning to look like "Good Prince John" was enjoying his role as resident king a little too much.

Chapter 13

Welcome Mats

Jasmine drew up and stared blankly at the scene before her. "What happened? I thought you said it would be vacant."

Moments earlier, they had crested the top of a small knoll, and came into sight of Robin's home. It was far different from what he expected. His assumption that silence, general disarray, and untidiness would be the main features had proven far from correct, and the actual appearance of the place was shocking. The Locksley mansion was alive with activity. Servants tending to the orderly, well-kept grounds, dogs running about, horses stretching elegant heads out of the back of the stables, ears up, staring at the pair of far-off figures on the horizon.

"I thought it *would* be vacant," Robin said, his answer slightly delayed by surprise. "There was nothing left here to keep anyone after my father and I departed."

Or so he had thought. Now it appeared his absence was just the ticket for somebody else to move in and make themselves at home. Aside from the fact that they'd kept the residence in tip-top shape, the concept was rather disconcerting. Robin sighed and absently patted the silky neck of his horse as the animal shifted beneath him. Things were different here. Very different.

They had reached the village of Nottingham by afternoon, and Allan-a-Dale bade them farewell on the outskirts, wishing them well in their quest and promising to start spreading the word about the required ransom. Behind him the town was bustling. As Allan's tall form melted into the gathering, the faint sounds of his lute rising above the activity, Robin cast a long glance over the town and smiled. There was the blacksmith's shop, the livery, the miller's store... it was all there, looking exactly the same as when he'd left. Unfortunately, he couldn't say the same thing for his home. Everyone he knew thought he was dead, and it appeared someone had taken the news very much to heart. Robin pointed to a large flag fluttering in the breeze.

"Look. The colors of Guy of Gisbourne." He dropped his hand to the saddle. "I should have known," he said resignedly. "He and DeMarke have been hovering over my father's shoulder for years like a couple of starved vultures."

And with his father – and supposedly Robin himself – now gone, the two cousins had wasted no time in setting up shop.

"What are you going to do?"

Jasmine's question was curious, and Robin just shrugged.

"Make myself known," he said. "They'll hear about it soon enough."

The two horses moved forward on command, trotting easily down the long, sloping incline toward the manor. The activity never lessened. A pair of carts thundered by to rumble purposefully into the courtyard, filled with foods and various manufactured goods. They were immediately swamped with bodies for unloading. A fancy carriage stood idly off to the side, by the stable wall, obviously soon to be in use.

A stable boy was the first to notice the visitors. He had emerged from the stables with a tall, dappled mare and was leading her toward the idle carriage when he saw the pair of horses coming his way, and turned to call out behind him. The news spread quickly. By the time Robin and Jasmine clattered into the courtyard, everyone on the Locksley estate was aware of their presence.

Including the trio of guards keeping watch at the front door. "Keeping watch" being a term used quite loosely, of course, as it seemed their true job was lounging on the steps, sharing a barrel of ale that sat between them and eyeing several of the female servants as the girls passed by. At the sight of the advancing horses, the biggest of the three set down his mug and swaggered forward. Beneath the helmet he wore, Robin could see a sprinkling of unkempt, red hair, matching a beard that stuck abruptly out of the chin. The guard held up a hand.

"State your business and be brief," he said brusquely, placing gloved hands on his hips. He looked at Jasmine. "Unless you'd care to start," he added, eyeing her openly.

"I wish to speak with Guy of Gisbourne," Robin answered without preamble.

"I'm sorry, his lordship is very busy." The guard wasn't even looking at him.

"I can see he is. Fixing this place for my return must be quite time consuming," Robin said smoothly, and an arrogant gaze was immediately directed at him.

"*Your* arrival," the guard said with a chuckle, and glanced amusedly over his shoulder. "And just who might you be, mate?"

"Does the name Locksley seem at all familiar?"

Apparently it did. The smile left faster than if it had been erased. Urgently he looked behind him again, this time seeking support from his cohorts, but they were as taken aback as he.

"John... fetch his lordship," the first said at last, prompting the smallest of the three to open the door and disappear.

"Thank you," Robin said placidly. The look of absolute astonishment before him was just too good to let go. "Was I not expected?" He asked in his best innocent tone, and saw Jasmine lower her face to cover a smile.

"Yes – uh, no –" The guard gave up and shrugged, his attitude doing a complete about-face. "My apologies... I was never told to expect anyone. I was told you were..."

"Yes, I am well aware of my supposed status," Robin finished for him. "Tell me, what is your name?"

"Gilderoy Ravens."

"Mr. Ravens, I shall commend you to his lordship for your competent and capable behavior regarding the safety of this door but now..." Robin gazed about. "I believe your presence would be better served elsewhere."

"Yes, sir, I –"

"That won't be necessary, Robert," a new voice said, cutting Ravens off mid-sentence. "I shall see to their placement."

Robin found himself looking into the cool, detached eyes of Sir Guy of Gisbourne, aspirant lord of the manor, as the same gave a quick study to both Robin and Jasmine before seeming to dismiss them both as mere pawns in a much larger chess game. He was clothed in regal attire, clothes suited to what he believed to be his distinguished position, clothes much too fine for the body they adorned. Even in their elegance, they were unable to hide evidence of an ample paunch surrounding Gisbourne's middle, or the pasty, sweaty appearance of his skin and pudgy fullness of his cheeks. Gisbourne was even more repulsive than he had been when Robin left. Just imagining Lady Ellen yoking herself to such a creature was enough to induce a slight gag reaction. Robin put the thought aside and plastered a smile onto his face; one, he was sure, reached no farther than his mouth.

"Gisbourne," he said. "It has been quite some time since I saw you last."

If the man was at all shocked by Robin's sudden – and very alive – appearance, he revealed nothing, matching Robin's phony expression down to the last tooth. The effort turned his face into something resembling a common toad.

"I must admit it is a surprise to see you, Locksley," he said. "My compliments. To return from war is indeed the feat of a man."

Robin left the comment alone. Condescending tone aside, it had all the hallmarks of being a jab at Robin's father, who had not returned and who, Robin knew, Gisbourne had never liked. But if Gisbourne was looking to get a rise, it wasn't going to happen.

"It pleases me to see this estate cared for," Robin said amicably, replacing his preferred remark with something safer.

"It is a good house," Gisbourne answered. "Built well. I enjoy it. And the lands are some of the best I have." Letting Robin digest this last without pause, Gisbourne shifted the topic with his gaze, which had moved to Jasmine. "Who is your lady friend?"

"Jasmine, meet Guy of Gisbourne," Robin said flatly.

"*Sir* Guy of Gisbourne, if you please, Robert," was the immediate correction. He looked Jasmine over carefully. "You are not English, my dear lady," he said. "Where do you come from?"

"I am a Saracen," Jasmine said simply, and Gisbourne turned to Robin with something of a mildly rebuking expression.

"Come, come, Robert. Must you bring their kind into our fair land? Surely you realize we went to war to rid ourselves of such barbarism."

"I didn't see you out there wielding a sword, Guy," Robin said. He was quickly losing the battle with that rise Gisbourne wanted out of him. "And it's *Sir* Robert, if you please," he added.

"Well, well. We have a fellow knight among us. Is there anything we can do for you, *Sir* Robert?" Gisbourne asked. "You have but to ask."

Robin choked down an insulting suggestion that immediately volunteered for active duty.

"I will come to the point," he said. "You have done an excellent job of caring for my land while I have been away, for which I thank you, but your stewardship has met its demise. I am home and can now assume responsibility. You have a month to gather what is yours, which I believe is more than adequate time, and at the end of that month I shall expect you to return to your home. I will compensate you for your trouble, of course."

Gisbourne's smile was even colder than before. But before he could say anything, the door swung open again and a young woman stepped outside. The threatening look immediately disappeared.

"Ah, my lady Ilene," Gisbourne said flatteringly, and extended his hand.

It was accepted gratefully, Lady Ilene blushing slightly as she looked into Gisbourne's eyes, absolute adoration shining in her own. He, in turn, was obviously just toying with her.

"I would like to introduce our guests," Gisbourne said at length.

"Yes! Please do!" Was the delighted answer, and Robin smiled into the direct, friendly gaze pointed his way.

"My lady," he said.

Lady Ilene of Derby was a beautiful woman. Fair of skin and regal of stature, her appearance was made all the more striking by the silken lengths of deep, auburn hair that nearly matched the redwood quality of her eyes. There was kindness in those eyes, yet also a certain amount of shielded ambition, ambition that undoubtedly aided Lady Ilene in keeping up the image she did, even as her family's circumstances descended. Her family was Norman, with lineage stretching as far back as the times of King Arthur. It was even said that one of her ancestors was a knight of Arthur's. Their status was far more humble and less gallant in current times; her father was only a minor nobleman who had inherited his title through blood, and then squandered what money the family did have in a vain and fruitless attempt to elevate his own station. Robin knew Ilene only slightly, for though her family was not above his, they had hardly ever moved in the same circles growing up. Among nobles, the rift between the Normans and Saxons tended to display itself through distance rather than bloodshed.

Lady Ilene was pleasant when Gisbourne introduced her; that she remembered Robin was obvious, and that she was at least intrigued by Jasmine was equally so.

"Your father was killed in the war, was he not, Sir Robin?" Ilene asked at last.

"He was." Robin answered her but he looked at Gisbourne. "It took fifteen men to bring him down, my lady."

"I'm sorry." Ilene's voice was sincere. "I owe your father a good deal," she said. "He offered his assistance to me when the wheel of my carriage broke in the middle of a rainstorm. I might have been out there all night had he not helped."

"He told me of that. It was an honor for him to have assisted you."

Ilene smiled, a surprisingly girlishness slipping into it somehow, and linked her arm through Gisbourne's.

"Sir Guy was to take me to Nottingham," she said, casting another adoring glance in Gisbourne's direction. There was just no telling what people would find attractive. "I do hope we won't encounter any calamities on the way."

"As do I." Gisbourne snatched at the way out and turned to Robin. "Especially since... your father... isn't here to save the day," he added suggestively.

Another dig. Robin kept his mouth shut.

"I apologize that I cannot be more solicitous," Gisbourne continued with assumed dignity, "but Lady Ilene and I were about to depart. It would, of course, be improper for me to turn you away from my door, after what you have undoubtedly been through. You are welcome tonight as my guests. The servants' quarters are –" He started to point, but stopped himself with a condescending expression. "Well, you know where they are," he finished. "And if that does not appeal to you, there is a pair of empty stalls in the stable that should be quite adequate for your needs."

Somehow, the idea of being a "guest" in his own stable was not very appealing.

"Thank you, but I believe we'll continue," Robin said. "Good afternoon to you." He nodded briefly to Lady Ilene. "My lady," he said, and led the way out of the courtyard, cantering across a wide, grassy field before vanishing into the thick woods surrounding the place. Once out of sight, he pulled his horse to a stop and looked back, through the shadows, at the manor still barely visible in the faded sunlight. "Jasmine," he said quietly. "I thought I hated that man before... I didn't even understand the meaning of the word. And to think Ellen –"

The inevitable gag reflex surfaced again as Robin realized exactly what Ellen's marriage would mean, what kinds of vile things she would be committing herself to, all of it safely ensconced under the umbrella of holy matrimony. The thought of Gisbourne even *attempting* to touch her...

Revolting, is what it was. There was only one man worthy of Ellen de Gant. And it sure as hell wasn't Gisbourne.

"So much for a joyful homecoming," Robin muttered. He'd hoped he could get at least *one* good night's sleep at home, even if he was required to share his bed with rats as he'd anticipated.

Jasmine was studying the light beyond the tree-line, her face pensive. Gisbourne had clearly made very little impression upon her aside from being someone to keep a very close eye on, but then, Robin figured she was well accustomed to dealing with people of such a caliber.

"Where do we go now?" She asked.

Robin considered a moment, weighing the options. They needed a place to go, his home was out of the question; time was running out... and he needed help. Robin made a resigned decision.

"There's only one place we *can* go," he said helplessly.

Robin wasn't sure what kind of reception he'd receive from Marian Fitzwalter, nor did he particularly wish to ponder the subject. The options for said greeting ranged from aloof to deadly. He didn't expect much; perhaps a cool smile, a quiet word, maybe nothing at all. All he knew was that it was necessary to see her. Marian was the only one he knew who was close enough to the queen to merit an unannounced entrance, and an unannounced entrance was exactly what Robin needed.

As Marian's home slowly began to some into view over the horizon, he felt the knot in his stomach grow a little larger, and wondered if this was really such a good idea. What would Marian be like now? How would she have changed? Robin hadn't seen her since he left, and that was a long time. Many things could have happened.

Or, worse yet, nothing could have happened at all.

How Marian would react to the news of her brother's fate was uncertain; she had suspicions, yes, but what would she do once she knew for sure? How could Robin even tell her? How would he break this, the most terrible news he could bring, to Peter's sister, especially with Marian hating him as she did? Honestly, he had no idea.

They were let into the courtyard through a pair locked gates by a youngster with a striped tunic and an unruly shock of brown hair who requested that they leave their weapons just inside. His tone was friendly enough. The crossbow he held denoted a greeting of a slightly different nature. The large, wooden gate swung open with a loud creak, and the horses followed along placidly as the two weary travelers walked inside.

Robin took in the familiar scene at a glance, his stomach twisting. It had been this very courtyard that saw his departure, when he left with Peter at his side, going off to a war neither of them was prepared for in the least. Now Robert of Locksley was back. But Peter Fitzwalter would never return. And still, Robin felt as though he was completely unprepared for the road being placed before him.

Lord, I need your advice, he thought silently.

He didn't actually expect a response. It was just habit. And he was right; no answer came. Robin was on his own.

"What do you wish us to do with our horses?" He asked as, with a swish of movement, the young man hopped from on top of the gate and advanced quickly.

"I'll take them," the boy said. "I apologize for any inconvenience, but we have had several uninvited visitors in the last few weeks."

"Uninvited?"

"The sheriff of Nottingham. And others. They've been –"

"Tommy?" A quiet, familiar voice called. "Thank you, I'll see to our guests."

Robin's stomach completed the square knot it was trying to tie itself into. As the boy called Tommy nodded and led the horses off, Robin looked beyond their moving backs toward the manor, his eyes seeking the open door. A woman stood in the gloom there, little more than a blacker image against the darkness, her face invisible for the shadow. Robin knew who it was. And he had a hunch that Marian Fitzwalter was none too pleased to see him.

"Robert of Locksley," she said. The voice was not kind. "I see you have found your way back."

"Hello, Marian," Robin said. "It's been a long time."

Marian Fitzwalter stepped forward slowly, out of the doorway, light sliding in muted shafts up her figure. And Robin knew as soon as he saw her that his previous expectations were far from accurate. "Little Marian" was no longer a child. She was no longer the girl he used to play with. She was a woman, and a beautiful one at that, endowed with grace and poise he had seen in very few places – or on very few people. Her hair had darkened over the years to a color nearly touching black, a contrast made all the more apparent by the cream of her skin and vibrant, sizzling green of her eyes. Robin could only imagine how easily those eyes could shift straight to blue with the right hint of color. Her figure was curvy without being too much so, imparting a willowy elegance fit for royalty, one that would surpass even the most perfecting of opinions.

If Marian noticed the slight look of surprise that crossed his face, however, she ignored it, sauntering casually into the courtyard with her arms hugged lightly to her chest. The expression on her face was tolerant enough, but far from welcoming. Not surprised at all.

"It has been a long time," she said as she reached them. "I believe the last time we met was the day you allowed my brother to accompany you on this suicide trip you called a crusade."

Robin knew he should have expected this; Marian hadn't changed in the least. Subconsciously he prepared for battle. Again.

"He made his own decision," he answered.

"He followed you," Marian said sharply. "He *always* followed you because he respected you." She surveyed him briefly, reading in his eyes what Robin couldn't say aloud. "He's dead, isn't he?"

Robin nodded.

"I should have known," Marian said, her voice edged with bitterness. "It was a fool's hope I entertained that you would look after him." She turned to Jasmine, who, though unknown to her, provided an adequate outlet for anger that had been pent up for a long time. "You may not know it," she added in an enlightening tone, "but you are traveling with a man who has managed to single-handedly take away the two things I held most important in this life, all within five years."

"I know little about him," Jasmine answered in Robin's defense. "Only that he has *given* me the thing I hold most dear. Freedom."

Marian rounded on Robin again.

"And just what is it you want to give me, Robert? Come to pay your penance?"

"I've paid my penance, Marian," Robin said, and he could hear the anger etched into his own voice. "I spent a year locked up with twenty other men who would have gladly given their lives for our king's quest, eleven of whom did, rotting away like rats in a cage while the rest of the army came home without a second thought. I watched men suffer and grow ill with fever, watched their hope slowly fade away until there was nothing left. I have seen war and killing and bloodshed, all of it locked away in my mind forever, never to be removed, never to be forgiven, so believe me when I tell you, Marian, *I have paid my penance.*"

Marian said nothing, regarding him with glinting eyes and lifted chin, the cross dangling from her neck beginning to flash as bright as her anger. The piece caught Robin's eye suddenly, and as soon as he saw it, recognition clicked into place.

"You... you were the second guard at Lady Ellen's carriage," he said.

Marian smiled coolly.

"You are sharper than I thought. Yes, it was I. And it took all of my resolve not to run you through, Robert of Locksley, the moment I saw you. I'm still wondering whether my restraint will pay off." She cocked her head to the side, inquiringly. "So you are a knight now," she added. "How splendid."

"Why were you there?" Robin asked, disregarding her criticism.

"I had some things I needed to do," was the evasive answer, "and Ellen allowed me to come with her. I have learned it does not pay to travel as myself." Marian sighed and uncrossed her arms, her eyes starting to lose their intense fire. "Well. Now that we have adequately reestablished our relationship, what is it you really want, Robert?"

Her voice was suddenly tired, as if she had used all the energy she possessed and just wanted to get this talk over with.

"Marian..." Robin ran a hand through his hair. "I didn't come here expecting a warm welcome from you. I know you hated me the day I left, and I suspected you'd feel the same when I came back. But I want you to know that I did everything within my power to protect your brother. The only reason he is not here now is God's Will deemed otherwise."

Why had he said that? It's not like he believed it.

"Please," Marian said wearily, and held up a hand. "Do not speak to me of God. He no longer dwells in this house."

Robin recalled saying something very similar to himself about three months ago.

"Peter was too young to die," Marian added softly. "All of you were, even the eldest among you. Life is too precious to throw away... it's just very hard to accept that one life is deemed to end before another, a candle to be extinguished in its brightest moments." She traced her fingers over the cross around her neck. "It makes God seem so cold," she said simply. "I wonder sometimes if he even cares."

It was the closest thing to either an apology or an attempt at peace Robin had seen yet. He didn't know which.

"I have heard our king is alive," Marian said suddenly, changing the topic, and Robin grasped the straw with both hands.

"That's why I'm here," he said.

"I see." Marian looked to Jasmine. "And how is it you came to be here?"

Robin and Jasmine took turns explaining the situation and their involvement in it, how they had gotten here, and what Robin had been instructed to do by the duke of Austria. Marian listened intently. Her innate hostility was put aside for the moment, possibly over-ridden by a hint of curiosity. Her face, however, revealed nothing other than the fact she was listening. Robin concluded the tale with a helpless shrug.

"Our very future rests on this moment," he finished. "I need an introduction to the court so I can relay what has happened, and you are the only person I know who can provide one." He looked at her imploringly. "Please, Marian. There may be bad blood between us, but don't let it affect the welfare of our king. Or our country. Their survival is far more important than our petty feud."

Marian was silent. For a moment Robin thought he might have used the wrong words, that she might refuse and tell him to get lost, then Marian nodded tersely, gesturing with a quick motion toward the stables at the far end of the wall.

"There is room for both of you in the stables," she said abruptly. "We will discuss this matter over dinner."

Another stable offer. At least it wasn't his own.

Dinner was a surprisingly civil affair, one in which the subject of the past was strictly avoided. And it was during this time of uneasy peace, that Robin learned a few more interesting – albeit, very troubling – facts about the present state of affairs.

"Before we depart tomorrow, I will give you some better clothes," Marian said, looking carefully over the long robe Jasmine wore. "There is no need for you to wander around in an old cloak any longer. And you, Robert." She turned to him with raised eyebrows. "How long has it been since you last had a decent set of clothing?"

"I lost track," Robin answered frankly.

"Then I will find something for you, as well. I still have some of Peter's things, and I don't imagine you'll find much at your father's house."

"I doubt it," Robin agreed. "Gisbourne isn't quite my size."

"He's no one's size," Marian said dryly, and played idly with a piece of food before her. "I assume you've heard the news, about his supposed bride to be..."

"Yes. He's got great taste, but no class to go with it."

"I have told Ellen time and again she cannot marry that man, but her father insists she should." Marian held her hands up in a helpless gesture. "She'll do as her father wishes, despite the stupidity and despite the danger."

"Danger?"

"Lady Ilene."

Robin nodded. Nothing more needed to be said on the matter. He'd seen the way Ilene looked at Gisbourne, knew already that Ilene was far from being above scenarios of intrigue to achieve her goals. For her to want something that Ellen, as a rival and a Saxon, was going to get just on principle, made for the beginnings of disaster.

"If she's so in love with him, why doesn't Gisbourne marry her?"

"Her family may be old, Robert, but the plain truth is she just hasn't the connections Ellen does," Marian answered. "That's what this is all about. Connections, power. I believe in this case it has something to do with land; perhaps Ellen's father will get a larger chunk than the rest of them for doing more to help strengthen their power."

Another "them".

"The rest of whom?"

"The committee."

At Robin's blank look, Marian settled down to explain. The committee, according to her, was a group of noblemen who had banded together in the last two years in the hopes of gaining control of the entire area. Guy of Gisbourne and the Sheriff of Nottingham were the leaders, along with Ellen de Gant's father and five or six others who were prepared to use whatever means they deemed necessary to achieve total control. Taxes had been raised to almost three times their original total. Mercenary soldiers provided means to strong-arm people into paying. Anyone who didn't would be put on display in the pillory on the first offense, with a second offense bringing a jail sentence and a confiscation of land, which would then be divided among the committee. Some were in such straits they were unable to buy food. And Sherwood Forest, the place many a young lad had hunted over the years, was suddenly off limits. Only the land of Maud de Caux, a wealthy widow with extensive holdings in the forest, remained open to hunting.

"But it is only a matter of time before even it is seized," Marian concluded. "They will find an excuse." She laughed softly, but without a stitch of humor. "It's ironic, really," she said. "Without the sheriff, this committee would just fade away. None of the others have what it takes to keep it going without him."

Robin fiddled with a piece of chicken.

"Your boy Tommy said something today," he said, "that I didn't quite understand. He said the sheriff had been paying visits here. What does he want?"

Marian sighed heavily.

"What has he always wanted from me?" She asked resignedly. It was more of a rhetorical question, but Robin still didn't get the connection.

"Always?" At Marian's quick look, he completed the thought. "*Always*... wanted from you?"

"You mean you don't know? The sheriff of Nottingham is Eustace DeMarke."

Eustace DeMarke. The man who had seen fit to remove from the picture the one love of Marian's life simply over the desire for power, was now the sheriff. Head of the notorious committee. They had this place under their thumbs so it seemed, DeMarke and his little band of power brokers. He had total control, had all the local power he could possibly want... and he had been coming around here. Hunting expedition, more than likely, trying to charm Lady Marian into accepting his ever-present proposals before he inevitably resorted to more drastic measures. Perhaps this was what Allan meant when he said: "It is only one of several." Ellen and Gisbourne, Marian and DeMarke... two of the most well-connected young ladies in the region being used as veritable pawns.

"Is that why you travel in disguise?"

Marian just nodded, staring at the table.

"How does this committee enforce their laws?" Robin asked. "I know DeMarke has soldiers, but a power play such as this would take..."

"Hundreds," Marian finished for him as Robin paused. "DeMarke thought of that, as well. He's turned his manor into a garrison and houses over three hundred men there, and about one hundred horses. I've been told he has enough torture machines to start a business. He keeps it all very spiritual, of course; Cardinal Warwick has made a habit of taking regular swings through the place. It makes DeMarke look good." She buried her fingers in her hair, brushing it back from her face. "I hate him," she stated flatly. "He comes here with his flowers and sweet words... but I am not such a fool as he thinks." She looked up suddenly from where her gaze had been fixed on the wood grains of the table. "The flowers and words are just a guise. He pressures me and makes threats. Nothing outright, of course, just subtle things. Little things. I had no idea the lust for power could drive a human to such extremes. But," she concluded, "DeMarke sees me as his opportunity. And he will stop at nothing to press the advantage."

Jasmine had watched the exchange in silence, but now rested her forearms on the table and leaned forward intently.

"Then you must press back, my lady," she said. "Give Robert what he needs and take him to your queen."

There was a slight nod, one half of resignation and half acceptance, before Marian went back to the food before her, deep in thought. There was quiet after that, broken only by the sounds of servants coming to and fro, plates being cleaned, the occasional scuffle of noise outside. All that needed to be said had been already. When the meal was finished, Marian saw them both to the door, holding it open with a delicate palm as Robin and Jasmine stepped outside.

"I will take you to Queen Eleanor," she said. "Our king's return is the only hope. Prince John is a helpless whelp whose sole calling in life is amassing riches, ignoring the plight of the people. He will do nothing to stop DeMarke or your Sir Guy of Gisbourne. It wouldn't surprise me at all if he were connected with them somehow." A slight smile crept into her eyes. "It appears you, now, hold the only hope for our nation, Robert," she said, and stepped back into the shadows. "Be ready. We leave at first light."

With that, she closed the door, and Tommy led them to their accommodations. The stables proved quite comfortable, actually, cared for well by someone who seemed to prefer the words "cleanliness" and "horses" to be in the same sentence, and the pair of stalls Robin and Jasmine chose to bed down in were tidy enough to rival the insides of most houses.

Robin stretched out with a tired sigh, glad to be off his horse and off his feet. He knew he should keep thinking, as he had not yet given much consideration to what he would actually say to Queen Eleanor when he met her; had nothing prepared. He had breezed along to this point, assuming his love for king and country and Eleanor's own happiness at hearing that her son was alive would carry the whole conversation. The more he thought about it, the more he realized it would not be so. There would be questions, accusations;

if not the queen herself, then certainly members of the court who were present. Robin had to be ready to defend himself.

But, at the moment, his mind refused to defend itself against anything more serious than a wandering bed bug. Robin snuggled deeper in the thick hay, under the blanket he had draped over his body, and prepared to enjoy the first real night of sleep he'd had in quite some time. He was just about to drift off when Jasmine's voice reached him from the next stall over.

"You were right," she said sleepily.

"About what?"

"She doesn't like you."

Robin rolled his eyes.

"Thank you," he said.

It was nothing more than he anticipated, of course, the reaction he'd gotten from Marian. Less, actually, considering he was still alive. But her bitterness alone was not what bothered him. It was the underlying sense of hostility he'd found in the entire country. Robin hadn't expected a warm welcome in the true sense of the term; not from Marian or anyone else, but what he received was not exactly expected, either. Instead of a country waiting with bated breath for news of their king, he found a place cold and detached, devoid of life, of love, devoid of everything except corruption. It was as if the people had decided to simply buckle down and deal with the trials put upon them; like they considered the tyrannical rule imposed by a couple of noble thugs simply another adjustment, and all they had to do was endure this new way of life they'd been given and just hope they could eventually learn to cope well enough to make it tolerable.

It was as if England itself had lost all hope for happiness. Robin determined right then and there that he would help them get it back.

Chapter 14

Opposing Forces

"Her highness, Queen Eleanor."

The distinct announcement was followed by the sound of whispering cloth as all assembled bowed low, eyes lowered respectfully as Queen Eleanor of Aquitaine entered the large room. She was a tall woman, proud, regal as the title she bore. Her hair was silvery and thick, twisted into a bun that was pinned sharply at the back, below the bottom edge of the ornate, gold crown that rested peacefully atop her head. The clothing she wore only increased one's immediate impression of authority. Detailed and intricate, it defined the term "royalty" and lent a commanding aspect to her appearance.

Eleanor nodded in appreciation as the court rose to their feet, then slowly sat on the large, engraved throne behind her. She had come here tonight because her presence had been specifically requested. Although she still carried the title of queen, Eleanor's status was purely that of a figurehead; mother to the true leader. She did not rule the country. Rather, that responsibility belonged to Richard, and, with his death, had fallen to her younger son, John. As such, it was with no small amount of curiosity that Eleanor learned neither the presence of her son nor his wife Isabella had been sought. Only Isabella's bodyguard, Lady Gwen, was in attendance, and Eleanor could not find her face in the crowd. Casting a quick glance over the people, she turned her attention to the task at hand. Before her, several steps below, was the reason she had come; or rather, the pair of reasons: two men who knelt silently, awaiting their summons to speak. Eleanor did not know who they were. She did not know what brought them here. She knew only that they had been on this last crusade with her eldest son, a mission ending in captivity when their ship went to the bottom of the sea, along with several of its sisters.

The brief hope that this visit might possibly be about Richard entered Eleanor's mind, but she dismissed it just as quickly. Richard was dead, swallowed up by the sea, his body never found. Even the rumors she'd heard since then could not dispel the truth of his fate from her mind. Rumors were always present; they were hardly ever true. She surveyed the men below her with shrewd eyes. What could they want with her that was so important? She could see little, just unclear features, as the sun had long since faded from a dark sky, and the room was lit only by torches and candles, creating a somewhat shadowed, if elegant, setting. But Eleanor was nothing if not a reader of people, and she could sense before her a certain sense of loyalty, a loyalty lacking in many of the members of her own court.

What had happened to the men between the dreadful shipwreck that cast them adrift and the present moment was unknown to her, but the state of both the messenger and the young man who knelt silently by his side was evidence enough. The messenger was young and slim, with a maturity about him that came from long days filled with battle and bloodshed, sleepless nights of watchfulness, and a long stretch of imprisonment. His face was lined with fatigue, his eyes with bitterness, but he was here, ready to serve his country yet again. His companion was smaller, hooded and cloaked, kneeling silently with his hands in front of him. In his hands he held a jeweled box, clasped shut in the front with a solid gold catch.

Eleanor sat back and studied them.

"Speak," she said quietly.

The taller of the two, holding a long sword in his hands, rose to his feet and took a step forward, a pair of grey eyes emphasized with sudden clarity in the candlelight.

"Your Highness," he said. "We come on behalf of our king."

***

Robin couldn't tell whether Queen Eleanor believed him or not, but she said nothing either way, so he kept talking, thanking his lucky stars that Leopold of Austria had miscalculated the impact Blondel's discovery of King Richard would have on the queen and her faithful subjects. Had the duke known of the cynicism and distrust that pervaded this country, Robin doubted he would be standing here right now. He told Eleanor of his imprisonment and that of his men, how Leopold finally came to get him and placed in his hands this mission. Jasmine was silent beside him, secure in her disguise, the cloak draped loosely over clothes given to her by Marian. Robin himself was in a tunic belonging to Peter, one Marian had unceremoniously thrust into his hands this morning before they left.

"I will not take you to the queen dressed like that," she had said. "Put it on."

And so, here he was, speaking to a member of the highest authority in the land, and he didn't know if she even believed him.

"Surely Your Highness heard the rumor," he ventured at last. "The rumor that Blondel found your son in the dungeons."

"I heard it," Eleanor answered evenly, speaking for the first time since Robin began. "But I am not in the habit of believing tales told by rambling troubadours. Blondel is a minstrel. A wandering musician. Many ballads may be composed of such news, and he would have much to profit by it."

"He would," Robin agreed. "And it is easy to understand why you overlooked his words. But they are true, Your Highness. I saw your son myself before I left."

Movement caught his eyes from behind the throne, and Robin glanced over momentarily. A pair of figures stood in the shadows there, disguised in darkness, the one on the right tall and wiry, the other shorter, more stocky. It was this second outline that gave himself away. He did nothing rash, nothing to set himself apart, but the small crown glinting on his head defied discretion. It shone dully from a ray of light that managed to find its way into that forgotten corner of the room, light that danced in flickering shades from its solid surface.

Eleanor had been regarding Robin wordlessly from her position, but now tilted her head to side curiously.

"And who are you, young man, to see my son?"

"My name is Sir Robert of Locksley."

"And how do we know that?" The shorter shadow behind the throne moved, and Prince John stepped into the light, eyebrows raised expectantly. "How do we know you are not another fortune hunter, if you will, ready to capitalize on my brother's adversity?"

A few scattered mumbles of agreement sounded throughout the room. So here it was, the session of probing questions Robin had prepared himself for.

"What proof have you that my brother is alive?" John continued.

"I have in my possession the seal of Leopold of Austria–"

"And how hard would it be to steal such a trinket?" John broke in. "Leopold is blind as a newborn mouse."

As another ripple of agreement floated about like leaves on a stream, Eleanor of Aquitaine said nothing in reaction to her son's behavior, her countenance displaying a sharp interest in Robin's response. She wanted to see how well his argument stood up to criticism. She wanted to see if he was for real. Only then would she see fit to find truth in his words. And so, Robin looked to her with his answer.

"Your Highness," he said. "As I was about to say, I have in my possession the seal of the duke. *As well as...* the seal of your son." He looked directly at Prince John as he said the last, and, reaching to his left into the box Jasmine had just flipped open, retrieved both pieces. At the appearance of the king's seal, the face of Queen Eleanor took on a look of complete shock. Someone behind Robin gasped audibly, someone else muttered in a suspicious tone, the rest were dead silent.

"May I see that?" Eleanor asked, and her voice was suddenly very soft.

Slowly, Robin advanced and knelt before her.

"I'm telling you the truth," he said softly. "I would not be here if I weren't."

The eyes of the queen met his for a brief instant, looking hard, before she accepted the pair of seals from his hands. Robin held his breath. For a moment, nobody said a word while Eleanor gazed carefully at the medallions in her hands, her eyes thoughtful, her face unreadable. Finally, she nodded.

"I believe you," she said, and Robin smiled.

"Thank you, Your Highness."

"What must we do for his return?"

Robin was about to answer when he was interrupted.

"Have you all lost your sanity?" Prince John demanded, and took to the floor. He could see his own ship of power sinking, quite rapidly, and sitting around to watch it go under was not his style. He was not quite ready to give up on the issue. "I see he has you convinced," he said knowingly, striding out into the center of the room. "All of you. You too, Mother. A few well-spoken words, a pair of seals any fool could take or replicate on a whim, and he has your full and undivided attention. Ask yourselves, what comes next? A ransom. My brother is *supposedly* being held prisoner by the Duke of Austria, who, naturally, will release him for a price. A price that, more than likely, will go straight into this man's pockets while the issue remains unresolved!" He spun around and pointed to Robin. "How do we know he's not lying? How do we know my brother is even alive? Anyone? Is there *anyone* who can vouch for the word of this... this *boy*?"

"I can."

The response was quiet, but it carried in the silent openness of the room. Robin glanced to his left, at Jasmine, who looked back at him in surprise from underneath the long hood she wore, before they both turned as the crowd parted and Marian stepped to the front. She curtsied quickly and smiled at Queen Eleanor, a smile that was instantly returned. The action caught Prince John completely off guard. He just stood there staring.

"Your Highness," Marian started. "I want you to know firstly that I have no reason to protect this man. I have no reason to lie for his benefit. The only reason I am defending him now is because he tells the truth, and I want to see his words acted upon. Your son Richard is alive. Our *king* is *alive*. This is a day our whole country has been waiting to hear of, and now that it has finally come, we treat it with skepticism and contempt, choosing to hear with our minds instead of our hearts." She looked quickly to Robin. "I know Robert," she added. "He and I grew up together, and I know how much he loves his king, and his country. He and my brother followed your son to the Holy Land that they might make a difference in this world, so that they might serve King Richard to the best of their ability. My brother is dead, Your Highness. He died serving his country. Robert spent a year in prison on the same account, and it was a year that changed him very much from when he was a boy. He has no reason to lie. I knew him then and I see him now... and I know he has seen and heard things that most people in this room would shudder to even think about. Yet he is here again, because he believes. Your Highness... I ask you humbly to accept what he tells you, for it is the truth."

She curtsied again, quickly, then looked to Robin with an inquiring expression, asking him wordlessly if she had been convincing. Robin thought so, but it wasn't up to him. Eleanor was still clearly a bit uncertain. She wanted to believe the news about her son, wanted to believe what Marian said. But she couldn't forget the warning that all of this might be an elaborate, cash-motivated hoax.

"Does anyone here see any reason why this man cannot be trusted?" She asked finally.

There were a couple of malcontents, but the general consensus that rumbled through the crowd was positive. Robin looked around him and saw many varying expressions, some of skepticism and some of confidence, some of suspicion and some of trust, but no matter the appearance, they all had one thing in common: a thin ray of hope.

Eleanor took it all in and smiled.

"What are the terms, Sir Robert?"

They would be departing shortly. It was early morning, still damp and cool, but the day gave the impression it would be quite nice later on. Robin had left his meeting with the queen yesterday a near hero, the bearer of long-awaited news that was received gladly by a faithful public. Maybe things weren't as bad as he first thought. At the obvious signs of defeat, Prince John had thrown up his hands in disgust and stalked from the room, tossing over his shoulder a remark of: "Don't say I didn't warn you", or something along those lines. No one noticed him. Nobody really paid attention to anything but the task at hand. They were too busy planning for their king's return.

The second figure behind the throne had not taken off when Prince John had; rather, he just stood there, as he had for the entire meeting, listening. Carefully. Finally, when the foremost issues of importance had been decided, Cardinal Doncaster Warwick took his leave, striding out of the room as silently as he had first come, blending into the gloom like a ghost.

Queen Eleanor declared an immediate state of emergency, sending messengers to all corners of the country to retrieve whatever funds they possibly could from anyone they could find. She then wrote out a brief letter of agreement to the duke of Austria, as per his instructions, and sent Robin on his way, his heart much lighter and his smile brighter than he'd known in some time. He tucked the queen's letter close to his heart, the letter and the kind words of gratitude she imparted to him.

"You are truly one of our great knights, Sir Robert," she said. "Your country thanks you."

With congratulation and praise they had left; he, Jasmine, and Marian; slipping out of the room as they had first come. They had just entered the large hallway directly beyond the pair of large doors when a figure stepped forward, the figure of a fair-skinned woman with blonde hair, wearing the clothing donned by the palace guard. Her features were distinctly Norse, from the braided hair that was almost white in color, and the light blue eyes.

"Robert of Locksley," she said quietly, "I must speak with you."

Robin immediately recognized Lady Gwen, Isabella's personal guard. He excused himself momentarily and followed her a few steps away.

"I cannot remain long," Lady Gwen said. "But I must warn you to be careful. Prince John will not be pleased with the news you have brought. The committee in Nottinghamshire is of his creation, and if Richard returns, all of his plans will be swept away. Prince John will do anything to prevent that from happening."

Robin nodded.

"Thank you, Lady Gwen," he said. "I will take heed."

With a brief, answering nod, Lady Gwen strode off down the hallway. Her puzzling statements had left Robin with more questions than answers, questions that, to this moment, refused to give up their secrets. He knew those secrets would be revealed in due time, when they returned to Nottingham. But there still one thing Robin needed to do before he left the capital, something he'd been thinking about for quite a while.

At the quiet knock, Bishop Paul Lorien let him in with a wary look, taking Robin's appearance in with some distrust.

"What can I do for you, my son?" He asked, probably expecting to be robbed.

Robin affected his best aristocratic pose and smiled.

"Can the son of an old friend trouble you for a word of advice, Bishop Lorien?"

The bishop eyed him for another moment, still dubious, then his face broke into a broad grin.

"Upon my – *Robin?* Is it really you?"

"It is," Robin said with a laugh, and answered the warm embrace given him. "You're one of the first people to recognize me."

"You really can't blame them," Lorien said as he stepped back. "Look at you!"

Robin didn't have to look. He knew. He said as much, causing the smile to slowly fade as Lorien once again ran a critical glance over his appearance.

"War has the ability to leave its mark upon a man," he said. "It has most certainly left its mark upon you."

"At least I'm alive to talk about it," Robin said bitterly.

"I am sorry, Robert," Lorien answered. "Your father was a good man."

"The best. We didn't always agree on things, but he... he never gave up on me. He never gave up on anyone. Except himself... and now he's dead."

"It is all in the will of the Lord," Lorien said sagely.

Robin let it go at that, quite confident the bishop would not want to hear his current opinions on the "Lord's Will".

"My... father wanted you to have this," he said instead, and pulled the ring out of his pocket. "It was one of the last things he said to me."

Lorien accepted the small token with a sad smile.

"Thank you, young Robin," he said. "I will always cherish this."

For a moment an uneasy silence filled the room as both tried in vain to bring some new topic to the forefront, then Lorien put on a jolly face as he laid the ring on his desk.

"Well," he said at last, in an overly-cheerful voice that failed to disguise the emotion it was meant to replace. "Tell me of your journey. Where did you come from and how in the *world* did you get here?"

****

The room was too dark to suit most people, but for the prince of England, darkness was his alibi. He had lived in it all his life, the darkness created by his brother's shadow, the lop-sided version of royal love their mother spread between them, by the very shadow of England itself. For the first half of his life, it was his enemy, something to be guarded against and made war upon, but in the last two years he and the darkness had become fast friends. It had been through this darkness that he was able to tap into the wealth of Nottinghamshire. It had been through this darkness that he managed to keep his mother blind to the true state of affairs there while he literally raked money in with both hands, using the natural greed of Eustace DeMarke and his cronies to his advantage. John charged a heavy price to those who wanted close proximity to his side; what they did, in turn, to get the money – and a little extra, to boot – was their problem.

John was content to live in the shadow of his brother no longer. Even with Richard himself gone, his soul seemed to remain, lingering in his mother's heart and in the hearts of people all over the country who would never be satisfied to have "John Lackland" remain in power. They wanted only one man, the man with a heart of a lion; no one else would do. So John had made his own plans.

He had known for many months that his brother was alive, alive and in prison. Truthfully, John had entertained the slight hope that Richard had actually perished on that tragic voyage across the sea, but he soon realized the current situation would be equally satisfactory. Leopold of Austria was a man known for his grudges, and he would not relinquish the object of his wrath easily. Richard would remain in prison until he died, the country would finally accept his fate and move on, and thus would begin a new and glorious title for Prince "John Lackland". He would be lacking nothing anymore.

At least, that's what the plan had been until today. John had been troubled when the rumors began circulating about his brother, stories brought to life in song by Blondel, but they were easily suppressed. Some skillful hinting on John's part, a little doubt thrown on the issue at convenient times... Blondel was made to look the fool. And the rumors went away. Any other tidings of such a nature, John had figured, could be dealt with summarily in the very same manner. It had all been so simple, seemed so easy... until last evening when that young whelp waltzed in front of the court with a skinny monk and a box, claiming to know the whereabouts of the long-gone, sorely-missed Richard *darling*.

His announcement – and the proof he provided – had sent John's plans for kinghood off into the wild blue somewhere. The only way his plan would work at all was for Richard to be gone. Completely, utterly, permanently gone. Otherwise Richard would do something. Something king-ish. And John would be back to square one, jumping at his own shadow that somehow managed to be just that much darker than the one he lived under.

"You're sure those were the terms," he said.

Cardinal Warwick's rasping voice almost echoed in the small room.

"Certain," he said. "If you wish to end this nonsense now, you have the means."

"Yes... so I do..." Prince John tapped his finger against the grainy wood of the table before him, deep in thought.

"I doubt your wife will listen if you told her," Warwick added, "but Lady Gwen is growing restless. She does not approve of your methods, and she knows about the committee. She could be trouble."

"If she is, we'll deal with her," John said absently, penning a quick note. "First we must conclude this affair. Then we can worry about Lady Gwen."

The letter Locksley carried could be the detriment of John's plans and the ruin of his life. But Cardinal Warwick was no fool, and he had made good use of his unknown presence before, listening well to the discussion between the young knight called Locksley and Queen Eleanor. John wished he had the clergyman's patience, but he supposed his lack thereof kept Warwick employed. Richard's release rested solely on the delivery of the letter just bequeathed to Locksley. And his release was the last thing John wanted. So, it was with absolutely no regrets that John Lackland, younger, ill-favored son of Eleanor of Aquitaine, sent a rider to Nottingham bearing a message that could would end the life of his only brother through its implications. It was a message that read simply:

Robert of Locksley must be stopped. Kill him and destroy the letter he carries.

No one need know what was in that letter; no one need know it was a letter of agreement, conceding to the terms set down by the duke of Austria. Not that Eustace DeMarke would care even if he did know. That was one thing John absolutely loved about Nottingham's sheriff: they both wanted the same thing and were willing to do anything short of jumping in front of a poisoned arrow to get it. Including sacrifice the lives of family. The letter had to be in Leopold's hands at the end of about twenty more days, or the deal was off. If it just happened to never arrive...

John smiled to himself. Well. In that case, the duke of Austria would take care of the rest.

****

Marian Fitzwalter was not proud of the chip she had on her shoulder concerning Robert of Locksley, but she didn't feel enough remorse to remove it. As she wended a careful way toward the chambers of Bishop Lorien, Robert and the negative space he occupied in her heart took up a great deal of her mind as well, bothering her for some reason she wasn't quite able to pinpoint. She was thinking so hard about it, in fact, she almost failed to notice when she reached her destination. The door was partially open as she approached. Marian heard voices from within, and as soon as she did, she stopped, realizing where she was.

"I am sorry for your loss, Robert," Lorien's kind voice said. "I know how hard it is, but you mustn't dwell on it. It is not what God would want you to do."

"I understand that," Robert said. His tone was lined with the same quality Marian knew her own had held for the last few years concerning that topic.

"And it isn't what your parents would want, either," Lorien added quietly. "I understand, Robin, how your thoughts on faith may not be very kind after what you have been through, but don't let hatred overtake your soul. If for no one else's sake than that of your parents. Let them see you as they should."

There was a moment of silence. Marian could almost see Robert nodding in concession. She stopped just short of doing the same herself, the bishop's words reaching her somehow though they were meant for Robert. There had been many a time when she wondered whether or not her own parents could see her, many a time she wondered what they'd say if they could. She had no time to dwell on it, however, for Robert suddenly thanked the bishop for his advice and angled quick footsteps for the door.

"Come see me the next time you're in London," Lorien said.

"I will."

Robert was smiling as he stepped outside. The door closed behind him, he turned, and Marian saw him jump as he caught sight of her standing in the hallway. She was suddenly struck by how grown up he seemed. His eyes were the same, fiery grey she remembered, but they were lined with compassion and understanding now, as well as a strange mixture of joy and sadness, and a good deal of maturity she knew had come from his days as a soldier; days that had made him grow up far too quickly. All of this she perceived in the split second it took for his surprise at her presence to flip all the way to resignation, as if he expected a lecture. Marian attempted a smile.

"We're ready to leave," she said.

Together they walked out to the carriage, keeping a respectable distance between them, and Marian resisted the temptation to move a step closer for measuring purposes. She had the distinct impression that Robert had grown while he was away. Marian clearly remembered being almost eye level with him when he left; now she had to look up. And look up quite a ways. As a matter of fact, his whole physique had changed, and even through the gauntness of his features, Marian could see a difference. He was less boyish, signs of physical maturity clearly visible around the face and through his shoulders, and he moved with more the agility of an adult than the awkwardness of adolescence. Yes, Robert was very different now, very different indeed. He was no longer the boy she had grown up with.

Marian suddenly wondered if her resident grudge should apply to the adult model.

****

The rider reached him at midday, having galloped hard, and by the time he left once more, Eustace DeMarke had the note from Prince John in his hands. He read it carefully, word for word, the two-sentence message conveying all the urgency of a two-page epistle written by a desperate man. The note left a lot out. But Eustace DeMarke was nothing if not a smart man, and he was well able to fill in most of the holes left open, fill them in and smooth out the seams to boot.

So. Robert of Locksley was back in town. DeMarke didn't need a rocket scientist to tell him that with Robert had come news, news that would require a response in the form of the letter DeMarke was supposed to destroy. That meant King Richard was alive; alive and possibly in prison, waiting to be rescued. Locksley was either let out or escaped, returning to his homeland and his queen for help. And with his return had come a bad situation. If Robert succeeded, King Richard would be back. If Richard came back, John would be in big trouble, as would all of those he associated with on the dealings in Nottingham and the surrounding areas. All of this effectively slicing DeMarke's cord to the throne, *any* throne, with no more difficulty than an arrow would slice a bit of fabric. For, DeMarke was realizing, his connections at this point were no more significant than fabric. They would need bolstering. He had an idea of where to start; two places, as a matter of fact, but first he had to deal with this matter.

"Guy," he said, and his cousin entered the room without a word. "Get the men. We have a problem."

"What kind of problem?"

DeMarke handed him the note without turning around.

"An old friend," was all he said.

"Ah, yes, Locksley." Gisbourne tossed the note back onto the table. "He came to his father's house the day before yesterday. Seemed very surprised to find it occupied."

"Why did you not tell me?" DeMarke asked sharply.

"Mere oversight, cousin," Guy answered. "It won't happen again."

"Be sure of that." DeMarke slid to his feet, extinguishing the small candle before him.

As Gisbourne disappeared, Eustace DeMarke strode across the room and slung a long cape around his shoulders, watching the bottom edge swish across the floor. Robert of Locksley... the skinny little brat who had been so stuck on Marian Fitzwalter before he went off to war. DeMarke had rather hoped he'd been kind enough to just disappear over there, but no such luck. DeMarke decided he was going to enjoy this. For, the necessity of the thing aside, he had his own score to settle. With Locksley, the situation, with Richard himself, who had suddenly shown up in spirit to pose a threat to DeMarke's plans. Funny, that it was guys named Richard who kept getting in his way...

With that, Eustace DeMarke stepped outside to go to war. What he didn't know, however, was by acting on this string of actions, he and Prince John were about to invoke consequences that would pull the entire temple down around them.

****

"It's not that I don't want you to come with me, Jasmine; I just don't think it will be safe for you. I don't want to see you get hurt." Robin sat back and studied her with care. "The duke already knows you're gone," he reminded her. "It won't take but one small slip for you to be discovered, and then what? He'll probably just kill you."

"He is right, Jasmine," Marian said. "This isn't your battle."

Jasmine nodded in acquiescence, although she was clearly vexed about not being able to do her part and accompany Robin when he took the queen's letter of agreement to Leopold.

"I must confess my motives were more selfish than anything," she admitted. "After what he did to me, nothing would please me more than to see the look on his face when he realizes he must release your king. But you are right. My imagination will have to suffice."

She stared out the window, her eyes dark and thoughtful, gazing at the scenery that rolled by on either side in an endless succession of trees. They had entered Sherwood Forest some time ago, following the road as it wound south toward Nottingham, the carriage moving close enough to the trees on either side it almost seemed one could reach out and touch the old, moss-covered trunks and rustling leaves. Many a robbery and many a murder had been committed on this old stretch of road, many a legend had begun here, many a traveler had simply disappeared into the sea of green. Robin was observing the queer, olive coloring of some unknown specimen of plant life when the peaceful sounds of twilight were suddenly broken by a ruckus farther up the road. He felt the carriage begin to slow dramatically.

"I think we have a problem, m'lady," The driver said quietly.

Robin leaned out the window, and immediately spied the road block, about a hundred feet up the road, where ten horses were visible, all ridden by men with purpose in their stature and crossbows at the ready.

"Robert, I don't like this," Marian said, and her face was edged with suspicion. "I don't think this is a random stop. They're looking for something..."

The roadblock came a little closer, and Robin spied a collection of yellow-and-black striped tunics.

"It's a posse," Marian said abruptly, her gaze fixed out the window. "I think DeMarke is with them, but I'm not sure." She looked at him quickly. "You should leave. Now. I have a bad feeling about this."

"We had better do as she says, Robert," Jasmine agreed. "What you have to do is far too important to allow for trust."

Robin didn't need to be told twice. The easiest way to solve a problem was to shoot the messenger.

"What about you?" He asked Marian, sudden concern for her surfacing as he realized what she'd be up against.

"I've dealt with DeMarke for the past several years, Robert. I'll be fine."

Robin studied her face briefly.

"All right. We'll cut through the forest on foot and meet you to get our horses. So don't sell them," he added with a grin. As the carriage rumbled closer to the barricade, Robin took a final, cursory glance at the approaching mob, which had now increased to fifteen, then opened the door as they passed through a deep portion of shadow. "Come along, Jasmine," he whispered. "Let us be on our merry way."

The door closed, the coachman smiled at them, and, as he increased the pace a bit, Robin and Jasmine slipped into the trees.

***

Marian tried to look casual as the carriage ground to a halt.

"Charles!" She called in her most genteel voice. "Why have we stopped?"

"I believe someone would like a word with you, m'lady," the coachman replied.

He had no sooner spoken than the carriage door whipped open and the repulsively handsome, sneering face of Eustace DeMarke filled the doorway. Marian could see his even more hideous cousin lurking about in the background, directing troops.

"Evening, my lady," DeMarke said ingratiatingly.

"Sir DeMarke," Marian answered in as polite a voice as she could possibly muster under the circumstances, and fought the rising bile in her stomach. "You're quite a ways from home."

"As are you," DeMarke answered. "What are you doing out at this hour?"

"I went to London," Marian answered.

"Ah, yes, of course. You took a friend there this morning."

Marian eyed him casually. She might have known.

"You seem well informed," she said. "Although if you had cared to dig a little deeper, you would have known the man I took this morning was no friend."

"Don't tell me Robert still holds a sore place in your heart," DeMarke said dramatically. He was letting Marian know where she stood... and how much, exactly, he knew already.

You hold an even sorer place, you revolting pig, Marian thought. Out loud, she said: "I think of Robert as I have always thought of him."

"Of course." DeMarke took a superficial look throughout the interior. "And where is our young friend now?"

"London," Marian lied. "He did not wish to some back with me tonight."

"Yes, London often has that effect," was the response. DeMarke leaned farther into the dim carriage, and Marian resisted the temptation to back away, suddenly realizing that compared to this idiot, Robert didn't seem so bad. "Tell me," DeMarke continued. "Where did Robert come from? I heard he was dead."

"He was in prison," Marian said. "He is here to negotiate the return of our king."

"His highness is alive?"

The question – and the attached expression of joyful surprise – was purely for show.

"Alive and prepared to take over the throne once more," Marian said. "Upon his return he will set right anything that is... shall we say out of place."

At her suggestive comment, DeMarke quirked an eyebrow and changed tactics.

"And... Robert holds the key to his homecoming, you say?"

"Yes."

"The note he's carrying, perhaps?"

So he knew about that, as well. How, Marian had no idea, but the implications were enough to cause no slight amount of concern to enter her mind. She said nothing. At her silence, DeMarke sighed, as if about to impart something truly agonizing.

"I surely hate to tell you this, my lady," he said, "but before you decide to give your life and reputation as collateral to protect him, I must tell you. It appears as though your hero Locksley has a little more up his sleeve than he told you."

"Such as?" Marian asked in feigned shock.

"Treason. Blackmail. Numerous other infractions of varying degree. Now that you know these things, and know that he is no longer the innocent, brave conqueror... has his location changed at all?"

"Perhaps by a few taverns," Marian answered dryly. "Other than that, no."

DeMarke seemed about to grill her further when, out of the blue, there was a loud yell from the trees to the side of the road.

"You, there! Stop!"

Marian heard the distinct sound of a crossbow firing, then another, and DeMarke flung himself backward out of the carriage to see what was going on. Marian heard him shouting questions. She already knew the answers to most of them. Anxiously she peered out the window, staring into the blackness, hoping neither Robert nor Jasmine had been on the receiving end of one of those arrows. There was nothing out there, nothing but darkness and shadows...

Her eyes caught movement. Deep in the forest, straight across from the carriage and in a completely different direction from where the sheriff and his men were looking, Marian saw a brief flash of light. She realized it was faded sunlight reflecting off the blade of a sword. And she understood immediately that it was meant to get her attention. As she watched, Robert rose stealthily from hiding, Jasmine beside him, and waved quickly, the gesture little more than a blacker shade of movement. Marian waved in return, but she didn't know if they saw her. For, without a backward glance, Robert and Jasmine turned and melted into the darkness of Sherwood Forest, little more than a pair of flitting shadows moving through the trees.

****

"Are you being serious?" Amantha asked, arching her eyebrows. "A history professor."

She'd come back down to meet Northam at exactly eleven am when he'd rung her requesting a positive ID; the description she and Jerry had given yielded results, and Amantha was doubly curious to find out who this character was. Aunt Marilla's story was still playing on her mind as she left. Somehow, just hearing it made Amantha feel closer to her mother, and now, listening to Northam's explanation of this man, Gregg Nicholas, it leapt to mind again. She wondered if he knew the story. She again ran her eyes over the photo handed her; she would have known that face anywhere. The blue-green eyes seemed even more vibrant than they were in person.

"What does he want, do you think?" She mused.

"Treasure, apparently," Northam said directly. "I spoke with someone this morning who has known Nicholas for quite some time. It appears he has been hung up on this 'legend', if you will, for the past twenty years or so, since high school."

There it was again: the treasure angle. Amantha had grown up hearing about it, knew her family's obsession. Nicolo had been doing his own research for as long as she could remember. But in the end it was this guy, Gregg Nicholas, who had found that secret room. Not Nicolo.

"Twenty years?" She asked. That would put him somewhere around forty, Amantha surmised. Twenty years of searching, sifting, and waiting all lead to the moment Nicholas broke into the dig. Clearly the man was dogged, and more than likely, had amassed a catalogue of leads, leads that Nicolo, for some reason, did not have.

If this treasure were, indeed, to be found, it would be by someone like him. Not Nicolo.

"You look tired," Northam said sympathetically. "You should go home and get some sleep."

Amantha laughed. She was tired.

"It was a long night," she said. "After I left here, I spent the rest of the night watching that interview again, over and over."

"I thought as much." Northam smiled. "Did you find anything useful? Or do you have anything you might be able to add about his behavior when you spoke with him?"

Damn, she shouldn't have said anything. Of course Northam would query her about it. Amantha paused. Only briefly, masking the gesture carefully. If Gregg Nicholas was to be Amantha's avenue toward revenge, he needed to remain off the radar. If she told Northam her suspicions now, Nicholas' hunt would be over very quickly, and Amantha wanted Robin Hood's treasure to be found, if it even existed. What she didn't want was for it to be found by a Goldstein. Gregg Nicholas was, at this point, the best hope of that. She knew he would go for the necklace next. It was the only option that made sense. As soon as Aunt Marilla had pointed it out on the telly screen, there was no other alternative; Amantha had known, from that moment, how Nicholas had found his target, and judging from the results he'd achieved even now, it was highly likely he was right.

With that in mind, she wanted to give him as much of a head start as possible. That didn't make her feel any better, of course; Northam was only doing his job, and she felt bad withholding information. He was, after all, not just an officer of the law, but a friend. Maybe someday she'd be able to apologize.

"No," she said after a moment. "I didn't find anything on the video… and Nicholas acted strangely normal toward me. Aside from giving me a false name, of course."

Northam nodded.

"If you do remember something, call me straight away," he said.

"I will." Amantha tried to keep her body language neutral. She chanced a glance at the stack of papers near her elbow, the stack from which Northam had produced the photo of Nicholas, and frowned suddenly. "Who is that?" She asked, retrieving another shot from near the bottom.

"Nicholas' accomplices," Northam answered. "We don't know who they are yet."

Amantha stared at the photo in silence, struck by a sudden sense of déjà vu. It depicted two men getting out of a cab directly in front of one of the many pubs bordering the construction site. The Pale Horse Pub, time stamped at 21:47. Of the two, one man was shorter, possibly around one hundred and seventy cm, but he wasn't the one she looked at. Carefully she studied the taller man in it, the one who had caught her attention.

"I think I know him," she said, placing her finger on the paper.

"From where?" Northam asked quickly.

"I don't know." But it wasn't good. Tall, strong jaw, big shoulders, posture that could only be described as military bearing. It wasn't a clear shot, the image she held. She couldn't see his face hardly at all... in fact if she had seen it fully she doubted this sense of déjà vu would have hit her as hard. It was in his outline, the way he stood, the angle of the shot and the distance... something. Something was niggling at the back of her mind. "It's probably nothing," she concluded, and laughed. "I think I need more sleep." Honestly, one all-nighter and she was seeing patterns everywhere. Six billion people on the planet and she thought she knew one of them from a bad photo? Unlikely.

A knock at the door broke the quiet.

"Commander... Marshal Gates is here, sir," Leonard Howell said, leaning in the doorway.

A touch of surprise hit Northam's face.

"Really. Well, show him in."

Howell nodded and disappeared.

"Miss Goldstein, unfortunately I need to excuse myself for the time being," Northam said apologetically.

"No need for apologies, Commander," Amantha answered with a smile. "I assume you'll keep me up to date... as much as you can, anyway?"

"Of course." Northam smiled in return and showed her to the door. He opened it to the presence of Howell and another man that Amantha didn't know.

"Ah, Marshal. Good of you to come," Northam said, shaking the man's hand. He glanced at Amantha. "Miss Goldstein, this is US Marshal Peter Gates. Marshal, Amantha Goldstein."

"Pleased to meet you, ma'am," Gates said as Amantha greeted him, and shook her hand. His voice, like his manner, was gentle. His accent was very similar to that of Gregg Nicholas.

"Well, gentlemen, I must be off," Amantha said brightly. "I can show myself out."

Waving farewell, she pulled the door shut behind her. A moment of silence, and then:

"What can I do for you, Marshal?" She heard Northam inquire evenly. His voice had changed: it was guarded, muffled through the closed door.

"I was hoping you might be able to tell me if you've found the information you were after," was the quiet reply.

"We've made some progress."

Another second.

"Can I be of any assistance?" Gates asked.

"I already extended that offer," Northam returned. "I wasn't under the impression you were interested. I know that you know more than you told me."

"Not for certain... I suspect, is all. I didn't want to jump to conclusions."

"What do you suspect?" This from Howell.

"That Gregg has contacted someone he shouldn't have," Gates said simply. "He's been after this legend for a long time, Commander; he's not a bad man but he's determined, and he has motive to see it through. You said this morning that he'd contacted the Goldstein family on several occasions after they found that necklace in Mexico, but was shot down."

Really? Amantha had never heard any of this. Maybe that was why Nicolo had suddenly become so animated about it; someone else was on the hunt, and he knew he had to move quickly or risk losing the lot.

"If that was the case," Gates continued, "Gregg might have felt like he had no choice but to do something before someone else discovered what he was after. Now I'm not saying this to make an excuse for his course of action; merely to explain my thoughts."

Amantha could almost see Northam nodding.

"Go on," he said.

"Gregg isn't a criminal, Commander. He doesn't have a criminal mindset. Breaking into a place like that would require help."

"You mean the man in the surveillance photo," Howell surmised. "You know him."

"I think so. If it is who I suspect, Gregg is in way over his head."

Amantha was prevented from hearing more as a secretary rounded the corner. She smiled easily and made her way out, deep in thought. This situation had just taken a very interesting turn. Gregg Nicholas had been tracking down this story for twenty years… he'd contacted her family when they found the necklace but got no response; after that, he'd broken into the dig by following some scrap of information only he knew, and succeeded in finding the body of Robin Hood. If there was anyone in this world at the moment who could possibly run that treasure down, it was Gregg Nicholas. Amantha wanted to see this legend, this treasure, brought to light. The chance to do so whilst rubbing salt in Nicolo's wounds was just icing on the cake. It was there, in that moment, that Amantha made up her mind. It didn't matter how many bad guys were involved or how scary this man was that Marshal Gates referred to a moment ago: when Gregg Nicholas went for the necklace, *if* he went for the necklace, she wasn't letting him out of her sight.

Amantha Goldstein was inviting herself on a treasure hunt.

****

The laptop screen cast a bluish glow over the room. Night had long since fallen. Ian Lowell sat alone in the darkness of the hotel room, silent, tracking down leads to Gregg's treasure. After Gregg and Jared had successfully escaped at the riverbank the night before, Ian and his boys returned to the hotel, casually checked out, and moved to a new location to launch their own search. It was with no small amount of chagrin that Ian realized the battle worn sword Gregg had left behind in the car was not the same one he had removed from the coffin; the clever professor had outwitted him. In doing so, Gregg had ensured that he was the only one with a true copy of the riddle.

Point for the education department.

But Ian was not as foolish as Gregg thought. He spent the better part of the night, as well as the following day, reacquainting himself with Gregg's quest, and had quickly found that there was indeed a method to the madness. Research into Robin Hood had immediately landed him in the middle of the history of a family by the name of Goldstein, and from their past to a string of current endeavors. He'd heard mention of these people through the years, of course, but as a man far more interested in living his own life rather than the life of someone else, Ian had taken very little notice of them. He paid closer attention now.

In the room beyond the connecting door, Troy and George were busy regaling each other with stories of wine, women, and wild nights while they waited for Rob to return with whatever food he managed to scrounge up at one am. Stan was with them, not saying much as was his way. They made for good team members; asked few questions, accomplished things quickly and efficiently, and were good blokes. Stan, Ian kept around simply because he had no other recourse at the moment.

He remained in thought as the front door opened to admit Rob, food in tow. He could hear him tossing a box of food into each pair of hands as Rob walked casually from the well-lit room into his dark cave. Rob dropped a box of Chinese takeout on the desk next to his elbow.

"Who's the chick?" Rob pointed to the screen, where Ian was studying the stilled image before him; two people, a male reporter and a strikingly beautiful woman, stood in front of the exact same section of wall Gregg and Ian had torn down the previous night.

"Gregg said she works at the museum," Ian said absently. Of course she was more than that. From his scant research into the family, Amantha Goldstein was at the forefront of the enterprise. She was rich, sought after, and Ian was fairly certain she was the woman Gregg had talked with before they broke into the dig. But, going into detail on a subject that wasn't their primary objective was counterproductive, so he kept it simple. At his basic response, Rob just laughed.

"Mate, I would have gone into museum work if my boss was as hot as that."

Ian said nothing, but the small smile on his face gave away his thoughts. Amantha Goldstein was an interesting woman. Classy, well-spoken, and smart. If it hadn't been for her visage, her gentle voice, distracting him at every corner through the broadcast he would have found this moment an hour ago. He studied the symbol Gregg had pointed out carefully, then slowly sat back in his seat.

"We need the necklace," he said.

"What necklace?" Rob was busy digging around in his own bowl of chow with a pair of chopsticks.

Ian clicked to the online version of an old newspaper article from November.

IS IT REAL? The digital headline queried. *Goldsteins uncover priceless necklace in Mexico, hint at ties to Robin Hood legend...*

Underneath was a photo of the jewelry in question. It took no genius to see the physical necklace matched the symbol Gregg had said was so important. The one visible on the wall of the tunnel. Silver branches woven in that strange formation, blue sapphire nestled at the base.

"Gregg said this symbol was the key to everything," Ian said quietly, returning to the original, stilled video. "It's how he knew where to look."

"He saw this on the news broadcast."

Ian nodded.

"Why does he need the real thing?"

"Because," Ian said, clicking to a text document, "he needs a blue stone of hope."

In the document was as much of the poem as Ian could put down from memory, as he'd seen it engraved on the sword. He was nearly one hundred percent certain the "stone of hope" referred to the necklace in the article, which tied in with the symbol that led Gregg to the dig. That necklace was now locked up in the Goldstein Museum. While Ian couldn't recall the entire poem, little bits of it had stuck out, particularly those which elicited a reaction from Gregg Nicholas.

The blue stone of Hope.

As soon as Gregg spoke of it aloud, his expression had changed. Closed off. Retreated. To his credit, he hadn't verbally given anything away when he figured it out; however, the look on his face, the same face Ian used to swindle poker winnings out of, proved his undoing. It was at that moment last night when Ian realized Gregg was going to be more of a problem than he reckoned at first, when he realized Gregg would intentionally withhold information if he could.

So much for friendship. It was almost funny: when he had received that call from Gregg a few days ago, he'd allowed a tiny sliver of optimism to take root in his mind. He'd known, when he walked away all those years ago, Gregg hadn't understood. He'd known Gregg was hurt, probably offended, and Ian was far from surprised when that little burner phone he took with him never rang. Then suddenly, ten years on, that phone started ringing and here was his long-lost buddy, contacting him for help. Ian thought for a brief moment that Gregg might be trying to reach out, extend an olive branch, and he had been hopeful. Then they had met face to face, and he knew something was wrong. They had broken into the dig, and despite the façade of friendliness between them the elephant in the room matured. When things turned sour, as Ian knew they were bound to, it happened fast, and it went down hard. Gregg hadn't held back with his opinions. That strange, inexplicable something had been niggling at his mind all night, and as he burst forth with that tirade about Ian and Rob and how they were no better than criminals themselves, Ian had understood what it was:

Fear.

Of him.

Gregg was afraid of him. The sheer realization was enough to both incense and sadden him, for the only other time Ian had seen that look on someone's face was the first time his own father had raised a hand to his little sister. Her countenance had held that same mixture of hurt, terror, and accusation as the blow struck home. Seeing it on Gregg's face and knowing he was the cause cut a lot deeper than he thought it would. And suddenly Ian found himself chasing Gregg down, half of his mind enraged with Gregg's accusations and the other half wondering why the whole thing was so damn funny. Even then, regardless of how true and how damaging words had been, regardless of the situation, the man he was after still was Gregg Nicholas, the guy Ian had grown up with and gotten in and out of trouble over the years. And even in his anger, he was very conscious of that. After all, when he started out on this long road all those years ago, it hadn't been to kill a friend.

"You want us to go check the river again?" Troy had asked upon reaching their new location, finding Ian on the shared balcony of the hotel.

"No need," Ian replied. He had only just discovered the true identity of the sword Gregg had left behind, and despite himself a grudging admiration took hold, reminding him of why he and Gregg had always gotten on so well. Aside from Rob, Gregg was the only one who was as sneaky as Ian was himself; possibly even more so. "He'll be long gone by now." He had paused and stared reflectively into the distance, resting his palms on the balcony railing. "In fact, if anybody's going to come out of this in one piece, it's Gregg Nicholas," he had finished.

And now, sitting in the darkness with the cursor blinking evenly next to the text he had managed to reconstruct and the little Clip-It entity staring at him intently from the bottom of the document, Ian stretched slowly. It was interesting to contemplate who would have won this race, given the chance. Having successfully completed the "Art of Crime 101" course, Gregg thought he had what it took to get the deed done on his own, without the use of any sort of force. Ian had been around the block enough to know that was impossible. But then… perhaps he had been using force for so long, he'd forgotten how to operate without it. It was a strange thing to contemplate. In the end, he supposed they would all find out soon enough which way was better, no matter what happened. Gregg needed time to cool off, and to ensure his cooperation to even a minimal extent, Ian knew he was going to have to get creative. Exactly how creative remained to be seen, but he had a few ideas.

"Where to next?" Rob inquired.

"Retrieve Gregg." Ian's voice was wry. "We need to keep an eye on the museum. I reckon that's where he's headed next."

"I'll get George on it," Rob answered. "You think bringing Gregg along is a good idea? He's liable to be a bit touchy."

"Give him time and he'll come around. We need him," Ian said. "He's the only one with a complete copy of the riddle. And as much as I would like to actually turn this into a race, I have other obligations to worry about. Gregg and his riddle are the only things that will see a quick end to this."

"If we can find him, we'll be able to smoke him out."

"Oh, he'll be there," Ian said thoughtfully. "Somewhere. The necklace is in the museum, and that's what he needs; we just need to be a little patient, a little creative… we'll get him back. He's one of the few things we can count on happening."

At the time, he had no idea how right he was.

The eagle may soar, but the weasel
never gets sucked up into a jet engine.

- *Anonymous*

Chapter 15

Jared's contact had come through. They had slithered like pond scum away from the riverbank, caught a cab, and sought shelter, winding up in a dodgy little hostel in a part of town Gregg was sure even Ian would avoid. Fortunately, it had wifi. Jared had connected up with the big, wide world of the internet and gotten in touch with his buddy here in London, and within a night, the wheels were turning for them. Jared's mate had come up with another mate who knew someone who knew a guy who worked at the museum; once that link was established, the techies all went to work on breaching museum security with the same gusto they might use in a Halo multiplayer game. It was like a little, underground network of nerds and hackers that Gregg was heretofore unaware of. Who needed Ian when he had an army of geeks on his side?

In his possession were timetables, blueprints, and security codes; he knew where to go, what to do, how long it would take him to get there, and more importantly how long it would take him to get out. And now here they were, rumbling down the street in front of the museum in a rented van, Jared sweating bullets and Gregg trying to be as stoic as he possibly could. He'd been woken promptly at seven am, with Jared tapping him insistently on the shoulder and holding up the day's paper.

Gregg was on the front, picture and all.

Well, that didn't take long.

He'd scanned the article briefly, the realization that all this would very quickly make its way back home creeping into his mind.

That was one thing he hadn't planned out all that well: what to do if he somehow made it out of this in one piece but got fired for it. If he had the treasure in hand, it wouldn't be so bad… maybe… but if he failed…

"After you drop me off, pull into that driveway over there," Gregg said. He was jittery and jumpy, and his hands shook as he tried to put his gloves on. He felt like the whole world was spying on him.

Jared pulled over in front of the museum, skillfully avoiding the two cameras mounted near the entrance. The van shuddered slightly as it slowed; Gregg hoped it wouldn't stall. It was a sketchy vehicle, to be sure, but the only one they could come up with. They'd tried numerous rental agencies, looking for one that would accept cash payments, but all for naught. After ten places turned them down, Gregg was on the verge of jumping off a bridge. He thought he had known frustration in his time, but this was ridiculous. He even considered the possibility of buying some small, cheap piece of junk just to get them through the next few days, but decided the possible ramifications weren't really worth it. In the end, Jared stepped up to the plate and paid a three hundred dollar bond on this old van; while Gregg was sure Jared was still off the radar – at least for the time being – seeing his credit card get processed was unnerving. He had a funny feeling that laser-printed card receipt was going to end up being their undoing.

"Are you sure you want to do this?" Jared asked worriedly, slipping the headset over his ear as the car ground to a halt. "I mean, it's a great movie idea, breaking in here and all, but let's be realistic just for a moment. They never get caught in the movies. What if you do?"

Gregg attempted an apathetic shrug. Opened his door. Put in the earpiece and connected the mic to his lapel.

"I should be out in ten years or so. You can come visit me, bring chocolate, whatever."

"Right. Yeah. Good plan."

Gregg stepped back to close the van up.

"Just one last question," Jared said as the doors swung towards him.

"What?"

"What if *I* get caught?"

"Then I'll send you some chocolate from South America."

"Gee, thanks," said an indignant voice in the earpiece.

Gregg stared at the building across the street from him. He was reminded of the White House. The Goldstein Museum was huge by anyone's standards, a testament to just how much money could accomplish when in the hands of someone wanting to do more than buy a superyacht and cruise the Med. It was bold, audacious, and built to impress. Even in the darkness it stood out, its white walls awash in the beams from external lighting and streetlamps, daring anyone to come closer. From the blueprints given to him by Jared's hacker friends, Gregg knew it stretched at least one level underground and two stories up; a cavernous, expensive space filled with nearly every historical treasure imaginable.

It was big. It was imposing. It was a fortress.

Gregg knew he'd be lucky to get in and out with his hair on.

The plan was to go in the back entrance through the underground parking lot, down the corridor directly inside, and into the main display area. Marian's Necklace was kept in a specially-designed case at the very center. It was surrounded by more than a dozen CCTV cameras. The corridor that led to it was also heavily watched. Jared's mates had made sure Jared would have access to the main security system, from which he could easily manipulate the camera feed and cover Gregg's movement through those two areas. Then, all Gregg had to do was avoid the guards, use the code provided to him to open the necklace's case, and swipe the jewelry before escaping back the way he had come. In theory, it was a solid plan.

If everything went well.

If Gregg didn't screw up.

If Jared didn't screw up.

If his mates even gave him the right codes.

Gregg made his way down the side drive, into the underground parking lot, toward the back entrance. Looked around. Punched in the code that theoretically unlocked the heavy, metal door. The buttons beeped, faded to silence, and the door buzzed as it opened. One hurdle down.

"Door's unlocked," he said quietly.

"Okay, give me a second…" Gregg could hear the clicking of laptop keys as Jared hacked into the security system and prepared to make Gregg invisible.

"Feed's looped... you're good to go," he said. Then: *"Good luck."*

"Thanks," Gregg said as coolly as he could, and pulled the door open.

Yeah. He was going to need it.

****

Northam nearly pounced on the phone when it rang.

"What do you have?" He asked.

"We found them." Howell's voice was mingled with radio traffic in the background. "You were right about the van, sir. Plates were spotted twenty minutes ago, and we have been shadowing them. Nicholas and Casey are in the vehicle... they've pulled over just outside the Goldstein Museum."

"Must have their opening hours confused," Northam said dryly.

"I would assume so," Howell answered in kind. "Nicholas has exited the vehicle and is making his way toward the museum now."

"And the kid?"

"Out of sight, but he'll be nearby."

"Find him before you move in. I'm on my way."

Northam hung up, then dialed Gates from his mobile. He impatiently shoved aside the report he'd been reading – a bizarre tale of woe from the US military claiming two of their Humvees had been stolen from RAF Alconbury near Huntingdon earlier in the day – and grabbed his coat. The Yank issue could wait; those people needed to learn how to keep track of their ordinance better, anyway.

"Gates, we've got him," Northam said as the other pocked up. "He's at the Goldstein Museum."

"I'll meet you there."

Northam flipped the phone shut and made for the door. He was suddenly energized. Nicholas had to be after that necklace the Goldsteins had found a few months ago, a hunch Northam had cultivated since the break-in (at which point he had placed some of his own men at the museum itself). Talking extensively with Gates had solidified the theory (at which point Northam doubled that security). Gates had been highly instrumental in filling in the holes

Northam was still dealing with surrounding Gregg Nicholas and his caper, and Northam felt he had a much better understanding of the man now. But Nicholas proved cannier than they'd first anticipated. Tracking him down proved to be a bit on the tricky side.

Busting the group through the thief from the pub, whose name turned out to be Ian Lowell, was no better a proposition. Northam had launched a search for Lowell as soon as Gates identified the man, but came up empty. He seemed to vanish into thin air after the dig and hadn't resurfaced; in point of fact, they could find no record of him even being in the country... or anywhere else for that matter.

A brief history of the man, also supplied by Gates, made Northam realize why the US Marshal was so uneasy about Lowell's involvement. Lowell had essentially been a fugitive for the past ten years of his life after embarking on a bitter campaign of revenge, triggered by the death of a mate but most likely established in undiagnosed post-traumatic stress from an event that happened while Lowell and Nicholas were serving in the US Navy together. PTSD was not something to be taken lightly, nor was a decade of retribution. Not only was Lowell himself liable to be a walking emotional powder keg, his associations with people outside the legal net could very easily come back to bite Gregg Nicholas in a nasty way. For example: if Nicholas actually found this vast treasure he was after and one of Lowell's shady mates (or worse still, shady enemies) happened to find out about it, then things would get really colorful.

Northam finally called a halt in the search for Lowell, as they were able to turn up nothing significant. In the grand scheme of things, Gregg Nicholas was the one they really wanted. At this point, everyone else was merely an accomplice, and for all intents and purposes, aside from that one snippet of video footage from a faded pub camera, Ian Lowell may as well have been nothing more than a ghost.

They'd caught their big break when they got a hit on a credit card belonging to Jared Casey, when he paid the deposit on a rented van not four hours ago. Casey had clearly and easily been identified by the pub's security camera as he made his way through on Lowell's heels, and a quick search for him through the wide world of international travel placed him on the same plane as Nicholas merely two days ago.

Gregg Nicholas occupied economy seat 7B on the British Airways flight from Boston. Jared Casey was in seat 7A. In Northam's book that was one hell of a coincidence. They combed through footage at the airport, and it was no surprise when Northam found the three robbers – Nicholas, Lowell, and Casey – meeting up in arrivals, sauntering out the door like they were best mates. Funny how the promise of getting rich quick seemed to solidify friendship.

****

"Amantha, you cannot expect me to condone this, really," Nicolo said. "We are trying to establish ourselves as serious, contributing members of the historical community. Not a group of fanatics searching for press at all costs."

So much for the "any publicity was good publicity" motto. Amantha sighed.

"It was not my intention to make the front page of a tabloid," she said. "I didn't even know they were there watching me."

"You should have known."

Amantha fell silent. She was in the security department of the museum, where Nicolo had summoned her merely a few minutes ago. In his hands was yet another article about Amantha's antics in the Spitfire, detailing an unfortunate incident where she had lost power midflight and had to make an emergency landing in a field near a primary school. The photos in the magazine showed Amantha exiting the plane, then sitting despondently beside it with her head in her hands; a schoolyard and a few images of crying children rounded off the story effectively.

In truth, Amantha had been sitting in said despondent state because it was hot, she was thirsty, and hadn't eaten in six hours; the school was three kilometres away; and she had it on good authority that children cried just because they felt like it and not for any serious reason. The incident was ridiculously exaggerated. As she had been taught to do from the beginning of her flight training, she had been constantly aware of her surroundings and landing options from the moment her plane left the ground. Due to the fact that she'd flown this particular route many times, she had the added advantage of knowing exactly where she was, and where that field was in relation to her position. When the plane went silent, she simply lowered the gear manually, spent some time looping in circles to lose altitude (working on her glider rating, as she'd heard it called a time or two), and coasted in to land. She'd experienced a rougher landing on an airliner.

The culprit in the power loss ended up being minor, and a simple fix; of course, the element being called into question was Amantha's ability as a pilot and whether or not money could buy the experience needed to fly something like a Supermarine Spitfire.

"Why didn't you inform me of this mishap?" Nicolo asked.

"Because there was no danger!" Amantha argued indignantly. "The engine cut. I glided for five minutes and set it down in a field. *Three kilometers* from the school. Even without touching the brakes I couldn't roll that far once I hit the ground; the kids never even knew I was there."

Nicolo was unmoved.

"That's not the point. The point is you were seen piloting an aircraft that went down unexpectedly. This is the result." He held up the magazine. Amantha once again got a good look at the photoshopped version of her visage plastered on the front, where she appeared to be wiping away tears of distress from a strangely grainy and pimpled face. "I think it's time we discussed alternative activities for you to participate in, Amantha," Nicolo continued. "Activities more suited to your abilities, and the image we wish to promote."

"I see. So the image of a woman piloting a vintage fighter isn't good enough for you," Amantha returned.

"It might be if she could do so quietly and keep it in the air without incident. And, to be honest, I have always had reservations about this... interest... of yours. It calls attention to parts of your past I'd much rather see buried."

Meaning her father. Internally, Amantha bristled at the statement.

"I highly doubt that is what people think of," she said tightly.

"Perhaps. But I don't need to remind you that the press is a funny thing."

Nicolo started on one of his explanations about the world and everything in it; Amantha tuned out. She stared at the bank of monitors behind him, watching the colors and numbers change over and over and over; every now and then a staff member could be seen on one of them preparing to leave. Soon the museum would be empty except for the security guards, and fortunately for her, that meant Nicolo would have to discontinue his speech long enough to walk out.

She hoped so, anyway.

In the next moment, staring over his shoulder at the screens, she saw the flicker.

In the lower-right corner of the wall, the second and third screens in bounced, ever so slightly, before returning to normal. Amantha stared at them intently, ignoring Nicolo as he continued to talk. She couldn't read the numbers time-stamped at the top of the screens; she was much too far away for that. But one thing she could tell, readily, was that they had ceased to move. The camera had been frozen. Amid the continual motion and activity of the remaining one hundred plus images, such a small detail would have been virtually undetectable. Amantha had just been lucky enough to see it happen.

She knew in that moment that Gregg Nicholas was in the building. He had come for the necklace. She looked at the newspaper folded along the surface of a nearby desk, at the headline splashed all over the top. Nicholas was on the front, as he had been on nearly every single daily news source that Amantha had seen. She'd been thinking about it all day, this hunt of his, and since that split second in Northam's office when she had decided to go all in, she'd been coming up with a plan. If this man was going after treasure, she wanted in on it.

She thought fast. Marilla was outside, in the staff room; Amantha couldn't leave her behind. First, she needed to get rid of Nicolo. If they were going off the grid, she'd need cash. That she could get from the museum safe – if she was going crim, might as well go all the way. Whatever she did, it had to be fast; Nicholas wouldn't be here long.

It was now or never.

"Listen," she said, holding up a hand to cut Nicolo off mid-sentence. "I need time to think about this."

Nicolo spread his hands in a placating manner.

"Very well." He rose. "I will leave you to think about it for a moment."

Of course, only a moment. And when he returned, Amantha knew what answer Nicolo was expecting. To his mind, aviation was a part of Amantha's past; her future was this museum. His museum.

Once again she found irritation quickly winning over common sense, as Nicolo's condescension and bullish attitude let her know exactly where she stood. She sat still, waiting for him to leave. His footsteps retreated, a door opened, closed. Amantha jumped up. As the room was emptied for their discussion, there was no one to interfere with her movements. Immediately, she crossed to the security counter. Located the original feeds from those two screens through the intranet, pulled them up. The hallway outside the main display area was empty. The display room had only one body in it: in the middle of the room, breaking into the case containing Marian's Necklace, stood Gregg Nicholas.

"Got you," Amantha said softly.

There was a third-party signal interfering with both cameras' connection with the intended screens in the security room. Overriding the signal, Amantha activated the hallway camera again, but left the one in the display room looped; if she wanted the opportunity to talk to Nicholas, she needed to have him trapped dead to rights in a place of her choosing. In the display room they might as well be invisible. She just needed to make sure he would stand still long enough to talk.

She had done her research on Gregg Nicholas; since learning his name from Northam, Amantha had hit Google and started running the man down. What she found was interesting, to say the least. Nicholas was a professor in California, after moving there from Texas. He was into hiking and horseback riding and fishing, and seemed to be a genuinely nice guy when he wasn't running around knocking people over the head and breaking into things. But, more than that, the man had found that room in the dig with little more than a symbol on a wall. Amantha didn't know how, but she had a hunch he was on to something. And she was going to find out what it was. She jumped as Nicolo's footsteps sounded on the far side of the room. She didn't have much time. Popping open the large combo safe in the corner with an ease borne from much experience, Amantha grabbed a wad of cash and ran from security, out to where Marilla waited patiently. She had accompanied Amantha to the museum when Nicolo called her in, and had been stuck in the staff room for nearly thirty minutes.

"What happened?" Marilla asked resignedly.

"We need to go," Amantha answered. "I'll tell you later." She grabbed her jacket and made for the stairs.

"Ammy, what are you doing?"

Amantha paused, cracking the door open. No one in sight.

"Remember the chap that broke into the dig?"

"Yes…"

"He's here."

"Here! How do you know?"

"I just saw him," Amantha said. "I'm going to talk to him… I want to see what he knows."

"To what end?"

Amantha grinned.

"I want to go with him."

"Ammy! This is not –"

"Aunt Marilla… if you want to know what just happened in there, I'll tell you. Nicolo wants me to sell the Spitfire. He wants me to engage in activities more suited to my 'abilities'." Amantha knew the anger in her voice was poorly disguised. "At the end of this thing, I may have no choice but to do what he says, but in the meantime, I concede nothing," she finished. "And I would like nothing more than to see Nicolo beaten soundly at his own game."

Marilla surveyed her momentarily. Amantha could see her thinking, weighing the options, concern over the future at war with the curiosity she knew her aunt must be feeling about the treasure, and the legend. It had been such a large part of both of their lives, for better or for worse. And she could see her aunt considering the point Amantha made about Nicolo. Marilla had her own feud with the man; although she was far too classy to wage out and out war on him for fear of a very public reprisal, opportunities like this for underhanded revenge were few and far between. In the end, it was too good to pass up.

"All right, then," Marilla said. "Just promise me you'll use your head."

"Of course!"

"And I'm coming with you."

"As if you had a choice," Amantha said wryly. "Anything would be better than being here when Nicolo realizes what's happened."

Together, they slipped from the staff room and down the stairs. Taking a roundabout way, Amantha wove her way through the opulent, overstuffed display areas of the museum, finally ending her trek just outside the main room.

"Wait here," she whispered.

Marilla nodded and stayed in the shadows, clearly quite a bit more excited than she was willing to admit. Amantha walked quietly forward and peered around the corner. She hoped she wasn't too late.

Bingo.

There was Nicholas, display case open, holding the necklace up in front of him. Against the bright, whitewashed walls and expensive trappings, his blue jeans and light jacket looked strangely out of place. As Amantha remembered he was quite tall, with a willowy build and a posture than hinted at a somewhat shy personality. It was funny to see him in this way, knowing who he was.

In the quiet, Nicholas said something that Amantha didn't catch; she noted the small microphone nestled in his ear, and realized his accomplices must be on the other end. She glanced at the camera on the far side and knew she had ten seconds before its eye would find her; mindful of keeping herself out of its sight as well and thus invisible until she chose otherwise, she stepped into the room, keeping well close to the wall.

She didn't know how this was going to go.

****

"You sure those cameras are off, Jared?" Gregg asked nervously as he stepped into the main display area.

"Gregg. This is me you're talking to."

It was silent except for the ticking of some far-off clock and the quiet hum of the cameras that swiveled in their bases along the walls. There had to be at least five of them. In theory, Jared was going to guide him through the ever-changing angles, depositing him squarely in the spot that was covered only by the camera he had disabled. Taking all of them out would have been too obvious, even for a few minutes. It would only take one eagle-eyed guard to spot the problem.

Gregg could see the necklace staring at him from its case in the center of the room. Maybe he should just take the chance and run for it. The blue stone, winking in the light, seemed to egg him on.

"Ok… wait for my signal," Jared said.

Gregg waited.

"And you're sure there's nothing else in here I can set off," he suggested.

"Nothing. The motion sensors come on after all the staff have left. Trust me on this."

"Of course," Gregg muttered to himself.

"Right, get ready. When I tell you, step exactly three paces to your right and stop. After that you will proceed directly forward. On my cue, of course. Now. Go."

Gregg did as instructed. Along the wall to the right, three paces, prepared to go forward.

"And five paces forward... go."

Thus it continued for the next three minutes, this dance with failure. Forward, to the right again, back to the left, forward, left. The necklace loomed. Gregg studied its detail as he moved, ran the security codes through his head again. It was with no small amount of relief that he heard Jared give the all-clear as he stood in front of the case. Now, assuming he could get this thing out without a problem, Jared would have time to guide him back through the camera frames and out the door.

"Eight minutes until the guard."

"Thanks."

That would be the last guard check for the night, the one where they came by and switched on the motion sensors throughout the display rooms as the remaining staff prepared to exit the building. Gregg needed to be out of here before that happened.

Eight minutes. Piece of cake. He punched in the code, and the case popped open on command. There before him, on the top shelf, was the prize. Gregg thought he'd never seen anything so beautiful in his life. Marian's Necklace adorned an elegant, marble bust, lying against the creamy surface with grace and delicacy. The large pendant was constructed of solid silver and inlaid with the blue sapphire that shimmered in the brightly lit room, enhanced by intricate patterns of two identical, leafless branches that wove around it, etched with character. Gregg grinned and leaned back so the camera Jared was watching could get a good look, pointing excitedly. They were on their way now.

"What, do you want me to take a picture?" Jared asked, and his voice held anxiety. *"Let's go, Gregg. I can see it later."*

Gregg turned back to the piece, suddenly loathe to touch it. Then, with gentle hands, he reached forward and picked it up. Carefully he draped the necklace over his hand, a feeling of exhilaration claiming him as he stared at its glittering surface. He touched the piece gently; it was cool under his fingers. The beautiful, engraved silver lay across his palm like a leaf, the vibrant, blue stone staring at him like the dark eyes of the universe. It trembled as his finger ran across its shiny surface. Gregg looked closer. Funny, it looked like that piece was meant to come out.

"Come on, Gregg... let's go, let's go."

Time to go. He could worry about the loose stone later.

"I'm on my way." Gregg dug out the small, plastic bag he had brought along, put the necklace inside, and closed the cabinet. "You ready to go after some treasure?"

"You bet."

"Very good, Mr. Nicholas. I must say I'm impressed."

Gregg spun around to find Amantha Goldstein leaning on the doorframe, ankles crossed, watching him. She was dressed casually in jeans and sneakers, a loose sweater, and a light windbreaker over the top. Her museum ID was suspended around her neck on a navy blue, AOPA lanyard. Her hair was loose, falling over her left shoulder, as she regarded him with a thoughtful expression. In all, she looked fit, athletic, calm, cool, and collected.

"Damn," Jared said in his ear.

Damn was right. Gregg wasn't sure if it was going to end up being the good kind or not.

****

Gregg Nicholas was genuinely shocked to see her. Already he was backing away toward the door.

"I wouldn't do that," Amantha said casually. "The video feed in the hallway is live. Even if you make it out of this room, it's a long run." The sudden look of near panic on his face was evident, and she didn't have to move closer to hear the startled exclamation piping in miniature tones through the speaker in his ear. "You can tell your friend to calm down; if I'd wanted to give you both up I would have already. I just want to talk."

"I don't suppose I could request a raincheck," Nicholas said dryly, finding his voice. "I'm on a bit of a schedule."

"So I see." Amantha pushed herself off the wall and walked slowly towards him, hands in her pockets, hoping the nerves she was feeling weren't as visible on her face as they were on his. He regarded her suspiciously. The necklace lay forgotten in the bag in his palm.

"You're on camera, you know," Nicholas suggested. "We've only killed one in here."

"I am aware of that, yes. Fortunately for you, I am a common sight in this room." Amantha made sure she stayed well within the live video feeds throughout; if she somehow stepped into the same frame Nicholas was in, she would disappear. And then the whole thing would be over. They were like a pair of fighters, circling each other in the ring, each waiting for the other to make a wrong move. "Tell me, Mr. Nicholas... what is your plan? I assume, if you make it out of this building, that you have a plan."

"Yes. Get as far *away* from the building as possible."

"And then?"

"And then I... hope to follow this map to the end and find gold – what is all this about?"

Amantha merely smiled at him.

"I get it. You want something." Nicholas threw his hands up. "What? You're obviously not here just to turn me over to your lackeys for lying to you before, so what do you want?"

"You said it yourself: you're going on a treasure hunt."

"If I can get out of here, yes."

"I want to come."

"No way, Miss Goldstein," Nicholas said flatly. "Not a chance."

"Why not?"

"You mean aside from the fact that you'd be, like, the hugest liability in the history of liabilities?"

"You're already on the front page of today's paper, Nicholas; I fail to see how I'd be the liability."

"It's way too dangerous." Nicholas sighed, his countenance changing slightly. "Look. I'm not the only one after this thing, all right? There's somebody else. And he's not as nice as me or Jared." He tapped the earpiece nestled in his right ear.

"Only two of you? I thought there were three who broke into the dig."

"And now there are two, and we have competition," Nicholas responded. "For the moment there's a good bit of distance between us, but if that changes…" He shook his head. "It won't be safe. *You* won't be safe. And I can't have that on my conscience."

The photo from Northam's office leapt, unbidden, to her mind. A hint of unease followed. Amantha felt it touch her mind and banished it roughly; she'd already determined that the uncomfortable sense of déjà vu she'd experienced was nothing more than fatigue clouding her judgment.

"I'm a big girl, Mr. Nicholas. I can take care of myself."

"I don't even know where this thing will lead," Nicholas said, almost helplessly. "It might be nothing, go nowhere. Then what?"

"Then we can deal with that when it happens." Amantha crossed her arms. "I suggest you make up your mind quickly," she added. "You only have a few minutes, really, before security finds you." She checked her watch. "Three, as a matter of fact. They come through this room at quarter past the hour."

"How did you know I was here?"

"I saw the cameras freeze. And I knew you were coming because we found a symbol that matched the shape of that necklace on one of the tunnel walls when I replayed the interview recording."

Nicholas regarded her silently.

"Why?" He asked finally. "What do you hope to get out of this that you don't already have?"

"I want your name in a history book, Mr. Nicholas," Amantha said simply. "I want you to be known as the man who found the treasure of Robin Hood."

"I bet your family would love that," he muttered, and Amantha grinned at him.

"Precisely."

He sighed. Fell silent. Thought.

"Well…"

The sudden sound of the burglar alarm shattered the stillness of the room. Nicholas and Amantha both jumped. In the wide, open-facing of the room, the alarm rang and echoed and multiplied on top of itself, bouncing off the bare walls and tiled floor like a myriad of tennis balls. The noise was deafening. Gregg shouted something into the microphone, then flicked a switch to turn it off.

"It looks like you've been found, Mr. Nicholas!" Amantha yelled at him. "What is your decision!"

Nicholas rolled his eyes.

"Fine!" He yelled back. "You can come! I'll see you outside!" They ran out into the hallway, where Amantha caught his arm as Nicholas started to turn away.

"Not without some insurance! Give me the necklace!"

"Why!"

"I want to be sure you're not going to take off!"

Nicholas hesitated. Then, with a sudden look of inspiration, he took the necklace from the bag and felt along the bottom rim of the largest stone. His fingers found something, pressed, and the stone dropped into his palm.

"Go!" He shouted, tossing the stone to her. "Meet me in the parking lot!"

Amantha had no idea how he knew that loose piece was there. She still had no idea how he even got into the building in the first place. She had no idea how the alarm had been set off. Who set it off. Why. How. Her mind was a mass of questions – most with no answers – as she ran to where Aunt Marilla waited for her.

"Come on, Aunt Marilla," she said. "We need to go, now."

"Ammy…" Marilla caught her arm. "Are you sure you want to do this?"

Footsteps sounded. Amantha turned to spy Nicolo rounding the corner, security on his heels. His face was chiseled in stone, and the rage in his eyes was tangible.

"I never thought this of you, Amantha!" Nicolo yelled. "Stealing from your own family!"

"You're hardly family," Amantha said to herself.

She and Marilla turned around and ran. Nicolo yelled something at the guards, and when Amantha glanced over her shoulder, she saw both of them coming after her. She daren't contemplate the irony of running away from her own building. Just down the hall was a side entrance to the museum; beyond that, a set of stairs leading to the driveway and the underground staff carpark. Where Gregg Nicholas would be waiting.

"Amantha!"

The shout reverberated chillingly through the empty room behind them, blending and cycling with the alarm, as Amantha dragged Marilla toward the exit. The door appeared on her left. The solid, metal frame slammed open under her palm and Amantha bailed outside into the yellowed semi-darkness.

"Whoa!"

The exclamation of surprise hit her ears at precisely the same moment she saw the man cresting the stairs right in front of her. He was too close to avoid, so close the door almost hit him; she was running too fast. And Amantha, unable to stop, found herself falling headlong into his arms. An iron grip settled on her upper body as the door whacked into the handrail, a pair of big hands capturing her with ease when Amantha tried to jerk back. The smells of coffee, peppermint, old leather, and a very inviting cologne hit her senses, then movement was restricted entirely as her arms were pinned to her sides.

"Let me go!"

Amantha squirmed furiously, completely unaware of the confusion that prevailed in the background as the alarm continued to screech. She knew Nicolo would be right behind them – she had to escape! She bent around, an angry retort on her lips, and looked up to meet a pair of the most striking hazel eyes she had ever seen in her life. She froze. The deadly kick she had aimed at his instep never materialized. She was caught fast by the magnetism of his gaze, looking into hers with such intrigue. A lock of chestnut hair draped carelessly over his brow as, with an interested expression, her captor cocked his head to the side and smirked at her.

"Well, hello, Beautiful," he said in a velvety Australian accent. "And who might you be?"

Amantha realized at that precise moment that she'd been holding her breath. She was suddenly very aware of his touch. The world, which for a split second had disappeared entirely, came crashing back on hand as Marilla descended on them like a frigate under full sail, clubbing the man back with her umbrella.

"Keep your hands –" *smack!* "– *off* my niece!" Another fearsome swipe emphasized her demand.

As the man recoiled, Amantha managed to break free of his hold and grabbed Marilla by the hand, yanking her down the steps toward the carpark entrance with Marilla still yelling and flailing the brolly. They reached the dim hole and Amantha stopped. Turned. Found the doorway.

There he was at the corner of the building, paused with a hand on the frame, little more than a shadowy figure doing the same as she: looking back. Looking for her. Even from here she could feel his eyes on her. Even from here she could feel the intensity. The light played over his handsome features in a faded, gentle pattern, shining off the leather of his flight jacket. Neither of them moved. Amantha knew, as soon as she turned away, that she'd never in her life see this man again; so she stood, took the moment. It was one of those instants no one could ever explain; a connection forged with only a passing glance, an understanding reached with hardly a word spoken. No names. Amantha wished she knew his name.

A racket sounded inside the building, and just like that he was gone. With a final backward glance he melted into the darkness, disappearing just as Nicolo's guards banged the door open. Amantha jumped backward into the carpark. Her heart touched with a strange sense of loss, she ran down the sloped drive behind her aunt, reaching the lower level where Nicholas was waiting impatiently in the faded light. Down here, the alarm was little more than a muffled ringing, like it was being routed through a tin can.

"Hang on a minute, you didn't say *anything* about bringing someone else along," Nicholas said testily as they approached.

Marilla eyed him in a severe fashion.

"If you think you are going to leave me behind, young man, I suggest you reconsider," she responded.

"This is my aunt, Marilla Clancy," Amantha said. "Aunt Marilla, Gregg Nicholas."

A shout above the surface echoed through the hollow, cement space.

"We need to keep moving," Nicholas said, looking around carefully. He seemed strangely calm now, as if the anticipation of being found out was far worse than the actual event. His blue-green eyes now reflected only caution.

"Where's your friend... Jared?" Amantha asked as they jogged along the length of the carpark toward the emergency exit at the rear. She wondered if she should tell him about the man she'd just encountered.

"In a van a few blocks away. I have the microphone off so he can't hear us right now – he's liable to get a little panicky if he hears the kind of ruckus we're bound to attract." This last was spoken wryly, with affection.

The three fugitives reached the rear gate, paused. A big panel stretched across the middle, decorated with a label that read: EMERGENCY EXIT ONLY – ALARM WILL SOUND. Nicholas was about to press the gate outward to escape when the burglar alarm from above shut off. Where once there was a continual background racket, now there was nothing. Silence. Utter, stony silence, broken only by the occasional stray shout from the building. Before them, the path was little more than a white strip of concrete headed into the unknown.

"You'd best have a very quick route in mind, Mr. Nicholas," Marilla said quietly. "With the alarm off, this gate will give you away in quite short order."

"That's what I'm afraid of," Nicholas answered. He was surveying the blackened pathway with palpable apprehension, hand on the bar. Still he hesitated. "This is too easy," he said shortly. "There is no way they'd leave such an obvious escape route unblocked."

Amantha knew Northam had this building under heavy surveillance. It had been that way since the dig was breached. She'd expected a virtual army of policemen to materialize as they fled the building, covering any available exits, including this one. Like Nicholas said: this was far too easy.

"They could have me dead to rights back there," Nicholas said. "The cameras were live everywhere, and they're all over this parking structure; all they had to do was track me. What else could they want to –?"

Suddenly, Amantha knew. And, by the look he shot her, Nicholas was thinking the same thing.

"The van," Nicholas said sharply, "They know where it is. They found Jared."

Almost on cue, a car shot into the building behind them, lights flashing, squealing to a halt as the doors whipped open and uniformed men jumped to the ground. Northam's men.

Amantha hated being right all the time.

"Jared," Nicholas said in a panic, turning on the microphone, "get out now."

"What? Now?"

"Yes, *now*, move! The car's hot!"

Even as he spoke, Jared gave a panicked exclamation, catching sight of something only he could see. Eerily, Amantha could hear his voice, accompanied by a horrible racket as he scrabbled out of the car.

"Gregg! Gregg they're all around me!" Came the frantic cry from the ear-piece.

"Get under cover, Jared! We're coming!"

"There's too many –"

The speaker was disconnected.

Nicholas swore soundly and pressed the bar. Another alarm started screeching madly directly overhead, this one higher and more penetrating, blending with the shouts and sirens and running footsteps behind them.

"Go, go, go!" Nicholas shoved them out the gate and slammed it shut, jamming a bin under the handle. "To the right! *Move!*" He shouted. He led the way, running into a nearby alleyway with Amantha and Marilla right on his heels.

****

"We've lost sight of them, sir," Howell said over the radio.

"Keep looking. They can't have gone far."

Northam and Gates jogged into the main road, a few blocks from the museum. The van was sitting before them, jutting from the earth with the doors open and the engine running, vibrating slightly as it idled in place. Four or five policemen scoured the area directly around. Leaning in the driver's side, Gates reached over and flicked the ignition off.

"Well, they can't get far without a ride," he said, pocketing the keys.

"Kneeles, stay here," Northam said, addressing the men around them. "The rest of you fan out and work your way back toward the museum."

Damn. They'd almost had this lot. If the alarm hadn't been triggered when it had, Northam would have had Nicholas dead to rights.

"Now the question is: who set it off," Northam wondered aloud, speaking to himself.

The inside of the car was a shambles. Equipment and clothing was scattered everywhere, like someone had rummaged through and grabbed only the absolute necessities of life before making a mad dash for the door. The occupants were gone. An overturned laptop lay between the front seats, humming slightly, connected to a pair of headphones with a speaker that dribbled over the edge and hung by its cord, swinging aimlessly. Northam lifted the setup, staring at it momentarily. He turned it, slowly, and held a finger to his lips as he gestured to the image on the screen. Before them was a hazy picture, obviously from a small camera, bouncing and skittering around as the owner moved restlessly forward.

"Somebody forgot to turn off the program," Gates remarked softly, and smiled as Northam slipped on the headphones. Heavy breathing was audible through the speaker in tiny, electronic vibes. The background was unclear, a hodge-podge assembly of street and buildings, but Northam was able to pick out a few significant characteristics. He waited silently, like a bird of prey, for information. Suddenly the camera he watched through panned right, sharply, and a second figure skidded into view around a corner.

"Jared!" A voice hissed close to the speaker.

That would be Jared Casey. Sidekick, college student, and apparently computer nerd extraordinaire, if the amount of tech gadgets on hand was to be believed.

"Gregg!" The kid dashed forward and reached him, clearly out of breath. Well, two out of three from the dig were accounted for; Northam wondered briefly where the third party was, the tall bloke with chestnut hair. The one Gates had called Ian Lowell. *"They almost had me back there,"* Jared said. Straightening, he looked beyond Gregg Nicholas, out of sight of the camera. *"Who are they? Dude, really, you brought tourists? What is this, an excursion?"*

"They're not tourists, Jared," Gregg Nicholas replied almost immediately, mantled with light traces of a Texas accent.

Northam arched an eyebrow as the camera turned around. The shadowed faces of Amantha Goldstein and Marilla O'Clancy stared back at him onscreen, looking around uneasily. Northam and Gates traded a look. What were *they* doing?

"We can't stay here," Amantha said directly.

"What about the van? Think we can go back for it?" The computer nerd asked.

"No," Gregg said. *"We'll just find cover and wait."*

"For what? Meal time? Dude, why don't you just call Ian? He's probably at a pub somewhere crying into his beer and waiting for something to do."

"I'm not quite ready to stoop that low, Jared."

"Come on, Gregg surely you have a better plan than just –"

Northam cleared his throat.

"Gregg Nicholas, am I right?" He cut in mildly.

The nerd broke off mid-sentence. Conversation ceased. Northam could almost imagine the frantically-waving hand signaling for silence, evidenced by the shocked expressions on the other three faces.

"Funny," Gregg's voice said over the line. *"Somehow I didn't picture God with an English accent."*

"No, I would imagine not," Northam answered. "Fortunately for you, I don't claim responsibility for making the laws. I only enforce them."

"Cop, huh?"

Northam saw the view shift slightly, angling away from the others.

"Commander Northam," he introduced himself. "Scotland Yard." He watched the camera suddenly give a spastic jerk as it was hastily unpinned from its mooring. "I trust this isn't too much of an inconvenience for you," he added.

"Not at all," Nicholas said, and with a sodden crunch, the sound vanished with the picture. The camera and microphone had both been smashed.

"Howell." Northam yanked the headphones off. "They're still in the area," he said. "Nicholas, Casey, Miss Goldstein, and her aunt. All four of them are together."

Gates was already going to work on the laptop. Pulling up the video from moments before, he sifted through it quickly and paused the clip right after Nicholas had turned from his companions. There was a sign visible in the background, illuminated by a streetlight, which Northam had seen but was unable to read for the distance. With a few quick keystrokes, Gates isolated that portion of the picture and blew it up.

"We've got them."

"Kneeles, stay with the van." Northam slammed the door and followed Gates away. "Howell, where are you?" He asked directly. "We're coming your way now."

"Yes, sir. We're at the northern end of the street. It looks like there's a –" Howell suddenly cut himself off. *"Wait, sir, something's happening."*

"What?" Northam stopped mid-stride. "What do you have?"

"I'm not quite sure. It sounds..." Howell's voice trailed off for a moment, then: *"John, look out!"*

Without another word, Gates and Northam ran for Howell's position.

****

Gregg tossed the broken shards of technology away, unnerved. The voice that had met him was unyielding, seeming cast from iron, the voice of one who would not give up until he had what he wanted. In this case, Gregg's head on a platter.

"That was close," Jared said, wiping a hand over his forehead. "Sorry, man, I thought I killed the program."

"It's all right, Jared," Gregg said. "But Miss Goldstein is right: we can't stay here. It won't take them long to find us. What I want to know is who set that alarm off."

"Well, they were about to shut down for the night. Maybe somebody walked past the wrong sensor."

"The alarm wouldn't have been armed yet, as there was still staff inside," Amantha said. "Someone set it off intentionally. The only place to do that is in the back of the building, near where I ran into that guy –"

"What guy?" Gregg asked sharply. Even as he said it, the situation became clear. Gregg looked at Jared, found him looking back, and slumped hopelessly back against the wall.

Ian. Ian was the guy. Gregg should have known he couldn't lose him for long.

"An uncouth beast," Marilla said indignantly. "Had his arms all the way around Amantha, he did. The poor girl was pressed against him like a grape."

"Yeah that sounds about right," Gregg muttered to himself as Amantha tried, rather unsuccessfully, to hide the blush coloring her fair cheeks. Even in the darkness her discomfiture was tangible.

Bloody Ian. He had set up this whole thing, waiting until Gregg was well and truly committed before setting off the alarm in the building and making things too hot to handle. Somehow, some way, he had known about the museum despite Gregg not saying anything, used the information to his advantage, and engineered a very slick job. He had set up the trap, sat back, and was probably somewhere nearby, just waiting for Gregg to call him for help. And by doing that, Ian would get his hands on what he really wanted: Marian's Necklace, and the riddle.

Add Amantha Goldstein into the mix, and Ian would think all his Christmases had come at once.

How had he known? How had he figured it out? Gregg sighed. Maybe, at the end of the day, Ian was just that damn good.

"What are you going to do?" Jared's question was quiet.

"You know what I'm going to do."

"Look... I know I suggested it, but I was sort of kidding. Are you sure that's a good idea?"

"Nope."

What Ian would do with them was uncertain. For all Gregg knew, calling him might be worse than taking their chances on foot. The problem was he didn't have a choice. Two men had just come into view through the gloom and found Jared's trail across the way, five more were fanning out along the street on either side. Flashlight beams were everywhere. Slowly, the entourage began to tighten their circle, heading right for the small alcove where Gregg and the others waited like so many ducks in thunder. One of them was pointing at the building across the street; it wouldn't be long before they closed in. And Gregg knew there was only one thing to do. He only prayed Ian wouldn't shoot him on sight.

"Who are you ringing?" Amantha asked as Gregg whipped out his phone.

"The bloody guy that got us into this bloody mess in the bloody first place," Gregg groused, and hit call.

"Who's that?"

"Ian Lowell."

Amantha glanced over.

"And who is he?"

A fighter pilot is a man in love with flying. [He] sees not a cloud but beauty. Not the ground but something remote from him, something that he doesn't belong to as long as he is airborne. He is a man who wants to be second-best to no one.

- *Brigadier General Robin Olds*

Chapter 16

Whoever this Ian chap was, he was only too happy to help. Gregg hadn't been inclined to discuss his identity much; all he'd said in response to Amantha's question was "the competition", and pressed the phone to his ear. And with that, Amantha knew she and Marilla were about to meet the third member of Gregg's dig team, the one Gregg had warned her about inside. The one who wasn't so nice.

Beside her, Jared mumbled something unintelligible, watching Gregg in resignation. He was a skinny kid, Amantha saw; eyes as blue as the summer sky and very perceptive. Dark hair, wavy, cut short enough to stay out of his eyes but still a bit on the long side. Geeky looking, especially with the glasses, but Amantha had a feeling he would turn out to be quite the handsome lad when he got a little older.

"Yes, there are four of us..." Gregg was saying into the phone, frowning. A second of silence, and: "What, are you worried about seatbelt regulations or something?" He snapped. "Of course we're fine to split up; just pick us up and we'll deal with it then. And... hurry, will you?" He sighed, hung up, and pocketed the phone. "Miss Goldstein, Mrs. Clancy," he started, "this is the last opportunity for you to get out of this mess, and I really wish you'd take it." He looked to them, pleadingly, eyes vacillating from one to the other. "Seriously," he added for emphasis. "It would go much better for you if Ian and his team never came in contact with you."

As if he wasn't serious enough already. Amantha shook her head, was aware of Marilla doing the same to her left. Gregg sighed again, heavily.

"Then welcome to chaos," he said. "I would advise you from now on to keep to yourselves and watch your step. The men we're about to team up with are no saints." He rubbed his forehead. "You in particular, Miss Goldstein." He studied her briefly, as if weighing a pair of unsavory options, then finally cleared his throat and glanced away. "Look, um… I don't want to sound melodramatic or theatrical or scare you or anything, but – I want you to do me a favor and stay away from Ian when you meet him," he said. "Just stay all the way away."

Marilla raised her eyebrows at him.

"Are you suggesting that my niece would prefer to do otherwise?" She queried.

"No, no not at all!" Gregg was clearly afraid of causing her offense. "He can just be very –" He paused. "Charming."

"'A mischievous rascal of a man with Rick Simon's eye for women and Indiana Jones' penchant for trouble'," Jared said, providing air quotes as he did so. He jerked a thumb at Gregg. "He said it first. I'm just quoting him because it bears repeating due to an inherent truth."

"I see… I will try to keep my wits about me." Amantha looked between them in amusement. She doubted very much that she'd be swept off her proverbial feet by something as universal as charming. If this chap Ian thought he was all that, God's gift to woman, he could keep on nursing that beer and dream. Amantha was just here for the gold.

"Oh. And for the record I'm sorry about before, at the museum," Gregg added. "With the..." He searched for the right phrase. "…fondling," he finished, awkwardly. "Some men have no sense of propriety."

"It's quite all right," Amantha replied, praying her obvious confusion with the issue could be attributed to aristocratic embarrassment; she didn't want to admit to him – or anyone else – what her thoughts were concerning that particular moment in time. It didn't matter anymore. The whole thing was over; she would never see the man again, and didn't even know his name; there was absolutely no need to dwell on it. Really, fancies such as the ones she was entertaining were positively... unsuitable. As well as ill-timed, considering they were unnervingly close to being run aground and all Amantha's brain wanted to focus on was a pair of hazel eyes. In the few seconds it took to call this Ian character and specify where they were, the circle had tightened still more, making escape almost impossible if their ride didn't show up within the next thirty seconds. A guy across the street was already scoping out their position with a bright torch.

"They'll be on us in a minute," Gregg whispered, ducking as the beam went right over his head. "Come on, Ian, where are you?" He slid to his feet, keeping in the darkness, and edged toward the street. "All right, look," he said. "I'm going run out and try to draw them off, but you-all stay put. When Ian picks you up, call me, and if I haven't gotten caught I'll tell you where to find me, okay? I have to get these guys out of here."

"Uh, no you don't. Not if that's Ian."

Jared's comment caused Gregg to fall silent. Off to the left, the low rumbling sound of a large motor was slowly beginning to disentangle itself from the ever-present hum of traffic, growing louder and louder. The three men down that way stopped. Even the two across the street paused. Amantha could almost see them asking each other what was going on.

"What is that?" Amantha asked.

Suddenly, a horn blared, a muffled yell sounded, and everyone in the street dove for cover. They lunged off the road, leaping headlong out of the way as, with a roaring of its giant motor and squealing of tires, a US military Humvee skidded sidewise around the corner and charged up the lane, another right on its tail. Streetlights illuminated the massive, camo-green vehicles, making them seem even larger as they bored through the night. Ian had made his entrance.

"What the *hell* – You've *got* to be kidding me!" Jared shouted.

"Come on!" Gregg leapt into the open, waving his arms wildly. In the beams of light spraying across the street, he looked almost comical. He yanked the door open as the first Hummer slid to a screeching halt right beside him, ladling the area with fine dust. "It's about time, Ian!" He yelled. "Where were you?"

The second Hummer skidded to a halt. Two henchman appeared, grabbed Marilla by the arms, and yanked her toward the car.

"Get in!" Amantha heard one of them shout. Then Marilla disappeared, doors were shut, and she and Jared were piling into the back of the first vehicle as the other shot by them, engine roaring. One door slammed. Another.

"Everybody in?" The driver, Ian, craned his neck around to have a look. Amantha suddenly felt her breath catch in her throat.

"You!" No. This couldn't be happening.

The man who had so unceremoniously broken her fall outside the museum glanced over and met her eyes, a genuine and playful grin suddenly lighting his face.

"Well, hello again, Beautiful," he said impishly.

Amantha was saved trying to come up with something to say as Gregg whacked him solidly across the back of the head and shrank down below the dashboard.

"Save it! Go!" He yelled.

Lowell punched it. The giant car plowed forward, whipping in a tight circle as it laid rubber on the street and sent men scattering. The noise was deafening. The Hummer's six point five litre, turbo-charged diesel engine shot up to two thousand RPMs and beyond, sending the great beast charging forward like it had been shot out of a cannon.

So this was Ian Lowell. Amantha didn't know what else to think. Literally, nothing else came to mind. Except at least she knew his name now. Amid the immediate and confusing mess of emotions that boiled to the surface, she tried to make sense of who this man was, exactly. Ian, the third member of Gregg's team, the man in the photo from Northam's office. Clearly Amantha had been mistaken when she thought she knew him. That photo may not have been the best quality, but if she had actually met Lowell before there was no way she'd forget him. He was much too…

Hot.

Amantha gripped whatever she could as the Hummer's back end spun crazily to the right, sliding over hard pavement; inertia soon had her following it around, crashing into the back of her seat when the vehicle straightened and leapt forward. Jared, not belted in properly, did an elaborate somersault in place and almost wound up in a hand-stand position on the floor. He clutched frantically at the belt as Ian jerked the wheel to the right and shot out into the chaos that was the main road.

"Ian, the bus!" Gregg yelled.

The Hummer lurched again, sending both Amantha and Jared against the wall. Amantha heard horns honking, tires screeching, and then a small car went zipping by below the window, untouched, its driver shaking a fist. Admittedly, Amantha was terrified. Even at this hour these streets were far too narrow and crowded for a crazed car chase, especially involving a vehicle of this size. They could all be killed! Her attention was drawn to the front, where Ian had picked up a two-way radio and was now driving with one hand while he talked easily with whoever was on the other end.

"Stan," he said, "we're on the move. Stay put until we're clear, and then come clean up." A crackling affirmative sounded as Lowell took a quick look over his shoulder, deftly switching lanes when the street widened to peel through a mess of cars. Streetlamps danced rhythmically over the windscreen. "King, where are you?" He asked above the bellow of the engine.

"Where do you think I am?" Was the crackly response. *"Dodging a few cops."*

"Yeah, we got a few of our own," Ian answered as lights began to dance across the ceiling, blending with the streetlamps. Suddenly, he laughed. "Hey, was that you?"

Amantha glanced right as, several streets over through a narrow alley, the back end of a Humvee and a cavalcade of police cars shot by, going the other way.

"Why don't you spin that thing around and we can have a little fun?"

"No!" Gregg shouted.

"You got it," the other said merrily. A few moments later, a jovial yell sounded over the walkie. *"Hey, Aussie, we're coming up on you now!"*

It was about then Amantha realized both of these men were completely mad. Lowell's voice radiated an almost suicidal excitement as he dropped the Hummer into a slide and skidded around a corner, positively cackling with glee. A stoplight loomed ahead, but, fortunately, remained green as they flew by, doing a slalom run through the traffic.

"Ian, watch it, or you're going to get us all killed!" Gregg's outline disappeared again as a sign missed the window by mere centimeters.

"Plenty of space, mate," Lowell said. "Rob, keep an eye this side-street to our left!"

"Why are you so blasé about this!" Jared shouted. He flopped against the radio unit, white as a sheet and seeming on the verge of cardiac arrest. Buildings flew by on either side; cars, trucks, signs, pedestrians all undamaged by the onslaught. Lowell could drive; Amantha would give him that.

She had no idea how long the insanity lasted – much longer than she thought, surely – before they reached a slip road. She clutched the seat as they rounded a corner, then clapped her hand to her mouth to stifle a yelp.

"What *is* that!" Jared yelled frantically.

A few hundred meters ahead, limned in the semi-dark under a series of fluorescent lights and the stream of headlamps on the motorway, their path came to an abrupt end in a mess of barriers and earth-moving equipment. The road was under construction. This could be a bit sticky.

"Well, we'll just see about this," Lowell said, almost to himself. As if to add insult to injury, four or five squad cars suddenly shot into view and skidded to a halt, trying to flank anything the ready-made wall of obstacles missed.

"You're on your own with this one, mate," Rob's voice cut in. *"I'm taking another route. We'll catch you at the target."*

Target?

Amantha glanced over her shoulder in time to see the Hummer cut a sharp dido behind them and spin around like it was on a tether, hurtling back the other way to blaze a trail through oncoming traffic. Several pursuit cars plowed off to the sides with tires squealing. Their own speed had increased. Amantha couldn't see the speedometer, couldn't see anything at all. There was the line of cars, the blockade, all of it coming closer... they roared by the vehicles and, at the last moment, Amantha flung her arm over Jared to keep him in place, clinging to the first stationary object she could find. Then they slammed into the barricade, the Hummer's giant grill sending debris spewing in all directions as it smashed out the other side.

"Anytime, baby!" Lowell shouted, and plowed through the mess to hit the motorway at high speed.

Amantha had been absolutely right. He was insane.

Dragging the cars by the barricade and at least three more who had been with them from the start, they shot onto the motorway, the Hummer's engine bellowing.

"Rob, I can see you. We're about half a mile back," Ian said abruptly, and there was a crackling affirmative.

"Coming up on target!" Rob called, far too jovially for comfort.

How the other vehicle had managed to get in front, Amantha didn't know. A couple of seconds later, she didn't care.

"Good luck!"

"Good luck?" Gregg and Jared asked in unison. Gregg looked forward and groaned, slouching down against his seat. "Oh no, Ian. Not again…"

Amantha peered over Jared's flailing arm just in time to see the other Humvee, pulling at least half a dozen cop cars, suddenly veer sharply to the right, cut across the lane, and aim its nose right for a slanted trailer that held down a position beside the central reservation. The trailer was surrounded by flares, spaced evenly and lighting the edges like a runway. The trajectory created by its angle aimed directly toward a sweeping curve in the barrier, beyond which were the opposite-bound lanes. A column of cars charged like Formula One racers toward the location.

He wasn't!

The Hummer straightened, headed right for the makeshift ramp.

He was.

The massive car powered up the incline, flew off the end, and went airborne. Tires still spinning in the light, it sailed over the reservation and a lane of head-on traffic before it crashed down and sped off again, weaving madly and cutting through the scattered cars. Headlamps wove crazy patterns as other drivers tried to avoid a collision. Another leap and it left the road to gouge its way through the fence surrounding a nearby park, skidding to a sideways halt with long black marks stretching out behind it in what would have been perfectly-manicured grass. Over the radio, Rob's distinct voice shouted victoriously. Amantha could hear her aunt screaming in the background.

Lowell stuck a fist out the open window with a wild war whoop as they reached the scene. They swept past the flares, onto the base of the trailer with a solid clunk and the Hummer surged forward, gaining momentum. A split second later, the vehicle shot off the end of the ramp and soared into the air.

Amantha could do nothing but stare. The earth seemed to disappear from beneath them, falling away, and Amantha felt her stomach drop down through the soles of her shoes. It was like taking off in an aeroplane, but with the knowledge it would soon turn into a roller coaster. Over the barrier they went, crashing down hard, and suddenly Amantha was staring at the bonnet of a huge lorry as it plowed toward them. It came closer, closer, enough for Amantha to pick out the Mack logo on the front, illuminated eerily. Then it was gone around the side. The Hummer fishtailed, wove its way around a covey of oncoming cars and, with another dive, sailed off the side of the road. It landed with a slam in the park. In the other Humvee, Amantha caught a glimpse of the man at the wheel, laughing at them.

Neither driver waited to see what kind of damage they'd caused. Lowell jammed the throttle to the floor and sped off, following Rob, grass and plants shooting out from under the tires.

"Thanks, Stan! Now get out of there!"

As her pulse began to slow a little, Amantha glanced back, staring at the motorway and a few shocked pedestrians in disbelief until a tree branch swept across the top of the vehicle, blocking her view. And as the whole chaotic mess faded out, Amantha knew she hadn't had that much fun in a car in a long time.

Not that she'd admit it, of course.

The rough journey continued for another few minutes. Finally, with a last bounce, they left the park and reentered the traveled main of surface streets. They received a few odd looks from passers-by. And everyone else. It seemed all around them was a sea of staring eyes.

"Are you all right, Jared?" Amantha asked.

"Yeah. You?"

Amantha just nodded, taking stock of their surroundings. Was Lowell serious? They were wanted. Criminals. Fugitives. But instead of running for their lives, they were instead gadding about with the utmost of nonchalance, winding through a typical London tailback ensconced in what could only be described as two drab packing boxes with wheels. It's not like they were invisible.

"Ian... has it occurred to you yet that maybe this isn't the best place for us to be?" Gregg inquired tactfully.

"Not nervous, are you, Genius?" Lowell and Rob dutifully came to a halt at a red light. Beside them, Amantha saw a small child staring up at the cars in shock.

"You know I hate it when you do that," Gregg said. "The car chases, squealing tires, going airborne and almost getting killed... I don't see why you find that so fun." He drummed his fingers on the hard metal of the door, attempting to be casual. "So... where'd you get the wheels this time?"

"Come now, Gregg. You know America has bases in every country in this world."

"You stole an active-duty vehicle? From a *base*?"

"Where else am I going to get one?"

"Can't you do anything without stealing it first?" Jared chimed in.

"If it's any consolation, it was in the maintenance yard, so it wasn't exactly *active*."

"How is that a consolation? It's stolen *and* might break down without notice! What exactly was your criteria for securing a ride?"

"It started. That was probably the biggest plus." Ian laughed at Gregg's continued alarm, his eyes shifting to find Amantha's in the mirror. "How you holding up back there, love?"

The question caught her by surprise.

"Quite all right, thank you," she said simply. Caution would be the key in dealing with this one, she thought, as the light before them changed to amber and they moved forward. She could feel the color creeping into her cheeks again. This whole situation had taken such an unexpected – and unnerving – turn; she wasn't quite sure what do. It was just hard to accept, this. Of all the people in the world, why did Ian Lowell have to be *him*?

"You were at the dig the other night, weren't you?"

"Yes... yes, I was." Amantha wondered at the inquisitive tone, watching him keenly. "Were you?" She asked in return. "I didn't see you anywhere."

"Well, you weren't supposed to," was the cheeky reply, complete with requisite grin. "Although I must admit Gregg had the better end of that deal. I was pulling Jared-sitting duty."

"Hey!" Jared protested, and Amantha stopped just short of rolling her eyes in amusement.

"I'm terribly sorry for the inconvenience," she said. "Next time you lot decide to break in somewhere I'll be sure to be on hand to give you an interview."

"Admit it, you would have enjoyed that."

"I guess we'll never know, will we?" Amantha's response was delivered in kind.

Lowell winked at her and pulled a small bag of what appeared to be peppermint candies out from under his seat, offering it around before taking one himself.

"Where to, Gregg?" He asked.

Gregg was clearly at a loss. Amantha felt bad for him, realizing just how out of his element he was. Well, she'd wanted to come along on this little jaunt; might as well make herself useful.

"I might be able to help with that," she suggested.

Gregg glanced back at her tentative statement, looking suddenly hopeful. The puppy-dog expression on his face was too much to ignore.

"Do you have a place we could go?"

"Maybe." Amantha thought for a moment, realizing she needed to get in touch with her aunt. The location she had in mind was Marilla's farm in Kent, the place where Amantha had grown up. The farm was in a trust, and still held the O'Clancy name. But, the Goldsteins had made Marilla drop that "O" when she agreed to rejoin the clan to be close to her niece, leaving her with just the Clancy; there was a chance, however slight, that the change would be enough to throw law enforcement off for a short period of time. Possibly. "May I use your radio for a moment, please?"

"Of course," Lowell said in response to her question, and handed the device back to her. "It's a bit old school but it does the trick."

"Thank you." His eyes were simply astounding. "Your friend's name is Rob, correct?" Amantha queried. "I assume it's not King."

"True, but if you call him King he'll love you."

"Please don't," Gregg pleaded.

Amantha smiled and raised the radio, pressing the large button under her thumb.

"Hello… am I speaking with Rob?" She inquired.

"You certainly are, darling, and who am I am speaking with?" The answering response simply dripped with male intrigue. It was accompanied by several catcalls and whistles from the peanut gallery. Amantha caught Gregg shaking his head and muttering something unintelligible. He seemed to do that a lot with this crowd.

"That's not overly important at the minute, I'm afraid, but I would like to speak with Marilla."

"And just who might she be?"

"Unless you have more than one woman in your car, I should think it's quite obvious," Amantha responded wryly. Already she could hear Marilla in the background, demanding possession of the radio. Rob and two others could be heard arguing with her before there was a moment of silence, followed by Marilla's voice.

"Ammy? Are you there? Are you all right, dear?"

"Yes, I'm fine… you?"

"Yes. Although I must say the gentlemen in my company are somewhat lacking in etiquette, not to mention vocabulary."

Another chorus, this one of dissent.

"Come on!" Amantha heard one of them gripe. American. Typical.

"Shush!" Marilla commanded. *"Clearly your mother never spanked you, but don't think I won't."*

"I'd rather get spanked by the other girl," the voice sassed teasingly, but got no further before there was a distinctive whumping sound and a yelp.

"Manners maketh man, lad, and you have a long way to go," Marilla answered. *"Are Gregg and Jared all right, Ammy?"*

"We're fine, Aunt Marilla!" Jared called, while Gregg chimed in from the front seat.

"Yes, but we have a small problem," Amantha said. "We need a place to go. Someplace we can spend the night."

"You're thinking the farm, are you?"

"Would you mind?"

Another pause as Marilla considered.

~ 311 ~

"All right," she said at last. *"But just for tonight. Tell the boys – nah! You watch your language, lad; and hands to yourself!"*

"Thank you!" Gregg called from the front, clearly relieved.

"Gregg says thank you," Amantha relayed. She bid her aunt good-bye, with Marilla still laying down the law with the henchmen and handed the radio back to Lowell.

"Sounds like she's busy making friends," Lowell remarked. He rubbed the back of his neck, where Amantha did recall seeing a particularly solid blow land earlier. "Who is that woman, anyway?"

Despite herself, Amantha laughed outright at his wounded tone.

"My aunt," she said amusedly. "Marilla."

"Mrs. Clancy to you," Gregg added.

"Unless I have a death wish."

"Precisely." Gregg's expressive countenance turned back to Amantha. "Where do we go from here?"

"My aunt has a small property in Kent," Amantha said. "About an hour's drive, barring traffic… longer by way of back roads, of course. It's under her late husband's name and was used by his family for some time, so it's not easily traced. Well…" She shrugged. "I would venture a guess that it would buy us tonight. If you'll turn left up here, Mr. Lowell, I'll show you where to go."

"You're in charge, love," Lowell said. He lifted the radio briefly. "Fall in behind and stick close, boys. Our lovely lady passenger is giving us a guided tour."

"We're on it," a new voice said. *"And can you please do something about this woman?"*

"Just mind your manners and you'll be right," Lowell said. "It's about time you boys had some performance management."

The Hummer in front of them pulled off, giving Ian free rein out front, and Amantha leaned forward to give directions. After that, it was just down to the waiting. Time passed slowly, the two vehicles rumbled along without difficulty. The ride was tense. They were far from being out of danger, as the streets of Greater London still stretched around them, and no one knew if, by some harsh stroke of misfortune, they might round a corner and come face to face with a cop car. Twice they did have to nip off into obscure niches to avoid detection. Darkness was their ally in this instance, but even it failed to disguise everything.

They stayed off the motorway as much as possible, which added a significant amount of time to the journey. Gradually, the city began to thin out, the spaces between houses became wider, the streets less official. When the ghosted portraits of sheep started to be framed in the window, it was clear they were almost home free. Streets became roads; towns thinned, became smaller. It was with a nearly collective sigh of relief that they all acknowledged they were out. The headlights illuminated the bitumen before them, which was deserted, as would be expected at this time of night, leaving them undisturbed.

And still, all Amantha could think about was: now what? Things had certainly changed tonight.

"Rob, you guys still alive back there?" Lowell asked after a good forty-five minutes of silence.

"Yeah, we're fine, Ian. George is asleep. Troy's still a little scared, but – Ah!"

A muffled thump and a yell cut off the teasing voice as, behind them, the second set of headlamps did a dido before straightening out again, skipping across the ceiling in a convulsive fashion.

"We'll be in touch," the other voice said, and clicked off.

Jared was squeezed into his seat and now sat silently, bunched up like a cold sheep as he regarded the whole setting with an aggrieved air. Amantha could hardly blame him.

"Gregg, you may not believe this," Lowell said quietly as he put the radio down, "but as we pulled onto the main road, I thought I saw Gates standing there."

Gregg moaned.

"Oh, I saw him too. I was hoping it was just my imagination," he said miserably. "You know, shadow games with the light or something like that. Paranoia gone wrong. You think he's helping them out? Would he even have authority over here?"

"I doubt it."

"But…?"

Lowell paused, glancing at a night bird that swooped low across the road.

"He's here," he said.

Were they speaking of Marshal Gates, the man Amantha had met in Northam's office?

"What should we do about it?" Gregg asked, and Lowell shrugged.

"Be more careful, I guess," he said. "You know Gates; he's like a dog with a bone when there is a riddle that remains unsolved."

"And where we're involved..."

"...he'll be twice as bad." Lowell smirked. "He has a reputation to uphold, after all," he concluded. "He'll be happy to run us down just on principle."

They were quiet after that. Gregg started to fade. The tires hummed easily on the smooth, winding road; the engine growled comfortingly in Amantha's ears as she took in their surroundings. Lowell was watching carefully all around, his eyes constantly shifting and leaving not a bush or a pebble unnoticed, updating the ever-changing picture that must be visible in his mind.

They continued on without speaking, and the world rolled by slowly. Amantha always forgot how dark it got out here, with no streetlamps to break the black expanse. She could see bugs fluttering in the bright beams of the headlamps; occasionally, a small animal would dart across the road. Behind them, the other Humvee rolled along unwaveringly, its lights casting shadows all through the interior of the front car. Jared was asleep. Gregg's head finally dropped permanently as he joined him, and Lowell glanced over, carefully nudging Gregg's sagging neck into a more comfortable position. Amantha thought she saw him smile a little, the type of expression an older brother might use on a sibling, but she couldn't be sure.

She knew little of this man – in fact, almost nothing – but Gregg's spare and heartfelt warning about him gave her pause. Not to mention her own chaotic mindset. It was amazing what a split second could do. She couldn't deny she was curious about Lowell; he was just one of those people that demanded attention simply by being present. From what she'd observed he was intelligent, adaptable, and had that unique ability to think quickly on his feet. A formidable foe, indeed. Funny though, when Gregg told her about "the competition", he had conveniently forgotten to mention that the two of them used to be mates.

"Are you an owner or enthusiast?"

Amantha turned forward to find Lowell's eyes on her in the rearview mirror.

"Pardon?"

He gestured to the lanyard around her neck, the dark strap emblazoned with the AOPA logo.

"Oh!" Amantha quickly removed her ID, placing it on the seat beside her. "I completely forgot I had this on. To answer your question, I am fortunate enough to be both," she said. "You might call me an enthusiastic owner. My plane is hangared not far from our destination, as a matter of fact. At Old Hay."

"Old Hay! Really!" An expression that seemed far too cheesy and boyish for a man of his dubious profession lighted Lowell's face. "Beautiful spot," he said. "I came to one of their fly-ins a few years ago."

"Are you a flyer?" Amantha asked, far more keenly than she intended. It was such fun to meet fellow aviation nerds.

"Since I was sixteen. Gregg and I started together."

Of course he would be. A hot guy with a great smile, and he was a pilot. Only drawback was he happened to be a crime boss and probably had a record rivaling the length of an unchecked tapeworm.

"I assume you own one," Amantha ventured. "A plane, that is. Considering… you know, the work you're involved in and the amount of travel you must do…" How else was she supposed to phrase that?

Ian chuckled at her attempt at tact.

"Gulfstream," he said. "Nothing fancy; it's not a G6 or anything, but it's functional and hasn't left me high and dry yet. You? What are your wings of choice?" This last was said with that same, cheeky smile.

"Actually, I… own a Spitfire," Amantha said. She met his gaze without reservation. "1944 Mark IX."

"No." His eyes lit up. "I thought you were going to say you flew an ultralight or something."

"Hardly."

"Shotgun start?"

"What else?" Amantha grinned back at him. "She's beautiful," she said simply. "And challenging. I've been flying since I was eighteen and have done my share of hours, but this was…" She shook her head. "Exhilarating."

There really was no other word.

"I'm sold," Ian said. "Don't be surprised if I come knocking on your door one day asking for a ride. I must say, that is impressive, Miss Goldstein. Only sixty or so of those birds left, and you fly one."

Amantha tried hard not to like the compliment. A good forty-five percent of her succeeded.

"Aunt Marilla's house is directly ahead," she said instead. She leaned forward along the wireless unit and pointed out the small, overgrown driveway, which was chronically shielded by rose bushes and other assorted plant life. "It's up here on the right. Watch it, it sort of sneaks up on you."

"I can see that."

Amantha glanced at him. Found him watching her, smiling. Hazel eyes, intense, edged with a strange gentleness, accentuating strong features. Unreadable. Intelligent. Gregg's warning about charm surfaced in there somewhere. With words suddenly fleeing her mind, Amantha sat back as they turned off the road to Marilla's house, unsure of whether it was fear or excitement she was feeling in the pit of her stomach. Maybe a bit of both. Logically speaking there should be no argument, of course, but then… Amantha had a feeling she was a bit past logic.

****

"Where is she?" The face of Nicolo Goldstein was an imposing one, to be sure, when he approached Northam and Gates in the foyer of the museum as soon as they walked in. Northam swallowed a sigh, borne mainly of irritation, and kept his tone as neutral as possible.

"Unfortunately they seem to have eluded us for now, but we'll find them. In the meantime, would you be good enough to answer a few questions?"

"Keep them short," was the terse response.

"Of course." Northam treated him to a still smile. "Let's start with where you were."

"Just outside the security department," Nicolo said. "I returned to the room to find the safe open, a large amount of money missing, and Amantha nowhere to be seen."

Behind him, Howell trotted down the stairs leading to the security department and gestured to Northam, indicating there was something he needed to see upstairs. Northam nodded briefly and continued the interview. As requested, he kept it to a minimum; Nicolo wasn't going to be much use anyway, as Northam was already fairly certain he knew what happened. He and Gates traded off asking questions, which Nicolo answered shortly, his voice lined with aristocratic condescension.

"And you say you saw her with the necklace?" Gates asked.

"No. But she ran from me, money is gone, and the necklace is gone." Nicolo checked his watch. "Is that it?" He demanded finally. "I have a meeting with my lawyer in five minutes to discuss our options for dealing with the press."

"Of course." Northam gestured to the door. "We'll be in touch," he said.

"How long until you have her in custody? I want that necklace back, and I want her in a jail cell."

To say he was gunning for Amantha would have been an understatement. Northam was beginning to understand why Amantha bolted when she did; to her, this wild caper may have been the only way to escape.

"We are doing everything we can to locate Miss Goldstein, as well as her aunt," Northam said patiently, reminding Nicolo that there were two women missing, not one. "For the time being, all I need from you is to remain calm… and please let me know if she contacts you."

"Find her. And the necklace. Quickly." Nicolo adjusted his coat and flicked a speck of dust off the sleeve. "The last thing we need is another headline like this with her in it," he said, flinging a magazine into Northam's hands. He stalked away without another word, leaving Northam and Gates looking after him with raised brows.

"Charming," Gates remarked.

"He always is."

"He's been accosting every cop in the place for information since I walked in," Howell added on. "Think he had anything to do with it? Insurance payout maybe?"

Across the room, Nicolo pushed his way through a small group at the entrance, flung the door open, and disappeared.

"No…" Northam shook his head. "We'll look into it, but I highly doubt he's involved." That, of course, would be far too easy.

He held up the magazine, frowning at the ludicrous smattering of text over the front.

CAN MONEY BUY TALENT? The headline read. *Amantha Goldstein crashes powerful aeroplane near children's playground, license now under review.*

It should be illegal to doctor the truth that much, really. Or a photo. Northam didn't know how Amantha coped with it; seeing his name crop up in a rag like this every other day would drive him mad.

"That was a good landing – I saw the story in the paper a few days ago," Gates said.

"So did everybody else," Northam said dryly. "Unfortunately, their news sources aren't always as reliable as yours. Read the right news, and Amantha nearly wiped out an entire primary school." He rolled the magazine up and threw it where it belonged: the bin. "She's a lovely girl," he added. "Doesn't deserve any of the bad press that comes her way."

Or the blowback from the family over it; it was, after all, the Goldstein name that made her such a target.

Northam and Gates had returned to the museum only a few minutes before, after catching the tail end of the wild car chase that ended with both Humvees flying through the air over the motorway. That was certainly something one didn't see every day. Every cop in the city and beyond was now on the lookout for the ragtag group of fugitives; with that many men and women on the hunt, aided by the extensive network of cameras, success would not be long in coming. Northam felt it best to return to the initial scene of the crime and try to reconstruct the drama from there.

They'd already established that Nicholas had been spooked by the burglar alarm, which had been short-circuited at the back of the building. But why? And by whom?

Northam was deep in thought as he and Gates followed Howell to the security level. A crowd had gathered around the bank of monitors along the wall; there must have been something uproariously funny happening, for the whole lot was nearly doubled over with laughter. Northam saw Shaun Howard on the far side, trying to keep a straight face but failing miserably.

"We just found this a few minutes ago, sir," he said, spotting Northam. He quickly introduced himself to Gates and led the two of them toward the screen garnering the most attention. Northam and

Gates eased their way through the bodies, trying to reach a point of at least comparable visibility. It took Northam only a superficial look to see what the entertainment was. He stepped to the front and looked at the display, just in time to see an older, very distinguished-looking woman literally beating the tar out of – was that Ian Lowell? – smacking him repeatedly with a black brolly before Amantha grabbed her arm and yanked her down the stairs out the back of the museum. The jerky, disconnected CCTV movements made the event doubly comical.

"Looks like we found Ian," Gates said dryly as the video looped and repeated itself.

Lowell could clearly be seen triggering the alarm behind the building. He then worked his way around the side, cresting the steps just as the door flew open and almost hit him in the face. Amantha bailed outside right into his arms. A brief struggle, and Marilla entered the foray like a tigress.

Northam glanced down to cover a smile. He'd heard quite a few stories pertaining to Amantha's feisty aunt over the years; whilst he'd never had the privilege of an introduction, he now believed every one of them. He looked over to find Gates hiding his face, laughing silently.

"What?"

Gates gestured futilely.

"If I could pick one scene that summed up Ian's love life…" He pointed. "This would be it."

Onscreen, Amantha fell into his embrace yet again, only to be extracted by her aunt as Marilla nearly leveled Lowell with a series of deadly strikes. She and Amantha could then be seen dashing down into the underground carpark. Several other cameras positioned around captured Lowell retreating into the darkness, presumably to retrieve his ill-gotten transport and assuage a wounded ego.

"Why would he set the alarm off?" Howell wondered aloud, and Shaun nodded.

"If he and Nicholas are working together, what would the point be?"

"Unless they weren't working together anymore," Northam said.

And that brought with it a whole new set of questions.

Another frame, from the back of the underground carpark, showed Nicholas leading Amantha and her aunt away from the building, in the opposite direction.

"Shaun, see if you can find footage of where Lowell disappeared. There were two Humvees involved in this chase; I'd like to see who was driving the other one."

"I'm on it." Howard took a final look at the video and strode across the room, pulling the door open. A body stood on the other side.

"Sir?"

Northam glanced over at Howard and nodded when he recognized the visitor. He took a final glance at the video, and left the room with Gates and Howell on his heels to speak with Jerold Henderson, a young detective. Howard closed the door behind them and trotted down the steps.

"What can I do for you, Jerold?" Northam asked.

Jerold regarded him in a somewhat cautious fashion. Northam had a sudden feeling the news was not going to be good.

"Sir, we just got word a few minutes ago... Bruce McFarland is here. In London."

"What."

"Yes, sir."

"You're sure?" Howell asked quickly.

"Yes, sir."

Northam and Howell traded a look.

"That can't be good," Howell said.

"No... no it most certainly cannot." Northam immediately put the current situation out of his mind as he tried to make sense of the information just handed him. Why now? Why would Agent Bruce McFarland of the FBI choose right now, this moment, to suddenly toss himself back into Northam's sphere? "He's after the Ernest Mansfield case," he said, almost to himself. "I would be willing to put money on it."

Howell sighed. Gates lifted an eyebrow.

"You mean..."

"Yes. That Ernest Mansfield. The bloke killed in the Heathrow shooting."

"And by extension you mean..."

"Yes. That Bruce McFarland."

"Brother, you have my sympathies. I've never met him myself but have a few friends who almost needed therapy after a run-in." Gates clapped a supportive hand on his shoulder. "You're sure he's after Heathrow? That was six years ago."

"And remains unsolved. By him." Northam rubbed his forehead. "I'd be willing to bet that's why he's here. He must have a new lead."

That didn't necessarily have to be the case, of course; clearly there were hundreds of explanations as to why the man might return to this part of the world, just as Gates happened to be in London right in the middle of a heist involving two of his former deputies. It could be anything; a wedding, family trip, funeral... even as he considered the options, Northam knew he would require significant proof before he'd believe any of them. McFarland was not Gates. And the McFarland he had come to know always had an agenda; was always after something; and never, *never*, did anything at random. Or for fun. As Howell quietly asked Jerold a few more questions, Northam remained in his own thoughts, and, for the first time in a few years, allowed himself to dwell on the case that had first introduced him to Agent Bruce McFarland, the unsolved case of Ernest Mansfield.

It was a Tuesday and Heathrow International was right in the middle of a busy afternoon, when gunfire erupted near a ticket counter and sent people screaming for cover. The bedlam that followed lasted for several minutes, and when things had finally been quieted, it was discovered that an American businessman and his young wife lay dead in the exact spot where they'd been standing in the queue, waiting to check in for their flight to New York. The ticket counter behind them was riddled with holes, as was a wall across the room. No one else had been injured. By the time Northam arrived, the area had been contained by airport police, and he was escorted to the scene. That was when things started to get weird.

Northam was informed on the spot, as they approached the bodies, that there were two victims, and that they'd both been murdered. Execution style. His job on the matter was described as relatively simple: identify the killer, find him, and put him behind bars. At the time, Northam's cynical half had wondered, silently, how they could be so sure it would be easy; it wasn't until later that he made the connection. After he'd been booted off and realized the whole thing was a setup.

From the moment he laid eyes on the gruesome sight, as explanations continued to be fed into his ears, Northam knew something was amiss. First, there was the scene itself. The position of the bodies was wrong; the witness statements – all of them – hinted at a fight rather than a cold-blooded killing; and it had been Northam's experience that when one came to the scene of an execution, one usually didn't find the deceased clutching an illegal, high-powered handgun in his fist with three rounds missing and fresh powder marks in the firing chamber. As for the girl, there was only one gun matching the bullet that hit her, and it was her husband's. If anyone was indeed, executed, it was her. It didn't help Northam's cynical half at all that, aside from a few stills printed off for the benefit of steering him down the right path, he was never allowed to see footage of the incident. Interpol and a few members of America's alphabet soup network locked it all down almost immediately. The whole thing was dodgy. It reeked of corruption.

Within twenty-four hours of setting up shop, Northam's team had already found and processed a complete fingerprint lifted from the arm of one of their victims, and had come up with an ID: Parker Lewis. At the find, upper management celebrated, but Northam's cynical half got more cynical. Heathrow was one of the most heavily-secured airports in the world. The queen herself had departed from it on numerous occasions. It was unable to be breached. For someone to get a gun *into* the airport in the first place required a sort of diabolical intelligence; here they had two men, two guns, undetected. Such ability spoke of expertise on the parts of both the victim and the shooter. So how would a bloke with that kind of street smarts manage to leave a complete print on the scene?

It was about that point when his corruption theory became fact, and when his investigative life slanted in a definite downhill direction. Looking back on it, he knew he should have kept his mouth shut and not rocked the boat; retaining compliance would have given him a longer leash to work on, and he could have possibly found the opportunity to learn what really happened. As it was, he shot his mouth off like a fool and ruined any chance he had of discovering the truth. His faith in his country and its system had been so strong, he felt there had to be someone who would listen to him; it never once occurred to him that, perhaps, the system was part of the problem.

He was educated very quickly, when he tried to proceed using the correct channels of communication. His concerns were simple: Parker Lewis, whoever he was, was *not* the one they should be after. Rather, given the circumstances, they should be having a closer look at Ernest Mansfield and what he'd managed to do to get himself killed after, it seemed, he murdered his own wife. Not only that, but why there seemed to be this incredible need to bury the whole incident.

The correct channels of communication closed up, and he was shot down. And the next morning, Northam awoke to find Agent Bruce McFarland of the FBI encamped on his doorstep, demanding any and all information he had on the case. Not that there was much to hand over, of course. McFarland was a bullish man, arrogant and totally assured of his own merit; from the moment Northam met him he had one goal, and one goal alone: find Parker Lewis.

When Northam objected to his intrusion, a wad of duly signed paperwork was shoved under his nose to ensure cooperation. And when Northam once again took those correct channels of communication out for a test drive, he was informed politely to behave and, after his numerous indiscretions, just be thankful to have a job. And of course, he was expected to keep his mouth shut and allow this new investigation to proceed uninterrupted.

So much for faith in the system. Lesson learned. Needless to say, with such a choppy transfer of power, the two men didn't part on the best of terms. Northam at least attempted to warn the FBI agent of his suspicions regarding the incident, but they fell on deaf ears. McFarland ignored him and raced off in a hail of red, white, and blue flares. He was obsessed with Parker Lewis, to a worrying degree, and within a few hours the man became an international fugitive. Thanks to some careful leaking of information and the dependable, gossip-hungry appetite of the media, Lewis became a household name overnight, feared by all with the same, ghoulish zeal as Jack the Ripper.

Northam didn't understand until that moment how deep the situation truly was. He'd known something wasn't right, but as he watched McFarland swagger away with his investigation under one arm and his pride under the other, it all became horribly, horribly clear. He hadn't been brought on board as an investigator; rather, at the time, someone was looking for a puppet. Someone to follow direction, reach preordained conclusions, and catch a preordained bad guy; to take a fight between two bad guys and turn it into a murder with one. There was only one reason to do that, and that was to protect the reputations of parties associated with the dead man. Northam had to wonder, briefly, what Ernest Mansfield had been up to and how many of those alphabet soup agencies (and perhaps his own bosses) were involved in it. He'd almost resigned after the incident happened, so shattered was his confidence in both the system and himself; to this day he wondered if he had made the right choice by continuing on.

But in the wake of his removal from the case, even the elaborate frame and McFarland's absurd level of fanaticism failed to yield results. After all the drama and pomp and circumstance had died away, the shooter managed to evade capture, leaving behind only a reputation, and in Northam's case, curiosity. It was an odd thing, really; never once did anyone, anywhere, get a good look at a photo of the man known as Parker Lewis, including Northam. It was all locked down, packed away behind the iron wall of need-to-know. Strange, that. It didn't stop the media from going to town, of course, spewing forth story after story and building the status of this madman to ridiculous heights; the fact that there was no physical image to tie it to made their scare-mongering all the more effective. Fear was so much more potent when it didn't have a face. After everything was said and done, it was the typical news blitz: lots of people ended up terrified over nothing, sales and ratings skyrocketed for that short period of time, and the man at the center of it all was just a name. A name on a scrap of paper, and an urban legend that had never really faded. Nothing more.

And now, McFarland was back in town.

"Know why he's here?" He asked Jerold directly.

"Not yet," Jerold said. "He landed about two hours ago."

"All right." Northam sighed heavily. This was one complication he didn't need right now. "Two hours ago, you said?"

"Yes, sir."

"And you have no idea where he is now."

"No, sir. Two men are on it, but no luck so far."

"Find him," Northam directed immediately. "I want to know where he's staying; who he's staying with; what he's doing here; where he goes; how he gets there; and every sugar-coated, cholesterol-filled, deep-fried American snack he scrounges up along the way. Got it?"

"Yes, sir." As Jerold beat a hasty retreat, Gates turned to Northam.

"How does all of this concern you?"

"I was the officer in charge to begin with," Northam said. "McFarland was…" He paused to ensure the remainder of his response was suitably diplomatic. "…a bit of a problem."

"And his timing now is legendary," Gates replied.

"Yes, it most certainly is." There was a reason Northam had demanded to know the minute McFarland stepped off a plane, any plane, in the UK. Because he was an absolute menace. Anyone in the law enforcement world would know who the man was, simply because of this case. It had been so big, so far-reaching, yet so shrouded in secrecy, it created a maelstrom of publicity that still cropped up occasionally to this day. And of course the bull-headed McFarland would find a new lead right now, when Northam was going to be too tied up on this jewel heist to keep an eye on him. Typical. It reminded him of his days bartending in uni: hospitality being the beast it was, his afternoon would often go from dead quiet to flat-out in a matter of minutes. Fifteen customers and a health inspector would walk in the door at the same time, he'd run out of change, and a fridge would break. This situation was turning out a bit like that. Northam sighed, listening to Howell's summary of the witness interviews after the shooting.

"A nightmare, that," he was saying. "We had three thousand plus witnesses in the complex; five hundred in the immediate area that actually saw it happen. Only a few ended up being truly reliable. Most were too panicked. Descriptions were wrong, information was patchy; people were more concerned about staying alive than taking note of hair color or brands of clothing. That was Jerold's first case as a detective; poor lad didn't know what to think."

Northam nodded silently; he remembered those long hours of interviewing, as person after person proved, once more, that the memory banks of the average individual don't function well under stress levels that high. There was a handful that managed to keep their wits about them; a few that stood out; one or two that proved truly useful.

And, it was while considering those one or two that Northam remembered something else: McFarland wasn't the only person he met as a result of the investigation.

"Commander?"

"Yes." Northam glanced up to meet Gates' curious gaze.

"Everything all right?"

"Yes… quite," Northam said distractedly, realizing his sudden concern must have shown on his face. "Just wondering what McFarland's up to this time. All right, let's get back inside."

He popped the door open and returned to the security department, directing traffic around the monitors. He had a theft/possible kidnapping to solve right now; McFarland would reveal the reason for his visit soon enough. But even as he continued sifting through videos, running down leads, his mind was busy elsewhere. There was another person involved that day, at Heathrow airport. Northam began to wonder: was this really a coincidence, or was that just too strong a word? What was the connection? Six years ago an investigation went unsolved, and a man framed for murder managed to slip through the long arm of the law. Now, at least three of the main players from that day were back, and once more entangled in circumstances together. Northam was the investigator. McFarland was the puppet who took over.

And Amantha Goldstein was a witness.

Northam suddenly wondered if Parker Lewis was lurking around out there somewhere.

Chapter 17

"Well, what do you think?" Lowell asked. He hopped out and slammed his door.

"No one will know the difference," Gregg answered. "Unless, of course, you think a small, British country home with a pair of US Humvees parked out front might arouse suspicion."

The other Hummer pulled into the yard and parked, idling momentarily before the driver killed the motor. The headlights were flicked off.

"Rob, leave the lights on for a minute," Lowell called, trotting over. "Just so we can see what we're doing."

And it was then Amantha got her first good look at him, as he stood in the bright beams that shot forth from the car once more. He was tall and slim, dressed in a faded, leather flight jacket and blue-jeans, wearing shoes that looked like a combination between a cowboy boot and hiking shoe. Broad shoulders. Posture that expressed confidence. A western-style belt buckle shone dully on his waist, half hidden by the jacket and the fold of a crisp, white shirt he wore tucked in. His hair was thick and wavy, disheveled in a charming sort of way, curling around his ears. At a question from one of the men in the car, Lowell pushed up his sleeve to check a dark watch on his wrist.

"Should be any time now," he said.

"Yeah." One of the American accents made itself known as the passenger doors popped open and two men emerged. "Unless he got caught."

"Or lost," the driver said dryly as he came around. That would be Rob. The other two must be George and Troy, but Amantha had no idea who was who. The trio walked over by Lowell, and the four men conversed in low tones for a minute or two. Their serious expressions indicated the big chase they'd just survived was probably the last topic at hand.

"You guys okay?"

A duet of mumbled affirmatives sounded in response to Gregg's query as Jared and Amantha slowly uncurled from their cramped positions, stepping to the ground, stretching after their long spell of idleness. No one tried to make light of the situation. Predicting a conclusion was impossible after this turn of events; they all knew it; what was the use of pretending it didn't matter? Their ship had been steered into rough waters, and the only lifeboat in sight was the familiarity that existed between them, as tenuous as that was.

Across the drive, Marilla hit the ground and walked briskly toward them, shooting a dour look at the two Americans.

"Are you all right, darling?" She asked, and Amantha just nodded. She ran a hand through her hair and took a deep breath of the gentle, night air, leaning against the Hummer's broad side beside Gregg. Marilla stood stoically. Jared sat down on the cement slab. A moment of silence. This was awkward.

"So…" Jared drummed his fingers on his knees. "I'm Jared. College student and future inmate."

The comment elicited a ripple of laughter. Marilla and Amantha introduced themselves formally, shaking hands with Jared where he was perched.

"How did you two meet?" Amantha asked finally.

"My computer crashed and I needed a techie," Gregg said. "This was the one that showed up. I've tried to get an upgrade since then, but no luck."

"Ha. Ha. Ha." Jared leaned back on his hands. "Do you know how many times you've used that joke?"

"Well, they hadn't heard it yet," Gregg defended. He directed his gaze toward Lowell's crowd, standing by the other car, his movement causing Amantha, Jared, and Marilla to do the same.

"Who are they?" Marilla asked after a moment. "Where do they come from?"

Gregg gave a noncommittal shrug.

"The British guy is Rob Dancer. He was in the Navy with us. I don't know the other two. There's a fifth one out there, too, somewhere but I can't remember his name."

"And... Lowell?" Marilla asked. "What about him?"

Another loose motion of Gregg's shoulders. Again, vague. He didn't want to talk about it.

Amantha surveyed the small group with a critical eye, intrigued. Her gaze lingered on Lowell as he spoke with his crew in the expansive glare of the headlights, taking in movements and gestures, trying to ascertain what went on inside that sharp mind. He was always thinking; that much she could tell.

"You said it was a long story," Jared said at last. "About Ian."

"Is that a question?" Gregg's tone matched his quirked eyebrow.

"Kind of. I guess... when you said you knew a guy who could get us into the dig, I was expecting something a little different. Somehow I don't get the idea that knocking off a couple safes in a café is what went down."

Gregg acknowledged the point, seeming reluctant.

"You're right," he admitted. "I... I'll tell you everything. You have a right to know. All of you. We're stuck in this now, so..." He trailed off.

Know your enemy, Amantha finished to herself. She let her gaze drift back to the small cluster of men by the second Hummer, listening to Gregg as he started, slowly, relaying the tale, every word seeming to grate on his consciousness like it was turning the key to an old padlock he'd hoped never to open again.

"You may not believe it now, but Ian Lowell was the best friend I have ever had," he said. "I've known him since I was five. We went up many a hill together as kids, fought many a fight together, shared many a victory and defeat. We rodeoed together for about ten years; joined the Navy when we were twenty and ended up flying Tomcats..."

"Wait. You flew a fighter jet," Jared said.

"Ian was the driver, so was Rob... that was how we met him, first day of basic. I was a RIO. Radar Intercept Officer. You know, like Goose. My eyes weren't quite up to scratch for the driving, but I did most of the talking. And I had control of the eject sequence, which was a bonus," Gregg added with a smirky look.

"Dude, I knew you were a Navy guy but I thought you were a cook or something. You do realize your cool factor just went up by, like –" Jared made a gesture and spread his hands out. "– that much."

Beside him, Marilla laughed quietly.

"Impressive, Gregg," she said, nodding in approval.

"It was pretty cool," Gregg agreed. "We were the elite. Kings of the skies."

"Is that where the names came from?" Jared quizzed. "You know. Genius, Aussie, King…"

"Oh." Gregg laughed quietly. "Yes. Those were our call signs. They might sound cool, but really it was the rest of the guys poking fun at stupid things we'd done, failings, that kind of thing. It's an old tradition – and no, you don't get to choose your own."

"Bummer," Jared said. "What if you get stuck with a lame one?"

"Actually, we flew with a guy whose name was, quite literally, Lame Duck. Anyway, we were based at NAS Norfolk, in Virginia, assigned to the Jolly Rogers. VF-84, on the *TR*."

"The what?"

"The *Roosevelt*. Aircraft carrier. We went overseas in '91… and I think that's where it all started for Ian. The downward spiral. At the time, of course, the Tomcat was beginning to be phased out of operation, replaced by the F-18, so our job wasn't as intense as the guys on the ground. We were there mainly as recon, strike fighter escort, bits and pieces. But things don't always go to plan. Not in a place like that. We were in the middle of an escort run when we got shot down."

Amantha glanced at him quickly.

"Really?"

"Really. Surface to air missile… came out of nowhere and knocked us right out of the damn sky. Ian managed to avoid a direct hit, but it took the wing off, and after that…" Gregg sighed. "That was it, really. No time to think. We ejected on impact, jet went into a spin and crashed; we hit the ground within a few hundred feet of each other, and Ian told me to run for it. If I'd been thinking straight I never would have left, but – I don't know what happened. I panicked, I guess. Survival instinct took over. Anyway, all I remember is

~ 330 ~

struggling to get away; I thought he was right behind me, and by the time I realized otherwise it was too late to do anything. Ian managed to hold them off long enough for me to get out… I crested a ridge, looked back… and there he was, huddled in a little crevice under some rocks. He was trying to buy me some time, and I will never forget the look on his face. It didn't take them long to overpower him. After that, he was held prisoner for a while, and – he was put through some tough stuff. He got discharged and shipped home to recover. I think it was only a matter of time before he snapped, really," Gregg said flatly. "We joined the US Marshals' Service, like I told you, Jared. But Ian wasn't quite the same. Never was, after he came home." He drifted off, his sentence dying with the awareness in his eyes as he became absorbed in the past.

"Was he able to get help for that?" Marilla asked.

"He's too proud. He had some serious problems when he went back stateside, but he never talked about it. Ever. We tried to get him into counseling; he wouldn't have a bar of that either. Told everybody it was no big deal. So in the end we went up that hill together too…"

"He was lucky to have someone like you," Amantha said quietly.

"A lot of good it did him in the end," Gregg said. "I tried, but… it was like trying to communicate with someone who no longer spoke the same language. It was sad to see. The tipping point finally came about two years after we joined the US Marshals. We were helping the DEA take down a drug ring that had taken over distribution of meth along the west coast, and we put together a sting in San Diego. Took us nearly a year to set it all up… within ten minutes it went bad. Bullets started flying, and we were caught completely unprepared. One of ours got killed. Ian got himself shot. And the guys we were after got out the back door and headed straight for South America."

"Graham Townsend," Jared said, speaking as if he had just collected the name from a closed vault. "He was the one who was killed, wasn't he?"

Gregg nodded.

"A very good friend," he clarified quietly for Amantha and Marilla. "Ian and I went to high school with him. He was the one who got us into the US Marshals." Another breath. "Anyway… that was when it happened. Ian never forgave himself; figured it was his fault, what happened to Graham. So, once he got back on his feet, he took matters into his own hands and decided to go hunt down the men who'd escaped. That was in 1994. December twenty-fourth... the day before Christmas."

"Have you spoken to him since then?" Marilla asked.

"Not until three days ago."

Ten years of hunting one's own kind. By now, Lowell would be an exact replica of the men he'd set out to destroy. Irony at its finest. Amantha felt a sudden pang of sadness, for Gregg, and for Lowell himself. She had a better understanding of that restless energy she got from him.

"What about the dog tags?" Jared asked. "I noticed Ian and Rob both have a pair."

Wordlessly, Gregg reached in the pocket of his jeans.

"You mean these?" He asked, letting a pair of military ID tags dangle from his palm.

"And... you have a pair."

"Are they yours?" Amantha asked curiously.

"No." Gregg brushed a hand through the hair at his temple. "The three of us swapped tags after we got out of the service... friendship thing, you know. Just in case we never got the chance to get together again. The ones I have are Ian and Rob's, Ian has mine and Rob's."

"And Rob has yours and Ian's." Jared sized him up a bit. "They still wear them," he observed.

"Well... I used to wear them, too," Gregg started, quietly. He seemed to be searching for the right excuse. His face was a study in weariness as he regarded the tags in his hand, sighed, and put them back in his pocket. "Things change."

He had given up.

"Don't blame yourself," Marilla said, seeming to guess his thoughts. "You cannot possibly control another's decisions."

"No, but..."

"There is no but, Gregg," Marilla said firmly. "You made your choices, he made his. Although I must admit it is a shame to see someone like that end up..." she gestured futilely. "As he is now. A very smart lad, he is... and clearly once he was a good man."

Gregg looked at her sadly.

"He was," he said. "Once."

Across the drive, Lowell stood on the far end of the group with his hands on his hips, doing more listening than talking as he stared out into the darkness, waiting for whoever it was that was due to arrive. His expression was unreadable. Amantha wondered what he was thinking about. Suddenly, she realized he had turned, away from the distance and gloom, and was looking right at her. Their eyes met briefly before Amantha dropped hers in embarrassment. She didn't see the smirk that started creeping across his face.

The sound of a motor hummed abruptly into range through the stillness, accompanying the pair of headlamps that swung up the drive. The lights went out on the second Hummer. Ian's group immediately ducked out of sight; Gregg, Jared, Amantha, and Marilla followed suit on their side.

"Now what?" Gregg muttered.

Jared peered around the wheel.

"Is it the cops?"

"Just get ready to run."

The car that entered the yard slowed up, its newly-painted, tan form sputtering and grinding to a halt, and Gregg's kind eyes widened in surprise.

"*Wow*. I never thought we'd see that hunk of junk again," Jared said.

"Is that your van?" Amantha asked.

"Yep. So he stole that too. Huh. I wonder if my stuff is still in there."

"Stan! You made it!" The lights came back on. Rob stood up easily, tucking a pistol in his waistband and following Ian over to where a fourth henchman hopped lightly out of Gregg and Jared's ill-fated rental. So that's who they were waiting for.

The henchman stepped to the ground. Closed the door. Amantha studied him silently, frowning. Her immediate reaction to the newcomer was: beware.

It was based purely on perception, an insight to humanity she had come to rely on heavily, and although far from admissible as hard evidence, it had never steered her wrong. Amantha knew people. She was a good judge of human nature, of individual character; her sixth sense was rarely off. And she knew she had just come across someone to be truly afraid of.

There was just something about him that didn't add up. It may have been his eyes, too small for his face, rather bug-like, rimmed by light eye lashes that gave him sort of a wall-eyed look. His hair was nearly white; cut short; sticking up in little, solidified spikes. Even his skin was unusually pale, almost translucent. Like an albino.

"Plates?"

"Taken care of," Stan said in response to Lowell's question. "No one will bother us."

"All right." Ian leaned in the passenger window. "Somebody swipe the keys?" He asked with a laugh. "Looks like we're down to hotwiring it for a while."

He and Stan ambled over to join them, Ian shoving his hands in his jacket pockets as he tossed a casual glance in Amantha's direction. Amantha tried not to look at him. Failed. Bloody hell, it was like the man was made of magnetic material.

"Well. I guess introductions fall to me, then," Lowell said, as the remainder of the group convened around them. "Here we have Rob, wheel-man extraordinaire; Troy, safe cracker, forger, and general mischief maker; and George… I guess he would be known as 'the scrounger'. Stan is the one who got that launch pad set up for us this evening."

Amantha looked in Stan's direction and inwardly cringed. The others didn't seem to be so bad by comparison.

"Team Gregg," Lowell continued. "We start with Gregg Nicholas, treasure hunter, teacher, and instigator; Jared, computer genius; Mrs. Clancy; and Miss Goldstein."

"Oh we know, Ian," Troy said cheekily, wriggling his eyebrows at Amantha. He was rewarded by a swipe across the shoulder from Marilla, who leveled a commanding gaze in his direction.

"I forgot to mention that Mrs. Clancy is Miss Goldstein's aunt," Lowell added smoothly.

"Oops." Troy attempted penitence. "Sorry, ma'am," he said.

"You're doing well tonight," George said. "A regular teacher's pet."

"And who are you, mate? I didn't quite catch it." Rob asked jokingly, inclining his head at Ian.

"I'm just the pilot." The answer was wry. "Mrs. Clancy, do you have space enough for all of us?" He asked. "If not, my guys and I can sleep out here in –"

"Certainly not!" The sharpness of Marilla's tone brought a look of surprised amusement to Ian's countenance, a sentiment that only increased as he observed her. If Marilla had been a cat, her fur would have been sticking straight out in righteous indignation at the suggestion. Agree she might not with the situation, but be deemed a bad hostess? Never.

"Sorry," Ian said, trying to keep a straight face. "You might be stuck with us, but I don't want to put you out any."

"Thank you for your consideration, Mr. Lowell, but it is unnecessary." Marilla's aristocratic sensibilities seemed assuaged for the time being. "I have extra bedding up in the loft," she said. "I'll unlock the door so you can get down what you need, and then I'll consult Mrs. Beeton for tea. I'm sure we're all hungry. And Gregg cannot be expected to lead us to treasure on an empty stomach."

"Speaking of which, we need to talk about that," Ian said to Gregg.

"Food first, Mr. Lowell." So saying, Marilla stalked back through the crowd and headed purposefully for the door, her manner reminding Amantha of an irate Bantam hen on the move. Amantha had to stifle a laugh, and glancing up just in time to catch Ian's conspiratorial wink made it even funnier. A grin of sincere amusement entered his face as their eyes met, and Amantha suddenly felt privy to a private joke. She couldn't help but notice how his face lighted up. His smile was just a hint cockeyed, tugging on the left side of his mouth, and quite sweet. He really was very cute.

Magnetic material.

"Amantha," Marilla said suddenly. "Let the gentlemen get their things. I could use your help, if you don't mind."

Her tone said it all. She was standing by the front door observing like a judge at a football match. As Amantha tried to swipe the persistent grin off her face, she could feel Gregg's gaze on her and knew exactly what he was thinking; when she chanced to meet it she found him playing with the tags in his hands, surveying her worriedly. His eyes held a mild accusation. Like Amantha was betraying him by paying attention to the enemy. Amantha didn't contradict him. She probably was.

Additionally, she noted that Stan, the newcomer, was watching her. Suddenly. Why, she didn't know. He had hardly even glanced her way when first approaching, but as soon as Ian looked at her, as soon as that connection had been made, he was on it. His gaze had hardly left her since then, and Amantha's unease increased. His expression was... she didn't know. It was a look she had never seen anywhere else. It made her nervous.

Marilla said nothing as she handed Amantha a key to the loft and set off toward the kitchen. Amantha unlocked the door and yanked it open with a heavy squeak of protest, trotting up the steps into the musty space. One by one, the boys followed her up and retrieved the pillows and blankets Amantha dug out for them from a pair of old trunks, trouping back into the living room to set up camp.

Jared and Gregg were the first up; Amantha bequeathed them with a pair of neon-colored sleeping bags, orange and green respectively, complete with inbuilt pillows.

"Lucky first," she said. "Everyone else gets flowers."

Gregg just laughed and took hold of the green one.

"Thank you for the consideration, Miss Goldstein," he said.

"Gregg. We're beyond the 'Miss' thing by now, really," Amantha retorted. "Call me Amantha or you get the flowers, too."

The American henchmen, George and Troy, were next to appear. George accepted the horsey blanket Amantha found lurking near the bottom, giving it a skeptical, sideways glance.

"*Muchas gracias, senorita,*" Troy said with a wide grin. He was clearly the less reserved of the two, and more opportunistic. "I assume you must be the owner of the sexy voice we were listening to earlier on the radio."

"Well I don't know how sexy it was, but I am the voice," Amantha returned. "You can call me Amantha."

"Amantha..." Troy experimented, drawing out the last syllable for a few seconds.

George and Troy were what Amantha would describe as "typical American": a bit loud, dressed in jeans and hoodies like gangsters, broad-shouldered and stocky. Friendly sorts, seemed to be, at least for henchmen; Amantha looked at the two of them, standing in front of her beaming like a couple of school kids, and couldn't for the life of her see them as anything else. She laughed to herself as they left the room and wandered down the stairs, elbowing each other and trading blows with the pillows all the way down.

Clowns. At least this team seemed to have personality, even if they were outlaws. She looked up from her continued rummaging to find Lowell approaching from the head of the stairs, and he smiled at her as she handed him a pile of floral fabric.

"Thank you," he said, accepting Amantha's additional offer of a baby-pink pillow.

"I hope the colors suit," Amantha joked. "I'm sorry, but all of our aviation sets are gone. Although, if you prefer…" Coyly, she held up a purple Barbie pillow.

"And I'll take that," Rob said, diving in to swipe the Barbie. He'd come up the stairs just as Amantha plucked it from the box. "If I can't have the real thing, she'll have to do." He rounded on her with what could only be described as a "chick magnet" smile. "Unless you want to take her place," he suggested in a put-on tone. "I won't tell. I promise."

"As if you could get a woman this good," Lowell retorted before Amantha could answer.

"Yeah righto, mate, as if you'd do any better." Rob's grin at Amantha broadened, enhanced by dark, expressive eyes that, Amantha could guess, would be quite irresistible to a girl under the proper circumstances. A small scar on his left cheek didn't hurt his cause any, as it turned into a rather charming dimple. Rob, she surmised, was less of a henchman and more of a "2IC". From what she'd heard earlier, he, Ian, and Gregg used to be nearly inseparable. Funny that he had stuck with Lowell through all this. She lobbed a matching blanket into his arms.

"Who am I to come between such a perfect couple?" She asked innocently.

Rob was unfazed by her refusal, casting her another flirty look as he made for the stairs.

"If you change your mind…" He suggested over his shoulder, and Lowell chuckled as he followed him down.

Boys. Some things never change. Amantha grabbed a sheet set for her own bed from the nearest trunk and closed them both up, glancing around a final time before she left. She'd just begun to make her way to the stairs when voices sounded in the entryway below, followed by footsteps; in the next instant, Stan rounded the corner and started upward. Amantha felt a slight falter in her stride. Her senses picked up the vibes she felt before. Mental warning bells were screaming at her. She tried to find a way out, around, away, but there was nothing. There was only one way in and one way out of this space: past him. Carefully, she stepped to the side of the doorway, staying well close, waiting for him to pass her.

Stan gave no indication he even saw her. He walked slowly, efficiently, staring at the steps beneath his feet, but a few paces from her he paused, glanced up, met her eyes. He didn't say anything, nor did he try to stop her in any way. He just looked. And looked. He was still looking when Amantha took the initiative and started to brush by him.

"I see you and Ian have found common ground," he said, quite unexpectedly. His hand reached out and touched the wall, blocking her exit. "Of course, he always manages to hit it off with the girls."

Amantha stopped. Reached up, removed his arm from her way.

"As I'm sure most men do," she responded, and kept walking as Stan opened one of the trunks and retrieved a bedding set, folding it meticulously.

"It must be... worrisome... for someone like yourself to be in this spot," he suggested. "Anything could happen."

"If I was that worried I wouldn't have come," Amantha said shortly. With half of the stairway separating them, she stopped and faced him. "What do you want?" She asked.

"Stan." Lowell's voice cut through the quiet, sharply; Amantha spied him immediately in the hallway at the base of the stairs, watching carefully. "I need someone out front at the head of the drive... you're it."

Stan's eyes never left Amantha's.

"Certainly, boss," he said in a tone that lacked some in the respect department. Slowly he closed the trunk, turned, and walked past Amantha down the stairs. His face was a study in satisfaction. Amantha had the sudden impression he'd spoken to her on purpose, just to feel things out. What? What could he possibly be trying to determine? She didn't know. But it was then, watching him retreat, that she realized exactly what that look he'd given her outside had been:

Calculating.

A nervous sensation started to twist in her stomach. If there was a way for a human being to be told with very few words that they were, in essence, no more than posh quarry, it had just been done. Amantha got the message loud and clear. This was not a supervised situation, nor could she expect aid from anyone. She was alone. If Stan decided that he wanted something from her, anything, there was no one to stop him from getting it. This wasn't a game, the spot they were in now; the men in charge were as unknown and dangerous as wild animals. As a female, and young, she would be a prime target. This was what Gregg had warned her about.

Ironically she considered the fact that it might behoove her to stick closer to Lowell when Gregg was not around; as the leader of this small assemblage, he might be able to exert more control. He, too, had kept a close eye on Stan as the man left and was still standing at the base of the stairs, leaned casually against the wall while he scrolled through messages on his phone. He'd taken his jacket off, leaving only the white, buttoned shirt with the top two undone and sleeves rolled up to just above his wrists. Very Fox Mulder. Was that supposed to be as sexy as it looked? The shirt contrasted sharply with the tan of his skin, which was quite dark even in the faded light from the hall.

Amantha reached the bottom and turned her attention to the door in front of her, which was protesting being pushed shut just as vocally as it had being opened. She quickly found herself in a bit of a bind trying to poke the key in the lock and hang on to the sheet set, which was commencing to slide off her arm. Rapidly. She realized too late her whole plan of attack could use some help.

"Oh, here, let me get that, love," Lowell said suddenly from behind her, and scooped the blanket up just as it dropped toward the floor.

Amantha laughed, securing the remaining stack as it started to topple.

"I was just trying to decide which was more valuable," she said. "Serves me right for trying to get it all in one go." She quickly locked the door, dropping the key in her pocket.

"Was he polite to you?" Lowell queried, inclining his head to where Stan had disappeared. Amantha noticed he'd already tucked the phone in his pocket to give her his full attention. "I didn't hear what he said, but the look on your face suggested not."

"He was as polite as can be expected," she replied. "I can't say I was anticipating deferential treatment from anyone here."

A smile, more than likely brought on by her forthrightness, tugged at his mouth as he looked down at her. At Gregg's height, he was quite a bit taller than Amantha was herself, but not enough to be intimidating, and as before his manner immediately put her at ease. He felt safe. Another ironic point considering who he was. No matter how many warnings were issued about him, Amantha couldn't go past the energy exuded by his presence.

"If any of these boys make you feel uncomfortable, you let me know," he said. "They're a decent mob for the most part... somewhat house trained... but throw a pretty girl in the mix and they turn into a bunch of tomcats."

With his gaze on her like that, sort of concerned and inquisitive and interested all at the same time, Amantha found she was quickly running out of things to say.

"I'll keep it in mind," she promised him.

Aunt Marilla saved her any further moments of self-discovery as she summoned the entire troupe for dinner.

"After you," Lowell said, gesturing Amantha in front of him, and followed her to the dining room. They dropped the small pile of blankets on the nearest couch and angled their steps for the kitchen, where everyone was already seated. Amantha saw her aunt eye Lowell severely over her head.

The table was quiet for a while. Even the chinking of silverware seemed strangely subdued. The pasta Marilla had whipped up was good; everyone present was hungry and not inclined to talk much; and then there was the problem of what to say, even if they were. No one really knew each other except possibly by name and status – Goldstein, Prisoner Three; or Troy, Henchman Two – no one really *wanted* to know each other, and they had nothing in common anyway. Except the treasure, and nobody really wanted to talk about that. It was, after all, at the root of this rather awkward situation. As such, communication was kept to a bare minimum, and a few mumbled phrases like: "Will you pass..." or "Are you done with..." were the only comments to break the silence.

Conversation finally started to flow a little more when Gregg, Rob, and the henchmen got on the subject of cars. Engine size, transmissions, and four-wheel-drive ratios started dominating the conversation as they compared notes on styles and personal preferences.

"Seven miles to the gallon?" She heard Gregg ask suddenly. "Are you kidding me? If I wanted that kind of mileage, I'd just buy a Hummer."

"Why not a hippie-bus?" Troy offered from the peanut gallery, and Rob looked at him tolerantly over a fork-full of pasta.

"I'm going to ignore that comment."

"Hits too close to home," Gregg snickered. "Why don't you ask him about the VW van he lived in during college, Troy? Complete with curtains and peace signs."

"Dude, were you a hippie?" Jared asked.

"Peace out, bro."

"You know I'm never going to let you live this down."

"You'd better, Chip, or I may not let you live."

Jared sighed.

"Chip. Please tell me this is not my – what is it called?"

"Call sign," Gregg supplied.

"And it is," Ian assured him. "You can thank Rob for that."

Jared took the teasing in stride and went back to threading his dinner around his fork.

"This is really good, Aunt Marilla," he said.

"I'm glad you like it." Marilla was clearly pleased. "It was a dish I used to make for my husband's family quite a lot... being Catholic, there were many mouths at every visit as you can imagine."

"I do apologize for presenting you with yet another army," Ian said from the end.

"He's not sorry, really," Rob said teasingly. "He just wants first dibs on dessert."

"Look who's talking. The ultimate schmoozer." Ian chucked a balled-up napkin at him. The banter seemed to break a little more of the ice, allowing a small bit of warmth into the room. A few scattered comments were attempted from one direction or another, then:

"My mum was the worst cook in the world," Rob said. "Rations tasted better than the stuff we used to eat at home." He chuckled. "It's why I joined the Navy in the first place."

"I thought your mum *was* the cook there," Ian said, and Rob tossed back the napkin that had been thrown at him earlier.

"Can it, Aussie. I never saw you wield a skillet with much success."

"Nor did you see the episode with the gas stove at my grandmother's house," Gregg slipped in around his fork.

Another fifteen minutes, and the food coma hit. The food was gone aside from the large portion set aside for Stan, the dishes were stacked by the sink, and the troupe sat in silence, contemplating the mysteries of life and crime and all that went with it.

"Now, who wants to lend me their assistance?" Marilla asked, breaking the silence. "I need someone with muscles. I have a large painting I've wanted to hang for quite some time but have never had the opportunity. It's been ages since there's been a man around here!" She looked expectantly around her. No one moved. "No volunteers? All right." She crossed the room in a couple of quick strides. "Since no one is inclined toward chivalry, I'll simply recruit someone. I'm stealing your henchman, Mr. Lowell." So saying, she took a shocked Troy by the collar and pulled him to his feet, steering him out of the room.

"Wait! What?" Troy's voice could be heard pleading over his shoulder. "Ah! Can't we just – talk about this... Rob! Ian! Help!"

"Well, how do you like that?" Ian shook his head, rising to peer out the door. "You give them an inch and they take your hired help. Mrs. Clancy?" He called. "Don't get too attached to Troy, love! We'll need him later!"

"Now don't you use any of your Australian charm on me, young man!" Was the tart, muffled reply.

Troy's ensuing pleas for help went unnoticed, fading away as he was ushered to the back of the house. Rob craned his head for a brief look, then shrugged.

"It's good for him," he said, and Amantha giggled.

"Maybe I'll volunteer you for duty when she comes back."

"Maybe I'll lock her in the pantry and save us all the trouble."

"Good luck." Ian's response was dry. Sighing tiredly, he leaned back against the bench and stretched a hand up to rub his left shoulder.

"Your shoulder again?" Rob asked rather shrewdly without turning. He was swilling his water glass in an absent manner on the table top. "Not quite like it used to be, is it?"

"Not by a long shot. I feel like I've just been spit out of a turbine. Oh, to be nineteen again... Hell, even thirty would be acceptable." Ian stood there massaging the offending shoulder for a moment, staring at the floor, a small chain visible under the loose collar of his shirt.

The dog tags. One from Gregg, one from Rob. They must have been close.

"Right. I'll be back," Ian said. He grabbed the extra plate of food and a pair of utensils, and headed for the door. Stan would have to eat as well, although such an action seemed far too human for someone like him. "Try not to burn the place down while I'm gone."

"No promises," George said.

A loud bang, followed by one of Marilla's distinctive howls of displeasure, announced the reentry of both her and Troy. They clattered their way back into the kitchen lugging what was indeed a substantial painting, mounted in a fancy, gilded frame that looked to weigh a ton. It was at least enough to make Troy struggle a little. He obediently held the painting against the wall, staring at the floor while Marilla marked out the location. His stance was almost birdlike. Between the posture and the hooded, greyish jumper he wore, he reminded Amantha very much of an irritated pheasant puffed up against the cold.

"If you'll place that on the floor," Marilla said. "*Carefully.*" This last uttered as the painting seemed to take a dive for the tiles. "You. Come help him," she continued, and pushed George over next to the wall. Eyeing the result to ensure everything was still intact, she reached down to pluck a small, grey device out of her pocket and turned it on, causing Jared to perk up instantaneously.

"What is that?" He asked, watching Marilla press the device against the wall. "You turning computer hacker on us or something?"

"Oh, heaven forbid! I wouldn't know a computer from a hole in the ground." Marilla held the instrument, which was about the size of an index card, out for Jared to see. It had two lights on it, one above the other, and was used, she explained, to find the studs, or supports, in the wall, so nails holding up a particularly heavy decoration could be placed properly. At the moment, the top light on the instrument was lit, flashing green, indicating no stud had been found. But, as soon as the instrument passed over a support beam, it could sense the difference in density and the bottom light would flash red.

"An American friend of mine once said it's known as a 'stud-finder'," Marilla said, the reserved smile she cast around seeming to expect trouble. She was right.

"A stud-finder! Really!" Rob ambled over with a bratty smirk inching across his face. "Let me see that thing." He took the instrument and held it to his chest. The red light flicked on. "Need I say more?" He asked, and took a bow amid the burst of humor and Gregg's droll remark of: "Oh, please; that is so old". Before he had a chance to bask in fame, however, Marilla reached over to snip the device out of his hand.

"Don't get too cocky, Stud," she retorted. "This thing has a history of malfunctions."

George and Troy seemed to disintegrate into peals of laughter, quickly diving behind Marilla's painting when Rob made a move in their direction.

"Now, now, Rob, you wouldn't want to damage this," Troy said over the top of it, peeping through a couple of carved circles in the frame.

"He won't have to," Marilla retorted as she drilled a screw into the wall. "You've done *quite* a good job of that already."

Rob was forced to cease his attack when Marilla herded him into work with the other two, standing by while they hefted the painting up the wall and hooked it into place.

"Thank you, lads," she said, then gathered up the small container of tools she held and bustled back down the hall to put them away. The peace of the moment was short-lived, however, as not a minute later she burst back into the room expectantly. "All right... who wants to wash up?" She asked briskly, picking up a long knife to twirl it around like a baton. Still no takers. Amantha wondered if they'd ever learn. "No one? Well, then I guess I'll just have to choose someone again," Marilla said loftily, clearly enjoying her streak of power. "You and you – who are you again?"

Troy twitched. Rob looked at her like she was nuts.

"You're joking, right?" Troy asked.

Marilla deftly flicked the knife in her hand.

"No, she's not, Troy," Rob said immediately, and dragged himself up again.

"But I helped last time."

"Man up, sunshine," Rob retorted, causing Marilla to nod at him.

"That's the spirit, Bob."

"Rob."

"Whatever. Come here, you're both on KP."

"Nobody told me there would be manual labor involved," Troy said.

"The inevitable price of crime," Marilla answered, unfazed. "My, but it *is* nice to have help around here. Now, the rest of you clear off. Once I have these two to task, we have a treasure to discuss."

She was really getting into this leadership thing. Rob and Troy exchanged a look over her head that clearly considered rebellion, then wisely reevaluated the idea and obeyed like a couple of faithful hound dogs. Marilla was still setting them to task and promising a slow and painful end if anything ended up broken as the remaining troupe lolled out of the kitchen. Amantha sank happily into the welcome softness of the couch. George grabbed the sleeping bag he'd been bequeathed earlier and found a parking space on the floor, while Gregg and Jared completed the semi-circle with a couple of chairs.

"Now. Gregg," Marilla said directly, marching into the room to take a seat beside Amantha. "Dinner is officially over. Tell us about this treasure hunt of yours."

Three additional pairs of eyes swiveled in Gregg's direction. Gregg nodded.

"All right," he said. "Where do you want me to start?"

"The beginning." Jared yawned sleepily. "They'll get lost otherwise. But keep it short because I'm close to checking out."

"Well… the beginning is: I have been researching this legend since I was in high school." Gregg rose and walked over to his bag, where it rested along the wall, zipping it open. "I had always loved the story, but first heard about the treasure when I was in eighth grade," he continued, pulling out a small packet of paper. "Up until then, I thought it was just a story. Then, when I became aware of the treasure component, a whole new world opened up to me. That was when I first read about the Goldstein family; your ancestor, Veit; and Marian's Necklace."

"I heard that you tried to contact us after the necklace was found," Amantha ventured.

"Yep. Many times. I just kept getting rejection notes back from your publicity people."

"Hence why, when the dig was uncovered…"

"… I broke in. I *knew* something was going on there," he said emphatically. "The timing was just too coincidental." He pulled out an old piece of parchment, on which was a drawing.

"Where did you get this?" Marilla asked, staring at the line drawing of the necklace, nearly identical to the one that appeared on the wall of the tunnel.

"I've had this piece of paper for ten years," Gregg answered. He continued his explanation, point by point, with the others sitting around him in silence, taking it all in. One thing could be said for Gregg Nicholas: no matter how random and spur-of-the-moment this quest might seem, it was anything but. He'd been researching this heavily for nearly half of Amantha's existence.

"So, you can see why I was so stoked when I saw that symbol on the wall," he said finally. "Now. Amantha. I would like to know: did *you* know what was in there?"

"I can't think of any time when the spokesperson for a brand knows anything more than what is necessary to sell the product. That is what I do, after all," Amantha said. "Sell the integrity of the Goldstein family name to the public. I was just as surprised as everyone else when the team discovered that hole in the ground. I knew there was 'something' there from the beginning, of course, as you did, but no more… no one but Nicolo – and maybe some of his closer investors – knew what they were looking for, exactly."

"Not even you."

"Especially not me."

"Of course you know that Amantha's mother, my sister, was supposed to be what Nicolo is now," Marilla said. "It was to have been she who became the 'head' of the family, if you will. Then things changed and Nicolo was given an opportunity."

"Control," Gregg said. "After Stephanie…" He trailed off. "After Amantha was born."

Marilla nodded. Clearly she appreciated Gregg's tact.

"He has taken that opportunity, and intends to see to it that Amantha remains under his management."

"Why?" George asked. He lay on his back with his fingers laced behind his head.

"That is a story for another time, I'm afraid," Marilla said. "Suffice it to say, Nicolo is a bitter man. He has lived his life since just before Amantha's birth with a giant chip on his shoulder. I would imagine he is fit to be tied by now, after tonight."

Gregg glanced at Amantha.

"That's what you wanted."

"That is exactly what I wanted," Amantha said softly. "Now if you can just find the treasure, Gregg, my day will be complete."

Gregg was watching her intently, seeming to take in her presence with a newfound sense of understanding. The sound of a plate clanging heavily off the benchtop broke through the quiet.

"Oi, you lot! Be careful in there!" Marilla threatened.

"Sorry, Aunt Marilla!" Troy's voice drifted in muffled waves through the door.

"So. Gregg." Marilla sat back. "We know how you found the dig. What did you find?"

Gregg pulled out another, scraggly scrap of paper, which crackled merrily as he unfolded it. The faded, white surface was full of wrinkles and water marks.

"This is a word-for-word copy of a poem we found, inscribed on the sword originally in Robin's coffin," he said. "This is what led me to the museum to get the necklace:

'This, a stone of Hope, a mirror to thine eyes
Blue as the endless seas, and deep as the midnight skies
May it speak of distance, as it was meant to do
The sentiments therein proving Truth to you'."

The first line reminded Amantha that she still had the loose piece from the necklace in her pocket. She continued to listen as she reached down and pulled out the blue stone; she was about to hand it to Gregg when she noticed, quite suddenly, that its shape was very familiar. Having it in her pocket for as long as she had after receiving it in such a rush, she hadn't had a chance to look at it properly until now. Quickly, she pulled out her mobile and started flicking through photos. Within moments she had found several of the bracelet from the dig, which she had taken when she got the piece home. The shape of that heart piece was eerily similar to the stone laying in her palm; the size was nearly identical.

"'This, an ivory piece," Gregg continued.
"Wisdom that shall grace your wrist
Such a work of divine craftsmanship
May it prove right for you, this from the lady of the sands
And narrow the distance for you to those foreign lands'."

Immediately, Amantha thought of the story her aunt had started telling her merely the night before. In particular the bit about Jasmine, the young Saracen girl who ended up accompanying Robert of Locksley to England. She would most definitely be considered a "lady of the sands"… and she had worn an ivory bracelet. Much like the one Amantha had found. Could it be? Surely not. Amantha looked at Gregg quickly, cast another glance between the stone and the small photo on her mobile screen.

"'This, the sword of Truth, which hath known its day
It will be used with Wisdom, but only once, I pray –'"

"Wait, Gregg, that's it!" Amantha sat bolt upright. "That's it! Wisdom!"
Gregg clearly had no clue what she was talking about. He raised his eyebrows, looking at her expectantly, but he didn't have a chance to ask before Amantha held up her phone.
"I found this bracelet in Marian's coffin," she explained excitedly, as Gregg played trombone with her phone to get a proper look at it.
"I saw this," he said. "Admittedly I didn't think anything of it at the time."
"Nor did I," Amantha said. "Until, that is, I picked it up and saw what was on the inside of the band." Excitedly she described it;

the shape, the size, the band engraved with strange numbers. "It was part of Aunt Marilla's story – this has *got* to be it!"

"What story?" Jared asked.

"Robin Hood!" Gregg exulted, his face lighting up. "Please tell me you have a Goldstein version!"

Marilla laughed.

"I do indeed, Gregg."

"But what does that have to do with the riddle?"

"In the story, Robin Hood befriends a young woman by the name of Jasmine," Amanth explained. "She is Arabic, also being held prisoner by the Duke of Austria; she escapes, and accompanies Robin to England. On her wrist she wears a bracelet that looks to be made of ivory. Think about it, Gregg: who *else* would be referred to as a 'lady of the sands'?"

"And you really think this story might hold some truth."

"Forgive me for sounding vain, but if there is a version that has the possibility of truth, one would think this might be it," Amantha said. "Whether by design or reality, the Goldstein family has a long association with the legend of Robin Hood."

"And you're certain this piece you have is ivory," Gregg pressed.

"Positive."

"Where is it now?"

"My flat."

"Ugh. Right in the middle of a hornets' nest," Jared muttered. "I hope you all like prison food."

"How about you shift your thinking, Chip, and start prepping your palette for some Five-Star Michelin?" George said cheerfully.

The small group was quiet for a moment, mulling over this new information, with only the sound of water and clattering dishware audible in the background. Amantha had a feeling things were going to get complicated.

"So… your family has its own version of the story," Gregg said to Marilla.

"We do, indeed."

"I don't suppose you could, you know, tell some of it… I think I've heard every version on the planet, but never from a descendant."

"That lineage has yet to be proven, Gregg," Marilla reminded him.

"If this bracelet angle works out, it just might be."

"Very well, then... I will tell you. As I explained to Amantha, however, it is far too long to be told in one sitting. I'll have to catch you up to where I left off last."

She briefly reconstructed the first part of the legend; as Marilla talked, Gregg's face became more and more animated. He started asking questions. Connecting dots. Nodding and agreeing with her assessment of people in the story, who he had clearly spent a good deal of time studying over the years. By the time Marilla caught them up to the present, Gregg was as excited as a schoolboy.

"'Wisdom that shall grace your wrist'," he said, quoting the riddle. "I think you might just be right, Amantha. The numbers on the back must be some kind of cipher."

"Coinciding with whatever that book is from the last stanza," Jared suggested.

"Probably."

"You think it fits?" George queried.

"Like a glove. That bracelet is the next part of our puzzle. It makes perfect sense, really; there is a theory that Robert of Locksley was not alone when he returned to England, and considering Jasmine's background, she could very well be his companion."

"What do you mean, her background?" Marilla asked.

"War crimes have been committed since the dawn of the war machine," Gregg said. "As long as there has been conflict there has been kidnapping and rape, theft, desecration of sacred objects. The way to get to the enemy is through the things he holds most dear. His wife, his daughter, young children, religious artifacts or possessions important to the culture."

"In other words, collateral damage," Amantha surmised.

"Somebody has to give. The way to win is make it too tough for the other guy to stick it out. I wonder if that sword we found in the dig was Leopold's," Gregg added. "The one he gave to Robin in your story." He leaned back, studying the pattern on the ceiling. "Strange, as well, about King Richard's impending move from Austria. I'll bet that's when he was taken to Germany. He was held there by the emperor until the end of his imprisonment, with the sum of seventy-five thousand marks going to Leopold for the honor."

"Boy, Leopold was making money hand over fist on that deal," Jared remarked.

"Someone has to. Okay, Aunt Marilla, yarn away."

"With pleasure." Marilla paused momentarily to pick up where she had left off. "After slipping out of the carriage," she started, "Robin and Jasmine raced into the nearby forest, where they were partially hidden…"

The door to the kitchen squeaked open.

"Can you talk louder?" Rob called, clearly trying to agitate.

"Yeah, we can't quite hear you in here!" Troy added on.

"If you'd stop running the ruddy water the whole time, you'd hear splendidly!" Marilla retorted, and a couple bird-like chuckles slanted through the open doorway. She sighed and looked at George. "Would you please tell your boss to control his minions a bit better?" She requested.

"He tries. We're like toddlers."

Marilla ignored him.

"Robin knew the sheriff would be after them," she continued, "and he was in a quandary. They still needed to get the letter of agreement to the duke, a task now made all the more difficult by the pursuit of a posse…"

Amantha had a sudden vision of Marilla telling this story to her mother, so many years ago, and felt a sudden bolt of excitement. She didn't know what was going to happen from here; all she knew was that her mum would have loved this.

Live daringly, boldly, fearlessly. Taste
the relish to be found in competition -
in having put forth the best within you.

- *Henry J. Kaiser*

Chapter 18

Taking Flight

Robin was glad he didn't believe in ghosts. Sherwood Forest was creepy enough at night without them. As he and Jasmine wound their way carefully through the thick, ancient trees and low-growing plants, he felt almost a trespasser, an intruder in a place that shouldn't be disturbed. The shadows were deep and endless, the fading light nearly unable to penetrate to the forest floor, the scene completely silent. Within an hour it was totally dark, and the two weary travelers crawled beneath the full foliage of a bush to get what sleep they could. Not that there would be much. They had left the posse behind, yes, but the soldiers would be back. Come daylight, maybe sooner, they would be on the trail, hunting down their prey with relentless force.

"You know you don't have to stay, Jasmine," Robin said as they took refuge under the spreading boughs.

"What? You want me to leave now, just when things are getting interesting? Come now, Robin, where is your sense of adventure?" Jasmine's answer was rather glib, one that didn't inspire much trust in its honesty.

"I mean it," Robin said.

"I know." This time the response was much more sincere. "But I want to help."

Her words were still on his mind later as Robin lay curled up under the bush. He finally managed to drift off in the early hours of morning, but didn't sleep well at all, waking up every so often at some noise that stemmed directly from his imagination. It was still shadowy when he woke again. Jasmine was asleep, burrowed in her cloak, her light, even breathing the only sound in evidence as Robin stretched silently, sitting up to prop his back against a tree. He turned around to find himself staring a loaded crossbow right in the face.

"Whoa!" Robin jumped, his action and accompanying exclamation bringing Jasmine awake with a start. They both plastered themselves to the tree with their hands up.

The owner of the crossbow, a round, rather swarthy-looking woman with brown eyes, simply eyed them without concern from behind her weapon. She was stocky, tough, dressed like an old maid in patched clothing and ragged shoes, with a worn, knitted shawl draped around her shoulders. Her eyes were hard, but not unfriendly, more an aloofness that came from seeing many a low-life traipse through her line of sight. She sized them up silently.

"I am Maud de Caux," she said after a moment. "This is my land. If you will be good enough to tell me your business, we may be able to reach an understanding."

Robin almost laughed in relief, dropping his hands to his lap. He had only met Maud once, many years ago, as she lived very much like a hermit and rarely set foot outside her beloved forest. But even a hermit was preferable to a posse.

"Am I glad to see you," Robin said. When Maud said nothing, he rose carefully to his feet, Jasmine standing beside him. "I doubt you remember me," he added, "but we met once when I was young. My name is Robin."

Another pause as Maud de Caux studied him.

"Locksley," she said. "Robin of Locksley. I remember you, young man. Your father brought you one day." She lowered the crossbow. "You look very much like him. I had heard you were dead, but then, I'm sure you're aware of that already." Without waiting for a response, Maud turned to Jasmine. "And who are you?" She asked. "You look Arabic." It was not an aggressive question, merely statement of fact.

"I am," Jasmine said. "How did you know?"

"I have not always been this reclusive. What is your name?"

"Jasmine."

Maud nodded thoughtfully. She was still detached, not quite trusting the situation.

"Who is it you run from?"

"The sheriff."

"What have you done?"

"Exist," Robin said dryly. "Actually, I believe we've thrown something of a large horseshow into his plans, and now he would like nothing better than to throw it back."

Maud smiled suddenly, quite a lovely smile for such an imposing woman.

"So you are the 'dangerous criminals' he was after, then."

"You've seen him?"

"Early this morning. That horrid cousin of his wanted passage through my lands with a small posse. Said a pair of dangerous criminals had escaped their custody, but I had a suspicion he was exaggerating. I came out to look for myself after I sent them off." She slung the crossbow over her shoulder. "You must be hungry. My house is not far from here, and it will do you good to sit for a time."

"We do not wish to impose," Jasmine said.

"Nonsense," Maud answered tartly. "You are two of the most polite trespassers I've seen in quite some time."

Maud's house was quaint, tucked deep in the forest, invisible as soon as one passed the tall line of trees ringing the clearing that surrounded it on all sides. Her hospitality was as warm as the fire crackling in the hearth. Robin got the impression she was glad for the company, something she perhaps didn't get very often except in the form of town folk skulking through her front yard with a side of venison.

"People have been coming and going," she had said as she led them along a skinny trail through the woods. "I just keep my mouth shut and pretend I don't know they're here. I feel it's the least I could do." She held a bush aside for them to pass, letting it fall into place behind them. "The ironic part of it is most of them are the people who told me to keep quiet when DeMarke first began taking power."

"How did he do it?" Robin asked. "Surely someone would have noticed."

"Not in the least," Maud said glibly. "Not until it was too late. He made promises of wealth and security, and they let him walk right in and take over. DeMarke was no fool, Robin; he knew what he was doing. The people were kept blissfully ignorant of his true intentions, and those of us who did know were touted as malcontents. Our own people turned on us. They wanted the easy life he promised, a life that needed no responsibility because everything was decided for them. Anyone considered to be a threat to that lifestyle was immediately silenced. It was the work of a master, I will tell you."

"But Lady Marian told us DeMarke was harming the people here," Jasmine said. "How could they protect him for that?"

"She is right," Maud said. "He is harming them. Now. But Marian neglected to tell you the whole story, of how he worked himself in the position to do that. What is happening now is the result of a silver tongue and willing ears. For a year or two, the people around here had it good. Very good. They were well taken care of, fat and healthy, and by the end of the first year DeMarke had them dancing on the end of his leash like a pack of happy hounds. Then he began his campaign. Oh, it started out innocently enough. A rule here and there to provide more security, keep thieves at bay or keep drunks off the streets. A curfew to keep the children safe." Maud smiled ironically. "That's how he went at it," she added. "Through the children. No easier way was ever found to manipulate a people than through the safety of their wee ones. Protect the children and you protect the future. Before you know it, we are a community without freedom, under the rule of a coward."

Her words were lined with bitterness. Bitterness for the sheriff, his power-grab, but mostly toward the people of Nottingham, who had allowed this thing to happen. They reached her cabin shortly after, traversing the last distance in silence. Treating her two guests to a hearty meal, Maud insisted they tell her everything, about where they had come from and how they got here, how they got away from the sheriff ... how they ended up with an entire posse on their tails in the first place after being in the region a matter of days...

"My land has proven sanctuary for many people in this last year," she said at last, when they'd finished their tale. "You are welcome to stay as long as you like."

"Thank you," Robin said, "but it may be some time before this situation is resolved; the queen may have agreed to the terms but the money still has to be raised, and doing so may prove difficult. We don't want to get you in trouble in the meantime."

"You mean more than I am?" Maud asked lightly. "I have men coming here every other day trying to lock me up for something. The sheriff has tried to arrest me on charges ranging from harboring fugitives to public indecency, and once tried to implicate me in a string of petty thefts that were committed in Nottingham. By his men."

Jasmine smiled.

"We wouldn't want to be the excuse they end up using," she said, and Maud conceded the point grudgingly.

"If I can't convince you to stay here," she said, "then I will point you in another direction of safety. There is a little church not far from here to the east, along the river, that should provide shelter. At least until you can plan what you are going to do."

And it was with her words of encouragement in their ears that Robin and Jasmine left the relative safety of Maud's small cabin and continued on their way. They traveled quietly, watching their steps. Although this was private land, privacy didn't seem to mean much to this current regime, and Gisbourne and his men could show up at any time. Robin knew they needed a place to hide; someplace untouchable. Just until tonight.

The line of trees broke before them, and the two travelers found themselves near the bank of a lazy river, the dark waters meandering languidly into view around a bend farther upstream. In the river was a man. A friar.

"Ah-ha," Robin said sneakily. "Where there is a friar, there is always a church."

The friar was a small man, round and jolly-looking, bald except for a thin, horseshoe-shaped smattering of hair, clad in a brown robe with a matching, hooded cloak draped over the top. The cloak fell free of the white, rope band he had tied around his waist, its featureless lengths drifting with the slow current of the river. And beyond it all was the church; a quaint, rock-formed affair draped with ivy and moss seated on the opposite bank on a hill, a mere stone's throw from where Robin and Jasmine stood now.

Bingo.

"Robin, look," Jasmine said suddenly. "The posse."

Robin spun around. Sure enough, the muffled sound of hoof beats and flash of yellow tunics announced the arrival of the men, an imposing cluster of stern faces and itchy trigger fingers. Guy of

Gisbourne was in front, recognized easily by his pudgy form and flapping limbs, followed by nearly a dozen soldiers on their matching horses, all twelve men sitting easily as the posse turned to follow the river downstream. Toward Robin and Jasmine.

"If we can get inside the church, we should be safe enough," Robin said. "We just need to figure out how to get across the river. I don't see a bridge."

Just then, the little friar started humming to himself, tromping around in the water.

"I'll just ask," Robin said.

"What will you tell him?"

"Nothing. He doesn't need to know."

"Be quick," Jasmine whispered. "We haven't much time."

Robin adjusted his tunic and stepped out of the trees, Jasmine beside him, approaching the river's edge. The friar didn't hear them, busy as he was splashing water over a bit of clothing he was trying to wash, humming his little tune with his back to the woods. He still didn't turn when the pair of shadows slipped across the water beside him.

"Excuse me," Robin said amiably. His sudden appearance caused the little man to jump, water splashing noisily as he spun around. "Sorry," Robin said. "I didn't mean to startle you."

"Can I be of assistance?" The friar asked. He seemed rather miffed as, once more, he lowered his gaze to the water.

"Yes, you can," Robin answered. "My friend and I are trying to reach the church. We wish to pray. But as you can see, we are somewhat at a loss. Is there no bridge?"

"Yes. Just around the bend," was the response. "It is not far."

The friar never even looked up. Robin took a quick glance in the direction he specified, determining quickly that the distance was a bit too far for what he needed, even as Jasmine stealthily slipped back up the bank to keep an eye on things. Her tense nod indicated the sheriff's posse was indeed getting closer.

"And that's the only way across?" Robin asked casually, turning back to his chunky informant.

"It is. Unless you wish to wade." The friar's tone was far too glib. Like he was only too happy to send Robin who-knows-how-far upstream.

Robin took a glance at Jasmine, who gestured for him to *hurry up.*

"Would you lend us the use of your back?" He asked quickly. "We don't have time to find the bridge."

He saw Jasmine roll her eyes and heard her mutter something in her native tongue that – he was sure – had something to do with men and their intolerable stubborn streak, at about the same time the friar slowly turned around to regard him with a mixed expression of disbelief and utter disdain.

"Do I look like a carthorse to you?"

"No, but what does it say in the Bible? Do unto others...?"

"It also asks if I am my brother's keeper, and I am not," the friar returned. "Especially when my good brother has two fine, working legs that can carry him upstream on their own."

"I'll pay you," Robin offered quickly, but his proposition brought only a look of even greater contempt.

"Let me put this in plain, Biblical terms for you," the friar said. "Thou shalt not."

With that, he went back to his wash. Robin crossed his arms. That's it; now it was just a matter of principle.

"I really didn't want to do this," he said dramatically, "but I am afraid you leave me no choice." He slid the sword out of its sheath. "A ride, my friend," he finished, eyeing the shocked friar with a smile. "If you please."

The friar was mere inches from the tip of Robin's blade, and could see the futility of trying to escape. Reluctantly the little man turned around, allowing Robin to climb aboard, and began the slow, sloshing trek across the river.

"If you will please drop me on the shore and return for my friend," Robin said persuasively, hoping the sheriff's men didn't come bursting into the picture at this particular moment. The water was up to the friar's waist and getting deeper, its dark currents rippling around the toes of Robin's shoes.

"Do you recall what I told you about not being my brother's keeper?"

They were almost to the middle of the river when the friar's voice broke into his thoughts.

"How could I forget?" Robin asked, tucking his feet up to avoid getting them wet.

~ 359 ~

"I meant it."

He leapt to the side, almost sending Robin into the river, and Robin yelped in surprise as he grabbed wildly for a handful of bulky cloak. His fingers found purchase, dug into the thick material... then, quite suddenly, there was nothing there. The cloak fell from the friar's shoulders, and Robin found himself falling backwards into the water. He landed with a splash and a yell, flailing around helplessly, and when he sputtered to the surface it was to find the friar looking down at him with a triumphant smile on his face and a rather large knife in his hands.

"I said let me down on the *other* side, not in the middle!"

Robin's attempt at bluffing produced only a hearty laugh.

"Now, my young friend," the friar said, "it is your turn. It seems I need a ride to the opposite bank." He grinned outright, clearly enjoying the payback. "What was that you said about doing unto others? The sword, please..."

Robin surveyed the ample character before him and realized he was more likely going to drown than get shot by the posse. Grudgingly he handed over the sword and turned around, cringing as he felt a pair of beefy hands clap solidly on his shoulders. The friar hopped onto his back, and Robin almost went down, stumbling uselessly as the weight threw him forward and the water prevented movement. He said nothing and managed to take one step, two steps, tripped over a pond plant on the third. The friar was humming again. Robin regained his footing and trudged onward, half of him wanting to make the shore and the other half tempted to go down just to get even. The ground began to rise under his feet, bringing the bank closer with each step.

Robin suddenly tripped and went down. Accidentally, of course. The friar must not have been expecting such a move, for he fell forward, tumbling to the ground, dropping both the sword and the knife as he tried to get clear.

"Ah-ha!" Robin snatched the sword and held it up, leaping to his feet with water spurting from the toes of his shoes. "You know the procedure, I believe," he said.

This time he was prepared for any trickery that might be present, but, surprisingly, the little friar cooperated. He carried Robin over to the far bank and let him down without protest. Robin set foot on land to find Jasmine standing there, arms crossed, shaking her head as she watched them with an amused smile on her face.

"How did you get over?" Robin asked in surprise.

"The bridge," Jasmine answered, completely unfazed. "It is amazing how much one can get done when one listens to advice."

The friar grumpily grabbed the tail of his robe to wring it out. Funny, Maud sort of failed to mention him in her little reference to the safety of the church.

The muffled clopping of hooves, coming at a rather rapid pace, suddenly cut through the forest.

"The posse!" Jasmine said softly in alarm.

"Come on, Jasmine, we have some traveling to do," Robin said, and took her by the arm. "Thank you for the lift," he added over his shoulder.

A surprised look crossed the friar's round face.

"You are running from the sheriff?" He asked, and Robin paused.

"Sort of," he said cautiously, not sure how much he should tell. "Maud de Caux sent us this way."

"Why didn't you tell me? I could have helped you sooner." The friar glanced in the direction of the approaching racket. "Come with me," he said. "Quickly."

To say Robin was surprised would have been a major understatement. Hastily the friar led them up to the church, opening the door to herd them inside just as the sheriff's men came into view along the riverbank.

"In here," the friar said, and moved a large tapestry aside from the wall, revealing another door. "Hurry, now. They won't be long." He stuffed them into a room and slammed the door, leaving them in blackness.

"Where are we?" Jasmine asked softly.

"I don't know... it smells like a cellar." Robin felt around with both feet and hands and, sure enough, discovered that they were standing on the top step of a staircase, which led into the unknown. The room was cool and dry, definite hallmarks of storage, but Robin could tell nothing about *what* might be stored in here. There were far too many smells to analyze.

A thud outside froze all motion. Muffled voices could be heard through the thick door, the voice of the chubby friar as well as that of the even-more-chubby Guy of Gisbourne, both of them sociable and friendly and seeming to get along very well. Far too well, as a matter of fact. Robin had a sudden, frightening thought. What if the friar was playing both sides? What if he had just led them into a trap? He suddenly realized the friar still had his sword, and all he and Jasmine had between them was that dagger she'd been carrying around. Good enough to nail the friar if things went bad, but what about the rest of the troupe? What good could a dagger do against crossbows?

The tapestry swept aside in a loud swish of fabric, and the door flipped open.

"They're gone," the friar said as he poked his head in, and Robin sighed.

"You had me worried, mate," he said with a tense laugh. "I started to think maybe you had other ideas for us."

The friar grinned as he held the door open to let them out.

"Friar Tuck is good as his word," he said. "Maud and I have aided many a fugitive many a time, and we will continue to do so until a resolution is reached. Is there any way I can help you?"

"Well, we need someplace to hide out," Robin admitted. "Just until tonight."

Friar Tuck spread his hands expansively, water still dripping from his sleeves.

"Mi casa es su casa," he said expansively, holding his hands out.

"What?"

"My house is your house," Tuck repeated in English. "I learned it from a Franciscan friar who passed this way a few years ago."

The friar turned out to be quite the talker. He kept them entertained for some time, regaling them with stories of people he'd sheltered to ways he'd diverted the attention of the sheriff and his "cringing cronies", as he called them, proving it was indeed possible for a one-man-army with a cause to make a dent in fascism.

Robin didn't tell him about their journey or King Richard's return. He'd talked enough about that already, and he figured it wouldn't be long before Friar Tuck heard it himself from some one or another. The news was bound to be all over the country by now. He and Jasmine took their leave just after sundown and ate on the trail, a simple meal that Friar Tuck had packed them at the church, then continued their journey through the shaded corridors of Sherwood Forest. They finally reached Marian's home in the middle of the night. They remained hidden for a time, watching their surroundings, just in case the sheriff had thought far enough ahead to keep the estate under guard, but nothing seemed out of the ordinary. The place was quiet. Robin could see the boy Tommy sitting atop the wall. Stealthily, he and Jasmine slipped across the openness surrounding the walled estate, sneaking around back to a place Robin had known about since he was a child and had used many times to slip inside. It was a small rain gutter, gouged under the wall and hidden behind a large bush, undetectable from the outside and almost so on the inside unless one knew where to look. It took only a couple moments to slide through.

Robin stood up and flattened himself against the wall, Jasmine to his left, and both looked around carefully before making a beeline for the stables. Their footsteps were soundless on the soft earth. Hugging the wall and the shadows it provided, they ran silently through the tall grass, squeaking open the stable door. Robin ducked inside behind and closed the door with a soft thud. At their entrance there was an immediate shuffling of movement at the far end.

"Who is it?" An anxious voice asked.

"Marian, put down whatever weapon you have in your hands and stand up," Robin said. "It's us."

Marian arose from behind the wall separating a pair of stalls, holding a candle in one hand and a large, very ominous crossbow in the other.

"What took you so long?" She said testily. "I've been waiting. I have packed some things for you, and I wanted to make sure you both got out all right."

"Why, Marian," Robin said dramatically. "You sound like you might actually have been worried about us."

"Please, Robert." Marian dropped the crossbow in the hay. "I have already lost one childhood companion; must I lose another? And it is only natural that I should worry about Jasmine," she added. "With you around she'd be safer jumping in front of a wagon. Especially with the sheriff being as he is now."

"How is that?" Jasmine asked curiously.

"In a rage," Marian said. "You made him look a fool."

"No large feat, believe me," Robin answered.

"I'm serious, Robert," Marian said sharply. "He has sworn to kill you on sight. If you don't leave now, it will only be a matter of time." She leaned back against the dividing wall behind her. "He knows about the letter. I don't know how..."

"I do. Lady Gwen told me that Prince John is the one responsible for the inception of DeMarke's committee."

"And he knows about the letter," Marian said resignedly. She crossed her arms, eyes flicking between Robin and Jasmine. "What will you both do now?"

"After we deliver the note? I don't know. I guess that safest thing would be stay as far away from here as possible." Robin chuckled. "My, my, we really stirred up a nest of hornets, didn't we?"

"Quite."

"Who would have thought I'd run more risk of getting killed in my own country than in prison?"

Marian smiled slightly, and perhaps would have said something when hoof beats – and a lot of them – filtered in muffled throbs through the thick walls of the stable.

"Someone's coming." Marian opened the stable door a crack, her eyes seeking Tommy's position momentarily, and took a glance before almost throwing herself back inside, her face losing about five shades of color. "It's DeMarke," she said fearfully. "We must get you out of here!" She cast her eyes to Robin. "The letter," she said abruptly. "Give it to me, and then get as far away from Nottingham as you can. It's too dangerous for you to go to Austria now. DeMarke knows what you look like, and he will be relentless in hunting you. If you show your face again anywhere before King Richard returns, you'll be seeing the world from inside a noose. I'll deliver the letter."

"You'll do that?"

"Yes."

Robin whipped the letter out of his pocket and flicked it to her, then he and Jasmine quickly saddled their horses, strapping on the packs Marian had made for them, and swung aboard as Marian opened the stable doors. She took a step forward, then paused.

"Where will you go?" She asked quietly.

"I don't know." Robin shrugged, shook his head. "Wherever it is, we'll be long gone by morning."

"Take care… both of you?"

"We will," Robin said, as beside him, Jasmine nodded.

"Will you come back?"

"Hard to say."

Another small smile, one Robin thought might hold a touch of regret.

"Give me a moment," Marian said. "I'll light a torch when the gates are open, but be *careful*. Tommy indicated there are at least thirty men outside."

"Thanks for the tip." Robin looked down at her, realizing again just how beautiful Marian was. "Good-bye, Marian," he said gently. "Hopefully I'll see you when this is all over."

"Yes. That would be nice." Without another word, Marian was gone, disappearing into the gloom just as an authoritative knock sounded on the gate.

"Hold on, Jasmine," Robin said. "I believe this is going to be fast."

The gates squeaked open. The torch lit up. With a wild yell, the two fugitives dropped the reins and gave the pair of frolicsome horses all the room they could ask for, barreling out of the stables to bolt across the open courtyard and out the gate. DeMarke's men never had a chance. Five or six had sprung aside at the appearance of the rushing bodies, rushing to get out of the way. Robin and Jasmine blew by them without a backward glance, the two horses galloping full-tilt, running over a horde of men and dogs and other horses packed around the entrance.

"Bye, Marian!" Robin shouted as he plowed through the turmoil.

The answering shout was slightly more masculine and sinister in nature, but it was lost for the wind.

Don't cry because it's over,
smile because it happened.

- *Dr. Seuss*

Chapter 19

Turning Outlaw

The next morning...

"Get him!"

"Don't let them escape!"

His horse bolted to the side and Robin barreled off as an arrow came out of nowhere to zing over his head, imbedding itself high in the trunk of a tree.

"You know the law, lad! This is the king's land!"

It took Robin a moment to realize that, whoever this was, they weren't after him. Hopping to his feet, he tied the skittish horse to a branch and slipped closer to the racket, running from tree to tree.

Morning had found him riding silently through the woods, keeping his eyes wide open for the sheriff's men as he headed for the church. He had come to say good-bye. He and Jasmine were going to take Marian's advice and disappear, but Robin didn't want to do so without at least thanking Friar Tuck for what he'd done. He was now on the hill directly beyond the church, but it appeared that good-bye was the last thing he should be thinking about.

"Get your hands off him!"

Friar Tuck's distinct voice cut through the air just as another pair of arrows whined off into the forest, their sleek, deadly forms zipping through the air.

Robin slunk to the edge of the knoll and peered over. Two young men, obviously on an expedition whose intent was slightly different than Robin's, were standing firmly over the carcass of a large buck, bows and arrows at the ready, facing down about twenty of the sheriff's men. Eighteen, to be exact. Two had already been decommissioned. They were on the ground, one holding his arm and the other his shoulder, cursing the boys for all they were worth. The rest of the posse was on the verge of bypassing verbal insults and going straight for those of a more lethal nature, leveling an arsenal of crossbows at the youngsters like they were going to pincushion both. There was only one thing that kept them from doing just that. In the middle of it all, looking like a bear with a very bad toothache, was Friar Tuck. He had parked himself solidly between the boys and the posse, brandishing a huge piece of wood, simply daring the soldiers to try and shoot *anybody* while he was there.

Robin quickly shucked an arrow and fitted it into the bow. He didn't know the two boys, but Friar Tuck was a friend. And Robin intended to help his friends. Carefully he took aim, right in the middle of the crowd of bodies, and pulled back on the flexible, taut string under his fingers.

The men below scattered as one of their own gave a sharp cry and fell back, clutching his right leg. Perfect shot. Robin zipped another arrow into place and let it go, striking a second man in the shoulder. Turmoil had erupted in the small clearing as the two young men started firing, dropping several unlucky posse-members. Friar Tuck went after the rest with that big stick. A couple good swipes sent any who had managed to remain in their saddles to the ground, and the three fugitives immediately swooped down on the hapless posse, using belts and tunics and anything else handy to tie them up.

The boys were young, younger than Robin although not by much, and were polar opposites of each other even at first glance. One was shorter, about halfway between Friar Tuck's height and that of their companion, rather stocky with a mop of blonde, unkempt hair that, at the moment was matted with leaves from having taken a tumble. His clothing was old, worn, patched in many places with fabrics that made no attempt at matching anything around them, and was likewise mantled with various plant material.

The other boy was quite tall, right around Robin's own height, slim, dressed in a faded red tunic that did, however, bear hallmarks of being well taken care of despite its hard use. His hair was dark and cut long, mussed from running around. He seemed quieter than his hunting partner, a bit more brooding; like life had dealt him a few blows over the years that he found difficult to recover from.

As the commotion began to die down, Tuck dropped the stick he held and turned in Robin's direction.

"Robin, I know that's you!" He called. "Where are you?"

"You lads looked like you could use some assistance!" Robin shouted back as he led his horse down the steep bank, hopped on, and eased it into the river.

"And just what gave you that impression?" Friar Tuck was grinning as Robin leapt to the ground again and dropped the reins.

"Nothing, really," Robin admitted, jogging over. "I was just looking for something to do." He clapped Friar Tuck on the shoulder. "You would have made a fine knight, my friend," he added, and turned to the boys. "You're both all right?"

"Fine." The dark-haired one answered first, fixing Robin with a pair of piercing, blue eyes. "Thank you."

"You didn't kill any of them," the blonde one said, surprised, looking at the covey of squirming men.

Robin smiled sadly.

"I've seen enough of that," he said quietly. "Tell me, lads, what brings you this far into the forest?"

"You're looking at it." The blonde one gestured to the buck at his feet. "We'd just downed him when the posse showed up."

"What's your name?"

"I'm called Much. My father's the miller in town. This is my brother, Will Scarlet. Well, we're not really brothers," he clarified. "Will was orphaned and my family took him in years ago. And you are...?"

"You can call me Robin."

"Of Locksley?" Scarlet asked immediately. At Robin's nod, he tilted his head to the side carefully, seeming to size him up. "I see," he said, rather slowly. "It's nice to finally meet you."

"So you're the one causing all the trouble," Much put in jovially.

"The very same," Tuck said.

"We thought you would have cleared out by now."

"If you really must know, I was about to."

"And let others die in your place?" Scarlet's young voice was serious, almost hostile, and Robin raised his eyebrows in question. "They're to be hung for poaching," Scarlet continued angrily. "Six men. They'd been caught and were serving time for it, but when you escaped last night the sheriff decided to set an example. They die tomorrow unless we can stop it." He crossed his arms. "You're supposed to be the escape artist, Locksley. Can't you do something?"

Robin couldn't figure out why he was suddenly so antagonistic. It was almost like Scarlet had a prior grudge against him.

"When is this to happen?" He asked, addressing Much.

"Midday. At the garrison."

Much, too, appeared rather curious as to what Robin would do. Robin just nodded and picked up a crossbow to look it over, deciding to give it to Jasmine. She needed something other than that dagger to defend herself with.

"I'll do what I can," he said at last. "But we need to talk at another time." He hoisted the quiver of arrows higher on his shoulder. "Friar Tuck," he said sagely, "I do believe, after this episode, that your time as clergyman has reached its end for now. You are welcome to come with me until this mess is over."

"An invitation I accept gladly, Robin."

"You lads," Robin added. "Take the carcass of this buck somewhere safe. If another posse comes by, you'll need to be out of sight. Friar Tuck and I will deal with these men. Meet us here tonight, just after dark. We'll talk then."

Robin knew as he spoke that his mission had just been altered. Indeed, it had been altered the moment he shot that first arrow. No longer would he hide like a coward; no longer would he let others fight the battle while he took the easy way out. No, he would fight back. It's what his father would have done.

"Tonight, lads," Robin said. "I have a plan."

****

Marian had no idea what the sheriff wanted from her, nor did she particularly wish to know. After Robert and Jasmine had escaped the night before, DeMarke had grilled her for almost an hour concerning their whereabouts and plans, stopping the interrogation just short of a strip search to get the information he wanted. Marian told him nothing. There was nothing to tell. Judging, however, by the rather abrupt summons she had received this morning, DeMarke believed there was.

Marian pushed aside the small knot of anxiety in the pit of her stomach and called for her carriage, focusing instead on things of a more promising nature. Her boy Tommy had departed early that morning, traveling light and swift, the queen's letter tucked in his pocket. No one was looking for him, and despite his tender age the lad was smart. With any luck, the letter would be in Leopold's hands within days, and Tommy should be back in a week. Then the country could begin the long, difficult road to completion.

Collecting the ransom promised to be no easy task; finding enough money to cover it would be difficult enough, let alone doing so in the face of the opposition they would undoubtedly face from Eustace DeMarke and his committee. Desperate men had been known to do desperate things, and as soon as King Richard's return became public, DeMarke and his men would, indeed, become desperate. Attempts to collect the ransom could easily turn into a small war.

Marian was glad Robert had agreed to relinquish his duty concerning the letter. He had enough to worry about right now, with all the trouble he'd unwittingly stirred up. Although half of her almost wished Robert would have decided to stay and fight, Marian was well aware of the possible consequences – more so than Robert himself would be – and she knew such an effort on his part could only end in tragedy. No, girlish fondness of heroism aside, it was far better that Robert and Jasmine were gone from this place; Marian was sure her childhood friend had seen enough fighting to last several lifetimes.

She reached the garrison shortly before midday, and watched out the small window of her carriage as the massive gate was lowered before her, chains rumbling and creaking over large, round spools just inside. The gate clunked down, forming a sturdy bridge over the moat surrounding the garrison. The water in the moat was green and very uninviting, home to who knew what, and littered with all sorts of disreputable objects on its surface. The carriage slowed to a graceful halt inside the gate, next to a wagon that had just arrived carrying payroll for the soldiers, and Marian stepped out, taking a look at the fortress that had, at one time, been a rich-man's manor. She'd never been inside before. She could tell now she hadn't missed much. Guards roved freely about the tall, imposing walls, looking like so many identical twins in black-and-yellow tunics armed with a spear and crossbow setup that were carried in exactly the same manner by each. The garrison itself was made up of three major structures: the main building, which housed the troops; the prison block off to the right; and the stable to the left, swinging around to follow the wall. The rest of the place was vacant except for a large storage room and, of course, various implements of torture and death, most notably the series of stockades and the ten-man gallows seated right in the center of attention. Through the line of coarse ropes swinging in the slight breeze, Marian could see the front of the main building, elevated, impudently elegant, fifteen or so stairs reaching up to the door with flagpoles bearing Eustace DeMarke's colors sticking out from the wall on either side. And coming down the steps, a glowing, sickening smile on his face, was the sheriff himself.

Yuck.

"My lady Marian," DeMarke said gallantly, pressing his lips to her gloved hand. "I am pleased that you have accepted my invitation."

"Invitation? I'd say rather threat," Marian said tartly, snipping her hand back. "If you please, sir, I have many things to do today, and this trip has taken time I do not have. I request that you be brief."

"Of course." A flash of irritation appeared, but was covered with great skill. "If you will please come with me," DeMarke said, and led her towards the steps he had just come down. Behind them, Marian could hear one of the guards directing her coachman where to wait for her return.

Assuming I do return, she thought mildly. She went anyway, trailing the sheriff by a few paces up the stairs, and had just reached the landing when a shout sounded below.

"Cousin!"

DeMarke and Marian paused in unison, turning around as a heaving, sweating Guy of Gisbourne managed to surmount the final step and walked swiftly towards them.

"If you will wait here, my lady," DeMarke said, seeming to sense important developments, and strode off a few paces. The conversation was quiet, meant to be inaudible to Marian's ears, but she heard every word, nonetheless.

"Cousin," Gisbourne said. "I just came from the stables. Blankeney and his troupe haven't returned yet."

"How long have they been gone?"

"Two days. They were supposed to be in last night."

DeMarke never had to answer. As if on cue, the large gate out front dropped again, settling over the moat with a solid clunk. A rag-tag group of mounted soldiers were on the other side, five in all, looking like death warmed over with ripped tunics and splotches of blood covering anything that wasn't in pieces. Their horses walked docilely, heads down, seven more being led behind. If Marian had to guess, she would say this was Blankeney and his much-missed troupe. Or what was left of it, anyway.

"I'll go see what happened," Gisbourne said, but DeMarke detained him.

"No. It'll keep. I may need you."

Marian didn't like his tone. Especially since he had been looking her way when he said it. Now even more dubious, she complied obediently as the sheriff approached again with Gisbourne on his heels, and gestured her toward the entrance. The doors opened before her, and Marian stepped inside, not even bothering to take a look around the shadowed interior. She simply followed DeMarke to another flight of stairs taking off to their left, which led to, she presumed, the top floor. After staring at DeMarke's rather unattractive latter half and listening to Gisbourne pant his way up the long flight of stairs, she was led into a dark, unlit room that held only three pieces of furniture. All chairs. The rest of the room was nothing but stone and rats. There was door on the far side, the light inching in beneath indicating it led outside. Probably to a balcony.

DeMarke gestured Marian to one of the chairs and pulled up another, far too close for comfort, dropping into it as he crossed his arms. Marian could hear Gisbourne sitting down behind her. She stifled the nerves beginning to creep into her mind and plastered a very bored expression on her face.

"Now, my lady," DeMarke said, leaning back in his chair. "What would you say if I called you a liar?"

Marian didn't even attempt insult.

"I'd have to ask the issue," she said.

"Locksley." DeMarke quirked an eyebrow. "Did you, or did you not, lie when you told me he was still in London?"

"I did." Really, there was no use denying it now. "But, you see, I had no idea he was as dangerous as you say," Marian said innocently. "Certainly I would have done something, otherwise."

A brief pause while DeMarke contemplated a spot on his robe, a pause certainly meant to freak Marian out. It sort of worked.

"And the horses he and his companion took from you?" He asked after a moment. Very condescendingly.

"Stolen, as I told you last night," Marian said. "They were gone before I could stop them. Surely you saw that; it was you one of them almost ran over."

"You must have some idea where they went."

This question came from Gisbourne, in the same condescending, irritating tone his cousin had been using on her.

"They're probably out of the country by now," Marian said. *Hopefully...*

She saw a look pass between the two men and knew they believed not a word she said. Well, couldn't blame a girl for trying.

"Very well, then," DeMarke said, and flicked his eyes toward his cousin, then the door, prompting Gisbourne to rise heavily out of his seat. "Since your memory seems to have failed you concerning this one man, six others shall pay in his stead."

"What do you mean?" Marian asked tensely. "How can I forget something if I never knew it to begin with?"

Gisbourne had, by this time, crossed the room and opened the door Marian had seen earlier, letting light stream into the small room. Several rats scurried for cover. Marian slowly stood up as DeMarke took her by the elbow, following him uneasily out onto the balcony.

"See for yourself," DeMarke said, and pointed with a flimsy, jeweled hand.

Before her was the gallows, and it was nearly full. Marian felt her mouth fall open in horror. Six men stood bound on the tall platform, nooses around their necks and blindfolds over their eyes, soldiers behind them prepared to push them off the front.

"No," Marian whispered. "Please, I don't..."

There was a little girl tied up in front of the gallows. She was crying. Her dark hair spilled in dirty, unkempt wisps through her fingers, which were gripped tightly over her forehead, her entire form shaking with violent sobs known only to those who were about to lose everything they cared about. Undoubtedly, one of the men to be hung was her father.

"Well, my lady?" Gisbourne asked.

"No, you can't –" Marian looked at them pleadingly. What kind of contemptible man would execute a father... and make his daughter watch? "You can't do this, please. I'll tell you what I know, I promise."

"Start talking."

"Robert and that girl –"

"Barbarous creature."

"– came to me late last night," Marian continued, ignoring Gisbourne's interjection. "They had just come back from London and needed help to get to Austria. He told me it was to deliver the queen's letter. I told him I would help him – as any of King Richard's loyal subjects would. He swore to me on his honor that he was telling the truth, and I believed him. That is all, I promise."

"Where were they going? By which road?"

"I don't know."

"Where were they going after?"

"I don't know!"

"How were planning to get to Austria?"

"I told you –"

"Nothing! You told me *nothing*, Marian!" DeMarke threatened, his limited patience exploding. "Nothing but lies! Tell me what I want to know! It's either Locksley or them, m'lady! Choose!"

"I have chosen! I don't know what else to tell you!" Marian stared miserably at the six men below her, at the little girl, desperate to save them but unable to think of a thing more to say. She saw DeMarke look at the gallows, nod his head, saw the soldier step forward to end a life Marian was dooming through her silence. "Wait! Wait, there's something else!" She was stalling for time. She didn't want to face the reality of what was happening. As the sheriff held a hand up, Marian pulled out her mental spinning wheel to feed a few more lies, feed them and hope they stuck. "They're in Spain," she said awkwardly. "I remember that now. Before they left, Robert said something about it briefly. He knew someone... they were headed

north and then across the channel… to Austria to deliver the letter…
then to Spain."

"Where in Spain?"

"A place called Tigre," Marian said, grasping at the only
Spanish word she knew and hoping somebody thought to name their
town after a large cat. "It's in the east, along the border."

DeMarke smiled coldly.

"Thank you, m'lady," he said, and looked to the gallows
again. "Proceed!"

"No!" Marian screamed. "You can't do that! I told you what
you want to know! Please!"

"Don't be ridiculous, m'lady," DeMarke replied. "Spain is
far too distant for an effective example; Robert will be brought to
justice, but these men have broken the law and must be punished."

"But you said they would live! You said to choose and I have
chosen!"

"I lied." DeMarke turned away. "Just as I am sure you have
lied to me again," he finished, and gestured for the execution to
continue.

The guard stepped forward again. Marian felt tears
streaming down her face. She was panicking.

"Stop!" She screamed again. "Stop!" She was just about to
take a wild leap at the hateful, sneering man before her when a sudden
uproar split the garrison. She spun around as a dozen loose, terrified
horses bolted through the center of the compound, dashing madly
through the area. And behind them came the riders. Four men, all
wearing earth-toned, hooded cloaks, spurred their horses and charged
into the foray, firing arrows from sturdy bows and dropping several
unlucky soldiers to create chaos. One had a crossbow. He fired again
and again, leveling the guards by the gate as two of his companions
made a beeline for the entrance, dropping the bridge so fast it almost
split in half as it hit the ground.

The men on the gallows were already on the move. Another
man in a faded, red tunic that was barely visible beneath his cape
tossed each a pair of reins as his cohort cut the prisoners free. Without
a second thought, they leapt aboard the horses and took off, a fifth
man tossing the little girl onto the payroll wagon before flinging his
round form on beside her to angle for the gate. The one with the
crossbow was still shooting. Marian was vaguely aware of the sheriff

and Gisbourne shouting orders, yelling that the payroll be rescued as the wagon and its occupants rumbled out of sight, was aware of soldiers beginning to pour out of doors and buildings and windows, armed to the teeth. But it was the man on the gallows who held her attention. Quickly he slit the last set of bonds, leapt on his horse, and reined the feisty animal into the center of the compound.

"Long live King Richard!" He shouted. "Long live Robert of Locksley!"

With that he took off, as his red-clad companion tossed a pair of reins to the prisoner, who hung on for dear life as his mount shot over the bridge.

A guard suddenly leapt out of nowhere and slammed into the outlaw in red. They fell free of his bay horse, rolling across the ground, and the lad's bow went flying as a hard fist slammed into his face, knocking him to the ground. The guard stood up, drew his sword, then gave a sharp cry and fell forward as an arrow slammed into him. Across the compound, the owner of the crossbow lowered the weapon. He spurred his mount forward, leaning down to swipe the fallen bow off the ground at a full gallop and tossing it to its rightful owner as the young man in red vaulted lightly on his horse.

Then they were gone. Hooves thundered on wood as the last two riders left the garrison at a dead run, their horses flying out of sight just ahead of a volley of arrows that split the air. Far ahead of them, Marian could see the others barreling toward safety. The wagon ran ahead, its frightened team pulling for all they were worth. A few moments more and the whole lot disappeared into the forest.

The dust settled slowly, sheets of it sifting gently toward the ground, descending on silence. No one knew what to think; half of them didn't even know what had just happened. Marian let out the breath she realized she'd been holding. She stared at the empty gallows, at the ropes swinging haphazardly in the breeze. Her soul was suddenly embraced by relief. Against all odds, the tables had been turned, and quite effectively; she doubted any of the sheriff's men had ever been debased in such a manner.

"Guy," DeMarke said frigidly. "As of now, Robert of Locksley is an outlaw. His punishment will be death. Wherever he is, whatever he is doing, we will find him."

"And these men?"

"I want them back on the gallows by the end of the week. Alongside their outlaw friends. Make it happen."

With that, DeMarke turned and stalked off, Gisbourne on his heels, presumably leaving Marian to find her own way out. Marian didn't mind. She stayed by the wall, watching the forest, remembering the last time she had seen Robert and Jasmine as they snuck off into its depths, how they waved good-bye before they disappeared. She was glad they were gone. They were safe and sound somewhere, waiting out this treacherous storm of justice, and Marian was glad for that. She wouldn't want them in the middle of this. She realized suddenly that, even though Robert himself was disinclined to fight, she was almost indebted to him for what he'd done, indebted to him for what he'd started. The news of King Richard's return was already generating a spark of rebellion against the tyrannical rule of DeMarke and his beloved committee, inciting the people to raise arms against an authority that had held them in chains for too long. And if it hadn't been for one man, it never would have happened. For the news would have never arrived. Robert had, in fact, opened the door for other men who were sick of oppression, men like the leader of the small band who had just saved the day, to make a stand.

Marian made a mental note to thank Robert of Locksley if he ever showed back up.

Chapter 20

Beginning of a Legend

Prince John made a mental note to kill Robert of Locksley if he ever showed back up.

A letter lay open before him on the desk, a letter from Eustace DeMarke, and its contents didn't inspire much confidence. It had been a little over a month since Locksley had disappeared into thin air, and the month had seen some disquieting developments. Despite attempts to thwart him, Locksley had somehow made it to Austria; as a result, the queen's letter of agreement had been delivered on time, efforts to raise the ransom were underway all over the country, and the people of Nottinghamshire were starting to revolt against DeMarke. It had all begun with the raid on the garrison. Five men had managed to spirit away six prisoners and a payroll wagon, a band of thieves led by a mysterious, nameless individual that was no doubt a protégé of Locksley. Since then, the group had morphed into a full-scale army. They had sworn, on their honor, to both aid Queen Eleanor's attempt to ransom her son and to protect the people of their region, through any means necessary. They spent the next month proving it. Already money from their heists had surfaced, in the hands of mere common-folk, returned to DeMark's grasp in the form of taxes or fines only to be snatched yet again by the elusive, green-clad bandits who struck fast and vanished into Sherwood Forest. Hundreds of these men now roamed the countryside; untraceable, unstoppable, totally in control. By loose estimates, they had already snatched over 10,000 marks and about fifty prisoners.

Prince John angrily crumpled the letter and threw it aside. It was all Locksley's fault. All of it. Had he not shown up in the first place, things would still be under control. But dwelling on his indiscretions would bring no results; Locksley had disappeared, drifting away like smoke the day before the garrison raid, leaving others to complete the work he had begun. He must have been told to split. But by whom? And the biggest question, the one everyone was asking: where was he? Robert of Locksley had incited a revolution. But where was he now?

John didn't care. He'd just make sure to be here if the boy ever resurfaced. Quickly, his face taut with anger, he whipped out a piece of paper to write a very direct, scathing letter to the sheriff of Nottingham: to do or die.

****

The sheriff of Nottingham's quest for vengeance against Robert of Locksley was short-lived. The letter had arrived on time; Locksley had disappeared; and, in truth, things were becoming too restless on the home front to worry much about where he was. Those disciples he'd left behind had grown significantly in number, and were causing a bit of a problem. The foremost of these had surfaced merely a week after the garrison raid. Within a week, this new villain had risen in Nottinghamshire, and the small, insignificant reward posters placed at throughout the county were covered over as Locksley became a thing of the past. Big, splashy works of art took their places, pieces that seemed to dominate the very area they adorned, inciting the general populace to rise up against this most recent rabble-rouser and put him in the noose where he belonged. The name? A quaint homage to Locksley.

Robin Hood.

****

The garrison had long since disappeared. Will Scarlet pulled his lathered mount to a stop and held the animal to a shifting standstill, a sadistic smile creeping across his face.

You will never win, he thought to himself, the hateful face of Eustace DeMarke – indeed, the faces of all Normans – dancing before his mind's eye. Scarlet hated the Norman people. It was they who were responsible for the merciless killing of his family, they who had taken everything from him but his life, they who had hunted him down like a dirty, Saxon dog until they learned the hard way that his teeth were much sharper than their own. It was on that day, the day Scarlet had killed the husband of one Lady Alicia, that he officially became an outlaw. The Normans were Will Scarlet's mortal enemies; how he would love to send each and every one of them to their graves. And Locksley...

Scarlet looked at their unofficial leader. Locksley was just as responsible.

"Here they come," Locksley said quietly.

They had left DeMarke's fortified manor in a cloud of dust, running for the cover of the forest, where they split up and left three separate trails to the church. And now, true to form, seven more horses cantered into the clearing, led by the cloaked, silent figure called Bob. There was no ceremony. There were no introductions. Locksley immediately began barking commands, ordering the wagon unloaded and the payroll packed onto the horses, evidence of passage destroyed. Once his directives were carried out, the wagon itself was abandoned, and the group of twelve riders and thirteen horses beat another hasty retreat.

The situation was an odd one. Twelve men and a little girl, all inexperienced in the ways of outlawry, almost all strangers to each other, united only by the fact that they were all fugitives from an unjust justice. No one talked much as they wound their way through the stillness; there was nothing to say. In the blink of an eye, their futures had changed, and the blank pages presented were uncomfortably devoid of hints.

Scarlet had to admit a slight astonishment when he saw the hideout Locksley had managed to dig up. Situated deep in the thick darkness of Sherwood Forest, it had all the vantage points one could ever want and was within sight of several more, higher-seated locations from which one could see a good distance in almost any direction. An added bonus, a tall cliff that was within a stone's throw was home to the headwaters of a river, flowing forth in the form of a majestic waterfall that plummeted into a large pool at its base. An old, distinguished tree grew right next to the falls, its roots forming part of the cliff. Above the falls was a large, wooded clearing in the thick underbrush, open enough to be usable but surrounded and dotted by trees of varying sizes.

Bob disappeared shortly after they arrived. Scarlet saw his slight form start for the river, and, after helping un-tack and rub down the horses, Scarlet set his small bundle of things aside and followed. Locksley's friend had saved his life back there, in the garrison, and the least Scarlet could do was offer his thanks.

As he left the camp and walked down the overgrown, steep bank, the waterfall thundered in his ears, drowning out all other sound except those near at hand and enveloping the place in a very light mist. He reached the base of the trail and headed for the river, several paces away. There was a woman kneeling at the water's edge. Scarlet didn't know where she had come from. She was dressed in a faded tunic, the back of which was covered with a sheet of black, silken hair that reached past her slender waist. Her head was bowed, her hands rested lightly on her knees. She must have caught a faint, reflected movement on the water, for she started slightly and sat up, like she expected trouble.

"May I help you?" She asked without turning.

Her voice was low and quiet, mantled by a strange accent Scarlet had never heard before. Whatever it was, he liked it.

"I'm looking for the man called Bob," he said. "I saw him come this way. Where might I find him?"

Still the girl didn't turn.

"What do you want with him?"

"I wish to thank him," Scarlet answered.

The young woman rose to her feet and turned around. She was very slender, tall; with dark, smooth skin and delicate hands, a kind of beauty that had a certain exotic wildness about it, something that defied control. Her features were striking; oval face and almond-shaped eyes, all of it framed by soft, black hair that fell around her shoulders in thick waves. Her eyes spoke to him of many things, though she said not a word, studying him with a curious, sensitive gaze that was hard to meet but even harder to turn away from.

Scarlet searched vainly for something to say. He failed. Uncomfortably he dropped his gaze to the ground, studying a crossbow that lay on the folds of an old cloak. It was a moment before he realized what he was looking at.

"You mean *you're –*"

She laughed quietly as he cut himself off.

"What? Does Bob not suit me?"

"Not really," Scarlet said, and sheepishly trailed his fingers through his hair.

"Well, then you must speak with Robin about it," was the humorous, if somewhat shy, response. "He is responsible for the adoption of such a name."

"What do they call you?"

"Jasmine."

"Jasmine..." Scarlet repeated the name quietly. "I like it," he said. "It suits you." He smiled, gesturing to the crossbow on the ground. "And thank you," he added. "You saved my life, Jasmine, and if there is ever anything I can do to repay you..."

The answering smile was gentle.

"Just promise me you will take care of your life," Jasmine said. "It is enough."

***

Notoriety has a funny way of attracting people, as anyone associated with it would be willing to attest. It also has a funny way of compounding itself. Robin had known, from the moment he fired that first arrow in protection of a pair of fugitives, his path had been altered, and with the moment of decision over he was free to let his imagination run wild. He was already an enemy of Eustace DeMarke. He would become the worst enemy DeMarke or his committee had ever seen.

Once the idea struck, there was no getting rid of it, nor was there any getting rid of the anticipation. Suddenly, and very clearly, Robin could see how best to serve his country. The people were living in poverty; he would give them aid. The queen was rallying support for the ransom; he would help. DeMarke was robbing the country blind; Robin would give him a taste of his own medicine. In other words, he would become a thief to defeat a thief. Fight fire with fire. It was a crazy scheme, he knew, but it wouldn't let him go, for he had finally found something worth fighting for, right in his own backyard. And fight he would.

He didn't know what the others would think. They would be skeptical no doubt, but he hoped receptive, once they saw the logic. And the potential opportunity for payback.

It was an odd assemblage that he addressed; Jasmine, an orphan, a miller's son, a friar, six prisoners and one little girl made up the lot. The prisoners themselves were just as varied in their identities. Four of them were, in all honesty, questionable characters, but their disgust with the system was fierce and their aim unerring, making them just what was needed for the task at hand. The other two had more substance.

Francis of Gascoyne had been a so-called political prisoner for two years. A carpenter by trade, he was one of the first arrested for poaching, when the taxes became too high to pay and he took to the forest to feed his family, learning the hard way that such behavior would not be tolerated under this new world order. He'd remained in prison for several weeks before DeMarke realized he was wasting more money on food than the cause was worth. Francis was let out, he and his wife Rachel struggling like everyone else to make ends meet, before Francis was finally caught red-handed again over the carcass of another buck. That was two weeks ago; he'd been imprisoned ever since.

Jonathan Lacey was a former knight, a man everyone looked up to both figuratively and literally. With a presence suited to a man of his position, he proclaimed his Saxon heritage through eyes of an icy blue that seemed almost capable of tearing an enemy limb from limb with a single glance. He was knighted at the age of seventeen. Patriotism was as air in his lungs; ever-present and indispensable, a love of king and country that prompted him to accompany his fellow countrymen to Jerusalem on the Third Crusade. Unfortunately, that sense of duty had not been enough to stir the conscience of Eustace DeMarke, nor was it enough to outweigh the tempting bottom line that was the Lacey family's holdings. Jonathan returned home to find his land confiscated, his parents dead from fever, and his little sister Alexis lucky to be alive, living under the guardianship of Ellen de Gant. Upon speaking out at the injustice of DeMarke's power grab, he suddenly found himself a target, a political enemy to the cause, completely stripped of title and rank and forced into near exile. His status switched to that of political prisoner when he, too, was caught poaching.

Robin remembered Sir Jonathan Lacey; they'd met briefly several years ago, and had shared a few pleasantries in passing. The day? A hot, tiring, and stressful Christmas Eve. The location? Jerusalem. Nothing more needed to be said. As he talked, explaining in detail what he wanted to do and what he hoped to accomplish by it, he could see he had everyone's attention. The faces before him were intent, watching Robin's every move while he paced back and forth, gazes never straying from his.

"We have two goals, gentlemen," he said at last. "One is to help the queen in her quest to collect the ransom, and the other is to give aid to the people. We take only from those who can afford it, and *never* will we take hostages. Of any sort." He crossed his arms, meeting each pair of eyes in turn. "If anyone has objections, now would be the time to speak, and if anyone wants out, I won't hold it against you. It's your decision."

A bird chirped somewhere in the forest. A twig snapped in Tuck's hands. The six prisoners exchanged a look, while Much and Scarlet waited in silence. Finally, with an air of decisiveness, Jonathan Lacey stood up and spread his hands.

"Lead the way," he said. There was no argument.

They went back to Nottingham that very night. Payroll in tow, they went from door to door in the darkness, leaving small bags of money on the front steps before giving a quiet knock and sitting back to watch the show. After that day, Robin was fanatical. Sort of like an infectious disease, the mood spread, the desire to do more filling each heart in turn. Robin and the others suddenly realized what they could do, and the feeling it inspired was unstoppable.

The beginning was slow, but accelerated quickly. And it wasn't very long before their actions saw results of another kind. As news of Richard's possible return spread – as well as a decent amount of good, old-fashioned coinage – people began to seek them out. Sick of fighting uselessly and sensing a potential ally in this anonymous, enigmatic vigilante, they pulled up stakes and made their way into the forest, ready to join forces.

The first showed up not three days after the garrison raid. Robin had just stepped outside when, across the clearing, he saw Friar Tuck and Much escorting someone into camp. The newcomer was in the middle, blindfolded, walking with his arms tied in front of him and both elbows gripped in a pair of beefy hands. Tuck also had a large stick for good measure.

"Who do you have here?" Robin asked as he strolled over. He saw the figure under the blindfold turn his way quickly, as if in recognition.

"Found him snooping," Tuck said suspiciously, prodding at his prisoner with the stick. "When he saw me, he started asking questions."

The blindfold was whipped off, and the man beneath it jerked his head back in irritation, a mop of mussed, black hair falling into his eyes.

"Allan!" Robin laughed outright, nodding to Much. "It's all right, you can untie him," he said.

Allan flung the ropes from his wrists, glaring indignantly at each of them in turn as he snatched his lute from Much, who had it strapped to his back.

"*You.*" He pointed at Robin. "You're not even supposed to be here," he said severely, but his voice held an element of amusement.

"I'm not?"

"Not according to the sheriff." A broad grin suddenly stretched across Allan's face. "It's good to see you, Robin."

"And you. Tell me, friend, what does a minstrel want in a den of outlaws?"

"Something to fight for." Allan's green eyes took in the whole scene at a glance, shifting easily over the camp. "I wasn't expecting to see you here," he added. "Someone said you left the country."

"Who?"

"You know rumors," Allan said in a non-committal tone. "Someone started it, someone passed it on, someone believed it. DeMarke is utterly confused, because he's convinced you're gone, but he can't find out the identity of the bandit who led the raid on the garrison." His smile turned pensive. "I heard that Lady Marian was asking about you, as well," he said. "She would be surprised to hear you're still here."

"Don't tell her," Robin said. "It's better if she thinks I'm gone."

Better for her, better for him, better all around. Robin was worried about Marian. He knew she was a tough and capable woman, knew Marian thought she was strong enough to handle DeMarke. And she was, but Robin didn't want to think about some of the tricks DeMarke might have up his sleeve.

"Allan," he said cheerfully, changing the subject, "welcome to outlawry. Let me introduce you to our gang, such as it is. This is Friar Tuck, Much, Will Scarlet... Jasmine, of course, you know already..."

Allan was introduced around, and it quickly became apparent that he had previous ties to at least one of the occupants of the small camp. Alexis literally shrieked when she saw him. Loosing her brother's hand, she dashed forward, calling Allan's name excitedly as she darted into sight.

"Alexis!" Allan said, and the words were filled with affection. As the girl tumbled into his arms, he snatched her up in a hug. "You've gotten so tall!" He exclaimed. "What happened to that little girl I found on the road?"

Jonathan Lacey had walked over slowly, smiling at his sister's exuberance, and nodded to Allan over the mass of dark hair.

"You must be Allan-a-Dale," he said genially. "Alexis has told me about you."

And so were the dots connected between Allan-a-Dale and Ellen de Gant. Allan had met her through this little girl, Jonathan's sister, Alexis' presence providing the vital link between two lives that, under ordinary circumstances, could never have crossed.

Allan-a-Dale took to the life of an outlaw just as he did everything else: with fun and a lot of spirit. His tunes brought to the camp a sense of home, a certain stability that only music can provide. As the population continued to grow, first with the addition of more men and eventually, their families, the music became a necessity.

Things changed rapidly with the entrance of women and children. A few came first, followed by many others, and the small, pokey camp the gang had been occupying to this point developed into a full-scale village. It was ringed by lookouts. Scouts roved the area, invisible, blending with the forest, keeping the enemy out and providing valuable information to those inside. Each was equipped with a bow and a series of arrows outfitted with small circular pieces on the head, which, when shot through the air, would whistle shrilly to announce its arrival. The arrows were then painted in different colors: red for enemy; white for friend; red stripes for an enemy posse and white stripes for a friendly group; and an alternating red-stripe, white-stripe pattern for unknown. This system became the backbone of defense for the small city in the woods, staving off many a close encounter.

The heists they pulled off became more and more sophisticated. From confused and disorganized they developed into intricate dances with danger, a ballet that balanced tactics and skill and timing to win the day. Many a nobleman lost a fortune on the stretch of road through Sherwood Forest. Many a young maid lost her heart. Many a ballad and many a legend were begun about these audacious, gallant bandits, a notoriety that took their deeds to new heights. A month had passed since six prisoners and a payroll had escaped from the garrison, and in that month, the gang that started out with twelve members, thirteen horses, and no plan had become a force to be reckoned with. The outlaws were famous. People loved them.

Considering the circumstances, it may have been desperation that fueled the decision to call an emergency meeting of DeMarke's committee. The meeting was supposed to be top-secret; so naturally, by the next day, everyone knew about it. A servant at the garrison passed the news on to another servant; that servant to their family in Nottingham; each family member to everyone they knew, allowing Much and Scarlet to hear it on their way back through town... They, in turn, brought it straight to Robin. They burst into camp late in the afternoon, Much intoning in a very serious, overly-dramatic tone the contents of a large poster in his hands.

"Hear ye, hear ye!" He shouted, striding forward purposefully. "Generous reward offered for the capture of the outlaw known as Robin of the Hood! Come one, come all, and see for yourselves what kind of monetary gains could be yours for cooperating with our dear Sheriff of Nottingham! Hear ye, hear ye...!"

Robin had been in the process of mending a broken harness when the racket broke his concentration, and set his work aside to saunter over, easing his way through the growing, laughing crowd surrounding the instigators.

"Robin of the *what*?"

~ 388 ~

"Hood," Much answered. "You know, famous outlaw, traitor to the crown..." He grinned and handed over the folded parchment. "You may not know it yet, but you're getting quite the reputation. Take a look."

Robin unfolded the poster to spy a drawing of a faceless, almost shapeless figure with a feather in his cap and a bow in his hand.

REWARD, the poster said, *FOR THE CAPTURE OF THE OUTLAW KNOWN AS ROBIN OF THE HOOD.*

"Robin of the Hood?" He asked skeptically.

"I don't know who started it, but somehow it caught on," Much said. "People are talking. The sheriff, of course, is taking it all far too seriously and had these made. They're being put up all over."

Robin was amused that he was becoming something of a local legend. He was even more amused when Much told him some of the stories people were spreading.

"A thousand paces?" He inquired wryly as Much tacked the poster to a nearby tree. "They said I hit a target from a thousand paces?"

"That's the rumor."

"That's impossible."

"Says who?"

"How did you even get a hold of this?"

Much looked insulted.

"I'm a thief, Robin, remember? I swiped it off the notice board in town. And that's not all we got," he added importantly. "Tell him, Will."

Scarlet tore off a chunk of bread from a small loaf in his hand.

"DeMarke is making a move," he said. "Your idea is starting to work." So saying, he told Robin of the sheriff's top-secret meeting that was to take place three days hence. In London. "I don't know who called them, but the entire committee will be there. Not just DeMarke. He, apparently, intends to travel up the day before." Scarlet smiled in satisfaction, crossing his arms. "I say we hit them on the road," he said. "Show those Norman swine who controls this forest."

Robin looked at him carefully.

"You forget," he said gently. "Lady Ellen's father is a Saxon. He's one of us."

"He's one of them!" Scarlet snapped. "He betrayed us when he joined forces with DeMarke! You even said yourself he's no fit father for Lady Ellen!"

He suddenly had everyone's attention. Much paused mid-tack and glanced over his shoulder in surprise, while Friar Tuck, who had come over just moments before, watched the incident with a strangely resigned expression, as if this outburst was something he had been expecting. Off to the side, Jasmine stood silent. She was clearly taken aback by Scarlet's fierce statement, but compassion outweighed her doubt.

Robin never took his eyes from Scarlet's. They burned into his like blue fire, demanding an answer, challenging Robin to find him at fault. Robin knew he'd have to tread lightly. Will Scarlet was impulsive, unpredictable, and his burning hatred for anything Norman made him bitterly aggressive, anger sometimes resulting in an almost animalistic savagery as he had proven on several occasions. He was, despite his young age, probably the most dangerous man among them. He defied authority – anyone's authority – with a vengeance, and took a particular delight in resisting Robin's, challenging him at every opportunity for reasons known to no one but Will Scarlet. Robin met this confrontation as diplomatically as he knew how.

"I don't disagree with you," he said. "I just want to be clear that, should we do as you suggest, we would be doing this for the right reasons." The irony of his own phrasing was not lost on him. "Our goals are to help those who need it," he added, "not aggravate a feud that is not only pointless but has already cost many innocent people their lives."

The look in Scarlet's eyes flashed into instant hatred, and Robin knew if one could kill by such means, he would have dropped dead right then and there.

"Pointless?" Scarlet asked, his voice barely above a whisper. "Those people killed my family. And there isn't *one* of them I wouldn't gladly kill just to see their blood cover the ground as their life ends. I don't care who they are, Locksley; Normans, and anyone associated with them are guilty. As is anyone who defends them."

"What of our king, Will Scarlet?" Robin asked gently. "He, too, is Norman."

Without another word, Scarlet stalked off, disappearing into the trees, leaving absolute silence in his wake. Jasmine took an impulsive step, then checked herself. Her dark, soulful eyes were fixed on Scarlet, telling him all the things she couldn't make herself say, showing visibly just how much she wanted to help. Friar Tuck put an encouraging arm on Robin's arm.

"I'll talk to him," he said. "But, reasoning aside, his idea isn't a bad one."

Truthfully, Robin had been thinking the same thing. What better way to prove to DeMarke that Robin of the Hood and his gang was, indeed, a force to be reckoned with?

"Tuck," he said, and smiled slightly when Friar Tuck turned to face him. "While you're talking to him, tell Scarlet to get his bow ready. We have a convoy to hit."

As soon as Robin accepted the idea, he knew they'd have to think up something incredibly clever to be able to pull it off. Up to now they'd been dealing with imbeciles in small packs, noblemen with a driver and a few guards; this would be very, very different. Twelve members of the committee, twelve egos requiring twelve separate carriages, each carriage requiring a large number of sentinels. It would be the most difficult heist Robin of the Hood and his gang had attempted to this point, and it would call for special means. As it turned out, Jasmine provided them with those means.

"What is that?"

It was a day later. Jasmine had just finished dribbling a small trail of a black, powdery substance on the ground and closed up the drawstring bag in her hands, walking off a few paces to set it aside.

"Watch," she said in response to Much's query. "But stay back."

Those present took the suggested, obligatory step, most with expressions hovering somewhere between curious and suspicious. Only Jonathan Lacey seemed to know what was going on; his face held a very satisfied smirk. Off to the side sat a small pile of a black, powdery substance, more of the mysterious dust, and it was given a wide berth as Jasmine removed a stick from the fire. Kneeling down, she touched the flaming tip to the powder, backing away. The trail instantly lit up, sizzling blue and white and green as the flame ate along its winding path, working its way toward its goal. It hit the pile and exploded with a poof. Smoke billowed outward, spiraling up as it enveloped bodies and hair and clothing, the pungent, stinging smell a detriment to the nose.

"It's called black powder," Jasmine explained casually through the haze. "My father taught me how to make it many years ago." She swiped away a thin film that floated around in front of her face, trailing her hand idly through the still air. "If you want a distraction, Robin, this will do it."

They did need a distraction. And this strange substance would, indeed, do the job.

Two days later, as DeMarke's committee snaked along the quiet, wooded road through the forest in a small procession, they were not alone. The way was lined with eyes. Robin and his cohorts hid patiently on the roadside, watching, waiting for the right moment to strike. There were at least ten carriages before them. True to form, every member traveled singly, and in opulence, the ten or so guards flanking each vehicle seeming to dare Robin of the Hood and his gang to try robbing anyone that day.

Robin turned to his right and nodded. Right on cue, Jonathan Lacey raised his bow to the grey clouds above and loosed an arrow. The arrow shrieked through the air, soaring skyward, its slim form little more than a black streak. There was a shout from the road. The convoy halted. Guards spread out, drawing their weapons, scanning the thick foliage attentively for any sign of movement. No one noticed the thin film of smoke slowly working its way long the roadside. Not, that is, until it reached its destination. A large pile of the powder exploded in a whooshing of smoke and bursting of flame, a column of black fog shooting out from beneath the base of a large tree. The horses bolted in all directions. Their riders gripped manes and saddles for dear life, voices shouting from the carriage windows doing anything but helping the situation as the noblemen demanded to know what was going on. The party was muddled, bewildered, in complete disarray and completely at the mercy of its attackers.

Another nod from Robin. Another arrow sent screaming through the sky. Farther down the road, Francis and twenty men darted into sight, their horses plunging and rearing crazily in the excitement, and their appearance was just enough to take the high emotion of the moment and send it skyward.

"After them!"

The guards never hesitated. Spurring their edgy horses, they charged down the road, shouting insensibly, chasing down the string of fleeing bandits heading the other way at a dead run. Their intentions were good, surely, but their judgment was far from sound. They lost sight of the convoy almost immediately. They lost their quarry in the woods. Irritated at the audacity of these outlaws and even more irritated at being evaded, they called off the chase and prepared to resume their journey.

They returned to a slight crisis. The convoy had vanished. Every one of the carriages was gone, with not even a wheel-mark to indicate passage, and the passengers, DeMarke's infamous committee, were having their meeting right there in Sherwood Forest. They were tied up, blindfolded, formed into a rough circle in the middle of the road. Anything of value had been removed, from fancy clothing to jewelry to shoes, and the aristocrats, these men of noble bearing, now sat in humiliation, adorned with only the barest of bare essentials. With exclamations of surprise, their faithful escorts fell to picking up the pieces. And, busy as they were attending the task at hand, not one man took notice of the silent, alert figure that crouched in the thick underbrush along the side of the road. Robin of the Hood smiled to himself, gleefully, and crept off into the darkness. The committee would be far from defeated by this simple embarrassment, but at least they might recognize exactly what they were dealing with.

When Robin reached the camp, he didn't go in right away. Instead, he stopped at the falls, walking carefully through the tangle of roots and vines that spilled over the edge, and followed a small alcove stretching onward behind the massive sheet of water. He had discovered this place purely by accident. Underneath the falls, the stone underfoot was worn by water and age, rounded, slick, not very inviting at first glance. But Robin wasn't interested in first glances. Another few steps, a turn, and he was staring into a darkened hollow, his goal. It was here, in this place, that the portion of their thievery set aside for the king's ransom waited; its location secret to all but Robin and Friar Tuck. The pile was small now. It would grow larger. Soon they would have enough; enough to call their mission completed, to deliver it to the queen, to bring their king home.

Robin gazed around, at the large, nearly-empty room. He was proud. Of himself, his men, the people. Finally, after years of forgetting, they were learning to fight again, and their efforts were paying off. In the space of about one month, everything Eustace DeMarke had managed to accomplish in four years was well on its way to falling apart.

Chapter 21

Enter, Little John

Robin was near the footbridge by the church when the stranger appeared. The man was tall, built like a two-legged ox, wearing an old, goatskin outfit and a pair of sandals, the goatskin cap seated firmly on his head covering a mop of blonde hair that fell in manageable straggles around his temples. A thick, blonde beard with mixed flecks of dark and grey mantled his chin. Robin guessed the man to be a good ten or twelve years older than he was himself, but tough, as evidenced by a pair of rough, work-hardened hands that gripped the length of a solid walking stick.

Robin ducked into the foliage and slipped silently to the edge of the bridge. It could be the man was a friend, a hunter, a potential ally. There were many of those. But it could also be true that he was not. Robin intended to find out which.

He had learned that most would shy away from a direct confrontation when they didn't have a personal stake in the matter. The trick was to find out whether they did or not; the easiest way to do that was initiate the confrontation. Laying aside his bow and the arrows slung across his shoulder, Robin shucked his green cape and took up the long pole of birch he had been packing around all morning, moving up to block the far end of the bridge. He had only a few moments to wait for developments. The stranger rounded the corner and stepped onto the footbridge, his feet making hollow thuds on the wood. He stopped when he saw Robin.

"There is a tax to pass through these parts," Robin said casually, leaning on the birch rod in his hands.

The stranger was unimpressed. And very much unfazed.

"And if I don't wish to pay?" He asked.

"You may always turn around."

"And if I don't wish to turn around?"

"You may always pay the tax."

"I see." The stranger sized him up shrewdly. "And you are the tax collector?"

"You're catching on," Robin said in approval. "Which will it be, my friend? The choice is yours entirely."

Another pause while the stranger assessed his general character, size, anything else beneficial to the argument. Robin got the sudden impression he may have made a slight miscalculation.

"Tell me, lad," the man said at last. "What would you say if I proposed a bet? If you win, I'll pay the tax. If I win, you pay me the same."

Robin cocked his head. Depending on the nature of the competition...

"I'll hear you," he said.

"Good." The stranger's smile was confident. "Birch poles," he said, and pointed to the water. "The first man to get baptized pays the tax. What say you, boy?"

Lad and boy; two words meant to sucker Robin into making a prideful decision. They worked. So much for the theory on confrontation.

"You've got yourself a bet," Robin said, grinning with far more assurance than he was actually privilege to. He looked at the dark water meandering below. Funny, this was the second time he'd been lured into a fight over this section of river. Oh well. He stepped to the center of the bridge, listening to it creaking ominously underfoot – wondering at the same time if it would actually hold up under a fight – and faced the man before him.

"I hope you brought an extra purse," he said jovially. "The tax doubles with every inconvenience."

"Does it, now," the stranger said. "Perfect. I could use the money."

He swung the pole. Robin ducked under what would have been a ringing blow and struck back, hearing the evil thwack of wood

~ 396 ~

as the two birch poles connected with a hard barking noise. There was power behind that other stick. Another swipe sent Robin leaping backward to get out of reach, blocking wildly to keep from getting whacked. His offensive hits didn't seem to be doing any good. No matter what way he turned, the stranger was ready for him, stopping any moves before Robin had halfway completed them. Then, suddenly he saw an opportunity. The stranger turned partially sideways to avoid a well-aimed hit, and Robin took the chance offered. He ducked, feinted to the right, straightened with a hard swing... and met the other stick halfway up. It smacked hard into his forehead to send him spinning around, and Robin dropped onto the bridge. He was seeing a lot of stars on the way down.

"Had enough, lad?" The stranger asked, far too genially, as Robin flopped over and sat up.

"Not at all," Robin answered, and dove back in the foray.

The move sealed both of their fates. Robin yelped in surprise as the bridge beneath his feet abruptly buckled, sending him flying forward. A massive splintering sound reached his ears, and he was vaguely aware of wood crumbling and supports collapsing, landing in the water with a sodden series of splashes. All of this he noticed in the split second before he himself was in the river. Again. He surfaced indignantly, sputtering and coughing, and flopped over to a shallow spot near the bank. The big stranger was directly across, slumped on a small collection of timber sticking partway out of the water. The two of them glanced at each other, looked up at the gaping hole in the bridge, still oozing silt that drifted down to mantle everything with a grey film, and started laughing.

"Vengeance is mine, saith the Lord," Robin quoted painfully, and tried to extricate himself from a pile of boards that floated on top of him. "I think this was a situation where we were both supposed to turn the other cheek."

His response brought another hearty laugh.

"Aye, but where would the fun be in this world if everyone turned the other cheek?" The stranger asked. "You fight well, lad."

"The last person told me the same thing. I was hoping never to test his claim."

"Well, what do you expect, taxing innocent people to use this – rather unstable... piece of artwork?" Was the replying question, punctuated by a brief pause as the stranger sized up what was left of the footbridge. "What is your name?"

Robin chunked a timber away from him with a splash.

"Yours first," he said.

"Very well. My name is John Little, but I've been called Little John a time or two, as well."

Robin couldn't see why. He surveyed Little John momentarily, lounging back on his palms while water began drifting over his stomach.

"What do you want here?"

"I seek the man known as Robin of the Hood."

After all that. Why hadn't Robin just asked in the first place? At least then they'd still have a footbridge.

And my head wouldn't be split in half, he thought. "For what reason do you seek him, John Little?"

"To join him," John said. "I've seen enough nonsense. Too many people have been turning the other cheek for too long."

****

Jasmine wended her way through the trees, a large pile of wood shifting in her arms. She was deep in thought, walking habitually and not paying much attention to her surroundings, and didn't see the person coming up the trail behind her. She didn't even notice movement until a figure suddenly appeared at her elbow.

"Let me help you with that," Will Scarlet said, and snaked a hand in for the stack.

"I can manage."

The top of the pile lifted away, and Scarlet allowed himself a small smile as he looked down at her.

"I know," he said kindly. "I just want to help."

Jasmine dropped her gaze and made no protest. She had seen plenty of Will Scarlet over the last month or so, and had developed the disturbing tendency of forgetting nearly everything on her mind whenever he popped into view. The present moment was a prime example; Jasmine couldn't recall for the life of her what it was she'd been thinking about.

Scarlet hopped nimbly onto a boulder that blocked their path and held out a hand. The gesture was one of courtesy, nothing more, but Jasmine caught herself glancing away shyly as she settled her hand in his and allowed him to lightly pull her up beside him. She thanked him quietly and, balancing the load of wood in her arms, started back toward camp with Scarlet walking beside her. He was quite a bit taller than she was.

"I've been looking for you," Scarlet admitted after a moment. "I hoped we might have a chance to talk."

Jasmine looked at him quickly and wished she hadn't.

"About what?" She asked, shifting her gaze away.

"I don't know," Scarlet said, plucked a twig from one of the smaller branches in front of his face. "Anything."

They reached the edge of the camp. Pausing at the small woodpile near the first building, they dropped the fresh bundles on top of the stack and continued on, sitting down on a large log nearby.

"What was it like where you grew up?" Scarlet asked curiously.

Jasmine thought a moment about the place she was born. What *had* it been like? Not like here... not like anywhere.

"I wouldn't know where to begin," she confessed.

It was a lazy day about camp. Francis was just leaving with a small group of the older children after being suckered into taking them for an exploration of the forest; Jonathan Lacey and Allan were entertaining some of the younger ones, faint strands of music drifting through the still air; several women were busy cooking up something over a small fire, the black, iron pots perched over the flames ringed in white steam. Jasmine looked around her, at the green trees and deep shade of the forest, so unlike the striking harshness of the place she had been born, lovely in its own right but lacking the wild, untamed beauty of the desert; looked at the people wandering about, nice, good people but lacking the rigid hardiness of her own; and looked at the young man who sat in silence beside her, watching her face carefully, his kind, discerning eyes meeting hers without the reserve or prejudice she was accustomed to. How could she describe such a difference? How could she even begin to make him understand?

"It was another world," she said at last. "Another life."

A look of understanding crossed his face. But before he could respond, an uproar at the edge of camp caused both to turn in that direction. Robin sauntered casually into sight with another, taller man by his side, both of them the immediate object of a good-natured round of banter. The reason was obvious enough. They were sopping wet, from head to toe, looking, for all intents and purposes, like they had decided to reach the camp by swimming upstream. Jasmine surveyed them skeptically as Robin led the stranger over.

"What happened to you?" She asked. "Or do I not want to know?"

Robin held up his long cloak and wrung it out.

"Remember that bridge near where we first met Friar Tuck?" At Jasmine's nod, he chuckled. "It isn't there anymore," he said.

"Thanks to you," his companion said. "You started it."

"You should have turned the other cheek."

"I did. You almost hit it."

Robin dropped his cloak onto the log with a grin.

"Such is the nature of a duel," he said. "Jasmine, Scarlet, I want you to meet Little John. He has just fought his way – and very handily, I might add – into our ranks."

The big man called Little John was friendly. His eyes were a deep brown, surprisingly sensitive for a man of his massive size, reminding Jasmine of a large, harmless bear. He took to the kids right off. The feeling was mutual, as youngsters were soon dripping off every strand of his bulky clothing, trying to steal his cap and begging him to join their group. Allan and Jonathan seemed glad for the company.

"Where is Francis?" Robin asked as Little John joined the small assemblage of musicians across the clearing.

"He took some of the kids out to play in the forest."

Robin sighed.

"We must be more careful," he said. "The forest is big, but it isn't impenetrable."

He was right, of course. Subconsciously, Jasmine supposed they all had begun to become complacent. And Robin could very easily end up being the scapegoat for all of them if something went wrong; he was, after all, in charge, and their safety was his responsibility. As he walked out of hearing, Scarlet shook his head, viciously snapping a twig in his hands.

"Should we all sign an oath of allegiance, as well?" He mused wryly, almost to himself. The traditional look of closed caution was back on his face. He sat with his gaze lowered and his fingers peeling the skin off the wooden remnants in his hands, flinging long strings of it away vengefully. Jasmine watched him closely. She had always been aware of the innate hatred harbored in the soul of Will Scarlet, had seen it at work several times when anger turned into out-and-out savagery. A week ago in town, a young man Scarlet knew had been hit by one of DeMarke's soldiers, and Scarlet saw it. Yelling something almost unintelligible about the dirty Normans, he jumped into the foray, mercilessly thrashing the guard whose hand had struck his friend, and Robin had to literally drag him off to prevent Scarlet from killing the other. Since then, Scarlet's relationship with Robin hadn't improved. Although the two of them had managed to reach a sort of tacit agreement, Jasmine knew Will Scarlet was far from being called Robin's friend, and he was far from wanting to be so. Once again, as she had from the first, she wondered what he disliked so about Robin, and what Robin could possibly have done to bring about this hostility.

****

The kids loved to be out of doors. They scampered about gleefully, the boys with stains on their clothes and dirt on their faces, the girls with flowers in their hands. It was a lively procession that made its way back toward camp. Francis led them quickly back the way they had come. He knew they shouldn't be out this far, and henceforth intended to keep these walks closer to home, but one, final jaunt couldn't hurt any. They were about halfway back, traipsing along through the pathless woods, when the silence was shattered by a loud clamor. Francis jumped.

"Children!"

The kids dashed over, huddling around him as the noise increased. Men shouted, bodies slapped branches, metal clanged. And a posse shot into view.

"Get down!" Francis hissed, and pushed them down into the safety of a thick bush, ducking in himself right behind. Too late. Someone yelled from across the clearing, and Francis knew he had been spotted. Quickly he looked at the children, panic touching his heart, and grabbed Alexis by the shoulders as the racket came closer.

"Listen to me, Alexis," he whispered. "Listen carefully. You need to get the children out of here. Right over this knoll is the western branch of the river. Follow it up until it comes together by the rock, then head straight east from there and someone from the camp will find you. Understand?"

Alexis nodded.

"All right." He patted her on the shoulder, looked at the others, and bolted from cover. "Go, children, run!" The last thing they saw of Francis was his slight, dashing form careening through the trees, being chased down by the yellow-clad men on horseback. Alexis herded the children before her, out of the cover of the bushes, and made for the river. They didn't look back.

Francis ran hard, putting as much distance between himself and the youngsters as he could. He knew it was only a matter of time before he was caught. Plants slapped at his face and body, his feet pummeled the ground, the iron hooves of the horses boomed ever-closer behind him. They were cantering easily, their riders toying with him, gaining with every stride but content to let Francis run himself to death. Suddenly he rounded a corner to find himself face to face with five more right in front of him. The posse closed in, cutting off escape from all sides, and Francis knew he was in big trouble. He stopped. The horses moved closer. The faces surrounding him were completely unreadable, coldly so; mere expressionless, emotionless faces staring at him from behind a bevy of crossbows. One of the posse members urged his horse forward.

"What is your name?" He asked harshly. "Answer!"

"No need," another voice said, and Francis spun around. "I know who he is."

Francis stared in horror as a man who had once been a close friend stepped forward, regarding Francis with no more affection than one would a trapped rat.

"His name is Francis of Gascoyne," he said. "Carpenter by trade. Or at least he was until he turned to outlawry."

Francis listened without protest, heard every detail of his life spilled out in one long, unhindered speech, wishing suddenly he had done as the others had and brought his wife, Rachel, into camp. He thought she would be safer on the outside.

"Where is the camp?"

"I'll never tell you," Francis spat, and received a staggering blow from someone behind him. Catching his head in his hands, he fell to his knees, listening to the clop of hooves as a horse approached him.

"Then you are dead," the soldier said. "Speak now or never speak again."

"Patience, man, patience. We may have a better use for him."

Francis looked up to spy Eustace DeMarke, sheriff of Nottingham, easing his horse to the forefront. Where he had come from and how long he had been there Francis had no idea, but he knew the sheriff had heard every word that was said. He glared at DeMarke in open defiance as the man stood over him.

"And just what might that better use *be*?" He inquired coldly.

DeMarke took his time considering.

"Your wife... Rachel, was it? Where is she?"

"I believe you heard already," Francis said.

"Ah, yes, that's right. In town. Out... of the hideout..." He executed the last in a very deliberate tone.

"Leave her out of this."

"I'd like to, but as it stands now, I can't," DeMarke said. "With your help, perhaps something could be arranged. You see, Francis – you don't mind if I call you Francis, do you? – good. The hideout is useless to us without the gold your friends took. Tell me where it is, and Rachel will be spared."

"I don't know where it is. Only Robin Hood and the friar know."

"And if you did know?"

"You have my wife's life in your hands, sheriff, what do you *think*?"

Francis apparently passed the test. DeMarke sat up on his horse, a slight smile creeping across his face.

"Good," he said in satisfaction. "We have made progress." He nodded to his men to lower their weapons. "I'll tell you what," he added. "I will have a talk with your wife on my way back through town, and see if she would be willing to keep us company for a while. Then, when you find the stolen money and report to us both its location *and* the location of the camp, I will let her go. Understood?"

"And if I can't find it?"

DeMarke leaned down in his saddle, close enough to look Francis in the eye.

"Find it," he said quietly, and somehow Francis got the impression he had just been issued a very sound piece of paternal advice. He nodded as DeMarke pulled his horse away "Let him go. We've got what we need."

Francis was flung to the ground as, with a rushing of bodies, horses rushed by on either side of him, heading west. DeMarke held his mount back for a split second.

"Remember," he said over the pounding hooves. "Your wife is counting on you."

And, as the posse rode away, Francis lay in a heap on the damp earth, cursing himself for a fool and begging Rachel for forgiveness.

"I'm sorry, Rachel," he whispered. "I'm sorry..."

Slowly, he rose to his feet and wiped the dirt and leaves from his clothing, his mind already planning what he needed to do next. He caught up with the children in a short while. And, when they asked him what happened, he said simply that he'd gotten away. When Robin asked him about it later, he responded the same. No one needed to know the rest. They didn't need to know that, thanks to Francis, their parents and friends and futures were about to be put in very grave danger.

The sheriff wanted a traitor. He wanted a mole. Well, for the price of one woman, he had just gotten it. Francis didn't have a choice.

****

Finally, for the first time since this fiasco began, Eustace DeMarke felt like he was gaining the upper hand. It had been one month since this mysterious Robin Hood had spirited away six men and a wagonload of cash, vanishing like a ghost with not even a footprint to mark his passage. Since then, the committee's goal had slowly but surely been uprooted, the complex tapestry that was their plan coming apart stitch by stitch by stitch. After the committee itself was ambushed on the way to London, even Prince John had joined the ranks of the dissatisfied, breathing down DeMarke's neck like an irate dragon to get this thing under control.

To do or die. In a nutshell – or even out of the shell – that's what his last letter said. Contain this rabble or be removed of command. It had seemed impossible. It had seemed that Robin of the Hood and his gang were unstoppable. Each robbery, each toe out of line, had brought more repercussions on the people of Nottingham, as DeMarke attempted to put an end to the outlaw gang's popularity. Higher and higher he had raised the reward on the Robin of the Hood, tighter and tighter he had cinched rules in the outlaw's name. Still people kept coming. Blatantly ignoring the inconveniences they suffered and the riches that would be theirs, they came from all over, flocking towards this new beacon of hope hidden deep within Sherwood Forest.

But now DeMarke had leverage. He had Rachel.

Francis' wife had offered no small amount of resistance when DeMarke's men came to collect her. She fought like a wildcat, kicking and screaming and leveling the ire of both verbal curses and hard objects at her attackers, unwilling to be controlled even after she had been securely bound and gagged. Considering her performance, it was all DeMarke could do to keep his men from exacting a little payback, a fact he reminded her of to ensure her future cooperation. Rachel was now safely locked away, and it wouldn't be long before her husband the mole would dig his way right into the treasure room. Until then, Rachel would have a small taste of the life awarded a captured criminal.

"How are plans for the collection coming?" DeMarke asked.

"All the nobles have agreed to contribute to the ransom," Gisbourne said, answering DeMarke's absent question. "The committee will give the most... knowing, of course, that it will all be lost on the way to London." He smiled. "That is some idea of yours, cousin," he said. "No one will ever know the difference."

"No, I should think not."

DeMarke poured himself a cup of ale, sipping it reflectively. He, too, liked this plan. Best idea he ever had, if he did say so himself. Bishop Paul Lorien was set to arrive in Nottingham within a few days, with the sole purpose of collecting money for the king's ransom. He would get plenty. Nobles, peasants, everyone would be there to give what they could, sending it all off to London with pitifully thankful hearts. But their hopes would be dashed somewhere in Sherwood Forest, where a small, specially-chosen group of DeMarke's men would relieve the convoy of its heavy burden, spiriting the precious ransom away into the depths of the forest... under the guise of Robin of the Hood and his men.

And thus the ire of the people would be turned against the outlaw. Then, once the mole Francis had revealed the location of the treasure and the camp, the rebels in Sherwood Forest would be no more. They would be hunted down and torn to pieces by their own kind, hung as the traitors they were, and silenced forever. The treasure they stole, of course, tragically, would never be found. The king's ransom, even more tragically, would not be raised, and Richard would be stuck in Austria until he rotted. Then things would go on as planned. By the time Cardinal Warwick, chief liaison between Prince John and DeMarke, came to town again, events of the last month would be reversed and things under control.

"Guy," DeMarke said in satisfaction. "We are gaining the upper hand in this fight. Now we must press the advantage."

Gisbourne rolled a goblet between two pudgy hands.

"How?"

"We had plans in motion before this began," DeMarke reminded him. "They must continue. Ellen's father has agreed to a marriage for a price. It would cost us now, yes, but in the future, such an alliance would be highly beneficial." He drank deeply of the strong-tasting ale before him, setting the mug down with a hard clunk. "You will marry her, Guy. Now, right after the collection. Do and we shall be one step closer to victory."

Chapter 22

A Woman Worth Dying For

Jonathan Lacey saw the woman long before she saw him. He was in the middle of a crowd, just another one of a thousand faces, just another one of a thousand peasants. He had been there almost all day. After Friar Tuck wandered stealthily around the village to deliver a good deal of monetary cheer to the townspeople, Jonathan had spent the rest of the morning watching those same people and others just like them, folks from all over Nottinghamshire, spend their last farthing on a hope.

Bishop Paul Lorien had been escorted into town the previous morning, and within a day of his arrival there were enough people wandering around Nottingham to stage a revolution. Pity that's not what they had in mind.

With Lorien watching the proceedings for trickery through the vigilant eyes of a kind hawk, purses of varying sizes and weights were brought forward, counted, and announced. DeMarke and his boys were doing their part, of course, each one eclipsing entire flocks of their peasant counterparts with a single donation and bringing the tally that much closer to the necessary mark. Jonathan wondered what they were up to; surely they weren't actually going to let that money just... walk off.

"Two hundred marks from William de Gant!" Eustace DeMarke shouted above the continual rumble of the crowd, and despite themselves, people cheered. Lady Ellen was standing off to the side, clearly trying to remain out of the limelight, smiling as her father approached.

Jonathan listened intently as the tally rose ever-higher. He leaned against an old, wooden board that sported one of DeMarke's infamous rewards, the poster advertising a £1000 reward for the capture of the outlaw Robin Hood. Jonathan smiled to himself. Robin was getting to be quite notorious. He was certainly popular. Half of the conversations rumbling through the assemblage had to do with "the outlaw Robin Hood", praising him for an angel of mercy in this, a most desperate time of need.

"Richard of Derby has given four-hundred and thirty marks!"

DeMarke's booming voice valiantly proclaimed the amount of the latest offering, and the benefactor bowed in assumed humility to the proffered applause before returning to the side of his wife and daughter. The daughter turned to face him slightly, smiling, and as she did, Jonathan recognized her.

Lady Ilene.

Jonathan glanced around quickly. He had met Lady Ilene of Derby only once before, at a tournament years ago, a mere two years after he had been knighted. He was nineteen at the time. She was a year younger. Their meeting was brief, one he doubted she'd remember now, but there had been a certain chemistry between them, he thought. Until, of course, she learned he was of the dreaded Saxon lineage and had immediately broken off the conversation. Yet even then, even as she walked away, Jonathan had caught her looking back a time or two, and wondered if she really believed her own reasoning. He had supposed he'd never know. Until now.

Blending with the natural movement of the people around him, Jonathan stepped out and eased himself forward, coming to stand directly behind Lady Ilene of Derby. The years had been kind to her; from lovely girl to beautiful woman, she had matured with grace, the sizzling defiance that had always been so prevalent in her stature only partially concealed by time. Even a glance would ascertain that she was still the same, fiery lass Jonathan had first met that day in the stable.

"My lady Ilene," he said, causing her to turn quickly. Seeing his attire, the openness on her face began to fade as she undoubtedly expected a request for money.

"Do I know you?" She asked, rather distantly.

"Our paths have crossed before."

She looked at him again, now intrigued.

"Such a mysterious response," she said, her redwood eyes searching his for a brief instant before traveling over his face and hair. "It must have been an extraordinary affair that allowed us to meet." Her response could have been considered condescending had not a humorous smile accompanied it.

Jonathan smiled in return.

"It was, my lady," he replied. "The honor was all mine."

He had her attention now. Curiosity, so often decreed a woman's worst trait, can often be a man's best ally. Ilene did want to know more, and may have pressed the issue further had not DeMarke's voice suddenly cut in.

"Guy of Gisbourne has given one thousand, five-hundred marks!" Came the exuberant proclamation.

Ilene immediately turned her attention elsewhere.

"Excuse me," she said, and, with a brilliant smile lighting her face, wended her way to the front of the crowd to meet Sir Guy of Gisbourne.

Gisbourne clumped down the steps, his face etched into a grin that, as Robin had put it on more than one occasion, turned him into the exact replica of a toad. But there must have been something in that amphibious persona Ilene found attractive, for Guy of Gisbourne was the man she ran for. Jonathan experienced a slight, and totally irrational, pang of jealousy as Ilene caught up with Gisbourne at the base of the steps. Already Gisbourne was scanning the crowd, looking for something or someone, and Jonathan knew that, whoever it was, it wasn't Ilene of Derby.

"Sir Gisbourne," Ilene started happily. "I thought it a wonderful gesture –"

She never had the chance to finish her sentence. Gisbourne looked down, dismissed her, and without a word, brushed by the hopeful figure to head straight for Ellen de Gant.

Ilene froze. Slowly, her mouth still opened to speak, she dropped the hand that had lightly rested itself on Gisbourne's arm, and did the only thing she could: stand there and watch him leave. Jonathan could see the pain in her eyes turn to undisguised hatred as she looked at Ellen, the ferocity of a woman who knew she, in and of herself, wasn't good enough to achieve her goal. Ilene turned her back on them and looked at Jonathan. When she saw him still watching her, she tilted her chin up defiantly to disguise the tears that had moistened her eyes, and met his gaze rebelliously, almost like she expected him either to insult or laugh at her. Truthfully, it appeared she was challenging him to do just that. But, as Jonathan looked at her, he saw nothing amusing. All he could see was hurt.

The collection was over by afternoon. Jonathan took his leave right before everyone else, intending to beat the rush out the square, and met Friar Tuck and Much at a small, noisy tavern near the outskirts of town. Much had come to see his parents, and now, with both he and Friar Tuck having managed to accomplish their various missions without getting caught or hung in the process, they seemed quite willing to go home.

Jonathan was still thinking about Lady Ilene as he pulled up a rickety chair and sat down. What could she possibly see in a man like Guy of Gisbourne?

"The more I see of this, the more I appreciate the forest," Much said, gesturing to the packed room, and Friar Tuck nodded in agreement.

"As do I," Jonathan said, glad for the distraction. He nodded to the pretty, young girl who brought them a pair of mugs, and leaned back. "How are your parents?"

"Starving," Much said bluntly. "I gave them all the money I had and some food, but it isn't nearly enough." He smiled in thanks as the mug in front of him filled with ale before the pitcher was set on the table. "Do you think it will work?" He asked. "The ransom? It's a lot of money to raise for one man."

"Eight," Jonathan corrected. "Don't forget the seven soldiers. And I don't know. You're right; it is a lot of money."

"If it is the Lord's will, then it will happen," Tuck said sagely.

The three of them went back to their own thoughts, looking around the room at the assortment of drunks and low-lifes, and Jonathan suddenly wondered why he was here. He didn't even like ale that much. His gaze passed briefly over a tall, carrot-headed youngster sitting with his friends a few tables over, who'd all had about a week's worth too many and were reeling around in their seats, then went back to his drink. Peace was short-lived.

"Hey... hey, friar," the carrot-top shouted, his speech slurred and barely understandable. "Say, friar, if Bishop Lorien wasn't in town, I should think your services would be in demand about now."

Jonathan just shrugged. Tuck emptied his mug and set it on the table, casting a patient glance at Much.

"What would merit such an opinion?" He asked mildly as he refilled the cup, not even turning around, and his question elicited a hearty, if very quaking, laugh.

"Where have you been the last few days, friar, under a rock?"

"No, lad, in a church."

"Well, it –" The kid swayed dangerously in his seat. "It amounts to the same thing, pretty much," he cracked. "Boring!"

His buddies got a kick out of the joke. Tuck didn't.

"What made you think I would be needed?" His repeated question was clearly just to receive the necessary information and thus put an end to the conversation.

"You m – you mean you don't know?" The youngster cut himself off as he almost tipped over. "Gisbourne finally conned Lady de Gant into marrying him."

Jonathan sat bolt upright. Tuck almost choked on his drink and put a sharp hand on Much's arm as the boy started to jump up.

"When?" He said sharply.

"Well I think it was supposed to be tomorrow," was the smiling response. "They want Lorien to perform the service but I bet if you want to watch and take a lesson –"

His attempt at humor, if indeed that's what it was to be, fell on deaf ears. Jonathan leapt to his feet, bolting outside to vault onto his horse. Tuck and Much were already slinging themselves into the wagon by the door. Tuck snatched the lines with a yell, slapping the hard, leather straps onto the horses' rumps with a loud crack.

"Get up, team!" He shouted as Jonathan shot past him. "Move!"

The horses were old and clunky and slow ordinarily, but they knew a threat when they heard it. By the time the echo had died away, they were already out of town.

****

Robin sat silently, tapping his finger along with the rhythmic beat and listening to the sweet sound of Allan's lute as the little instrument sang its heart out on command. Little John was beside him, busy working over a long, flexible piece of wood he hoped to turn into a first-class bow. They were far back from the group, leaned against an old log, light from the fire dancing off their clothing and skin in faded patterns as it reached outward from its bright center, highlighting the forms of about thirty children who sat in a circle around Allan. People roamed quietly around them, around camp, the hum of conversation creating a very peaceful, homelike atmosphere. Robin could hear a few humming along with the tune Allan played; a soft, gentle melody that floated and twirled around camp like a piece of silk aided by a midsummer breeze.

It was dark out. Night had set in some time ago, settling in a solid blanket over Sherwood Forest, and with the night had come the doubled guard against intruders. Men were scattered all over, invisible, keeping watch. Robin could see Will Scarlet standing in the shadows to his left. *Supposedly* he was pulling guard duty, but his shift had come and gone some time ago, leaving him free to do as he pleased. Any excuses he had departed shortly thereafter. Robin smiled to himself. Scarlet was waiting for Jasmine to return.

Robin had noticed a distinct change in Scarlet over the last few weeks. He had mellowed some, lost some of the intense fire that made him so unpredictable, indeed, lost some of the hate. Robin had even seen a smile cross Scarlet's young, serious face a time or two.

"Coming in!"

Robin started at the yell, which was accompanied by the sound of a high-pitched, piercing whistle. Moments later, an arrow smacked into the ground. White.

"Must be the lads coming back," Robin said, rising. "We'll soon see how the day went."

They heard the wagon before they saw it. And Robin could tell just by listening that something was very wrong. It rumbled loudly over the ground, wood creaking and wheels rattling, the hooves of its team slamming into the ground and Tuck's loud whistles overriding it all. In the next instant Lacey blew into camp on his tall, grey mare, and skidded off to the side. The wagon was right on his heels. It tore into view at breakneck speed, scattering people, and Friar Tuck hauled it to a rough stop before he barreled off the tall vehicle. He landed with surprising agility.

"What happened?" Robin asked, immediately going on the defensive.

"We have a big problem," Lacey stated.

"It's Gisbourne," Friar Tuck said breathlessly. "We came as soon as we heard..."

"What –"

"He's forcing Lady Ellen to marry him," Much supplied from the back.

Robin turned around at the sound of a breaking string. Allan had gone dead white, rising swiftly, his eyes blazing in the firelight with something bordering on uncontrolled fury. Robin had never seen such an expression on his face before.

"When?" The question was far too quiet.

"Tomorrow."

Allan never hesitated. Without another word, he set down the lute with a careful, deliberate hand and walked to one of the small corrals at the edge of camp.

"Allan, what are you doing?" Robin asked, leaving the others to jog over.

"Saving her life, Robin." Allan grabbed a bridle off its rack and opened the gate.

"You'll get yourself killed."

"I don't care," Allan said as he caught the first horse he came across. "So long as she's free of that monster." He slipped the bridle on and started toward the gate, holding the prancing, head-tossing animal easily beside him. "I *will not* stand silent and allow her to give herself up to that beast like the spoils of war, and if I get killed, then so be it. I should have done this long ago."

He stalked outside, grabbing a saddle, but Robin held out a hand.

"Allan, wait. I'm coming with you."

***

The day was either perfect or absolutely horrid. It all depended on the perspective. Robin couldn't imagine a more lovely, clear day to set things right; he was equally certain Allan couldn't imagine a more awful conflict between the beauty of the day and the misery of his own spirit. The wedding was to take place at Gisbourne's newly-acquired residence; a.k.a., the former Locksley manor; and, to Robin, no better place could have been chosen. He knew the place inside and out.

The courtyard was crawling with people, and the confusion created by hundreds of milling bodies only added to the perfection. That was the funny thing about this sort of occasion: no matter what stake people had in it personally, they were always on hand for the entertainment. And the food. It made Robin's task that much easier; with so many people about, who would notice the scant few who actually had mischief in mind?

Robin and Allan waited just inside the wall surrounding the courtyard, perched comfortably and quite invisibly atop the stables behind a large statue. Robin hadn't been the only one to want a hand in the situation. Everyone did. They had slipped in one and two at a time, staking out positions all around the grounds, and if all was going according to plan, they should be ready to roll. Scarlet and Jasmine were across the courtyard, seated by the door; Much was with Tuck out back; Jonathan Lacey was keeping Little John company along the east side. Francis was just outside the back gate, holding the trio of horses that would take Robin, Lady Ellen, and Allan away from the manor, and several other men were out front taking care of the remaining mounts. In other words, Robin Hood and his gang had the place completely surrounded.

Allan sighed as he surveyed the scene, looking to Robin with an apologetic smile.

"Robin... thank you," he said. "For doing this. You didn't have to."

"Yes I did." Robin's answer was spoken lightly, but with complete sincerity. "Ellen is a friend of mine," he added on. "I want to see the two of you *live* happily together, not die happily in each other's arms. Besides." He peered innocently around the statue. "I imagine our friend Sir Gisbourne has a substantial chunk of cash lying around this beautiful estate... and I'm sure it could use a new home."

Allan glanced at him quickly, humor flicking momentarily across his face.

"How do you plan to do that?"

"I've already worked it out with Little John and Lacey," Robin said. "The wedding will be a distraction. While we're in getting your girl, they'll be leading the others in to get the gold."

Movement suddenly caught Robin's eye on the balcony above the front entrance. The door opened slowly, almost hesitantly, and Lady Ellen de Gant stepped outside, making her way to the wall over the courtyard. She was dressed beautifully in a long, white gown that seemed almost to shine in the late-afternoon sun, made, Robin was sure, of only the finest materials. Her blonde hair was pinned up, neatly and securely, the golden waves enhanced with a few sprigs of delicate flowers. But Ellen's countenance belied her lovely appearance. Her eyes were hopeless, even from here, reflecting a lonely, almost forlorn grief that shadowed her spirit, leaving her outer beauty completely empty. She was looking for Allan. Just as he was looking for her.

"Allan," Robin said quietly. "I think someone's thinking about you." As Allan spun around, Robin placed an encouraging hand on his shoulder. "Don't worry, my friend," he said. "We'll make sure she's safe."

The door opened again, this time without indecision, and Bishop Lorien wandered onto the balcony, joining Ellen with a quiet greeting. Although the conversation was lost to Robin at this distance, he could clearly see the kind worry on the face of his father's friend, and knew that, for now at least, she was in good hands. Lorien was the one man he knew would understand.

"You never told me," he said to Allan, settling back. "How you met Ellen."

"There's really not much to tell," Allan responded embarrassedly.

"Depends on who's listening."

"Well..." Allan considered a moment, holding onto the little instrument in his hands. "I guess I should start with Alexis, then," he said. He began to trail his fingers across the lute in an idle manner as he spoke, almost like he would get lost in his tale without the accompanying music. "I was traveling at night," he started. "It was starting to rain and getting cold, so I ducked under the branches of a tree near the side of the road to wait it out."

Allan's account of the matter was brief. It unfolded simply yet dramatically, the story of a love that had begun by sheer chance,

~ 415 ~

because of the little girl called Alexis and a cold, bitter night that saved her life and brought two more together.

"It was a fool's hope I had," he said at last, "that anything could come of it. I knew I had to leave. But I will never forget the last time I saw her, the way she looked..."

He broke off and dropped back against the wall.

"Beautiful," Robin agreed.

"I love her, Robin," Allan said softly. "More than life itself." He shook his head slowly, closing his eyes. "She's the only woman I ever met worth dying for."

Chapter 23

My beloved bride, the light of my life
These tokens have I for thee, who hast been my wife
May they guide thee on thy long road, through the sands of
time
For now I give them all to thee, these things that once were
mine

The darkness of the tunnel was around him once more. Gregg's voice echoed like that of a ghost throughout the room. As if it were happening all over again he recalled the moment he'd discovered the poem, read it, recited it aloud. Faded light from torches bounced off the walls, illuminating the text before him, scrawled so perfectly, so concisely, on the blade of the ancient sword that lay tranquilly in the coffin at his feet.

This, a stone of Hope, a mirror to thine eyes
Blue as the endless seas, and deep as the midnight skies
May it speak of distance, as it was meant to do
The sentiments therein proving Truth to you

This, an ivory piece, Wisdom that shall grace your wrist
Such a work of divine craftsmanship
May it prove right for you, this from the lady of the sands
And narrow the distance for you to those foreign lands

This, the sword of Truth, which hath known its day
It will be used with Wisdom, but only once, I pray
To serve as a dais for Hope, your guiding light
Washing away despair, fear of loneliness and night

And this, the book, fit for one of sovereignty
The words of wisdom have been good to me
Leading me towards the light of hope and truth
Guiding my steps, showing me what to do

A torch burnt out; the light receded. The poem became a little less legible, its intricate characters beginning to be lost in the twilight of the cavern.

May these treasures, these things that once were mine,
Help thee on thy long road, through the sands of time
May they light your way and help your quest
Toward richness in spirit, faith and happiness

But what did it mean? What secrets was this mysterious, elusive riddle trying to tell him? Gregg closed his eyes, trying to imagine himself as the writer of this enigmatic piece of literature, and what he would be trying to convey.

May it speak of distance…
May it prove right…
May it help thee… on thy long road…

A loud snore broke the stillness and Gregg's vision burst into nothingness with a nearly-audible poof. Nope, nothing had changed. He was still sitting; hunched, cramped, basically blind and showing mild symptoms of DVT; in a shadowy corner Marilla Clancy's living room scoping the poem out with a pen light, while Henchman Troy was stretched out; comfortable, oblivious, and snuggled up with his favorite firearm and a box of grenades on the couch.

Yep. Living the dream.

Gregg would never admit it, but he was envious of Henchman Troy; after helping Rob finish the dishes, Troy had wandered into the living room, sat down, and promptly fell asleep.

While he drifted off into la-la land, Rob joined Gregg and the others listening to Marilla tell the Goldstein's tale of Robin Hood for another hour or so. Now the entire group – minus Stan, who was on watch and Ian, who had disappeared – was dispersed around the living room, talking quietly, and Troy was still dead to the world. Damn those who could fall asleep simply because they were tired.

Gregg sighed and went back to the poem. He was worried. No, scratch that; he was on the verge of panic. He was panicked because he realized the necklace he'd just gone to great lengths to steal wasn't the only thing his group would need in order to continue. They, in fact, needed four objects, the objects listed in each stanza of the poem: the stone, the sword, the bracelet, and a book. So far, Gregg had one of these in his possession. He'd thought that was enough, those few, short hours ago when they'd tromped so tiredly into Marilla's house. Then Amantha showed him that bracelet, and Gregg started to worry. He looked at the poem again, much closer this time, and officially came to the understanding that he was in way over his head.

He was only one-quarter of the way there. The sword of "truth" was being held hostage in the dig, and the bracelet of "wisdom" shown to him by Amantha was in limbo somewhere in her apartment. And as for the all-important fourth object? Gregg had absolutely no idea.

A book, fit for one of sovereignty...

What even was that? Gregg tapped the pencil against his chin, resisting the age-old temptation to gnaw on the eraser. It was odd, really; the rest of the poem was so specific, describing each piece of the puzzle nearly down to the last detail. The book was the only thing not mentioned as anything else. He'd slaved and guessed and wracked his brain for any conceivable option, but still the answer eluded him.

Two yellow and water-smeared pieces of paper consisting of the four stanzas lay side by side on top of the dark, walnut coffee table under his elbows, their combined mass constituting the best hope he had of reaching his goal. He had just read the poem for what had to be the hundred and fiftieth time, and honestly, at this point he didn't know which was worse: the fact that he was stuck in this mess, stranded on an island of despair, with no help and absolutely no hope of escape... or the fact that he was just plain stuck.

"I must have missed something when I wrote it down," he muttered to himself, and tossed his pencil irritably on the table. "But what?"

What. Had. He. Missed. Gregg now found himself under enormous pressure to figure this thing out, and soon; by tomorrow morning, his face would once again be plastered over the same newspapers it had been today, plus any that had been missed, and the target on his back would get bigger. Seated here in Marilla Clancy's quaint country home, the inherent peace of his surroundings was a direct juxtaposition to the chaos in his mind. He'd gone from treasure hunter and master of his own destiny to chief problem-solver in a matter of hours; from the moment he'd given in and dialed Ian, huddled outside the museum like a lost lamb, he'd signed the contract, and was stuck seeing it through. It was like one of those end-user agreements full of fine print.

Slapping the poem to the table, Gregg stalked to his feet and made for the front door. He needed air; his brain was fried. He gave the handle on the front door a violent twist and yanked it open, storming outside onto the yellow-lit porch.

"Late for a date, Genius?"

Gregg snapped his gaze up. Ian stood alone, leaning against the wall, hands in his pockets. Under the faded light that managed to somehow illuminate the place, he looked almost ominous, a shadowy, sinister figure that was just waiting for Gregg to make a wrong move. It was so hard to compare this hardened, calculating man with the roguish mischief-maker Gregg had grown up with.

"Hey," Gregg said. "Planning our next move?"

Ian shook his head.

"Nah, just... taking a break. I'm tired," he said with a fatigued smile, and shrugged closer into his jacket as he looked off in an absent fashion.

Gregg paused. He didn't really want to talk now; it was inevitable, he knew, that they would be forced to discuss the current state of affairs, but exhaustion – plus as a decent amount of survival instinct – lobbied for procrastination. He didn't want to dig up the hatchet and risk effects similar to those he'd experienced before. The sudden realization that this was the first time they'd spoken alone, properly, in ten years crossed his mind; how time had flown. Outside the pale ring of light, a lone owl hooted dismally close to the house, and Gregg sighed, clunking the door shut. He had to get this over with. Then he would be able to see where they really stood.

"Look, Ian," he said. "I wanted to apologize for... what I said to you and Rob. It was way out of line."

Ian nodded silently, leveling one of those powerful, Scorpio gazes in Gregg's direction. His face was unreadable. Shadowed with nothing but varying patterns of light, it expressed only mild indifference as he contemplated Gregg's apology, seeming to process it for sincerity.

"You did what you thought was necessary."

It wasn't an *out*-and-out reciprocation, but it was a start, anyway. They were quiet a moment, listening to the crickets in the grass, the owl, the hum of voices inside the house. It wasn't a comfortable silence, however; both were just waiting each other out, seeing who would give in and ask the first question. Finally, Ian got tired of the game and crossed his arms.

"All right, Nick, you win," he said. "I'll talk first. What do you know about this mess that I don't?"

"Not much, apparently," Gregg said ruefully. "You knew enough to get ahead of me tonight."

"Wasn't hard. More guesswork than anything. Unfortunately, the museum and that necklace was as far as I got, so what else do we need to make this thing work? Seems to me there's more to it, or you wouldn't be out here looking like you want to pull your hair out."

"You're right; it's more complicated than I thought," Gregg said. "So, in a nutshell, we need four things: a stone, a bracelet, a sword, and a book. The stone we have, as it is the one from the necklace."

"And I assume the sword is the one you left in the dig."

"Yes," Gregg admitted. "I think so."

"Right. Makes it easy. Good on you for leaving it behind."

"Good on you for giving me a reason."

Ian ignored the slight.

"And the bracelet?" He asked instead.

"Miss Goldstein has it in her apartment. Long story, but she found the thing in the dig and it matches up with this story her aunt has been telling about the legend... I'm certain it's what we need."

"What happens when we have all this stuff?"

"I don't know yet. It's some kind of map, I think. Miss Goldstein said the bracelet has numbers on the back, which I assume is going to provide us with instructions, but we need a reference point."

"The fourth object."

"Correct." Gregg rubbed his forehead. "And for the life of me I can't figure that one out. All I know is that we need a book; I don't know which one, which version, what it will do… I've been reading and rereading that damn riddle out for hours now, and nothing is clicking."

Ian crossed his arms, shaking his head with a resigned smile.

"I thought you had this thing all lined out."

"Well, not *all* of it, clearly," Gregg said shortly. "I thought we were going to find the gold in the dig, not a map to it. There are still a few holes in my theory."

"I hope they're not too big, mate, because we don't have the luxury of time."

"I'll have it sorted by tomorrow," Gregg said. "You just worry about how to get your hot little hands on everything, and let me deal with the riddle."

"Fair enough." Ian quirked an eyebrow at him. "How did the girls end up in this, anyway? I leave you alone for barely over twenty-four hours and you come back with a harem."

"Again, it's a long story. Now." Gregg held his hands outward in an open fashion. "At the risk of rekindling the hostilities," he started, "that does bring up a good point. To the matter of our presence – Mrs. Clancy, Miss Goldstein, Jared, and myself. I'd like to ask what you plan to do with us."

The answer was predictably spare.

"That depends on you," Ian said.

"I see. So, all those years you and I spent together, all the things we did, none of it means anything anymore. You're just… going to push all of that under the rug so you can kill us with a clear conscience if it comes to that."

"Says the bloke who didn't call for ten years until he needed something," Ian retorted. "I didn't hear you talking lifestyle choices when you needed my expertise."

Ouch. That hurt.

"Like it or not, this is who I am now," Ian continued. "I make a living stealing things and dealing with people who are somewhat less than what mother would approve of. Until you've lived like this, Gregg, you wouldn't understand."

"You could change. What's stopping you?"

"I haven't finished what I started."

"Oh, pardon me; I forgot. Your crusade against humankind continues." Gregg made no attempt to curb the sarcasm slipping into his voice. "If you're looking for pity, you've come to the wrong guy; you made your choice when you turned in your badge. Tell me. How many men have to die before you can stand to face up to your own conscience?"

Ian never batted an eye.

"There will never be enough for that," he answered. "My conscience and I haven't spoken for a long time. Sorry to disappoint you, but things change. I have no reason to go back. Nothing to go back to even if I did. All of that vanished a long time ago."

"Yeah, that's great," Gregg snapped. "Blame your failings on something else. That always works a treat."

Ian stood up straight, his eyes darkening perceptibly.

"No one takes the blame for my failures but me," he said. "And I'm warning you right now not to push me too far."

"What are you going to do, shoot me? I'm terrified," Gregg said flatly.

"I just might." The answer was far too indignant to be taken seriously. "If I wasn't so damn tired I'd say let's take this out into the carpark and sort it out."

"What, the fact that you tried to kill me once already. And Jared."

"Come now, mate…" A knowing smile. "If I'd really wanted you dead I would have done it when I was standing right over your head on the riverbank. Jared is good at hiding, but he needs to learn to control his breathing."

Gregg sighed. So Ian had known they were there. Of course. Was there any point when he *hadn't* been one step ahead?

"Why did you let us go?"

"Why not? You needed time to cool down, and I knew you'd be back."

"Right."

"Well, I reckoned it was kind of like... parenting teenagers or something. You can fight with them all you want, but until you step back and let them let them experience failure on a personal level, it doesn't stick."

"I'm really not sure where this is going... neither Jared nor myself is pubescent."

"Could have fooled me." Ian rubbed his eyes and leaned back against the wall. He looked worn down. For the first time since this hunt began, Gregg took the time to really look at him; noticed the lines around his eyes. Worry lines. Those same shadows that had so convincingly displayed his dangerous side now served to show just how exhausted Ian was. Not only physically; it was the kind of fatigue that stretched from one's soul. Proof that Ian was slowly, surely, running himself into the ground. How much longer could he keep this up?

The front door popped open, and Amantha stepped outside.

"I do apologize, am I interrupting?" She asked as she caught sight of them.

"Not at all, love." Ian's countenance brightened immediately as her pretty face came into view. Gregg saw the look that passed between them, one that expressed both intrigue and a strange understanding. His antenna were starting to pick up signals he hoped were wrong. He'd woken briefly on the car ride in and caught the tail end of the conversation about Amantha's plane; he'd forgotten she was a pilot. Forgotten that she liked cars. Forgotten that she was just the kind of girl Ian would have fallen hard for ten years ago. He was beginning to sense a similarity in energy, in character, between these two people he'd inadvertently brought together, and his unease concerning Amantha heightened. This was an avenue he hadn't anticipated. He knew from experience how charming and irresistible Ian could be to the fairer sex, something he'd tried to warn Amantha about on no uncertain terms; what he hadn't counted on was the two of them having so damn much in common. That was as much unexpected as it was unnerving.

Amantha pulled the door shut behind her and approached them in a somewhat reticent fashion, nervously tucking a strand of hair behind her ear.

"I must admit I feel a bit silly," she said, addressing Ian. "We've spoken several times this evening, but I haven't introduced myself." She held out a hand. "Amantha Goldstein."

Gregg mentally rolled his eyes.

Can we please not do this, ladies and gentlemen?

Too late. Ian accepted the proffered hand, smiling down at her almost curiously.

"Ian," he answered. "It's nice to finally meet you properly." He had that tone in his voice. That look in his eyes. Direct, focused, unwavering.

Interested.

Okay, you can both let go now, Gregg thought to himself.

"Gregg was telling me about you before," Amantha added. She quickly stuffed her hands in the pockets of her sweater.

"Oh was he, now?" Ian shot Gregg an entertained look. "Isn't he just a wealth of information."

"He is," Gregg returned. "Gregg knows many things about a wide variety of topics."

"He also told me a little about you," Ian said. His intent gaze was back on Amantha. "He said you work at the museum, but my research tells me you do more than just sweep floors in that place."

"You were researching me," Amantha said in amusement.

"Only in relation to the museum, of course," Ian said smoothly. "Bachelor of Science… archeology major… seems to me you are one important girl."

"You might say that," Amantha responded modestly, a small, very sexy smile playing at the corners of her mouth. "When I'm not gallivanting all over the country engaging in illicit activities, I play at being curator. Only the last year or so. The project needed someone the public could identify with, and I agreed to help; I finished my first stint in university just in time to go back."

"Back. What were your original studies?"

"What, your research didn't cover that?" Amantha teased. "I studied engineering the first time. Mechanical. Masters in aerospace."

Ian's expression took on even more of a keen glint, if that was possible.

"And she's smart, too," he mused playfully, his "come hither" tone causing Amantha to laugh. To her credit, she held up well under circumstances that had most girls salivating by this point.

"It was nice to make your acquaintance, Mr. Lowell," she said.

"Likewise."

"Anything we can do to help?" Gregg added as she made for the stairs.

"No, no, I can manage," was the cheerful reply.

"Say, you're not trying to take off, are you?" Ian queried. "I mean I'd... hate to have to chase you down and pack you back in over my shoulder." This last was said flirtatiously.

"What makes you think you would even be able to catch me?" Amantha shot back as she left the porch and angled her steps around the side of the house. Gregg saw her glance back just before she vanished into the darkness. He frowned. Looked at Ian. He was kind of smiling to himself, pushing a leaf back and forth with the toe of his boot.

Bloody Ian. Trust the man to take *One Flew Over the Cuckoo's Nest* and turn it into a *Days of Our Lives* rerun. At least he was still limiting himself to the occasional teasing comment and wasn't trying to help her with things yet; with such innocuous behaviors, Gregg could be assured he merely found Amantha a nice distraction and was just playing around. The minute he got all cute and shy and started trying to pull the knight in shining armor card, trouble was on the horizon. Attraction did funny things to a guy. Some men turned possessive, some turned silly and outgoing. Ian Lowell became the undisputed master of accidental encounters and carefully plotted, stolen moments. Mr. Boy-Next-Door-Helpful himself. The irony of that drastic change had never been lost on Gregg, as when they were in school together – and he would hazard a guess, even now – Ian could have had pretty much any woman he wanted. When there was nothing at stake but a good time, a farewell, and a quick getaway down somebody's fire escape at six am, the ease and confidence with which he plied his trade was enviable. Then came the few times it had been real, and that confidence was stripped away. Ian became just another guy with a crush on a girl, unsure of himself and how to go forward. The trick now was finding out which category he fell in to at the moment; find out, and nip any eventualities in the bud.

"So… what do you think of her?" Gregg asked, trying to be casual.

The question elicited a quiet chuckle. The leaf moved again.

"Honestly, mate, I'm trying not to," Ian said simply.

"Good. Keep it that way."

"Still, she's… unique." Ian looked over his shoulder, to the spot Amantha had disappeared. "Did you know she flies a Spitfire?"

"Fabulous."

"A *Spitfire*, Gregg. This is not some little two-seater Cessna we're talking about here. Do you realize the kind of power that thing has?"

"I know, Ian. Incredible. I get it. She's a pilot. And a stunt driver. And she did some kind of fashion thing with Victoria's Secret last year –"

"What?"

"Never mind. You don't need to know."

"Was she a model?"

"Yes!" Gregg said in exasperation. "She walked the catwalk in this feathered cape-like thing."

"Was she hot?"

"What do you think?"

"I like feathers."

"Everybody likes feathers. Even people allergic to feathers like them. Just leave her alone and don't get any ideas."

"Come on, mate, give me a little credit!"

"I did once," Gregg said dryly. "Remember that cowgirl at the rodeo in Amarillo?"

"You had to bring that up. That was one time."

"Don't forget Kaycee, Wyoming. And your little fling with the mayor's daughter in La Junta… *And* the escapade in Vegas, where we spent a few days in the clink because you decided to take on that three-hundred-pound hulk of a sumo wrestler who didn't like you messing around with his girlfriend and just happened to be related to the chief of police. Face it, Ian, track records say a lot."

Ian was in the midst of trying to assemble an appropriate comeback when Amantha returned.

"Do we have a plan for tomorrow yet?" She asked, trotting up onto the porch.

"A rough one." Ian hooked his thumbs in his pockets. Gregg could only speculate what he was thinking about, but was fairly certain it involved feathers and lingerie. "It's only partial until Genius here figures out the rest of the puzzle."

"I told you I'll have it done by tomorrow," Gregg said.

Amantha nodded, swinging the door open to return inside.

"Good luck," she said. "And you'd better not leave without me."

"Wouldn't dream of it, Miss Ammy," Ian replied.

This time Gregg's eye roll was in plain view. Ian noticed it. Fortunately, Amantha didn't.

"Miss *Ammy*?" Gregg hissed as soon as she was out of earshot. "Ian, do you actually know who the woman is?"

"A fascinating blend of beauty and brains, Genius." Ian wasn't really paying attention, distracted as he was by Amantha's retreating figure, visible through the long pane of glass in the door. He caught sight of Gregg's condescending look and returned it in kind. "Of course I know who she is," he said. "I can read."

"Then even you must know 'Miss Ammy' is not a term most people would use on her," Gregg said. "She's a lady. In the truest sense of the word. I've done a lot more research into these people than a Google search so take it from me, she's off limits. You're type of... temporary affection... is something she doesn't need, kapish?"

Ian held up a hand.

"Gregg, I promise *on my honor* that I will behave," he said. He took a step toward the door, paused, and leaned in to look at Gregg conspiratorially. "Of course, I... can't guarantee that she will."

Gregg gave him a blank look.

"Your ego knows no bounds."

Ian just grinned at him – that cocky, flyboy nonsense he'd always used when on the prowl in some city dive – and strolled into the house. Presumably to research feathers.

Gregg just shook his head and let him go. What had he done to deserve this? It was like...

Honestly, this whole caper was like herding cats. How was he supposed to solve a riddle under these conditions? He was now saddled with not one, but two "tourists" (one of whom was famous enough to warrant military intervention); he only had a partial set of answers to a problem that needed to be solved yesterday; and to top that off, this whole Ian/Amantha scenario was not an avenue of thought he wanted to pursue.

Gregg wished he had that moment in the museum to do over again; he would have said no to Amantha's request to join him, and stuck to it, no matter what happened. Then, at least he would have only been a criminal. Now, not only was he a criminal, he was potentially responsible for the derailment of the Goldstein family future. What would happen if Ian proved that little bit too irresistible for Amantha's sensible nature? Gregg felt his stomach take a dangerous plunge as he thought over the possible consequences of such a situation. There was no conceivable outcome that boded anything but disaster, if Amantha's own history was anything to go by.

How the *hell* had he gotten them all into this?

It was one of those moments when he didn't know what to think, when the present contradicted the past and neither seemed willing to negotiate their positions. The future was nothing more than a blurry collection of "what if's", milling around beyond the horizon. Despite the uneasy truce he and Ian had managed to reach, Gregg knew nothing had changed; this hunt no more belonged to him than the patent for super glue. At the end of the day, he was still a theoretical slave, and Ian was still a criminal mastermind. He was still "the bad guy". He was unpredictable and, above all else, a man with his mind on revenge. Gregg knew he had best remember that if he wanted to get out of this in one piece. He stood there a moment, taking stock of the night, then, with the sobering weight of reality nested firmly in his head, trooped fuzzily back in the house to save his own life. Tomorrow would come a lot sooner than he thought, and it was going to be a rat race from here on in.

So much the better.

****

Amantha stepped out of a piping hot shower to tug on a jumper and a pair of pajama bottoms, padding into her bedroom past all the boys, plucking the sheet set off the couch that she'd discarded earlier. Marilla's living room resembled a teenage sleepover party.

Blankets and pillows were everywhere, and boys were perched, in varying degrees of semi-consciousness, throughout the room.

George was bundled lifelessly in the horsey blanket on the floor with his head nearly buried in a fluffy pillow, Jared sat cross-legged on one couch with a whirring laptop on his knees, and Gregg straddled the back of a tall chair he'd pulled up beside Rob, who had commandeered Marilla's recliner with his Barbie ensemble. The two of them were continuing their discussion about all things vehicular, rattling off the specs of an old muscle car featured in the latest issue of *Hot Rod* magazine. Troy lay spread-eagled on the floor beside them. His bare feet were propped up on the table with heels resting on the wood and toes pointed out at odd angles, hands behind his head. Beyond him, the table now resembled something of a wartime cache, as the henchmen had divested themselves of weaponry and extra ammunition and plunked it all down in piles that managed, through it all, to remain quite tidy. All that was missing from the setup was the proverbial box of dynamite and a few grenades. Amantha wished she had a camera.

"Night, lads," she said, yawning into her hand.

The answering chorus was muffled. In the chair, Rob tucked the Barbie pillow close to his chest and wriggled his eyebrows at her.

"You know where to find us," he said mischievously.

"How fortunate for me," Amantha returned. She was tired. She had a hunch she was going to feel every single bounce and jolt tomorrow. A strange sense of sorrow had settled on her heart as Aunt Marilla's story ended, dampening the curiosity and excitement she'd felt earlier. It was nights like these when she really missed her mother; nights when she was a bit lost and a bit confused, when she just needed her mum.

Dropping her old clothes in a small basket along the wall, she set about brushing her hair and removing from her bed the myriad of decorative pillows Aunt Marilla kept adding to. The collection had grown some over the years until it filled nearly half the surface.

Amantha's room was a small, homey hollow; during the day, a wisteria could be seen stretching along the eve of the house just outside the divided window pane, its white blossoms dripping prettily. Beyond was the large, fenced paddock where Amantha had kept her horse, Mystique, surrounded by the typical, lush countryside England was famous for. Her room itself was cozy, filled with memories and feeling. She and her mother had often come here when Amantha was little; while recollections from this time were fuzzy, what she did remember was filled with sentiment. Peace. Vague images of her and her mother sharing the tiny, single bed while Amantha slowly fell asleep; the smell of her mother's shampoo; the sunrise slowly filling the window. Then had come the day when Amantha occupied the room permanently, and her attachment to it had deepened. Little had changed in here since then.

Pink walls, hardwood flooring, stuffed animals in a little chest near the window, photos and posters covering the walls. Amantha had never really been into the band scene like her friends at school; instead, her photographic memorabilia consisted mainly of horses and aviation. Posters of the Red Arrows and the Breitling Jet Team rested alongside horse photos, interspersed with a few drawings Amantha had done herself over the years. She had moved to the university campus directly out of high school, and her room had remained nearly untouched. She would come home for a week several times a year, put on a fresh set of sheets on her arrival, and take it off when she left, leaving the bed bare but for the outer quilt and a mattress cover. That continual cycle had become part of her life. She always felt different, young, when entering this space. It was where she had grown up, and it was where she returned when she needed time away from the world of adulthood.

That world had certainly dealt her an unexpected hand today. She had started the day with the intention of going on a treasure hunt; when she found Gregg in the museum, she was thinking only of the legend, and the possibility of using him as a tool to beat Nicolo to the prize. Then she had met *him* and everything had changed.

The boss. Ian. She'd known from the moment they locked eyes that he was her "type". Of course that was before she knew who he was: the man Gregg had spoken of, the former team member who was not so nice and was now the competition. The one who could be "charming". Amantha was very close to classifying that description as the understatement of the century.

What was Lowell really like? She couldn't help but wonder. She'd been warned about him, both directly and indirectly, but still failed to match those up with what her intuition told her was true. There was so much more than just what appeared on the surface. The way he walked; the way he talked; the set, determined look in his eyes. Amantha had seen it before. On the faces of firemen and policemen, men like Northam and Marshal Gates who had spent years deliberately staring death in the face and daring it to come closer. It was the mark of a soldier.

But Ian's face held something else, as well; a certain hardness, a certain aloofness, like he had built a wall around himself and refused to let anything or anyone get close. Even when he smiled it was there, that detached sadness, allowing nothing more than a momentary, superficial façade of humor. He'd seen a lot in his time; had been handed a good deal of hurt. That the last ten years in particular had scarred him was apparent, and Amantha wondered briefly if it was even possible for a person to come back from something so drastic, after having conditioned themselves to kill for so long.

She was still suffering from the incredible urge to talk with Ian, that interesting paradox she always found herself in when she desperately wanted to say something but couldn't for the life of her think of anything *to* say. She just hadn't expected him to be so charismatic. Hadn't expected to share so many common interests with him. Charming she could handle; after all, it was mainly words with little substance, and something she dealt with successfully on a regular basis. But this fascinating combination of ex-US Navy pilot and horseman?

Amantha stripped the quilt set from the bed and dug into her pile of clean linen for a fitted sheet, unfolding it absently. Charming quite frankly failed to cover those bases. A quiet knock sounded on the door, which was still open; she looked up to find Lowell standing there. She smiled, probably far too quickly, even as her heart jumped into her throat. Was it bad that she was almost ridiculously happy to see him?

"Are you the new butler?" She joked.

"You know, Miss Ammy, sometimes it feels that way," he answered in mock distress. "Butler, nanny, and unofficial cheer squad." He held up her ID tag from the museum. "You left this in the car. Thought you might need it."

"I wondered where I'd put that," Amantha said, and accepted the lanyard from him. She ignored the sensation when his fingers brushed hers.

Ian was busy surveying the room in curiosity, taking in the blend of mechanical and equestrian hobbies that decorated her walls.

"And here I was expecting to see posters of the Backstreet Boys," he said. He gestured to the sheet she still had bunched in her palm. "Want an extra pair of hands?"

"Why, have you got a pair for sale?" Amantha asked lightly.

He eyed her a bit roguishly and held out a hand.

"Toss me a corner. Let's do this. It's no fun fighting with these things alone."

Amantha obliged with a laugh, and they went to work muscling the cover into place. Amantha would be the first to admit that fitted sheets were the bane of her existence, for the simple reason that one never could tell if the thing was on the right way or not until it was too late. She soon found herself giggling almost uncontrollably as first her corner, then his, then both, sprung from their moorings and catapulted inward, foiling their attempts to bring it under control. Ian joined her as the sheet shot off his side and ended up at his feet, pooling over the floor.

"It's war now," he laughed, and leaned down to grab it. A second later, and: "Is that a stack of firefighter calendars under here?"

Oh no. He'd found her stash. Amantha had forgotten she had that collection. A few scraping sounds and crackling of paper and Ian reappeared over the edge of the bed, holding the sheet in one hand and Mr. June from 2001 in the other, smirking at her. "Why, Miss Ammy," he said cheekily. "You are just full of surprises."

"They were out of puppy calendars," Amantha said by way of defense.

"For five years in a row?"

"Yep."

Lowell amusedly returned the calendar to its perch and went back to stretching his corner of the sheet over the mattress. It was with no small amount of satisfaction that they finally declared victory over the obstinate material and jammed it into place.

"Gregg said the two of you used to compete in rodeos," Amantha said interestedly, reaching down to grab the flat sheet.

"Yeah. Now that was a while ago," Lowell said frankly. "We team roped together, Gregg did steer roping, and I rode a few bulls on the side." He reached up to offhandedly catch an edge of the fabric

Amantha fluffed into the air. Together, they flattened it out with a soft whooshing sound.

"Is that where you got the buckle?" Amantha asked, tucking her side in.

He nodded. In the bright, interior light, the engraving of a large, Brahma bull poised mid-leap, with the rider on its back hanging on for dear life, was clearly visible.

"Actually..." Lowell finished his half and reached in his back pocket, pulling out a three-fold, leather wallet. "I have a photo from that day," he said. "It was the last rodeo we competed in before we joined the Navy." He popped the wallet open to a small selection of pictures in the back and handed it to her.

Amantha laughed aloud as she saw the one he indicated. It was of Gregg and Ian, much younger, and judging by the cheerful grins on their faces and the self-assured, almost cocky way they interacted with the camera, they had just won their event.

"Look how young you both are," she said in amazement, studying the pair of faces that couldn't be past twenty. Broad-brimmed cowboy hats perched on their heads, Gregg's tipped forward a little and Ian's tilted back in an impish manner, a few tendrils of hair curling out from underneath. His face was shadowed; she was sure he had never been a carefree person. But it was less so. He was slender, willowy, young, built more like a boy than the man he was now; his shoulders not as broad, his face not as filled out, the smile lines not as deep. His grin was still cockeyed. And his eyes, too, were very familiar; bright and alive, sparkling with that same, mischief-seeking glint Amantha recognized. "Did the horses have names?"

"Gregg's was Ace," Ian said. "Teepee was a little mare I'd had for about ten years."

"Teepee?"

"She came with it. Seemed to suit her so I didn't bother changing it." He gathered the quilt from the floor and deftly flicked it into the air, letting it settle into place over the small, single bed.

"Thank you," Amantha said as he dropped the other edge and held up his hands in a team-roping "time" gesture. "I literally would have been here all night."

"No worries, love."

"You're good at that." Amantha lifted the corner of the quilt and took stock of the perfectly-executed hospital corner underneath.

"I used to help my sister."

Amantha wouldn't have admitted it, but she was simply dying to have a look at the rest of the photos in the small packet she held, of which there were at least five. Did she dare look? Would it be right? She got the distinct impression she shouldn't and, no, it would not. Nothing about her interest was right. The only problem was she couldn't help it; curiosity may have killed the cat, but it would have been an exciting way to go. She glanced up at him, finger tipped to turn the page.

"May I?"

"Be my guest."

Slowly Amantha leafed through the pages, the images of Ian's past, people and places and events coming to life momentarily before her eyes while he described them for her. Occasionally he would reach over and point out a small detail. There were several of Gregg and Ian, some alone, some with Rob; a landscape shot of a charming house somewhere in the country; one very amusing photo of a group of officers – all men – waltzing on the flight deck of an aircraft carrier. Amantha could only imagine how entertaining the scene was in real life; she was fairly certain she saw Gregg in the background getting twirled by his partner. She flipped the page and paused at a picture of two young, energetic girls near the end, both reclined nonchalantly on the hood of a classic Ford Mustang and laughing gaily as if they knew how much trouble they were in for tampering with such a vehicle. The caption at the bottom read: "Punch a hole in the sky, flyboy! From your sisters and Sadey."

"My first car," Ian said. "Found her as an old rust bucket parked out front of a feed store when I was fourteen."

"She's beautiful... are those your sisters?"

"Arielle is. She's the dark-haired one." Ian pointed her out on the right. "She's a wild one, that girl, a real rebel," he said, and the affection was evident in his voice. "God would have been shaking his head the day he put her together. She can ballroom dance like a queen and is a better mechanic than most men I know. Charisse is my half-sister. Straight as a pin, very smart. She's a vet nurse now."

"What does Arielle do?"

"Well, Ria is…" He inclined his head back and forth non-committedly. "She's a bit like me."

Cat burglar immediately leapt to mind. Amantha tried to keep the delight off her face. So Lowell had family. Two beautiful sisters, cowgirls by the looks of them, dressed as they were in jeans and t-shirts and boots; sisters who obviously thought quite a bit of their flyboy brother. It was comforting, somehow. It took away from the aloofness Amantha sensed about Lowell, made him a little more accessible. There were more photos behind, but she didn't want to appear too involved, so she flipped the wallet shut and handed it back. He accepted it gingerly and tucked it in his pocket.

"Is that you?"

Amantha glanced at the photo he indicated and nearly died.

"Yes," she said, making a face. She and Mystique stood side by side, the horse's bridle adorned with a blue ribbon, while Amantha cuddled his large head, grinning like an idiot.

"How old were you?"

"Thirteen." That had been… fifteen years ago. Amantha had been fit at the time. Very fit. But, thanks to her body type, it also meant she had been skinny as a rail, bony, gawky, and frail-looking. Her hair was bad, her teeth were worse, and even a trowel full of makeup had been unable to hide the pimples on her teenaged skin. "Wasn't going to win any beauty contests in those days," she said with a nervous gesture, retrieving the picture from her bedside table to tuck it close to her chest. She almost wished he hadn't seen that.

"I don't know, I thought you were kind of cute," Ian answered. His tone was sheepish.

It was about then Amantha realized how close he was. He had moved while she surveyed the photos and now stood just off her left shoulder, right beside her. Close enough to touch, almost. The fact that they were standing this near while inside the confines of her bedroom was a point Amantha's mind chose right then to manifest. Lowell glanced down at her, then stepped back deliberately into the doorway, out of her personal space. He tapped a hand on the doorjamb. He must have sensed her sudden discomfiture.

"I should…" He gestured over his shoulder, paused momentarily, looked at her. Was he stalling?

"Then I will see you in the morning, Mr. Lowell," Amantha said shyly. He might not be, but she was. As the formal title left her lips, he smiled, looking at her steadily.

"I have a first name, Amantha," he said gently.

Amantha felt herself blushing under his gaze. Properly. Why did her name have to sound so good when he said it? Why did that smile of his have to be so cute? Oh, this was bad; really, really bad. She dropped her eyes to the floor and bit her lip, realizing just how much trouble she was in. When at last she forced herself to look back at him, the smile on her own face refused to be kept at bay.

"Ian," she replied, barely above a whisper.

At that precise moment, Aunt Marilla swooped into the middle of the discussion.

"And just what do we have here?" She demanded, taking in the scene, countenances, and atmosphere in one glance before boxing Ian solidly around the ears. He ducked out from under the blow, but was only partially successful.

"Take it easy, Mrs. Clancy," he said humorously. "I was just going."

"You most certainly are, young man," Marilla agreed. "Amantha needs sleep, and from the looks of you, Mr. Lowell, you should have gone to bed three days ago." She took him by the collar and steered him away. Ian didn't protest. He glanced back once, grinned at Amantha over his shoulder, then went along willingly and allowed himself to be herded into the living room like an errant teenager. Marilla could be heard depositing him on the nearest couch with strict instructions to go to sleep before turning on Gregg, Jared, and the henchmen to shoo them all off to bed as a mother would her wayward children.

"Put that riddle away, Gregg, or you'll go blind," Amantha heard her say, followed by: "Bob, sit down. You – minion – go back to bed. Jared, if I catch you on that phone one more time, it's mine! Where did the other henchman go? There were three of you before."

It was most entertaining, listening to her aunt chivvy along a group of supposed tough guys, directing traffic like a true professional. If anyone had thoughts of disobedience, such ideas were wisely kept secret.

Her charges adequately taken care of, Marilla returned to Amantha's room and gave her a quick hug.

"Sleep well, darling."

"Good night, Aunt Marilla," Amantha returned, rather distractedly, and sat down on the edge of her bed. She held the photo away from her and stared at it. Lowell's words came back to her. She hated this photo, really; the only reason she kept it was because it was the only thing she had left of Mystique. This photo, and an old, faded blue ribbon tucked in a box in her closet.

"Amantha."

Amantha looked up to find her aunt regarding her intently, with concern.

"Mind what Gregg said and stay away from that lad," Marilla said gently. "His kind brings only heartache. We are not safe here." She closed the door deliberately walked away, leaving Amantha alone.

Slowly, Amantha rose and turned out the light, crawling into bed. She suddenly felt... lonely. The hint of sorrow returned, chipping away at her heart. She could have sworn she caught a light scent of peppermint on the sheets.

After that, it wasn't long before the house was quiet. Amantha could hear minute stirrings every now and then, footsteps treading just outside, the occasional click of a door. A bag snapping open quietly. One of Lowell's men was on watch right now, maybe Lowell himself, keeping up a guard rotation that would last all night long. Amantha lay still and listened, to the sounds of the night and the sounds of people moving throughout the house, the magnitude of the situation not lost on her.

So they were really going on a hunt for gold. Ok. What had started out as a lark had quickly escalated into a full-fledged mission; from now on they would be evading both cops and Goldsteins, living as fugitives, existing on the edge. Poor Gregg. Amantha had a feeling he hadn't quite realized the can of worms he'd be opening when he started out.

Would this quest of his go the way he hoped? Of course Amantha had been subconsciously aware of the concept of a great treasure since childhood; it was what her entire family history was built on. But it had always seemed to be a little like Santa Claus. Something one might believe as a kid but discard as age, wisdom, and life pulled them in another direction. The theory of actually setting forth to prove, beyond a shadow of a doubt, that it was real, had honestly never entered her mind. Where this new road would take them, Amantha had no idea, but follow it they must. There was no going back now. Whether the treasure was real or not, Gregg had committed himself to continuing, to following this puzzle through to the end even if all they turned up was a piece of parchment that had: "You lose, suckers" painted on it in Medieval neon. He had little choice anymore. As of this afternoon, he had resigned his commission as project manager, and was now merely a passenger, just like the rest of them. And the man now at the helm was a different kettle of fish entirely.

Ian. She liked his name; it was simple, strong, uncomplicated. Like the cloak of approachability he wore. Amantha guessed that to most, he was simply a handsome man who possessed that something: that passing, intangible something that required a second glance. But not to her. She knew who he was, what he was. Just below the surface of his character was a band of solid iron; unbendable, unbreakable; shielding carefully from view elements of the explosive, dynamic nature that was, in essence, his soul. She could see it in his eyes; the passion, the energy, deep emotions that lurked like demons beyond the gates of hell; dangerous, volatile, unyielding. It made her doubt whether anyone could ever truly understand a person of his nature. Notice? Yes. Most definitely. Know? Maybe, but no better than he wished. He was a master of restraint, adept at traveling incognito; too proud, too confident, too stubborn; larger than life and towering far above the edicts of mere mortality.

Put simply, he was invincible. And he would always remain an enigma.

Movement caught her eye to the left; a shadow crossed before the window. Like the silhouette moving over her sight from outside the cool breadth of glass, so Aunt Marilla's words of wisdom moved across her mind, Gregg's words of experience, Gates' warning to Northam, blocking out the charming deception of moonlight Amantha had allowed into her mind and exposing for what it was the perilous shadow lurking beyond. What was she thinking, playing around with something like that? It made no difference what Amantha thought or felt or wanted to believe. First impressions meant nothing. It made no difference that she found Ian to be an exciting, compelling man, one of courage and gallantry despite his faults. It made no difference that he had little moments of kindness, moments of compassion, that showed through his tough exterior. It was probably all a ruse anyway.

The man couldn't be trusted; she had only to look at what he did for a job to know that (if being a crime boss could legitimately fall under a work category). It was just stress getting to her, was all. How many times had she read of the potential, sometimes inevitable, bond someone in her position would develop for the individual in charge? It was certainly not a new premise; in the blink of an eye, one suddenly discovers they have been thrown headlong into a scenario they hadn't anticipated, and is literally, both in a mental and physical sense, weakened in will by the strain. Then suddenly, into the chaos, comes someone who knows what he's doing. He is talented, charismatic, a leader, strangely kind in a mysterious way, and possesses that singularity that sets some men apart from their peers. But more than that he has control. Power. Steadiness. The ability to take this frightful dragon of a situation and render it harmless; becoming, in effect, a knight in shining armor.

The fact that said knight would vanish without a trace once life returned to normal was something the mind never seemed to grasp, assuming both parties lived long enough to see the day. The pragmatic half of Amantha's brain presented its case well, lobbying for common sense, and with its guidance Amantha was able to drag her wayward emotions back into line. There was no reason to fret. She'd be fine. Really. Her romantic side would settle down and this would all go away by morning.

But even as she tried to convince herself, it was a rather helpless tone that showed its pitiful face. For in the end, despite her mind's assertions to the contrary, Amantha knew in her heart that no argument, however intended or however menacing, would do her any good now. She knew her own resolves were futile. Because she knew; pretense, uncertainty, and propriety aside; that it wouldn't take very much of a push for her to fall in love with Ian Lowell.

This hunt couldn't end soon enough.

THE HUNT CONTINUES IN 2016!

Forever the Horizon, Part II

TRAILS OF THE PAST

THE HUNT: How much can one human mind endure? That is Gregg's question of the century as he continues to battle time and his own limitations to solve the mysteries hidden in the riddle, all the while hoping the answers won't lead his small troupe into waters they'll regret entering later. The game has changed now. The stakes are higher With Ian in charge, anything can – and does – happen, his dual traits of ingenuity and menace first aiding in the achievement of miracles and then reminding Gregg of why they split in the first place. Gregg know he must tread lightly. Even when he finally succeeds in unraveling the mystery, his victory is still shadowed in uncertainty; the knowledge he gains works against him, serving only to plunge his quest even further into the unknown. The drop is sharp, the waters troubled. And Gregg knows all too well they might regret it. The trails they follow are paved with memories, and it isn't long before he realizes Robin Hood's past isn't the only one they're digging up.

THE LEGEND: Robin Hood and his gang have proven themselves as a force to be reckoned with. But now comes the most challenging part of their battle yet. Notoriety brings its own problems; the more important one becomes, the more enticing – and necessary – it becomes to take them down, and DeMarke tries a new tactic: turning Robin Hood's faithful public against him in an effort to flush the outlaw gang out of hiding and right onto the gallows. His plan brings a wagonload of trouble to Robin's doorstep. When King Richard's ransom mysteriously disappears on the road through Sherwood Forest, the very tenets of Robin's outlaw identity are challenged, leaving all but the bare fact of his existence open to speculation. His loyalty is questioned. His patriotism is on the line. His neck is nearly in the noose, but it isn't the noose that has Robin running for cover in the end; rather the prospect of confronting a new challenge that suddenly presents itself, one in which he is forced to face down his most formidable foe yet: Marian Fitzwalter.

ABOUT THE AUTHOR

Colorado Marshal was born and raised in rural California. An avid storyteller, she has been writing for most of her life. A wide variety of interests and hobbies gives her plenty to put on the page, and themes ranging from aviation to equestrian vaulting are all likely to crop up in her books at some point or another. She currently divides her time between her adopted home of Margaret River, Western Australia, and California.